SHADOWS WITHIN THE FIRE

Volumes of Elementum

Volume I

Megan L. Adams

Shadows Within the Fire
Volumes of Elementum
Volume I
by Megan L. Adams

Published by Golden Tome Press
First published in the United States 2024

Copyright © 2024 Megan L. Adams
Map Copyright © 2024 Megan L. Adams

No portion of this book may be reproduced in any form or by electronic or mechanical means, including information storage and retrieval systems, without written permission from the author, except as permitted by U.S. copyright law. Please do not participate in or encourage piracy of copyrighted materials in violation of the author's rights.

This is a work of fiction. Names, places, characters, and incidents are the product of the author's imagination and are fictitious. Any resemblance to actual persons, living or dead, events, or establishments is solely coincidental.

Editing by Kyla M. Cullinane, LLC and Katelyn Washington

All rights reserved.

ISBN: HB: 979-8-9899327-0-2, PB: 9798867022747
eBook ASIN: B0CRF734R1

To my little sister Emily, who gave me the push and confidence to become a writer.

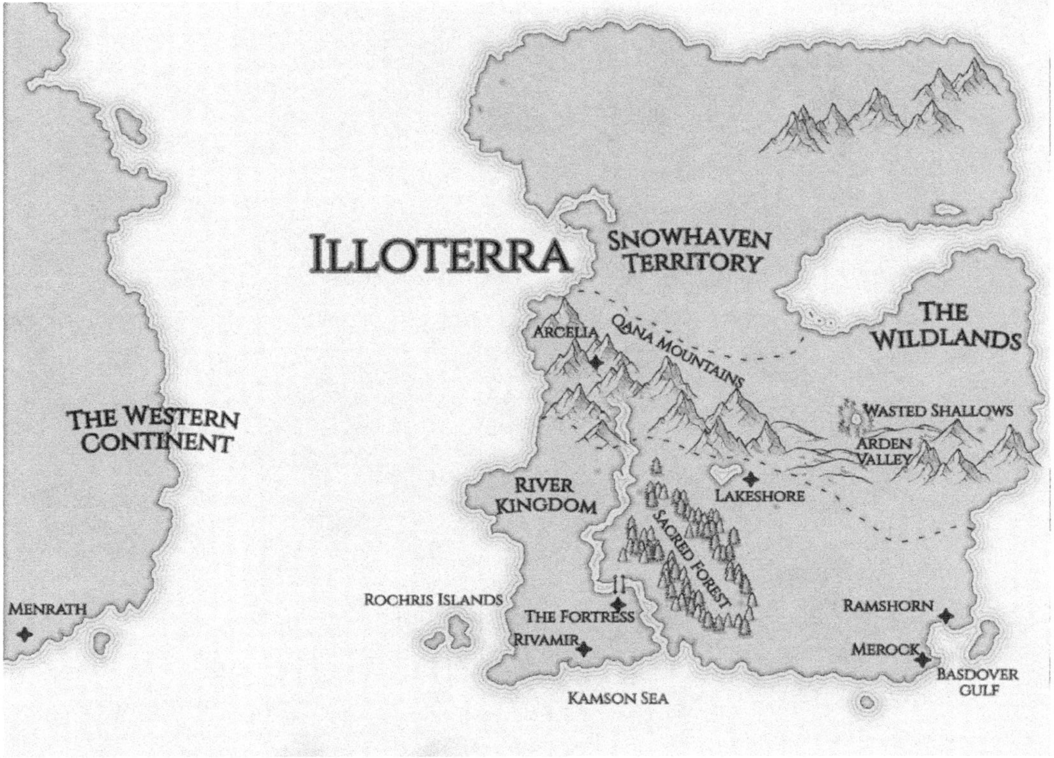
ILLOTERRA
SNOWHAVEN TERRITORY
THE WILDLANDS
ARCELIA
QANA MOUNTAINS
WASTED SHALLOWS
ARDEN VALLEY
THE WESTERN CONTINENT
RIVER KINGDOM
LAKESHORE
SACRED FOREST
MENRATH
ROCHRIS ISLANDS
THE FORTRESS
RIVAMIR
RAMSHORN
MEROCK
BASDOVER GULF
KAMSON SEA

CONTENT WARNING

For those readers who do not want to read explicit romance scenes, skip the following chapters:

Chapter 40
Chapter 48

Shadows Within the Fire

Volumes of Elementum
Volume I

PART ONE

MEGAN L. ADAMS

ONE
EVREN

"The High Ruler is summoning you...again." A voice swept across the grove, carried on the wind.

I couldn't see where it came from, but I knew he was coming. He always knew where to find me. Warmth seeped into me as a content smile came to my lips.

"Of course, he's looking for me again," I said under my breath, releasing a sigh. "I need to find a new hiding spot."

From my perch on a thick branch, high above the rest of the trees, I had freedom. Wind sweeping from the north brought a smell of rain, pushing away the salty brine coming from the sea. I filled my lungs, trying to soak in every last bit of sun, relishing its vibrant light. A bead of sweat rolled down my back from the end-of-day heat. The last few weeks the summer humidity made wearing long sleeves stifling but I didn't have a choice in my attire. I'd taken to hiking my long skirts up while I sat in the branches of the trees. There were no wandering eyes this far from the house that lingered in my peripheral. Especially this high in the air. People rarely looked up, oblivious to their full surroundings, and I had no qualms with taking advantage of their ignorance and lack of concern. I, on the other hand, didn't have that luxury. I had to always be on guard, constantly watching my back. Our home was supposed to be the safest in Illoterra. Supposed to be, but things have changed. My sanctuary has transformed into a prison.

"He said it's important. Tonight is a big deal." He drummed his fingers on his arm as he paced below me. His footsteps were muffled on the freshly trimmed grass. Maybe if I ignored him, he'd go away and pretend he didn't discover me. Perhaps if I just kept my eyes closed and my face turned to the sun, the gusting wind would carry me away. A stray cloud floated across the powder blue sky, darker than the charcoal on the page before me, obscuring the sun in thick shadow in its wake. I frowned as a shiver went through me at the sudden loss of warmth.

Adaris cleared his throat. Even without looking at him, I could see my brother in my mind—arms crossed, feet in a wide stance, face serious, trying his best to put a look of tolerance on his face. I didn't want to trade my afternoon outside for the stuffy gloom that awaited me inside the house. I wanted nothing to do with those stone walls that leeched all the warmth out of the day and kept the melancholy in, threatening to smother me.

"Of course, it is." I slammed my sketchbook shut, "Every dinner is a big deal." I tucked my charcoal pencil behind my high, pointed ear, rolling my eyes. I picked at the peeling leather cover with charcoal-stained fingers that had seen the many years of my attempts at creativity. "Mother will have me prepped and powdered to perfection right on time."

I didn't mind the flourishes. I didn't even mind the extravagant ruffled dresses. Arabelle Byrnes, my mother, always ensured I looked flawless while at the same time pretending I didn't exist. She had the particular talent of overseeing my evening preparation without actually glancing in my direction. It used to bother me, but now it was expected.

For the last two years, my father, Cadoc Byrnes, High Ruler of the River Kingdom, had been parading me around for all the worthy males in the realm as a potential bondmate with fancy dinners. Long tables covered in ridiculous amounts of food, that no one actually finished, and overflowing goblets of wine, that everyone *did* finish. I made polite conversation with whichever male Father has deemed worthy for that particular evening, all while trying to maintain a healthy distance from groping, wandering hands. Week after week after week of the same, monotonous meals. Nothing ever came from them. Just another night of boisterous laughter from drunk guests, fake smiles from me to appease Father, and no bondmate in sight.

Our family dinners were once a quiet affair. Just the immediate family eating as quickly and quietly as possible before slipping away to our individual spaces. Adaris and I kept our thoughts to ourselves so as not to attract attention from Father. Father was usually ruffling through work papers and correspondence he'd brought to the table, or discreetly discussing matters with high-ranking guardsmen. Mother sat, face solemn and blank, merely pushing the food around her plate before dismissing herself. But my approaching twenty fifth birthday meant finding a bondmate.

As a child, the storybooks Mother would read to me always said bondmates were like two halves of one soul. They were meant to be a gift from the gods, a way to bless our kind and live out our long, long lives in happiness. Father said it was all a load of crap—childhood stories to fill the heads of younglings with false hope. Bondmates were meant to align powerful families and create heirs to the kingdoms of the High Fae. All the males he brought to introduce me to were indeed members of powerful High Fae families, but were much older, friends of my father, looking to align themselves with our infamous lineage. The Byrnes family was the most well-known High Fae family in the realm. Our bloodline could be traced all the way back to the day the Powers Above gifted the Fae with powers. That didn't deter my father from collecting more allies to expand his reach, and he wasn't above using me to do so. My future was simply an afterthought.

Adaris moved closer, breaking into my thoughts. I glared down through the sparse branches of the tree I'd claimed as my own as he halted below me. The gentle wind mussed his usually perfect dark chestnut hair. I preferred the windswept version of him; it was closer to his true nature than the uptight heir that many knew him as.

"Evren." His voice was stern, his lips quirking to fight a smile. "Your duty is to marry a wealthy male from a strong family and produce tons of tiny male offspring that will continue on long after you have passed to carry on the Byrnes bloodline." He waved one hand through the air in a broad, sweeping gesture, the other hand glued to his hip.

It was uncanny, and slightly disturbing, how, at times, Adaris's voice mimicked our father's.

"Proper females shouldn't be lounging in trees and drawing pictures in the margins of her brother's books."

Well, that time he sounded like Mother.

I'd love to smack that smug look right off his face. I tipped my chin in a mocking way. In return, he bit his cheek to hold back a smirk. He always knew how to brighten my mood. I snapped a piece of gray, splintered wood off the branch and tossed it down at him. The flimsy piece hit him in the chest, and he feigned a dramatic groan, covering his heart and stumbled back a few steps.

"This isn't even your book," I retorted.

The distant blow of a horn tore both of our attentions, our heads turning in unison towards home. The cheerfulness melted away, replaced by bitterness filling my mouth. "I'm assuming Renwick will be there." I could hear the hollowness in my voice.

Pure disgust bloomed in my gut just speaking his name. It was like acid on my tongue. A chill unrelated to the passing cloud tickled up my spine. Although I hadn't told Adaris why I did my best to avoid Renwick, I was pretty sure he'd figured it out on his own. The bruises were getting harder to hide. Mother was the only one they were invisible to. If she had noticed my regularly discolored skin, she never let on. And the maids were smart enough to keep their mouths shut. I couldn't blame them though.

"Considering he's the Head of the Black Guard, I'd assume so." The planes of Adaris's face hardened, the sun casting shadows of the firm lines. His body stiffened with the almost unnatural stillness of the Fae. I knew he was trying to regain control of his emotions. The only time I ever saw him lose his temper was in regard to Renwick.

I gazed down at my brother again in fondness. I wouldn't say we looked alike, but I liked to believe we did. Adaris Byrnes was older than me by fifteen years, but he had been my confidant and companion my entire life. My protector. His strong, angled jaw gave him a sense of arrogance, but he was far from it. He was at least a foot taller than me, and where I was on the smaller side with curves, he was lean and muscular. The only similarities we shared were our dazzling violet eyes—a trait passed from our mother—and our pointed ears proving our High Fae bloodline.

He was squinting those ethereal eyes at me now, trying to read my face. I'd climbed high into the tree, making it difficult for him to see me. He was at least twenty feet below. The sun left a dappled shade across his skin.

I sighed into the sun again, shining like a gold coin in the sky, and took one more look at the beauty around me. From this height, I could see the entirety of the River Kingdom. My family home, or the fortress as Father called it, stood high over the city of Rivamir to the south. Smoke-gray stone walls towered, reaching up into the sky. The stone leeched the color from the surrounding landscape.

The sparkling teal waters of the Kamson Sea surrounded Rivamir from three sides. Along the sea, a fleet of ships lined the sheer shores. The largest fleet in the realm. It had come in handy during the war, or so I'd read. Cream-colored sails painted the horizon; they stood out against the bluer-than-blue sky that was peppered with fluffy, fast-moving clouds.

The fortress was separated from Rivamir by a grove, where I currently rested. A patch of twisted trees, their branches tangled into intricate knots, obstructing anyone's path that wasn't welcome. Adaris told me the trees the grove was older than the fortress itself.

Directly north of the fortress was the Great River, the waters dark and hostile. The river was supposedly impassable, though it was a common playground for me while growing up. The only way in or out of the River Kingdom was the massive bridge that stretched from one side of the river to the other. It was only large enough for a single wagon to cross at a time, which didn't truly matter to the people of Rivamir. No one from the city left using the bridge. Travel by sea was preferred. The bridge was guarded round the clock by the fierce Black Guard, and most would rather face the open waters than the Black Guard.

I turned to face the northern horizon, where the Sacred Forest and the Qana Mountains stood. The forest stood guard over the snow-tipped mountains, the Darkwood trees like mysterious sentinels. The rugged cliffs divided the realm of Illoterra in half—the Southlands and the North, the tamed and controlled south versus the unruly, frigid north. The sprawling territory to the north, covering nearly the entire northern part of Illoterra, was ruled by the Snowhaven Fae and unending winter. It was a savage wasteland, and not many dared to explore it. Legends of the Snowhaven Fae were told to me when I was young—legends of their harshness, of their unforgiving and torturous ways.

Villages were scattered here and there between the larger Fae kingdoms; lower beings inhabited these dilapidated areas. To the east, past the river, lay open land and the valley. The wildlands lay past the valley. Of course, I'd never seen any place other than the fortress. I studied maps and stared off into the distance using my imagination. I doubted I'd ever see the rest of Illoterra. Father wouldn't even let me visit the city. It was unspeakable for me to leave the grounds. Adaris was encouraged to travel our world, to learn and explore. And I was encouraged to be seen and not heard and follow the orders of my father.

How did my life become so predictable and mundane?

Well, it's always been on the dull side compared to Adaris. Each morning I woke and had breakfast in my room. Then I moved to the library for my morning lessons. If my tutors were in a good mood, I could sometimes convince them to move to the adjoining terrace, but it wasn't often. Adaris tried to have lunch with me when he was home. The rest of the day I devoted my time to drawing and wandering the grounds of the fortress. There was very little variation in my routine.

Adaris cleared his throat, dragging my attention downward. I plucked the pencil from behind my ear and tapped it on my bare knee, delaying the inevitable return home.

Adaris's eyes followed the movement and a line formed between his brows as he scanned my skin. He hardly missed a thing. Sometimes I wished he did. It wasn't that he thought I was being improper by showing my legs; it was him looking for anything out of the ordinary, any new and unexplained marks. My skin heated under his gaze, shame coming to me. I hoped he thought the reddening of my skin was a result of the summer heat, but I was never able to hide anything from him. I swallowed and tugged the hem of my skirt down to cover my legs and bare feet. I tugged my sleeves down past my wrists, too. Even though none of my most recent bruises were visible, I was still self-conscious, as if he could see all the old bruises that once were there.

Adaris bent to the ground with such grace and scooped a handful of dried, nutrient-depleted dirt into his fingers. The thrum of his magic appeared in the air, like a tiny spark of energy. My meager magic hummed in return deep inside me. A delicate flower sprouted from the dirt, and a gentle bloom opened. I sighed as I slipped from the high limb, climbed down to the ground, and landed with quiet grace in front of Adaris. I wiggled my toes into the soft grass. He offered his raised hand to me with a smile. I picked the dainty cream flower from the dirt, lifting it to my nose to smell the sweet aroma—jasmine, exotic and lovely. He gave my hand a tight, encouraging squeeze before offering his arm to lead me back to the house. I hesitated just a moment. I didn't bother suppressing a groan as I took his arm—accompanied with a dramatic eyeroll—and we turned toward the house.

Adaris was wise well beyond his years. Forty was young for a Fae. Especially a Highborn Fae of powerful bloodlines, like our family. While Highborn Fae were considered immortal, they could still be killed, unlike the gods. Along with extensive lifespans came strength, powers of varying abilities inherited through generations, and the capacity to heal ourselves quickly. High Fae produced very few offspring during their lifetime, some not even at all, which makes my brother and me unique. Common Fae and lower beings, such as sprites and humans, lived a normal mortal lifespan. All Fae of the Highborn Fae Families had powers, and I was no different...or so I had been told. Adaris had conjuring magic. Father could reach into other's minds. Mother could create shields with the air. Tutors came from all over the realm to teach Adaris and me to use our lower powers and perfect our higher abilities.

At twenty-four years of age, I had almost reached maturity but still hadn't come into my powers. Most Highborn Fae reached full maturity between the ages of twenty-three and twenty-five with their powers well developed by then. I remembered Adaris's powers started manifesting when he was young, much younger than most. He said they were weak at first but grew in strength slowly with time and practice. He honed them by training with the most influential teachers our father could find. He also learned to fight with a sword and hand-to-hand combat.

Adaris even went through The Trials at the early age of twenty-three. I was too young at the time to truly grasp the danger he'd been in. The Trials were an ancient tradition among the Highborn Fae. Those of High Fae families could choose to set aside their powers in an annual gathering to prove their strength, courage, and resiliency. Without their powers, they essentially became mortal. It was dangerous. It was bloody. Many were injured, and some even died, but those that walked away were given the highest respect for their entire lives.

My powers, on the other hand, seemed to be nonexistent. The Byrnes bloodline was supposed to be filled with strong Fae, long histories of shadows, and mind control and strength. And here I was, barely able to light a candle. I couldn't even heal a papercut, much to the confusion of my tutors and healers. I had to rely on the healers in Rivamir for healing, much to the embarrassment of my father. Adaris reminded me often that my powers would soon appear. I just needed to be patient and practice. Honestly, I was worried that the Byrnes powers somehow skipped over me being a second born. I tried to sneak in and listen to Adaris's lesson, hoping that I could pick up on something, anything to help, but it never did. Once Mother caught me spying during one of his daily sparring lessons with the weapons master. I hid off in the shadows, mimicking each step Adaris took. Advance. Retreat. Strike. Mother snuck in behind me, grabbed me by the ear, and dragged me from the room.

"Proper High Fae females don't need to be trained in combat. Your sole duty was to honor our family with your mind, not with a sword." She hauled me away to my tutor to pour over Fae histories.

At this point, I could hope for was a bonding with someone who was kind. Someone who could take me away from the strict hand of my father. A gentle male who I shared interests with. And maybe, just maybe, having a bondmate would give me a sense of purpose and fill this hole inside me. However, the Powers Above didn't seem to find favor in my thoughts for a bondmate. Everyone Father had suggested so far was either older, had a sour attitude, or was simply seeking an elevation in status. Not that I had any say in the matter. Father had already told me *he* would have the final say in who was selected for my future. It was tradition, after all, to be bonded by twenty-five, no matter how much I opposed the idea. Tonight presented another opportunity to find a bondmate to meet my father's high standards. I gulped down a lump in my throat as we moved closer to the shadows reaching across the grounds from the fortress.

Adaris patted my hand that had been resting on his arm. "Don't worry. We have a plan. I will keep you safe." But I still couldn't steady my trembling nerves.

TWO
EVREN

As Adaris and I walked arm in arm toward the massive stone fortress we called home, I peered over my shoulder back to the grove. My chest compressed and my breathing turned shaky.

Two years.

The grove and the winding gardens had been my haven, my escape from my bleak future. Nothing mattered and everything was left behind when I stepped into the fresh air. Two years ago, I found my secluded tree, one with a sturdy limb high in the air. At first, Adaris thought my discreet spot was clever. He only grew suspicious when I still preferred hiding in my tree when dark clouds released their downpours and lightning streaked across the sky. As if on cue, thunder rumbled from the north. The tingle of energy from far-off lightning made chills spring up on the back of my neck like an ominous warning of what was to come tonight.

My thoughts turned back to Renwick. Renwick Ashewood was appointed by Father as Head of the Black Guard toward the end of the war. Since then, he'd visited our family home on and off whenever Father didn't have him running all over the realm. However, two years ago, Father summoned Renwick to the fortress to stay. He lived in the house and managed the Black Guard, from the daily watches to the training of new recruits. He blended into our family seamlessly.

At first, our run-ins seemed accidental. He popped up in the hallways when I would turn a corner or walk by the room I was lunching in. He would slip into the library during my tutoring sessions to sit and just watch me. When Father asked him to join family meals, I couldn't escape his wandering eyes. His particular obsession with me soon became unbearable. I wasn't sure why the Head of the Black Guard showed so much interest in me. Maybe it was to get under Adaris's skin, or maybe I was seen easy prey. His twisted mind found enjoyment in harassing me, cornering me in dark alcoves and the more I pushed back, the more his interest increased. What started as distant staring and whispering inappropriate words morphed into rough hands that left bruises. My only escapes were my rooms or the grove.

The first time Renwick hit me, I cried to Father, but he brushed it off. He didn't even glance up from his work as he said, "What did you do to provoke him?" as if I deserved the blow. "It doesn't matter. Nothing matters except duty and your responsibility is to pair with whomever I see fit and to produce male heirs to carry on our bloodline." Clearly, my happiness or safety were of no concern to him. "Maybe you should focus on that instead of getting in the way of the guards." With a dismissive hand, he waved me away, returning his attention to the pile of papers and maps littering his desk.

I wasn't sure why I assumed Father would care. Father had a bit of violent streak in him too. It hadn't taken me long to learn to stay out of Father's way as a youngling, especially when he was drinking. His hands were quick to lash out if I got too close or spoke too loudly.

I was startled from my brooding as the doors to the gardens exploded open, slamming into the walls as loud as a clap of thunder, and the High Ruler of the River Kingdom burst into the garden. His entire form filled the door frame. His presence seemed to darken the sun. He was a bear of a man. His broad shoulders and stocky frame gave him a foreboding appearance. His thick mahogany hair was cropped short, though a lone wavy lock fell onto his forehead. His thin lips curved downward into a frown, his brows furrowed, and he bore down on us. His blue eyes would be striking if he wasn't furious. I tried my best not to shrink into myself with each step he took. Adaris's arm didn't waver a moment and provided me stability.

"Where the hell have you been? You were supposed to greet our guests an hour ago," he barked at Adaris, tiny droplets of spit coming from his mouth. "And you," he snarled in my direction, eyeing the dirt coating my bare feet and charcoal smudged on my fingers. I drew back under his scrutiny. "You shouldn't be wasting time out in that damned grove. You're always wasting my time."

My mouth opened and then snapped closed again, knowing I shouldn't say anything.

"I'll deliver her to her rooms now Father," Adaris said as he took a half step forward.

While Father was always red-faced and looking tense enough to detonate, Adaris was his opposite. Adaris stood tall and confident, his hands loosely clasped behind his back most of the time, giving him an air of dignity, refinement, and control.

"She's at *least* capable of walking, Adaris." Father's face flared crimson as he turned and stomped back into the house. He snapped his fingers twice in the air above his head to signal Adaris to follow him.

Adaris gave me a swift kiss on the cheek before striding after our father. "I'll see you in a little while."

I wrapped my arms around my sketchbook, clutching it tight across my chest before taking a deep breath and stepping into the dimness of the house. Even with sconces lining the walls, giving off gleaming yellow light, it took my eyes several moments to adjust. With the sun no longer warming my skin, I prickled with chills. I kept my pace quick, taking the fastest route possible to my rooms on the third floor, straining my Fae ears for any sound that I wasn't alone in the halls. Chatter from the servants filtered from the Grand Hall where dinner was being prepared. I usually tried not to wander the halls alone. I was a target in the eyes of prey when I was alone. My feet padded softly on the crimson carpeted floor. Almost there. A flight of stairs and one more turn separated me from safety.

    I took the stairs two at a time and rounded the corner. A door slammed down the hall, making me turn my head to look over my shoulder. A split second of distraction. I slammed into a solid, unyielding body. I stumbled backward, but firm hands caught my wrists before I fell to the floor. My sketchbook made a muffled thump as it landed near my feet. The firm body stepped closer, crowding me until I was forced back against the wall, my arms trapped by my side where the grip on my wrists tightened the barest amount. I tried to swallow the lump in my throat. I couldn't tell if my fear was squeezing my chest or if it was the weight of the body steadily pressing against me. The weight on my chest holding me to the wall was unbearable. I was trapped. Again.

    "Where have you been?" A gruff voice as sly as a viper. "I've been searching for you since I returned a few hours ago." A smug smile appeared on Renwick's face. I could hear it in his voice even though I refused to look up at him. Leather, sweat, and whiskey invaded my senses.

"Avoiding you obviously," I stammered under my breath, my voice dropping off at the end, failing in my bravado. I hated how his presence made me feel like a simpering idiot.

He lifted his chest off me briefly, then shoved me hard, my back and head smashing into the stone wall and his chest pinning me against him, towering over me. All the air was punched out of my lungs with a huff, and blinding pain shot through my skull making me see splotches of white.

"Feeling courageous today, I see." His mouth was so close to my ear that his hot, moist breath skated down my neck. "That's okay. I prefer when you put up a good fight." He grazed his nose along the arch of the shell of my ear, and sour bile rose in my throat. "It makes my endeavors so much more enjoyable."

A huge hand landed possessively on my hip and then greedily traveled up my side to my chest. He let loose a soft chuckle, and I clenched my teeth. I knew he could taste my fear. His hand moved to my throat, and I felt him drag a rough thumb across my jaw. I turned to move away, but his monstrous hand tightened its grip on my throat, holding my head in place, forcing my chin up to look at him. The soft yellow light from the sconces around us made his amber eyes glow fiercely. A thin black ring circled his irises. The coloring was odd, even for Fae. Even the golden streaks in his copper hair were gleaming.

I squeezed my eyes shut. I prayed to the Powers Above that someone would stumble upon us in the hallway. "You're hurting me." He gripped my throat tighter, and I held back my whimper of panic.

"If you didn't resist me, I wouldn't have to be so rough. You bring this on yourself." Those amber eyes searched my face for my reaction. He fed off my dismay and anxiety. "I missed you these last nine days." His mouth was so close to me, his voice barely over a whisper. "Particularly at night."

I hadn't missed him at all. I depended on those long stretches of days when Father had Renwick travel to oversee something or other. It was my only reprieve from his cruelty. I held my breath, waiting—waiting for what always came next. My insides curled inward, trying to anticipate whether he'd continue groping at me or strike me with another blow.

"Ashewood!" Cadoc's voice boomed from the stairway. My heart skipped a beat. I'd never been so thankful to hear my father's voice before.

Renwick froze as annoyance passed over his features. A deep growl came from him as he ran his tongue up the side of my neck before saying, "No worries, my pet. I'll find you at dinner. And then afterward we can have a proper reunion." That sick smile twisted his features again. "We will have a reason to properly celebrate after tonight."

A sharp slice of teeth stunned me as Renwick sank his teeth into my earlobe, pulling roughly as he ground his hips and erection into my stomach. He pushed away from the wall and stalked down the stairs. I remained plastered to the stone at my back, begging my shaking legs not to collapse, gulping huge mouthfuls of air. I couldn't lose myself. Not yet.

One. Two. Three. Four. Five. Run!

I ran straight for my rooms, abandoning my sketchbook on the floor, and startling several maids as I burst through the doors where I emptied the contents of my stomach into the trash pail on my bathing chamber floor, not even making it to the toilet.

THREE
ADARIS

I followed quickly after my father. Cadoc Byrnes hated to be left waiting. I didn't like leaving Evren standing alone. I knew she preferred to not be alone, especially when there were guests staying at our home. She never felt safe, though she wouldn't ever go into detail. She didn't need to. I'd seen the bruises she tried to hide from me. I was disgusted with whoever did that to her, but I hated myself more that I couldn't prevent it. The bruises and injuries had grown more frequent over the last two years, and I had a hunch as to who was to blame. I tried to shadow her as much as possible, but it was growing increasingly more difficult with Father passing on more roles to me within the Black Guard.

I knew I was supposed to greet our newest guests when they arrived earlier today, but I wanted to find Evren before Father did. Father insisted on having his heir meet any important visitors. I would have sent Renwick, but he'd disappeared...again. So, I sent Captain Whitt in my place. He was another of Father's favorites. Father would probably punish me later for abandoning my post by the gate, but I knew he'd be infuriated if Evren was late to dinner. I'd take the punishment if it meant she was out of his line of fire.

I paused just outside my father's study, straightened my jacket, and took a deep breath and slipped on a mask of disinterest before entering the crowded space. Normally the monthly Black Guard meetings took place in the Grand Hall, but with the servants preparing for a feast to rival all feasts, we had to make do with the study. At least ten high ranking guardsmen were scattered around the room, armed to the teeth, keeping close to the wood paneled walls while a few essential heads of families from the kingdom were seated on the two lush, leather couches near the fireplace. It was summer, and yet Father insisted on keeping a roaring fire going throughout the day and well into the night, which made the atmosphere stifling despite its large size.

Cadoc made his way to the enormous desk against the back wall, ignoring everyone, even those that stood to greet him. They quickly stepped away, dropping their hands in embarrassment. He spread a well-worn map of the realm across the smooth surface, holding the curled edges down with various paper weights. His favorite was a chunk of unpolished darkstone. Darkstone was one of the rarest materials in the realm, and yet Cadoc had a hunk of it on his desk being used as a mere paper weight. Darkstone was a precious material sent down from the Powers Above when they created our realm. It was scattered far and wide, so that all the lands had access to it and its potential. Many High Fae families had it mined, hoarding it for themselves and forging it into deadly weapons. With the magic of the Powers Above embedded in the stone, the weapons were the strongest ever made—never tarnishing and never needing to be sharpened. Over centuries, weapons, and collections of the darkstone were either lost or hidden making, it even more valuable than gold. It was extremely rare to see it in its raw, unpolished form. It was almost disrespectful how he treated such a gift from the gods.

    I made my way through the throng of people, all who ignored me, and came to a stop in front of my father's desk to the left. I stood with my hands clasped behind my back and patiently waited for my father to begin. The whole room became silent but buzzed with nervous energy. The heads of the families tended to be fidgety around the Black Guard. I couldn't blame them. Over half the males in this room wouldn't balk if their leader gave them the word to disembowel the one standing next to them. Their only allegiance was to their High Ruler and the River Kingdom.

Renwick Ashewood slipped in behind me and, head held high, made his way to stand sentry just behind my father's shoulder. His narrow eyes made contact with mine, licking what looked like blood off his bottom lip before a self-satisfied smile curled his mouth. The Head of the Black Guard stood like a Qana mountain cat, taking in his surroundings. He wore black leather armor, head to toe, except for the blood red cape secured to his shoulders with a steel epaulet in the shape of a snarling fox head with his rank below. Though it was the uniform of all the Black Guard, it made his presence more dominating, more formidable. One gloved hand was tucked behind his back, hidden beneath the cape while the other was draped casually on the hilt of a short dagger at his waist. I knew he had many more blades hidden on his body, but his hands were his most powerful weapon. I'd seen him from across the battlefield snap an opponent's neck with a flick of his wrist. Just another prize that my father collected for his personal arsenal. Those hands, I suspected, were the ones marring my sister's fragile frame.

Renwick was orphaned as a youngling and dumped into the Black Guard training camp as a slave like many strays were. That probably explained why he was the sadistic ass that he was growing up in such a harsh environment. No one knew his true lineage, but he did have the High Fae traits of prominent ears, healing abilities, and powers. The guardsmen and fellow slaves abused him repeatedly, taking advantage of his small size. From a young age, he'd learned to fight back when he was picked on and was known for being ruthless during brawls, biting and clawing his way free from his opponents. He was small, but he was quick and could slip through anyone's grasp. By the time he'd reached age twenty, his powers were strong and it was clear that he had great potential. The guardsmen were terrified of him after he killed a fellow slave for tripping him in the hall one day. One moment the males were laughing and pointing at Renwick sprawled on the floor. The next, the one who'd tripped him found his airway was cut off and the bones in his neck crushed. He was dead before his broken body hit the floor. That's when Cadoc and Renwick became quick friends and Renwick was promoted from slave to guardsman. Father witnessed the whole thing and had no problem convincing his father to promote Renwick from a slave to the lowest rank in the Black Guard. He worked his way up to the top. Father and Renwick still laugh remembering the moment as if it were a fond memory between the two of them.

  The rest of the Black Guard were just as fierce a group of males. The highest-ranking guards possessed strong, unique powers of one kind or another. Each member went through brutal, vigorous training to become skilled killing masters. Then a year probation period before they were initiated into the life-long service of the guard. They were then branded with the symbol of a Black Guard warrior on the side of their necks. Whether it was hand-to-hand combat or whatever weapon they were given, the guardsman were professional killers through and through. Power and fear were their mantra. No one came out of the other side of training without seeing death and lusting for more bloodshed. Except me, apparently. I would rather go through The Trials tenfold than attend Black Guard training ever again. Father had forced me into the training just days after I completed the Trial. Subconsciously, my fingers traced over the brand that was burned into my skin as well. Father had done it himself. He was so proud at the time that his only son and heir to the River Kingdom had mastered such a feat. I shuddered slightly at the memory of the back-to-back events and the recovery that took me months.

"We have a new shipment of potential trainees coming in from the Kamson Sea in two days. I need all hands-on deck patrolling the area. Captain Whitt, we need to move them to the training camp as quickly as possible." Cadoc spoke to a brutish looking guard member standing off to the side.

The Guardsman stepped forward, dressed in the same black and crimson uniform as Renwick. "Yes, High Ruler," Captain Whitt replied with an incline of his head.

"Whitt, you'll follow the trainees to base camp to get them settled." Cadoc ran his finger along the map, moving east. "We also need to get control over these smaller villages and territories. We've had a few rumors we cannot let get out of hand. We need a group of guards stationed at each village. Kines, Burford, and Giles."

Three more guards stepped forward. One of the ivory-haired elderly Fae seated on the couch jumped at their sudden movement.

"You three will select a small group each and take up these locations, here, here, and here."

"Yes, High Ruler," the three males said in unison before they stepped back into the shadows against the wall.

"Do we really need Black Guard presence in those villages?" I asked.

"Of course, we do," Renwick answered for the High Ruler.

Presumptuous prick.

I took a calming breath and angled my body more to face my father. Although Renwick was Head of the Black Guard, I still outranked him as heir to the River Kingdom. Renwick tested those boundaries any chance he got. Cadoc spun a small dagger, its hilt against a single finger and the tip dug deep into a point on the map. It looked to be a simple dagger, but was very dangerous to Fae. The blade was made of iron which would not kill a Fae immediately, but injuries from iron weapons would not heal as quickly. And if left to exposure, iron made all Fae powers weaker until they were nonexistent.

"But it's just rumors. There haven't been any uprisings or issues," I said, directing my words to my father instead of Renwick.

"Exactly. We need to keep it that way. They need to understand the laws I'm putting in place and know the penalty for breaking them," Cadoc said.

"Of course, building an alliance with those in the Wildlands would be a *much* better choice."

Cadoc paused the dagger, looked up from the map and glared at me.

"I'm not going to bond just for the sake of an alliance, Father...I mean High Ruler," I said.

Renwick grinned smugly behind him. Cadoc scowled at me, holding eye contact for several long seconds before turning back to his map.

"We'll discuss this later," Cadoc said under his breath, the cords of his neck straining as he held back his anger.

He'd been forcing the issue on me for years now. If I selected a bondmate from one of the territories that weren't giving into his pressures of taking over, I'd be able to sway them into submission. It didn't sit right with me, nor did I want to have a bondmate that I didn't even like. I also didn't agree with my father's "strategies" for controlling the surrounding territories. He'd been trying to expand the River Kingdom since he returned from the war. I'd tried everything I could to save Evren and myself from such matches, but Father wouldn't budge. In the end, I'd throw myself to the wolves before allowing Evren to suffer in a loveless match. I would go to the ends of the realm to protect her.

Renwick leaned in close to Cadoc. "Sir, and the crates from Menrath?"

Cadoc waved his hand to brush Renwick away, "Of course. We have slaves standing by at the docks to move the crates."

"Yes, High Ruler," Renwick replied as he stepped back again.

"That's all for now." All the guardsman snapped to attention. "Be sure to remain alert tonight. Don't let *anyone* go wandering around the fortress and grounds. We don't need a repeat of last month. You're dismissed."

A bustle of movement and whispers spread, then dissipated as everyone filed out of the study. Only Cadoc, Renwick, and I remained. I knew it was pointless to try to persuade my father from changing his plans, but I could at least try. The Black Guard didn't need a presence in villages with lower beings as he expanded the kingdom. All they would do is torment the residents and stir up trouble.

"Father…" I began.

"Why aren't you in uniform? The guardsmen look up to you, see you as their leader since you are my heir. If you aren't going to step up and take a serious role in the welfare of our kingdom, you at least need to dress the part," Cadoc said.

"Me mating with the daughter of another kingdom or land won't persuade them to join our cause," I said with an eye roll.

Cadoc slammed his fist on the desk, and I felt a swell of his power rush through my body and mind like a wave. "Why are you so fucking stubborn?"

I didn't reply. I knew I'd eventually lose this fight, but it wouldn't be tonight.

"You have so much of your mother in you," he sneered. "Such a waste. Such a disappointment."

It wasn't the first time I heard him say these words, but the blow was still there. I was too soft, too compassionate. I needed to be focused, deadly. That wasn't in my nature, and I was thankful to the Powers Above for that.

As the firstborn and only child, I was the heir to the River Kingdom once my father passed on. Then Mother got pregnant right before Father left for the war and gave birth to a rare second child, a girl. He didn't even know Mother was pregnant when he left for the Western Continent. Evren turned out to be just another disappointment according to my father. A second opportunity for a strong heir, but instead, he got Evren, a weak and powerless child. I had no doubt that if Evren had been male, he would've killed me just to be rid of me.

"Go get dressed. And don't forget your sword. We need to be a united front. I can't have these fools thinking we aren't a strong unit."

I gave a small bow before turning to leave, my boots muffled by the ornate rugs covering the stone floor. Renwick was still poised behind my father's right side like a loyal dog.

"I'll see you at the feast," Renwick called out behind me. His voice grated on my nerves. "I'm looking forward to your father's announcement. It's been a long time coming."

I clenched my fists tight but didn't bother responding as I strode from the room, leaving behind the two males alone in my father's study.

FOUR
EVREN

"**R**eally, Evren. Again?" Mother pursed her lips, turning to the lady's maid that was fussing with my hair while I sat in front of the mirror at my vanity. "Be sure *those* are hidden." She pointed a long, bejeweled finger at me before stepping away.

The disgust in Mother's voice was palpable. It hung like a cloak of shame on my shoulders. I didn't bother responding to my mother's exasperated response to my new injuries. The pitiful maid had just finished buttoning me into my gown before Mother started barking orders at her. She gave a timid curtsy before sweeping my hair in a new direction and securing it to cover the bite mark on my earlobe. I wasn't sure why Mother didn't allow the healers to close the wound. They were never allowed to hide the marks that Renwick so generously gifted me. The high curved points of my ears poked out through the layers of jeweled pins and curls. Mother typically preferred my ears to be on full display as a show of our power, but that wouldn't be possible tonight. Another maid dusted a pale powder across my neck to cover the purpling fingerprints beginning to show.

Mother had ignored the bruises and injuries I'd accumulated from the very beginning. The only evidence she noticed the abuse were the new dresses that appeared in my wardrobe—long sleeves to cover my arms, darker fabrics to cover the discolored skin on my shoulders and back. I'm convinced that was more for appearance than actual concern. If she were truly concerned, she would've acted on my behalf. Renwick was always so careful where he left marks on me. He wouldn't want to be caught in his actions, would he? He'd never hit my face. I almost wished he would so that I had proof of his brutalities. Leaving visible marks on my neck was new for him, either in show of lack of control or in blatant possessiveness, I wasn't sure.

Mother hadn't always been this way. Before Father returned from the war, we were inseparable. As any mother and child should be. But with the return of the head of the house, a rift formed. I didn't understand what had changed. Since then, we'd lost the close bond we shared. Now she went out of her way to spend as little time in my presence as possible. I could go days without seeing her. She preferred leaving my care to tutors and servants.

When Father announced I was to have a bondmate, she'd made an appearance again, but truly just sat on the chair in the corner while my lady's maid transformed me into the ideal Highborn Fae lady—pinching here, fluffing there, to make me look like a bonded-to-be. Mother may have looked at me but never saw me.

♀

Two colossal, intricately carved steel doors opened into the Grand Hall. The massive room looked stunning, just like every other feast Father hosted in hopes of finding me a bondmate. A long table with elaborate decorations ran along the back of the room in front of a monstrous fireplace, flanked by floor-to-ceiling glass doors thrown open to the night. Crimson velvet curtains trimmed with silver rustled in the breeze. The bubbling and splashing of water from a fountain in the adjoining courtyard floated like music through the opened windows. The gardens were beloved by our guests not only for the lush blows and vibrant colors but also the captivating view. The cobblestone patio looked out over the Great River. The Qana Mountains painted a panoramic view across the sky in the background. The sun was retreating off to the west, decorating the sky like a majestic canvas, and the two rose gold moons hung low in the east, followed by a blanket of stars. Thick clouds nestled above the ridgeline foreshadowed how the evening would end.

Lit torches were evenly spaced between the windows lining the entire dining hall. Despite having electricity throughout the fortress, Father liked the atmosphere the flames gave to the room. A darkstone and steel chandelier hung from the ceiling casting the hall in a bright, warm glow. Its center was twisted steel that matched the trees in the grove, the branches reaching out with candles on the ends of each one. Crystals made of darkstone dripped below the candles and sparkled in the firelight.

Delicious smells of meats, bread, and herbed potatoes wafted through the air as servants milled around making final adjustments on all the round guest tables spread around the perimeter of the room where the lower guests would be seated. The more respected guests would sit at the long tables positioned at the center of the hall. Most of the time, the guest list didn't change. The only alteration was whichever honored family Father had selected that week. Mother always made sure we arrived before my father, and that we were in place near the head table.

The Byrnes Family crest—a crimson and steel shield with the head of a snarling fox engraved in the center with long swords of darkstone forged in the god's fires crossed behind the shield—hung above the mantle behind my father's chair. The words *Power and Fear* curved along the bottom of the shield.

"Stop fidgeting. It's growing tiresome," My mother's voice hissed.

The first words she spoke to me since we entered the hall. We arrived almost half an hour early.

Mother was particularly irritable that evening. Her eyes made contact with the marks hidden under layers of powder before quickly moving away and pressing her lips into a thin line. My hand fluttered at my neck for the briefest of moments before I brushed my hands down the front of my full, burgundy skirts. The soft silk was smooth and delicate under my fingertips. My matching slippers were already pinching my feet. The long, flowing skirts had layers upon layers of fabric that made my bottom half look triple its regular size. The dress Mother had selected for me this evening was *not* one of my favorites, but it offered full coverage, which I craved right now. Even with the neckline covering up to my collarbone and flowing all the way to my wrists, I still felt exposed. At least she hadn't seen the fingerprints encircling each wrist. I hated that my fair skin bruised so easily and that I couldn't heal the marks. I couldn't stop my hands from quivering after my interaction with Renwick just an hour prior. I pressed my palms to my stomach. I tried to stifle the suffocation crushing my chest, but the bodice encrusted in delicate garnet jewels seemed to grow tighter with each breath, exasperating my panic.

"Powers Above! Evren, just go sit already," Mother said.

I didn't question her, just jumped at the chance to get off my shaking legs and away from the crowd that began to pour into the hall. A cloud of perfumes accompanying the lavishly dressed ladies gave me a headache. Hopefully, the fresh air flowing in through the open windows would provide some relief.

Over the last two years, it had been the same. Refreshments and alcohol kicked off the night while guests gathered and chatted. Light music played in the background, but there had never been dancing. Father despised dancing. A servant would ring the gong, and everyone would take their seats. Course after course of food was served, followed by dessert and the whiskey and wine ever-flowing. By the end of the night, most of the guests were tipsy enough for me to sneak away undetected.

Each week, Father presented me to a potential new bondmate. The male usually ignored me through dinner, choosing to speak to my father about their achievements and ideas to improve our realm. I preferred it that way. The handsy ones were the worst. One male from the Wildlands had no problem attempting to staking his claim by running his hand up my thigh. Adaris put an end to that by staking his dagger through the back of the male's other hand that was propped on the table. After that, Father made Adaris move to the opposite side of him next to our mother so he couldn't cause anymore disruptions.

I found my place at the head table, two seats down from my father's chair. I dropped into my seat, immediately reaching for a glass of water and taking a big gulp to try to calm my nerves as I peered around.

You'd think I'd be used to this by now, but…

Something was different. I placed my glass down on the table and took a closer look at my surroundings. There were twice as many servants moving around the hall than usual. More tables were set up as well, boarding an open space. The lights reflected off the freshly polished floor like the stars off the river waters outside on a clear night. Even a small orchestra was warming up in the corner compared to the normal quartet. My stomach sank like a stone had dropped in it. My palms began to sweat profusely. I clenched them into fists and placed them in my lap. Whatever Father had planned this evening made me on edge.

Several minutes passed, and after slow, deep breaths, I finally began to relax a little.

Father arrived, stopping at the entrance of the hall. He'd added the Black Guard cape to his attire as well as a deadly looking longsword on his hip. His hand rested casually on the hilt and his chin was lifted high. Every guardsman jerked to attention, their heels snapping together, and a fist placed over their hearts in salute. Then Adaris stepped up beside him.

Adaris and I locked eyes briefly, and the stiffness he held in his shoulders subsided. He wore the same breeches and boots from earlier—I could still see a fleck of grass in the heel of the boot. But he'd replaced his unbuttoned shirt with a crimson evening jacket. The dark, blood-red material stood out among all the bright gowns and jackets of the other guests. The silver buttons and thread glittered.

I smirked at his small defiance. Father preferred him to be in his full Black Guard uniform, but Adaris usually found a way around that.

All eyes turned to Adaris once Father made his way into the crowd. A couple rushed past the throng to be the first to greet him. He smiled with a wink at me before turning to chat with the overly primped duo. Even with my sharp Fae hearing, I couldn't hear across the hall with all the background buzz of chatter, but he made a polite bow to the female who had red-painted lips and the male who was already swaying on his feet. Based on the empty crystal glass in his hand, I'd say he'd already enjoyed plenty of whiskey. Both bowed low in greeting to the River Kingdom's heir.

I watched as servants moved from table to table, lighting the final candles that were decoratively placed as centerpieces. They each carried a long wooden stick with a flame bobbing on the end to set the wicks aflame. As a servant passed close by, I was mesmerized by the luminous glow. It was so similar to a dream I'd been having recently. I couldn't remember when they started. I didn't have the dream every night, and it was a dream more of shapes and shadows than anything. Images flashed through my mind like a book—strong yet gentle hands caressing, flashes of dark eyes and full lips, and ethereal fire. The liquid flames and streaks of darkness caressed my body the same way the hands did, but never burned or left a mark on my skin.

Suddenly, fingertips brushed along the nape of my neck. My breath caught in my throat and panic shot through me. My neck and shoulders went taunt. So unlike the touch in my dreams, this contact was far too familiar and made me cringe with dread.

"I told you I'd find you again, my pet."

Ice filled my veins as Renwick pulled the chair out between mine and my father's and sat down, draping his arm along the back of my chair. I stiffened at his closeness, keeping my eyes focused on Adaris as he moved around the room, silently pleading with him to rescue me.

"Lucky me. I get to have you as company tonight for dinner." He trailed a thumb across the patch of bare skin on my shoulder.

Renwick was a favorite among the ladies. His copper hair was cropped short, showing off his chiseled jaw and pointed ears. His golden eyes twinkled in the chandelier light. He wasn't a tall male or sculpted like many of the other guardsman, but he held himself in such a way that made him the center of attention. His full lips lifted in a dazzling smile that would make many, males and females alike, swoon at his feet. He was attractive and brilliant and charming...until he wasn't.

What was he doing sitting here? The seat between my father and me was reserved for my potential bondmate, not Head of the Black Guard. Powers Above, please someone tell me he's playing a cruel joke.

A dinner gong sounded, making me jump, and the crowd began making their way to their seats. The dull roar in my ears blocked out all other sounds until I blinked and Adaris was standing in front of me.

"Evren?" Adaris looked like he would explode at any moment. His eyes danced back and forth between Renwick and me. "Evren, are you alright?"

"She's just fine," Renwick spoke before I could and brushed his hand on the nape of my neck again. He winked. "I'll take good care of her tonight."

Adaris pulled his lips back, baring his teeth, about to say something, but he was interrupted by our father.

"Enough you two," Father hissed between clenched teeth.

A surge of power from Father rippled in the air pushing space between them. Both males quieted but Renwick was the only one that relaxed. Adaris remained rigid as he took the seat beside our mother.

⚲

Dinner carried on as usual. The servants served each course precisely as Father liked. Father and Renwick carried on a conversation despite my presence, though Renwick's possessive touch never left me— whether his fingers brushed mine as he grabbed his fork, or his knee making contact with my thigh, he made it a point to touch me all throughout the meal.

Tonight, I only had to make it through dessert. I'd hardly touched the food placed before me, afraid that if I did, I wouldn't be able to contain the contents of my stomach.

Father stood to my right, raising his glass to make his regular pre-dessert speech. The guests laughed and clapped in all the proper places, but I kept my face cast downward. I'd heard the same speech over and over; I could probably recite it by memory.

"Our realm is strong, but the River Kingdom will make it stronger... With the right allies, anything is possible..."

Blah blah blah.

My eyes were drawn to scattered droplets of wine on the cream tablecloth. They resembled drops of blood.

Suddenly, the entire hall burst into an uproar of shouts and applause.

"Evren? Evren, are you paying attention?" Water sloshed into my mouth from my raised cup, and I choked.

I blinked up at him, still in shock that he acknowledged me in the middle of a crowded room, before returning my gaze to my plate.

"Bondmate," Cadoc repeated, his nostrils flared.

Did I hear him correctly? He has seriously lost his mind.

I cleared my throat from the water I'd choked on. I dabbed my mouth with my napkin and placed my glass back on the table.

I didn't meet his gaze. "I'm sorry?" My hushed words were almost inaudible. I didn't want to anger him. Anything above a whisper would likely set him off based on the tension radiating from him. My breath stuck in my chest.

He had gone mad!

He was leaning with both hands splayed on the table now. He drummed his fingers on the table impatiently, his rings knocking against the fabric-covered wood in a rhythmic thump.

The expansive room seemed to hum with energy in the silence.

"I have selected a bondmate for you." Father's tight tone didn't hide that he was obviously annoyed with having to repeat himself. He cleared his throat and rolled his eyes in exasperation. "General Ashewood." He puffed out his chest and clasped his friend on the shoulder. He ignored my reaction, unfazed by my sputtering. "And there's no need to wait. We can have the blood binding ritual taken care of by the winter solstice."

My mouth hung open in shock, my head shaking from side to side. I couldn't look at him. I just stared down at my unfinished plate of food. I didn't respond. I *couldn't* respond. I knew my father had been looking for a bondmate for me. It was all he spoke about lately. But to suggest that I attach myself to Renwick Ashewood was insane. Not only was he much older than me, but he was a horrid, vile male, with a disgusting sense of humor—and his need to dominate and abuse those around him, including me. I had spent the last two years hiding from him. Why on earth would I want this monster to have a permanent place in my life? He isn't even Highborn! Father always preached about how important bloodlines are, so why was he brushing that aside now?

"Father, you can't be serious?" Adaris stood, his chair scraping on the stones as it slid back before falling over with a crack.

Gratitude filled me; my brother, always my protector.

Our father's fist slammed onto the table, sending plates and utensils scattering to the floor. I tensed and flinched away from him. "The decision is final." His voice amplified from the high, stone ceiling and an outpouring of magic. There wasn't a sound in the hall. Not a single sound. Not even a whisper. The only thing I could hear was my ragged breath.

Father raised a glass and chatter began to fill he room again. He turned to his friend, but Renwick wasn't paying attention. He had a wicked smile painted on his face, and his eyes wandered across me, down my body, devouring me with his eyes. He seemed to enjoy the horror that wafted from me. He slid his hand under the table and along my thigh. I tried to not physically heave the scant amount of food in my stomach. I was suddenly grateful that my full skirt prevented me from feeling the heat of his hand. Father knew of Renwick's character, of course. They were best friends, after all, and had been since childhood. They were similar in their savage way, which was the reason he was his right-hand male. Of course he'd found a way. He wanted him bound to our family.

My mother remained oblivious to the whole conversation, as she usually was. Seated at my father's right side, she pushed her food around her plate, a blank stare at an invisible point before her. She always seemed to be in some sort of trance, distracted from what was going on around her. Her eyes were glazed and unfocused on something far away.

My eyes finally left my plate, but instead of looking at Renwick or my father, I found my brother's eyes. Adaris's face was heavy with sadness. I saw the slight incline of his head before he turned to our father, pretending to listen to their conversation. Tonight had to be the night. An unspoken agreement we'd spent months preparing. We had to act as soon as possible. We knew it was a possibility, but we didn't think it would be so soon. I turned melancholy with the realization that this could potentially be the last time I saw my brother and mother. And that's even if everything fell into the proper place.

Adaris knew of my dream to have safety and security in life. To have a bigger life than to breed for the sake of a bloodline. He didn't want me to live a life like our mother. Neither of us wanted that. A life full of uncertainty and fear, an oppressed life, having to peer around every corner and tiptoe around to not anger her bonded would not be my future. My father wanted me to bear an heir and be a trophy. I didn't see why anyone would ever want to live like that. So Adaris and I had devised a backup plan, in case the male that our father selected for me was unsuitable. And Renwick was unsuitable.

I flinched when Father slammed his fist to the table again. My breath caught in my throat. This time, though, it was in response to a joke Renwick whispered in his ear. I wasn't sure how long it had been since the room resumed its festivities. I gulped back the emotion that was building in my throat, and I felt my chest tighten. I clasped my hands together under the table, twisting my fingers into knots. Overwhelming panic was threatening to break free, the loss of control. I had to be brave. My life depended on it.

♀

Adaris and I waited until after dessert when our father had finished a few goblets of wine and had moved on to whiskey. The entire room was absorbed in the celebration of my upcoming union. Father reclined in his chair, head thrown back in laughter at some barbaric joke between him and Renwick.

"Excuse me." I spoke more to myself than to anyone else.

No one batted an eye when I snuck from the Grand Hall. Not father, not mother, not even the ever-present guardsman who stood like statues at every exit. I slipped from the hall and darted to my room to change out of my evening gown.

For once, I wasn't afraid of what lurked in the shadows as I ran through the fortress to my rooms. Nothing was worse than the males I'd left behind at dinner. Adrenaline pulsed through my system. I pushed the door closed behind me once I made it to my room. I rushed to get out of my gown and into the disguise I'd hidden under my bed.

It wasn't until I stood in the middle of my room that everything came crashing back down on me. My feet moved in a slow circle, my boots whisper soft on the plush rug, and took in my bedroom one last time. My gown and silk slippers were discarded in a pile near my bed. The gems and pins that adorned my body were scattered on my vanity. Nothing here held any importance anymore. This room used to be my sanctuary. My favorite velvet chair was tucked near the fireplace, a shawl draped across the armrest. My bed was covered in blankets and pillows. The twin doors leading to the balcony where I painted and sketched were closed tight against the night. The double moons were no longer visible in the cloudy sky, and darkness had blocked out the stars. I used to feel safe here, but now, as I looked around, all I saw was a future that was a prison. I would not be a prisoner any longer.

The only thing I needed was my dagger. Rather, Adaris's dagger. Father had given it to him when he completed The Trials. The dagger was given to our father from his father. An heirloom passed down from generation to generation. And Adaris had given it to me.

Rushed footsteps coming down the hallway made me snatch the dagger from under my bed and hid it behind my back. My hand cramped from my tight grip on the leather-wrapped hilt. I prayed it wasn't Renwick that followed me. The door cracked open, and my heart froze as I prepared to strike. I knew I was no match against him, but I wouldn't go without a fight. Then Adaris's head popped into the room. I let out a breath of relief.

"We need to go. Now."

FIVE
EVREN

Even with the feast winding down, the night of celebration had only begun. The sweltering kitchen was a flurry of activity. The copper sink was overflowing with dishes, pots, and pans. The substantial butcher block table in the middle of the space had desserts of all kinds cluttering its surface—tarts and miniature cakes, slices of pie, and assorted pastries. Several servers were carting the desserts on large, round platters into the Grand Hall and returning with even more dishes. The scullery maids, sleeves rolled to the elbow, didn't bat an eye as more items were dumped onto the endless pile. They scrubbed and rinsed in a rush to prevent the stack from getting out of hand. Other servants shouted over each other, jokes and laughter filling the space, as they picked at leftover scraps of the dinner. No one bothered to pull their attention from their task as Adaris and I quickly made for the servant's door that lead out back to the river's edge.

Reaching his hand into a concealed crack in the stone wall, Adaris pulled out a weathered satchel. He'd hidden it weeks ago when we pieced our plan together. The satchel was light, with only a few days' supplies. He opened it and dropped a parcel of food into it before closing it again.

"Once you cross the river, run to the trees. You can camp there tonight. At first light, hike toward the mountains. There is a village not too far, Lakeshore. You can stay at an inn there. I'll come to find you," he said as he helped me tighten the straps of the pack across my shoulders.

I nodded my head. We stood sheltered in the stoned archway, the wind bringing the incoming storm swirled the dark grasses at our feet. There was a faint hoot of an owl off in the distance. Adaris held my shoulders, arm's distance away, and searched my face.

"Are you sure you want to do this?" Deep lines formed between his brows; the corners of his eyes turned down.

"Yes, I'm sure." My answer was out of my mouth before he even finished his question. "I cannot go through life with him. I cannot live in constant fear."

I cast my eyes down to my feet, pulling at the sleeve of my shirt to cover the purplish-green bruises staining my fair skin from this afternoon. Anger flashed in his violet eyes. I unconsciously brought my hand to my side where an older bruise yellowing with time marked my ribs. Renwick had cornered me in the library before he left for his last trip. He hadn't been thrilled when I refused his lips on my neck. I had jerked away from him when he slammed his mouth against mine, shoved against his chest in protest. As repayment, he threw me against a nearby table. I was surprised it didn't crack a rib. Had a servant not walked through the door at that moment, there is no telling what he would've done.

Renwick didn't need to use his fists to hit me; he just preferred to. There had been plenty of times he'd used his mind to hurt me. With a simple look he could have me pinned against the wall or tossed like a ragdoll across the floor. Even worse were the times invisible hands caressed my body from across the room. That power, those invisible hands, were the exact reason my father had named him Head of the Black Guard. His power and skill made him invaluable.

I tugged at my shirt again. I felt uncomfortable and exposed in the pair of pants that clung to my hips. The young stable boy Adaris had taken them from did not have the shapely hips I did. I couldn't possibly run in a dress, much less cross the river. The thin, flowy material of my tunic billowed in the breeze.

I sighed. "There must be more to life than binding myself to a male that doesn't give a damn about me. He only wants me as a prize and a punching bag." I bit down on my lower lip. It was the first time I'd admitted to Adaris out loud what Renwick was doing to me. But I needed him to understand why I couldn't turn back now. "I'm just a way for him to stay close to Father. I'd rather face the unknown than a future of torment."

My heart thundered in my chest as lightning forked across the sky, sending a crackle of energy through the air.

I lifted my face to his, my eyes burning as tears threatened to fall. My brother was my best friend and had been my guardian for as long as I could remember. I did not want to leave him. I remember Mother telling him, "Adaris, always protect your sister, no matter the cost." But he was powerless against our father and his desire for me to fulfill my duty. He knew it. I knew it. Adaris enveloped me in a tight hug, lending me his strength, and bringing me the smallest glimmer of hope.

"You can do this Evren. You are stronger than you think." His timid smile didn't quite meet his eyes. "Besides, it's a perfect night for a swim."

I attempted a smile in return but failed. Then we snuck wordlessly down to the river's edge. I looked back at Adaris one more time and saw his lips moving, the roar of the water drowning out his last words to me. That was for the better. Even another minute could have had me second guessing myself.

During the summer months, we would spend hours swimming in the Great River. Followed by baking in the hot sun on the shore. The water had turned frigid even though summer hadn't ended. The snow up in the Qana Mountains where the river originated within the lofty peaks had already made it an almost unbearable raging beast. I wasn't sure how Adaris had convinced me that swimming across the river was a good idea, but I waded into the rushing current anyway, the icy water chilling me to the bone.

The water was like knives piercing my skin as I stepped further and further from the shore. The water crept up my stomach, and I sucked in a deep breath. Then there was a sharp drop, and the ground beneath my feet vanished. My head sank below the surface, and the current dragged me downstream. My lungs burned, desperate for air. I struggled against the weight of the pack on my bag, arms flailing through the water, grasping for anything that would save me as I was pulled deeper and deeper. My feet hit the muddy bottom, and out of pure instinct, I pushed hard against the sludge, propelling myself upward to the surface. Just when I didn't think I could hold my breath for a second longer, my head broke through the surface. Air rushed into my lungs and then my head slipped underwater again. Over and over, the torrent slammed into me, attempting to crush me. I wasn't sure how I'd survive this. I couldn't tell how far I needed to swim to reach the other side. All I saw was darkness. The water pounded against my ears. It would almost have been easier to just submit to the water and let it take me. No more pain. No more fear. But that would be like Renwick winning, like my father winning. I'd barely lived a real life. So, as my feet found purchase on the bottom of the river once more, I used all my strength to burst through the surface, arms dragging through the frigid waters and swimming to the shoreline. Never give in. Never surrender.

It was only by a miracle from the Powers Above that I crossed the river. My hands were stiff and achy as I climbed from the water, my boots slipping on the wet rocks and mud. My clothes clung to my body as I heaved myself up the opposite shore. I remained on my hands and knees as I tried to catch my breath. I looked over my shoulder back to the fortress. The water had dragged me further downstream, but Adaris was there. As soon as he saw I was alive, he disappeared back into the darkness of the fortress to cover my trail.

With great effort, I stood. And then I ran. As fast as I could. The mud squelched with each step and splattered up my legs and onto my hands. Mother would be furious at me for racing through such sludge. She'd be furious at me for running. *Never appear to be in a rush,* she always said but survival trumped manners at this point. Survival was my only focus. Surviving long enough to make it into those trees ahead.

Straight for the trees, across the open grasses between the river and the Sacred Forest. The last light of the day danced in the wind, turning the world all oranges and reds. The incoming storm gobbled up the colors and light as it approached. Blood pounded in my ears. I imagined the guards raising the alarm as they looked for me, but I knew that wouldn't happen. Adaris would cover for me.

The further I got from the water's edge, the more solid the ground became underfoot. One hundred yards to the tree line. My legs burned, but I pushed myself harder, faster toward the trees. The wind whipped past my face, dragging strands of sopping hair across my eyes. They stuck to my cheeks and lips. I didn't dare look back over my shoulder. Fifty yards left, my heart was beating fast. I had to keep running. My legs burned with the effort. A clap of thunder shook the earth. Lightning crackled in the sky.

I had to make it to the tree line. That's what Adaris had said.

"Just make it to the trees and you can hide. I'll tell Mother you weren't feeling well and needed to lie down. They won't notice you've gone missing until the morning and then I'll lead them south, toward the city. You've always wanted to see the city, after all."

I glanced up to see the mountains towering in front of me. The storm was approaching quickly. The air was thick with moisture as tiny drops pelted my face. Black clouds dominated the horizon. White-capped peaks stood out in stark contrast to the clouds.

Keep moving. Keep going. Stop for nothing.

A sea of thick, dark trees surrounded the base of the mountains, making it look as if the peaks floated. Those ancient trees, overgrown and wild looking. For a moment, I hesitated, my steps slowing just a touch. The stories my mother told me of the horrors in these woods swept through my mind. There were beasts that would eat children if they wandered too far into the darkness. Wicked creatures of all kinds that gave a fate worse than death lurked there. Creatures that would lure you into their caves with light, airy songs before devouring you alive. But the horrors that hid were nothing compared to what I faced back home.

    I picked up my pace again as I entered the woods. No regrets. No hesitation. Thick brambles tore at my pants, slicing into my skin. Layers of leaves and twigs covered the forest floor, covering thick, warped roots that erupted from the ground. My foot caught onto something and I crashed to the ground. My arms weren't fast enough to catch me. The side of my head and shoulder slammed into a nearby stump. A sharp pain surged across my head, and the tang of blood filled my mouth. Tears erupted from me, as a haze covered my eyes, my mind surrendering to swirling darkness.

SIX
EVREN

I tried to open my eyes. Blood coated my lashes of one eye. Mossy earth and decaying leaves filled my nose as I wiped my face, cringing as my fingers brushed the cut on my temple. Even in the dimness of the woods, the light sent streaking pain through my head, causing me to wince. My whole body ached from the impact of the ground. My foot was tangled with a root hidden in the underbrush. As if it was holding me, pinning me to the ground. I pushed my hands against the sodden forest floor and brought myself onto my knees. The world spun in a haze around me as I attempted to orient myself. My eyes squeezed shut to stave off the nausea. It was useless. For the second time that night, my stomach hurled its contents until the only thing left was watery bile.

How long was I out?

It couldn't have been long. The sun's light was a thin line on the horizon. The storm had passed quickly. I stamped down the fear trying to bubble to the surface. No one would follow me tonight.

My shirt was torn, and blood had begun to dry from a deep gash in my shoulder. Everything dripped with the fresh downpour, and the air was much cooler in the shade of the trees. The forest grew dimmer with each passing second, dark shapes and shadows already playing tricks on my eyes. I couldn't stay here; I was too close to the edge of the forest. I had to keep moving. I had to find some sort of shelter. If I didn't, there was no telling what creatures would find me. A shiver of fear shot down my spine. Still, on my knees, I looked around. The movement made my stomach twist again. The metallic tang of bile threatened to come up again, but I took a steady breath through my nose. The only thing as far as I could see, which wasn't very far, were trees and more trees. I hadn't realized how dense the forest was. Just to the left, I spotted a tree that had fallen from rot, leaning against a large oak that formed a makeshift lean-to. I whispered a quick thanks to the Powers Above.

I yanked my ensnared foot free, then struggled to stand. I had to grasp a nearby limb to steady myself. The pack Adaris had strapped to my back was leaden with river water but still attached to me. How the in circle of dark hells had I not lost it? I've never been very religious, but I found myself thanking the Powers Above for the second time in the last two minutes. The gods of this world were never a concern to my parents. They considered the belief system antiquated and a waste of breath, though my tutors had drilled me on the Essence Scrolls anyways. Only wealthy families had their own copy of the Essence Scrolls, which clearly laid out the rules of all life. Common Fae and lower beings had to visit the Temples of Anruin, which were scattered across the realm, to study under the priestesses. One tutor scolded me daily of how privileged I was to have access to such knowledge and to stop complaining.

The Powers Above consisted of four gods: The God of Earth, the God of Fire, the God of Air, and the God of Water. Long ago, the gods blessed the Fae with aspects of their divine powers, gifts to bring them joy and help maintain peace in the world. Even some lower beings were gifted with small powers. However, some of the Fae became power-hungry, wanting to possess all the power from the gods. When the gods refused to give more power, four Fae, one for each of the gods, gathered and led a revolt, The Uprising, combining their powers to unleash darkness and chaos into the world. The Great Chaos came into this world and threatened to destroy it. Since then, the world has been in a constant battle between chaos and good.

I could only hope the gods were on my side tonight. I limped over to the fallen tree covered in mushrooms and peered into the makeshift shelter. Soft, green moss covered the inside of the shelter, and wet leaves piled against the trunk. I ducked my head as I climbed into the closeness and dropped my sopping pack onto the ground with a sopping thump. My body began to tremble with the dropping temperature. I quickly unpacked my bag, not only to dry out my belongings but to create an extra barrier against the wind. I hung my clothes and my one blanket from the knots and broken limbs along the fallen tree. I never knew what was legend and what was the truth when it came to the Powers Above and the gods, but tonight, I would pray to them to keep me alive.

I took a deep breath and examined my surroundings again. As children, Adaris and I had spent many days wandering through the grove that surrounded our home. With Adaris by my side, I was fearless. Even with our age difference, Adaris still spent most of his afternoons with me. We'd build forts and have sword fights to guard our kingdoms. He'd tell me about his school lessons and teach me how to skip rocks across the water. But the giant trees of the Sacred Forest were like nothing I'd seen before. The forest was a whole new creature itself. It breathed with the wind that whispered throughout its canopy, like a pulsing presence. Eerie noises came from deep within it like a foreign language I couldn't understand, beckoning me to go deeper.

Legend has it that the Sacred Forest was a result of the gods. The Darkwood Trees had bark black as midnight. Branches spread low and wide, some even sweeping so close to the ground I could perch on them. They intertwined and stretched to the sky. The trunks were thicker than the stone pillars holding up the bridge leading to the River Kingdom and they reached well over fifty feet. The canopies of the Darkwood trees consisted of dark green and brown leaves as large as my hand. Deep veins ran through the leaves like veins in an arm. If you held it up to the sun, they almost appeared to be pulsing. When The Great Chaos was first released, the gods sat back and watched as all the Fae and creatures of the realm fought the Uprising. But seeing they were on the losing side, the gods came down and fought alongside them to contain the spreading darkness. Each tree was said to be an evil being trapped forever by the God of Earth. It's why the black bark was twisted and gnarled as if it something was reaching to escape something. The gods left the forest stretching across our realm as a reminder of the Chaos and what happens when those revolt against the gods. They then banished all the dark magic to the circle of dark hells where it is still trapped today.

 I slumped to the hard earth. Water dripped from my body and clothes onto the dirt and leaves. *Drip, drip, drip.* I dropped my aching head down into my hands. Strands of my damp hair that were pulled free during my crossing stuck to my hands. I tried not to let myself think of Adaris and what would happen to him when our father found out he helped me escape. No. I couldn't think like that. Adaris was smart; he would find a way to protect himself. He could talk himself out of any situation. It was one of his many talents. I wanted to start a fire for heat and light, to chase away the shadows, but I didn't want to attract more attention to myself. I also had no knowledge of starting a fire. Maybe I should've learned something so vital to my survival. Too late now.

Loneliness began to undo me from within. The grief. The pain. The loss. Wariness overwhelmed me as I swallowed back the emotions. There weren't any sounds in the forest except the rustling of the leaves and the whistle of the wind as it moved through the Darkwood trees. My eyelids drooped heavily, but I was too fearful to sleep. I wrapped my arms around my knees, rocking back and forth. I clutched my dagger in my hand and couldn't help slipping into a restless sleep.

SEVEN
EVREN

M*other was a nervous mess, pacing back and forth in the entrance hall, pulling at her fingers. Every few minutes, she'd stop in front of the grand clock and mumble something to herself before resuming her pacing. She'd dressed me in my best that morning. She even snapped at me over breakfast for not being able to sit still. Father returning home had her on edge.*

I, on the other hand, was thrilled to finally meet my father. I was only seven years of age and eager to finally meet the male that Adaris had told me about. My stomach fluttered as my mind raced with visions of our first interaction. Would he be formal and stiff like the High Ruler I imagined, greeting me with a kiss on the hand? Or would he be playful and joyous like Adaris and toss me in the air, wrapping me in his embrace? My excitement made it nearly impossible to sit still as Mother had instructed me.

Adaris, as usual, was calm and collected, leaning against the banister of the wide staircase leading up to the family quarters. His arms were loosely crossed over his chest, and he winked at me when he caught me staring at him.

"You look beautiful, little sister," he said to me.

I looked down at my dress and smoothed the lilac fabric with my fingers. It was one of my favorite dresses because it made my eyes stand out, or at least that's what my maid told me. My mother had twisted and braided my long, silver hair down my back and Adaris had tucked a jasmine flower behind my ear. I'd never felt so pretty as in that moment. And I knew Father would approve.

My head shot up when I heard laughter and boisterous voices before the mammoth steel doors exploded open and a burly male stepped in and froze. Servants scattered, leaving only the four of us standing in the foyer. Father's round face was covered in a thick muddy brown beard, and his eyes were blazing aqua pools like the sea. His broad shoulders blocked out the sunlight behind him casting him in an almost shadow. His gaze first settled on Adaris, who'd straightened and taken a step forward toward our father.

"My son," he said, his voice deep as he clasped Adaris on the shoulder.

The male towered over Adaris a good foot and a half. Then he turned to Mother.

"Arabelle." There was no love in his voice, but rather contentment. "You look lovely as always."

When he swooped down for a swift kiss, she kept her eyes away from his face but tilted her head, offering her cheek to him.

"What is it?" he asked, confused.

And then he spotted me. I scrambled to my feet, all long limbs and clumsy. The anger I felt from him seared at my skin worse than a burn. Fury came at me like a wave. My throat went dry as I tried to speak.

"I..." *I cleared my throat.* "I'm your daughter, Evren." *I took a sheepish step forward.*

"Arabelle. What is this?" *His voice was deathly quiet. His face turned scarlet as he dragged his gaze to Mother.*

"I can explain, Cadoc," *Mother spoke softly, keeping her eyes down, her hands folded tightly against her skirts. I'd never seen her look so small.*

I knew he was referring to me, but I didn't know what I had done wrong. Even Adaris was confused by our father's reaction. I took a step back, the tips of my pointed ears and cheeks reddening.

"Father," *Adaris started, but Father cut him off.*

"Shut up, boy!"

I could taste the rage in the air, the tension so thick that not even a blade could slice through it. Adaris moved closer to me, gently pulling on the back of my dress and pulling me to him.

"You bitch! How could you? Do you even know what you've done?" *Father's voice shook the walls.* "How could you bring such shame down on this family?"

He threw a backward fist at my mother. I heard her teeth snap together as she fell to the ground.

"I didn't know until after you left." *Mother's voice was brittle.* "I swear."

Adaris didn't hesitate as he grabbed me around the waist and pulled me away, spinning me away, and shielding me from the sight. I was too afraid to fight against him, I just buried my face into his shirt, squeezing my eyes shut tightly. Terror welled up inside me like a wave.

"You should've had her taken care of! Did you even think?" our father bellowed.

Another wave of terror hit me as I heard a sickening thump and a bubbling gurgle of pain come from my mother. I pressed an ear into Adaris's chest, trying to drown out the sound that kept echoing in my mind.

"Cadoc please!" I heard my mother's pleading voice.

Another wave as a blood-curdling scream pierced the air. Then bright light and warmth hit my face, but the warmth of the sun couldn't take away the ice in my blood.

This was not the male that Adaris spoke of. He wasn't the proud, doting Father Adaris told me about. A male of honor. A male of integrity. One that was widely respected all across the River Kingdom and throughout Illoterra. A war hero.

My mother's screams haunted my dreams for years after that. I don't even know how long Adaris held me, cradling me against his chest deep in the grove. Even that far from the house I could still hear her screams. She was never the same after that day. It was like the light that lived inside her had been snuffed out. She grew quiet, distant. Her face glazed over as if under a trance. And I never saw her use her powers again.

♀

I jolted upright, flames flashing in my mind. Fire and anger and power. I gasped for air, my throat burning with a scream I hadn't realized was coming from me. The scream I dreamt of coming from my mother was mine. My mind whirled as my eyes adjusted to the dimness and I remembered where I was. Not in my soft, warm bed but rather in the Sacred Forest. A thin sheen of sweat covered my skin. The morning's first light peaked through the tree branches. Dew from the night covered every surface, giving off a moist, woodsy scent.

For a long time, I sat there, listening to the sounds of the forest around me, too afraid to move. My body ached from sleeping on the ground. Or was it from the running? I stretched my legs out in front of me, flexing the muscles in my legs, and they roared at me in protest. A bird's call overhead startled me as it twittered into the morning. Crickets chirped, and the leaves above me rustled with a soothing rhythm. How could a place be so quiet and still, yet be so full of movement? It disturbed me in a way that I didn't understand, and yet the longer I sat and just listened, the more tension eased from my shoulders and neck.

Exploring the surroundings of my tiny shelter, I saw a small cream flower peeking out from beneath a fern. I reached out and plucked it from the ground, turning it in front of my face. Adaris handed me the same flower yesterday in the grove. My chest tightened and I sucked in a breath, compressed with fear and guilt, threatening to split me apart. What had I done? Had I actually run away? How could I have just abandoned Adaris? I knew what our father was capable of.

I had two options.

One. I could return home, pretend I had gotten lost in the grove, and fallen into the river. Accept my fate of binding myself to Renwick and slowly melt away into nothing like my mother.

Or two. I could keep going, keep pushing through the briars, and face the unknown.

The weight of such a decision hung above me. I clutched the petite flower to my chest. I had made it this far. I had made it out of the fortress and across that river. I couldn't give up now. I shivered in the chilled morning air, my muscles and head aching.

I stretched my arms over my head, leaning to the left and right to loosen the muscles in my back. The gash in my shoulder had stopped bleeding though it still ached and throbbed. I needed to get it clean somehow. I sighed, releasing a long breath, and watched that breath turn into a cloud in front of my face. It was too late now. I'd made my choice. I had to keep going.

I survived the night. That must have been a sign. The wind that followed the storm blew all night, mostly drying out the clothes and blankets that had been soaked in the river. Damp was much better than sopping wet. I peeled off my still-wet clothes and replaced them with drier ones as quickly as possible. As I repacked my travel bag, my stomach grumbled. I reached for one of the glass jars that Adaris had packed food in—chunks of cheese and bread (I'd have to eat these soon), nuts, and dried meat. All of that seemed too heavy for my sensitive stomach this morning. I dug a little further and found an apple. I bit into the crisp peel and savored the sweet and tart flavor. I knew I needed the energy. I wasn't sure how long the hike to the village of Lakeshore was from here. I didn't even know what direction the village was in. Adaris had said to just go north.

I crawled out from under my fallen tree and stood. Nothing but towering, ebony trees as far as my eyes could see. The mountains were nowhere to be found, not through the denseness. I spun in a small circle. It was morning, and the sun was still fresh on the horizon. I knew from spending so much time in the grove that the closer the sun got to the top of the sky, the later in the day it was. I turned into the streaked light and let a beam warm my face. If the sun rose in the east, then I knew which way was north.

I can do this.

I would make it to Lakeshore, and Adaris would find me. I tucked the porcelain white flower into my waistband before setting off, praying to the Powers Above for another day of safety.

EIGHT
DELRIK

I stepped out into the morning sun, thankful to be out of the dark, foul-smelling tavern. I squinted and raised my hand to shield my eyes as the sunlight temporarily blinded me. The ungodly aroma of vomit, urine, and Powers Above knew what else filled the air, but the Wild Boar Tavern was the cleanest in the village, which said a lot about this village. It was all I could afford though.

I shouldn't have wasted the money. I should have slept in the woods and saved that last copper for food.

The storm last night was what pushed me to spend the money. The lumpy mattress was better than being drenched in the downpour. Wheels from a nearby cart clattered, and water splashed onto the street from someone emptying a dirty pail. I needed to find my next bounty if I wanted to eat something other than squirrel and rabbit. I plunged my hand into the hidden pocket of my sable cloak. Only two small coins remained. Just enough. I could stretch them, make them last if I kept to the forest and hunted for my meals as I made my way back home.

There were some things that I couldn't get past when traveling. The stale air of pubs, too full of overindulged, sweaty, and unbathed males, drunk with greed and ale, was one of them. I much preferred the forest.

Bounty hunting had been slow in recent months. Things had been quiet, which never sat right in my gut. The last time it was this quiet, war stirred across the sea. The War Across the Sea lasted almost seven years. Our realm came together as one to aid in an uprising in the western part of the world. Crime rates decreased as those strong enough to fight were shipped off to the shores of a distant land. I had even been summoned to fight in the Arcelia Legion. Those left behind were either too weak or too poor to cause any trouble.

The war had been over for almost eighteen years, but I still had memories of the years I spent fighting. The carnage and barren landscape left behind were not things one could easily forget. Once the war was over, I returned to the mountains. Even though I was given the honor as a commander in the Arcelia Legion, there wasn't much to do in the city hidden in the heart of the Qanas. So, I wandered, only returning every few months. Hunting down criminals for a bounty kept me occupied and still answered my inner call to protect the rugged peaks I had come to call my home.

I pulled the thick hood of my cloak over my head to cover my pointed ears and shadow my face. Between the scar stretching across my eye and my Fae ears, I stood out like a beacon in the crowd. The morning air had a bite to it, nipping at my ears and nose so I didn't mind the protection. Fall hadn't even arrived, but the mountains were already unleashing snow. A light wind blew down their steep slopes into the village. It wouldn't be long until snow covered the ground here too.

The village of Ramshorn was located on a main trade route across our continent of Illoterra. A lot of lowlifes and thieves loitered here in hopes of a quick coin. Or if they got lucky, a temporary job. The streets, even in the morning, were thick with beggars and prostitutes. Thankfully, most were smart enough to leave me alone this morning. I wasn't feeling very generous after such shitty sleep. Dreams of darkness and strange voices and a small flame flickering in the distance just out of reach kept my mind unrested and wary.

A gust of wind kicked up dust, and the hem of my cloak billowed around my filthy, mud-coated boots. A piece of sun-worn parchment nailed to a tree caught my eye from across the dusty road as it snapped about. An official seal of the High Ruler stamped across the top meant it was something to pay attention to. Or so the High Ruler wanted everyone to believe. The High Ruler, as he called himself, was Cadoc Byrnes. He ruled the River Kingdom, and he was a sadistic ass. Cadoc was a male who took what he wanted and didn't ask permission first. He didn't ask for forgiveness either. Whether that be food during a harsh winter or the taxes he had enforced on all the common Fae and lower beings living in the southern parts of the realm. And those that didn't comply were publicly punished by his Black Guard.

Cadoc only cared about two things—power and purity of the Highborn Fae bloodlines. He didn't take kindly to them being polluted by outsiders, by lower beings, especially humans. Over the years, the Fae's powers had been diluted by "crossbreeding" as he called it. As Cadoc's control of territories outside the River Kingdom grew, even before the war, the suppression of crossbreeds and lower beings increased, even to the point of slavery.

The humans, along with many lower beings, had been caught in the crossfire during battles. Not many humans existed anymore, at least not in Illoterra. A large portion of their populations had been collateral damage during the seven years of the war on the Western continent but several small cities were able to bounce back. The loss of so many human lives was an unfortunate cost, as Byrnes had said with zero remorse. I heard his guards on numerous occasions laughing about slaughtering humans just for fun.

I shuttered at the memories. I worked hard to clamp down my emotions when it came to Cadoc

Byrnes and how his rule has directly impacted my life.

Although Cadoc wasn't officially appointed as High Ruler over all of Illoterra, his family had seized control right after the war. No one had stepped up when disorder was breaking loose across the realm. Many believed, being from one of the oldest and most powerful High Fae families, he could return the realm to its prior order. The Byrnes family had always held positions of power and respect dating back thousands of years. And when Cadoc married Arabelle Halloran of Kilnard, a city on the western continent, that reach grew even further. Cadoc took it upon himself to appoint the Byrnes Family as High Ruler, unopposed by anyone south of the mountains. Those north of the mountains chose to remain secluded and out of the fuss.

Such a position of control shouldn't be given to a single family, in my opinion. Especially a family that oppressed those it ruled over.

The Qana Mountains hadn't always been my home. I couldn't remember where I was born, but I did remember coming to the mountains as a young child almost 120 years ago. My parents were hiding from the High Ruler. He'd sent his Black Guards all over the realm to enforce his laws. We hid in the foothills, but the Black Guard tracked us down. My father hid me in the caves. That was the last time I ever saw them. They never returned, and I lived on my own until I found the Mountain Fae.

The parchment snapped in the wind again, drawing me from my thoughts, and curiosity had my feet moving forward. The High Ruler typically didn't bother himself with the villages that surrounded his kingdom. That's what his Black Guard was for. He preferred to keep his hands clean. Unless there was something he wanted, of course. He'd stationed groups of guardsmen in all the larger cities and towns south of the mountains after returning from the war under the pretense of offering support. But now, even the smallest villages seemed to be occupied by at least a dozen of the crimson-cloaked bastards.

My boots kicked up chunks of dried mud as I made my way at a casual pace across the road for a closer look. Conversations quieted, and lower beings and Fae alike moved away into the shadows and shops as I neared. I'd become accustomed to them moving out of my way. The Hunter was the name they whispered as I passed. It always made me smile. I didn't mind. I preferred the name to the one given to me during the war. At least they left me to my peace.

Wisp-like clouds drifted across the cerulean sky. I snatched the parchment, yanking it down off the rusted nail buried deep into the tree. A drawing of a young Fae female looked back at me.

High Fae female, goes by Evren
24 years of age
Silver hair, violet eyes
Dead or Alive
1,000 golds rewarded by
High Ruler Cadoc Byrnes of Illoterra

    Odd that a female was being hunted for a bounty. It was rare, for sure, but the reward was large. "Dead or alive." I tipped my head to the side, again finding it strange a female was being searched for. Most females kept to the kitchens or ran small shops. And Highborn Fae females were too busy hosting parties and making small talk to commit crimes worthy of such a sum. She must be a cunning creature of great power or committed a great atrocity to have the High Ruler's interest. I loathed the idea of assisting the High Ruler with anything but if he was hunting her down, she must pose a great threat. And I couldn't let her endanger my home. I had pledged to protect the less fortunate from such danger. I floated on a dangerous line of protection and vengeance, honor, and rage. A mischievous smile curled my lips as I tucked the parchment into my cloak and disappeared into a passing shadow. No one was successful at escaping me once I had my eye set on their capture. She didn't stand a chance.

NINE
EVREN

The village of Lakeshore was not as nearby as Adaris had suggested. Either that or I was walking in circles. It took me three days of trudging through the forest to get there. Even during the day, shadows and light played tricks on my mind. I'd imagined I was being followed or I'd spot a figure just out of sight, only to find nothing. I frantically peered over my shoulder at each tiny crunch of leaves or snap of branches. The forest was deceptive, with its strange noises, and ever-changing light. My arms prickled at the slightest sound. I was being paranoid, but I couldn't help it. Maybe traces of the dark magic still lingered in the leaves and trunks of the Darkwoods.

    The increasingly sharp hunger pains drove me to keep moving forward, despite not being certain of my direction. I used the sun's position each morning and evening to guide me. I had eaten my last bit of food the previous night, and my stomach protested. Though what pushed me on was the fear of being in these woods for too long. I hadn't run into anyone or anything during my three days, which I found strange. My only companions had been the birds drifting from branch to branch. I was due for trouble.

The trees became sparse, and the narrow path I had been following became wider. A rush of relief filled me at the sight of a well-worn path ahead. A hill rose before me, and I spotted the pitched rooftops of a village. The lack of tripping hazards on the smooth road allowed me to examine my surroundings rather than focus on my weary feet. The number of times I'd fallen over hidden things in the underbrush was evident on my filthy knees and the torn skin of my palms. My mind wandered as my stomach growled yet again. I'd been hungry before. Withholding food was a favorite punishment of Father. No food until I had gotten through my studies.

"This is important. You will not have supper until you have all the Highborn bloodlines memorized. No one wants to be bonded to an idiot."

Then he would storm from the library, the shelves quaking with each stomp. The names of the surrounding villages and kingdoms of our continent would have been more useful now than all those far-off lineages I no longer remember. I continued my slow trek toward civilization ahead. Education had been important to Father. My successes were one of the few things I could do that brought him satisfaction. With that satisfaction came a bit more freedom in the days to follow. Servants, tutors, and Adaris were my only interactions, so I never despised studying day in and day out, no matter how much I put up a fuss, but those days of freedom made it all worthwhile.

I pulled myself from my thoughts as the village came into view. Nothing special, a simple street with simple homes. Simple storefronts of various kinds around a simple town square. And yet, it was charmingly perfect. It was an ideal place to lie low until Adaris could find me. I didn't know what Adaris's plan was after we were reunited. All I knew was to wait for him here in Lakeshore and he'd bring me to safety.

A place to rest hadn't been hard to locate. The Blue Stag Pub and Inn was one of the only buildings that were larger than a single story tall. I meandered down the street toward the inn, moving quickly so I wouldn't attract unwanted attention. I'd even pulled the hood of my cloak over my head.

I pushed open the heavy wooden door and stepped inside. It took my eyes a few seconds to adjust to the lack of light when I entered the pub. I removed my hood and repositioned the pack on my shoulder, wincing at my sore muscles. Even with the windows pushed open to let in a breeze, the smell of the previous night's ale hung in the air. The dilapidated, mismatched tables and chairs scattered around the room and the bar against one of the walls was vacant of any patrons.

A common Fae male was the only one there when I walked in. He sat behind a low desk tucked into the corner near the door. He raised a brow as he examined me up and down. I peered down at my dirt-stained attire and fought the urge to smooth back my rumpled hair. After traipsing through the woods for days, I'm sure I was a sight.

"I'm sorry to bother you, but I'd like to rent a room if you have one available, please."

He blinked at me once, then twice. His body was stiff and unreadable.

"Um...I'm sorry. Are all your rooms full?" I took a step away, turning my eyes to the floor.

The male jumped, almost as if he broke from a trance. "Yes, dear. Sorry," he said in a thick accent I didn't recognize. He shook his head. "We don't see many Highborn in these parts." I fought the urge to pull my hair over my ears as color crept up their tips. "We do have a room."

"Perfect. Thank you." I smiled at him.

He dug through a drawer and pulled out an old brass key tied with a burlap string to a piece of wood. The number six was carved into its surface, though it was worn smooth with use. The male walked around the desk and toward a hallway.

"This way," he called over his shoulder.

I followed him up the rickety set of stairs to the second-floor hallway. The floors had a thick layer of dust where the wooden planks met the wall and undisturbed cobwebs hung in the corners. The dim light filtered through a foggy window at each end of the hall, illuminating the dust motes floating in the air. He stopped before the last door and used the brass key to open it.

He swung his arm in a grand sweeping motion, inviting me into the cramped room. A bed, a copper tub, and a table with a washbasin were stuffed inside the too-small space. But at least I didn't have to sleep on the ground anymore. My aching back was thankful. And unlike the hallway, it was clean. I almost wept at the sight of the tub, too. I'd never been this dirty in my life.

"How long will you be staying?" He studied me again as I turned to face him.

I was suddenly uncomfortable under his scrutiny. I took a step away from him. "I'm not quite sure. My brother will be joining me in a few days."

"Well, it will be five copper pieces a day, six if you need meals. And I'll have one of the girls bring up fresh water."

"Thank you," I said as I handed him the coins to cover a week's stay.

His doughy fingers counted the coins eagerly before slipping them into his pocket. He nodded his head at me and then shut the door. I quickly moved to the door and snapped the lock into place. The lock looked like it would do little to keep anyone out who really wanted in, but it was better than nothing. I turned back to the room, leaning my back against the closed door, and let out a slow breath. I'd made it this far, and at least I wasn't still trudging through the forest.

A soft tapping came to the door, causing my heart to jump into my throat. I opened the door just a crack, worried that the innkeeper was back to ask another question. Instead, a small girl, a slave, stood before me with two pails of water. If her frail form and tattered clothes weren't clues enough the brand burned on the inside of her slender wrist made it obvious to everyone that she was property. My stomach clenched at the sight of her. She gave me a slight bow without lifting her head before she entered the room, not daring to look me in the eye. I didn't know what to say as she filled my tub in silence.

By her third trip, I couldn't bear it anymore.

"That will be fine. Thank you," I said as I pressed a copper coin into her hand.

I tipped my head down, trying to encourage a response. Her sad hazel eyes widened at the coin and then finally met mine in a silent thank you as she bowed out of the room.

I knew slavery existed throughout Illoterra. There were even some that worked at our home in Rivamir. I'd seen that brand on many wandering in and out of the fortress over the years. Father had forbidden them from being seen, though. I learned about them from sneaking into the kitchens for snacks and spending late nights in the library. I didn't like the idea of slavery, and I hated that I had been so sheltered that I couldn't see what was going on right in front of me for a long time. It wasn't until I witnessed a young slave girl being beaten for stealing a chunk of rotting bread from the trash. I couldn't bear to watch the brutality, but I felt shame that I didn't stand up for her. I never saw her in the fortress after that.

I tried to shake the growing anger rising in me as I moved to the tub. I stripped off my soiled clothes and discarded them in the waste bin. No amount of washing could restore them to a usable state. The cuts and scrapes had begun to heal and were now puckered, angry scabs streaked across my pale skin. The bruises were still visible but had turned from a deep plum to a greenish-brown color. I avoided the aged, fogged mirror above the washbasin. I knew the bruises were still on my ribs, too. I didn't need or want to see them. I padded over to the tub, leaning one hand on each side. I gingerly lowered my body into the tepid water. I sucked in a sharp breath, unsure if it was from the temperature or the pain from the injuries I'd accumulated. I leaned my head back against the edge and closed my eyes. At least, for now, I was safe.

☥

A few days passed with still no sign of Adaris. I had nowhere to go. All I could do was wait, but I was growing restless. The first day I slept. It wasn't until the slave girl knocked on my door again to offer dinner that I realized I'd slept through the entire day.

I spent yesterday wandering from shop to shop, keeping my head low. Squat brick houses and shops lined the cobbled streets. Tiered gardens smelling of dirt and fresh growth overflowing with herbs and vegetables. Vines with squash and beans stretched up trellises. Open fields stretched all around the village. Creatures of all shapes and sizes milled about, some minding their own business while others stopped to chat with one another. I'd never seen a village before. I had been forbidden from visiting Rivamir, the large city at the heart of the River Kingdom.

 I tried not to draw attention to myself as I moved through the village. Even dressed in pants and a flowing tunic, my high-pointed ears and silver hair attracted stares. I should've brought my cloak, but the sun warming my skin was wonderful. I wanted to soak up the last rays of the summer sun. Winter would arrive before I knew it.

 Everywhere I turned there were tempting displays—pastries, hats, blacksmiths, books. I stopped in front of each window, pressing my fingers to the sun-warmed glass. A flutter of excitement at experiencing something new made my heart drum excitedly inside my chest. A breeze brought the sweet smells from the bakery that made my mouth water.

 Was that chocolate?

 A bookshop stood out from every shop, tucked away in the corner of the village. The scent of paper, ink, and vanilla filled my lungs when I pulled open the heavy door. A bell trilled from above when I entered the shop. Floor-to-ceiling shelves stretched the length of each wall, all crammed full of books. The space was tight and cluttered. It was far from extravagant, but there were small personal touches all around. My fingers danced over the leather spines as I made my way deeper into the store. One volume caught my eye: one of Adaris's favorite books. I'd seen him read and reread the tome many times. So much so that the binding had come loose and the cover was worn. The golden letters of the same book glinted in the dusky light. I pulled it from the shelf and opened the cover. The smell of the new pages, the smoothness of them under my fingertips, brought me unexpected bliss, reminding me so much of Adaris. My chest tightened as the sadness of his absence filled me. I prayed to the Powers Above that he was safe and on his way to me.

    I peered over the top of the book's cover out the window overlooking the street, blinking back the tears that sprung to my eyes. Three little faces were peeking over the sill, their tiny fingers gripping the edge. I wiggled my fingers toward them in hello. Their giggles at being caught filtered through the door as another customer opened the door to leave. I smiled at their curiosity.

    I'd never been a big reader, but Adaris would spend hours lounging in the oversized wing-backed chairs, reading books from our father's library. I tried to follow in his footsteps, often taking books from our library, but I never found anything of interest. I preferred drawing. Books were how he survived loneliness. I had Adaris, and Adaris had his books.

Although Adaris never seemed lonely or bored when he was with me, I also knew he wanted more for his life than being stuck in Rivamir. When Father gave him a position in the Black Guard after he passed through the training, he was so excited to begin traveling.

"Finally, Evren! He finally has the faith in me to serve a purpose, to become something more than just his shadow."

"You know, you could just find your bondmate like Father asked you to years ago," I stated.

"And you know I have no interest in all that bondmate crap." He reached over and playfully pinched my chin between his thumb and finger. "Besides, that's your job, little sister."

I swatted his hand away, scowling at him.

I'm not sure how the loneliness hadn't beaten him, made him bitter. But it didn't. Somehow, he had driven on. So, I gave the shopkeeper a coin in payment, tucked the book into the crook of my arm, and stepped back out into the afternoon sun.

TEN
EVREN

The next day while walking through the village, a little boy came up to me. He didn't speak, just looked up at me through thick blonde lashes, his bright blue eyes watching me. Light freckles speckled along with cheeks and across his nose. There was no fear in his gaze, just innocent interest. I plucked a flower from a nearby bush and offered it to him in a gesture of friendship. He examined the delicate petals, turning his tousled ash blonde head to the side. Then he snatched it from my fingers, tucked it behind his ear, and ran off with a huge grin plastered to his dirt-smudged face. My heart warmed at the joy and innocence the child held. The world wasn't all cruel, was it? Just the world I had been born into.

Not sure what to do to fill my day, I'd asked the innkeeper for a quiet place to read. He pointed out a shady patch of trees that seemed inviting enough to spend a few hours. I figured since I wandered yesterday, I could relax and enjoy more sunshine today. With my new book, the one with the gold lettering, my sketchpad under my arm, and a charcoal pencil tucked behind my ear, I strolled out the door.

I spotted an old oak tree with a long limb hanging low, extending a few feet from the ground. The light from the sun shone in patches on the ground from the leaves floating overhead. I stood in awe of the tree. The limb was split from the main trunk, and new growth had curled around the damage, anchoring it back to its base. It experienced some severe damage at one point in its many years. A lightning strike or perhaps an ax. The resilience of this tree was breathtaking and struck a chord inside my heart. If a tree could not only withstand such trauma but thrive after, surely, I could survive the storm of life too.

I climbed up and stretched myself along the length of the branch and withdrew my dagger to slice an apple I'd swiped from the inn's kitchen. I ran my finger across the flat edge of the blade. The coolness of the blade was a stark contrast to the midmorning heat. The night Adaris had pressed the leather holster and sheath into my hand was the night he first noticed dark splotches on my upper arm. We hadn't spoken a word about how I'd gotten them, but he knew I needed protection. The curved blade was made of darkstone and was sharper than anything I'd ever seen. It felt weightless in my hand without the sheath. I'd kept it hidden under my bed with the stolen pants and tunic. I couldn't conceal it under my dresses while at home. I hadn't wanted to get caught with it, but I took comfort in knowing it was close by if Renwick ever decided to visit my rooms.

"Never give in. Never surrender," he'd said before kissing my forehead and leaving.

This was the first time I'd used the blade. It peeled the apple with little effort, a smooth clean cut. I studied the weapon in my lap as the black blade absorbed the sunlight. The upper spine of it had vicious serrations etched into it and its hilt fit perfectly in my palm. Holding the dagger in my hand left me heady with strength, which is exactly what Adaris had wanted.

My confidence had grown over the last week as did my strength. I slept through the night, waking each morning refreshed and well-rested. The bone-deep weariness after the perilous hike through the forest had evaporated completely. The cook's food brought out my full appetite, though I was afraid to ask what exactly was set in front of me each day.

The still waters of the nearby lake held the reflection of the sky on its glassy surface. The looming Qana Mountains were mirrored on the smooth surface. A ripple broke the surface sending expanding circles across the water. I didn't see what disturbed the water, but the way the midmorning sun sparkled on each expanding ripple like stardust had been poured into its waters was brilliance itself.

Past the lake, the base of those timeless mountains, swallowed up the shore. They looked as if they held all the secrets of the realm. The sheer rock shot straight up from the ground where snow permanently covered the highest peaks. A gust off in the distance sent swirls of snow billowing into the air. A large hawk soared through the sky and landed on a rocky precipice, his distant cry barely reaching my ears. Harsh cliffs jutting into the clear, blue sky. Their size and splendor made me pause and just soak in the breathtaking view.

From home, the far-off mountains looked smooth and uniform—a steel-blue mass rising from the earth. But up close, I could see the individual peaks and crevasses. The shades of grays, browns, and greens on each slope were as unique as each creature in the realm. No two were alike. I didn't ever want to forget the appreciation of seeing the legendary mountain range up close like that. The rugged harshness surrounded by beauty. I wanted to imprint it in my memory. I felt ridiculous getting sentimental over a tree—now the mountains—but I couldn't help it. This would forever be my favorite spot in the whole realm.

I sighed and relaxed my back against the trunk of the tree. My sketchbook was propped in my lap and Adaris's favorite book wedged next to me. I fliop0l;opl0cked my charcoal pencil back and forth in a steady rhythm on the edge of the paper. No amount of skill could capture the view before my eyes. I didn't even try. Next to the pressed jasmine flower, the strip of torn paper was tucked into the cover with a note written in Adaris's handwriting:

I found this on the floor outside your room. I knew you wouldn't want to leave it behind. I'll see you soon. Stay strong. - Love you little sister, Adaris

I was thankful that the pages had dried out from the plunge in the river. Only a few drawings had been ruined. But I refused to tear them from the book. I traced the letters of his name with my finger and tried not to let my sorrow ruin a perfectly fine day.

Suddenly, a movement caught my eye. A dark figure exited the inn and began to move toward me, keeping to the shadows of the scattered trees. The male was too tall to be Adaris, his shoulders too broad. I swallowed a hard lump in my throat. I remained seated and tried my best to control my breathing. His cautious pace made it obvious he didn't want to be noticed. How could someone *not* notice him? Between the brooding shadow on his face and that rather aggressive-looking bow strapped to his back, he wasn't a male that could go unseen. The black travel clothes he wore clung tightly to his muscled form. While his clothes weren't the same finery as many in Rivamir wore, he didn't match the shabbiness of the villagers. That body was used to physical exertion. The sleeves of his shirt were rolled to the elbow, revealing bronzed skin. Tattoos, starting at his left wrist, traveled up his forearm and disappeared under the fabric. His dark hair was sleek and poured over his shoulders. The front was pulled back, away from his face, into a knot at the back of his head. His eyes, which were as dark as onyx, carried a predatory gleam made more prominent by a deep scar arching through his thick eyebrow and dragging down over his eye and right cheek. I wondered briefly what horror he had faced to receive such a battle scar. He had probably fought in the war. Thankfully Adaris had been too young to go with our father during the war. Most males in the River Kingdom that departed on the many ships bound for the Western Continent hadn't returned home. And for those that had, their wounds went deeper than just flesh.

The stranger had an air of confidence that made me dislike him immediately. That sense of haughty arrogance didn't mesh well with me. Many suitors my father introduced me to had that air about them and they were worthless piles of crap. They were selfish and greedy, only seeking what could elevate them, only seeking more power and running after lust.

Why do males seem to look at me like I'm something for them to devour?

I was not in the mood to deal with this male right now. I was too frustrated with Adaris. I told myself it was frustration, but it was more concern than anything. He should've been here by now. It had been over a week. Deep down, I knew something wasn't right.

There was something about the way the stranger's body moved that had me intrigued despite his sneaking. The wind shifted as he moved closer, and his scent hit me like a tidal wave—a crisp woody scent with a touch of citrus. But there was something else there, something that tugged at a dormant part of my spirit. My breath caught, and a sudden surge of dizziness hit as my pulse raced. I rolled my eyes, pushing that unknown tug away and keeping my gaze focused on the mountains in front of me. I slipped my dagger into the sheath I had strapped to the inside of my calf and curled my foot underneath me. I didn't want to reveal I had a weapon. I had a hunch that I would need it. I tossed my apple core down to the ground.

Never show hesitation or weakness.

ELEVEN
DELRIK

Tracking the female hadn't been difficult. There were only two villages that were a few days' walk from Rivamir. And since she wasn't in Ramshorn where I had been staying, she had to be here in Lakeshore. The hike between the two villages was enjoyable. The summer giving way to fall in the evenings made sleeping out under the trees easier to clear my mind and refocus on my mission. The trees were familiar and offered the comfort of home. I know the Darkwood trees of the Sacred Forest were feared by most thanks to the legends spread to scare children, but to me, these trees meant safety. I spent much of my childhood in the woods, using the caves carved out of the mountains as my shelter. It was a quiet life, lonely most of the time, but I had grown to respect the creatures that lived among the trees alongside me. There was a fine balance in this world. I learned to hunt only when I needed to eat, and I left the creatures of the forest to themselves otherwise.

Lakeshore was a familiar stop for me since it was the last village before reaching the mountain trails that led me home. It was run down from decades of taxes from the High Ruler. Most of the areas throughout the southern lands of Illoterra were, and this dilapidated village was the last place I wanted to be. I preferred the north, preferred the shelter of the mountains and trees to being in the southlands. At least it didn't smell as bad as Ramshorn. It was probably due to the lack of pubs and gambling dens. The shop fronts were weathered and in desperate need of repair. The bricks were crumbling away from their foundations. Windows streaked with cracks and grime did little to encourage shoppers to enter. Children ran freely through the streets barefoot, and scrawny as starved rabbits. I wondered how many wouldn't make it through the winter.

Shoppers roamed the street. Someone shouted about the price of eggs while another couple argued over the last sack of potatoes. Just like in Ramshorn, people moved away when they saw me approaching. Most villages weren't all that welcoming to me. You'd think they would be grateful to me for pulling criminals off the streets. Instead, they just feared the rumors of death and destruction I left in my wake. Rumors left over from the war mostly. War had a way of bringing out the worst in people, even when one was fighting for the right side.

It only took me asking around at a few shops to find the female was staying at the Blue Stag on the edge of town near the lake. Either she didn't know there was a bounty on her head, or she wasn't that bright, or maybe both. The inn she had selected was one that was frequently used by wealthy travelers. It wasn't a great place to remain hidden.

The dust from the road coated my cloak and boots as I walked into the inn. The innkeeper greeted me without glancing up, too preoccupied with counting a teetering pile of coins on his desk. Mid-morning light filtered through the only two windows by the door. Dust floated in the dank smelling air and the floor was sticky underfoot.

"How can I help ya?"

He spoke in a friendly way, but when he looked up and saw me, the smile on his face vanished, and the tower he'd been stacking toppled over when he nervously bumped into the desk. That happened a lot…the shock at my appearance. Maybe it was my shorter-than-normal Fae ears or the bow strapped to my back, or the savage scar across my face. Another gift from the war. The older male stood from his stool so as not to be at a height disadvantage. It didn't make a difference. I was at least two feet taller than him, and I didn't bother hiding a satisfied smirk.

Nice try.

"I...I'm not looking for trouble," he stammered.

His thick accent was one from Merock, a small coastal village on the Basdover Gulf that was a regular trading post. It wasn't uncommon to hear accents and languages from across the realm while visiting those posts.

"I'm looking for someone. A young female." I showed him the torn piece of parchment. I had removed the information about the bounty and that she was being hunted by the High Ruler. I didn't want to raise any alarm. I also didn't want anyone else to know she had a bounty on her head. I didn't mind competing for my wages, though. It kept me on my toes and my senses sharpened, but I wasn't in the mood to deal with anyone getting in my way today. After being on the hunt for the last month, I wanted nothing more than to be home soaking in a steaming bath and enjoying a hot meal.

He seemed hesitant to give me any information, keeping his lips in a tight line and humming nervously to himself. I leaned a palm on the desk and flipped a small bronze coin his way. Money always made people talk. I was no longer shocked by the information I could weasel from people with a simple bronze coin. The piece made several flips in the air, winking in the sunlight coming from the front windows. His thick fingers fumbled as he caught the piece of metal. He held it up, squinting to examine it better before slipping it into his pocket.

"Ah. That lady has been staying here. She just left a little while ago to take a walk." He pointed out the door at the back of the inn. "Said she was waiting for her brother."

Did he even feel guilty for giving her away? Or was he so desperate for money he'd say anything? People would do anything to survive, including giving away the whereabouts of an innocent female to a stranger. His round stomach straining against the buttons on his tunic made it clear he wasn't struggling to keep food on the table. It always rubbed me wrong. The deception. The lies.

Someone had deceived my parents and now I was alone. This is the reason why I was never short for work. Faded moral lines left plenty of criminals that needed to be held accountable for their actions.

I didn't thank him as I pushed off the desk, swiping an over-ripened pear from his lunch pail at his desk. I took a bite before tossing it back to him. The too-sweet taste made me want to gag. My boots were noiseless on the scratched wooden-planked floor as I slipped out the back.

♀

I spotted the female propped on a low-hanging limb of a large oak tree. A pair of worn boots were discarded in the grass at the base of the trunk. One foot was tucked under her, and the other one, bare, dangled lazily down below her. That tiny foot swung back and forth as she twirled a pencil in her fingers.

She wiggled her toes as a light breeze ruffled the leaves and twisted pieces of her silver hair. Her gaze was focused on the mountains above her. She seemed deep in thought, like she had no idea how to truly capture the scene stretched out in front of her onto the paper. She glanced at the pencil before tucking it behind her high arched ear. She leaned back against the trunk of the tree with a deep breath, the swell of her breasts rising and falling. A book lie tucked against her hip. For someone being hunted by the Black Guard, she didn't seem to have a care in the world. She sliced a piece of apple with a dagger—a dagger made of Darkstone. Why did this female have one? Where did she get it? Had she stolen it?

Her pink lips parted as she slipped the sliced fruit into her mouth, unaware of the droplet of juice that dripped down her chin. I groaned.

I'd like nothing more than to lick that juice off her chin.

I shook my head, trying to stop my mind from wandering down *that* inappropriate path.

I watched her for several minutes, studying the way she sat. She appeared to be a typical mannered High Fae. She didn't seem like a criminal or someone of great power. She also didn't fit into her surroundings. Her hair reminded me of beams of moonlight spilling from the heavens above and reflecting off the River of Naraina on a winter night. The long silver strands were loosely braided down her back. Stray pieces curled and framed the profile of her face. The tip of her braid reached her curved hips. Those hips, I noticed, were made more prominent by the snug pants she wore. Even in the lower villages, females didn't wear pants. But Powers Above, they fit her like a glove.

I crept my way over to her, following the line of trees to get a better look while being sure to stay out of her line of sight. She tossed her apple core onto the ground and sheathed a dagger along the length of her calf. I smiled and made note of the weapon's hiding spot. That sly motion was the only thing that gave me any hint that she wasn't an ordinary female enjoying the sun. Streaks of sunlight fluttered across her body as the breeze rustled the leaves above her.

I silently joined her, leaning against the neighboring tree just outside of her peripheral. I explored the profile of her face—full lips formed a perfect cupid's bow, shoulders held back as if it was bred into her. Her petite nose fit perfectly on her face and had a slight turn upward at the end. Her cheeks held a pinkish color in them from the sun. She was remarkable. A small white flower was tucked between the pages of the sketchbook. Her finger brushed the petal, the gentlest of touches.

A flare of violet light flashed, distracting me from my examination of her. Had I imagined it? The light must have been playing tricks on me. Looking around, there was nothing around me with that vivid hue, but the sun had a way of tricking a hunter's eye if you weren't careful.

Focus!

I ran my hand through my hair. How would I get my hands on her? I didn't have all day to sit and marvel at her, no matter how much I wanted to. I pulled my attention from her profile with a shake of my head. It would be effortless to knock her off the low branch and grab her, but something held me back. Something held me transfixed.

"I've never seen the Qana up close before."

Her voice. Powers Above, her voice was like a lark singing, it was so light. Quiet, yet assertive at the same time. The soft notes broke into my hypnosis. She spoke with eloquence and poise. The corners of my mouth lifted as I followed her gaze out over the scenery. The shimmering lake reminded me of home. Of course, the River of Naraina, not a lake. It was rather how the water glimmered with the sunlight. The smell of the water. The lake looked warm and inviting. Naraina was never warm. It was always bitter cold, which made fishing a miserable task. That was the only redeeming quality of the Southlands—warm waters and now this beautiful being.

She turned her gaze to me when I didn't respond to her comment, and all the air left my body—I was struck breathless. Violet eyes bore deep into my soul. Surrounded by lush, long lashes, her eyes glowed, illuminated by the midmorning sunlight.

It had been her. The flash of violet light. I had thought I succeeded in sneaking up on her, but she had known I was watching her. Her brows rose, and a slight tilt of her head told me she was waiting for my response. She had a smile on those tantalizing lips, but it didn't reach those pools of amethyst. She was cautious, untrusting. Her smooth, creamy skin heated high on her cheeks as my eyes dropped to her lips and then back up.

Why is she so calm? Why isn't she afraid? Powers, why is she so damn beautiful?

I finally released a breath I hadn't realized I was holding. I had to take her before she decided I was a threat and ran. I knew I could outrun her, no one could match my speed, but I didn't want to draw attention to us.

The innkeeper said she was waiting for her brother. I could use that to lure her away. I wouldn't usually talk to one of the creatures I hunted. Too much effort. And they always tried to talk their way out of the crimes. The worst were the ones that begged like cowards. It was much easier to take them by surprise.

But she...she was different. Not sure why, but she was. Maybe because she was a female. Maybe because she seemed so ethereal in the morning light. Maybe because she was a gift from the gods to realm itself...

Snap out of it!

"I've been looking for you. Your brother sent me ahead of him." I was still leaning against the tree next to hers, my arms folded across my chest. I thrummed my fingers against my upper arm. Her gaze dipped to my fingers, then back to my face.

She dropped to the ground, placing her books beside her shoes, and turned toward me, still casual.

Her delicate bare feet made no sound when they hit the earth. She stood tall, shoulders pulled back in confidence, and turned to face me head-on.

Damn.

I was brought internally to my knees. Something shifted in me; something shifted in the whole realm. A tether grabbed hold of me, and my magic thrummed in response to her. Could she feel it too? That switch awoke something primal and alive deep inside my body and I would never be the same. I'd never see this world the same way again. This beautiful creature, full of grace, altered my very being. I could see a wildness burning inside her. She had me entranced with a single look.

This may be more difficult than I thought.

She tilted her head to the side, her brows knit together in confusion, then concern. She inched back the barest of steps. And I smiled.

There it is. It's about time. I was starting to think this was too easy.

"He didn't tell me he would send someone ahead of him." Her voice was quiet but didn't waver. She stared hard into my eyes, questioning my truth. Her gaze didn't falter.

Could she read my thoughts?

"He told me to escort you to the next village and wait there."

She took a breath.

A moment passed. "No."

Pure defiance. My blood roared with heat.

Did she really just tell me no?

The corner of my mouth lifted into a wolfish grin. I let my eyes rake down her body and then back up to her face.

"No?"

She pulled the thick silver braid over her shoulder and twirled the end around her fingers, twisting it tight before letting it drop to her chest. The motion threatened to distract me again, dragging my focus to her breasts.

"You heard me. No. He said he would come himself."

The calmness in her voice was deceiving, the way she lifted her chin in confidence. But I could see her pulse beating wildly below the thin skin of her throat. I could smell the fear, could taste the hesitation. I might not be full Fae, but I had that keen sense of smell.

She turned her back on me, that braid swinging with the movement. I wanted to wrap that braid around my fist. She bent and picked up her boots and books and walked away.

Did she seriously just turn her back to a stranger? To me?

Who was this female, and where did she come from? I had never met someone so trusting in an unfamiliar place. I had the urge to grab her arm and tell her how reckless she was being, how there were evils in this world, true evils, that would do anything to get their hands on her. How *I* was someone to be afraid of. So why did I have the urge to protect her? The internal battle between taking my bounty, protecting her from an unknown danger, and devouring her raged inside me. I raked a hand through my hair.

What the fuck is wrong with me?

"Evren," I called after her, my voice a bit sharper than I meant it to be. Her name was delicious on my tongue.

She froze. The muscles in her back tensed and her fists clenched around the laces of her boots. Instinct, I could see, told her to run but her feet seemed fixed to the ground. Like some unknown force was holding her in place. She whipped her head around and our eyes locked and held. I didn't move toward her. Not yet. This female was in danger; true, life-ending danger and I wasn't quite sure what to do. Anger began to fill me. Not anger at her but *for* her. I knew I could not leave her here for someone else to find. Someone would find her eventually. I had to get her somewhere safe until I figured out what to do.

I could see her decision as if she spoke it out loud, the moment she decided to run from me. A dark internal chuckle came to me as she turned to bolt. In a flash, barely a blink, I was standing in front of her, her attempt no match for my speed. She let out a squeak of surprise. Well, that was adorable. Thank you, Mother, for my unique gift of speed and agility. The look of shock on her face was priceless as she sucked in a sharp breath. Nobody could match my speed, it's what made me such a lethal opponent in the war. I was deadly.

Alright Delrik, don't play with your prey.

"Not so fast, Ev." I took a step closer, reaching my fingers toward her arm. She matched it with a step back, trying her best to maintain the distance between us.

"How do you know who I am?" Her eyes darted around my face searching for answers.

She tried to hide the emotion on her face. Tried to look impassive. She was failing. Miserably. She crossed her arms over her chest, craning her neck to meet my eyes. She was much shorter than me. I almost laughed at how high she had to tip her chin up now that we were closer. I smiled charmingly. She didn't budge. Not even a single inch.

Hmm. Bold female.

"There's someone looking for you. I'm just helping out a bit."

Her breath caught for a moment. She sidestepped. I matched it. She tried to cut to the left, but I seized her wrist before she could even move an inch. The moment my fingers closed around her wrist, a wild sensation sent a flash of heat through my entire body like a fire pulsing through my veins. I felt how smooth and soft her skin was under my calloused hand. Her gaze flickered to my hand as she dragged in a sharp breath. She must have felt it too because she dropped her boots. She looked down to her leg, giving away her next move. The dagger wouldn't save her now.

Wow, she is not good at this.

"Oh, I don't think so little one."

TWELVE
DELRIK

Overpowering her had been a breeze; hands-down the fastest hunt ever. Even compared to that one satyr a few years back. The blithering idiot thought he could outsmart me by hiding in a cave. The cave belonged to a pack of wolves. The wolves that roamed the Sacred Forest were vicious creatures and would eat practically anything. Thankfully, they got bored pulling his body apart and left enough of his head that I could still collect my bounty. A win for both the wolves and me.

Evren's resistance was useless. She didn't stand a chance to escape from the firm grasp I had on her arm. She was a slight thing; the top of her head didn't even brush my chin. She thrashed and kicked against me, swinging her petite fists against my chest as I dragged her back into the trees. Such a noble fight, but no one was around to witness her disappear.

"Cocky bastard. Prick. Asshole. Let me go." Her voice was muffled by my large hand I clapped over her mouth but I appreciated the effort she put into the name calling.

"Such a foul mouth for such a lovely creature," I purred into her ear. "I'm sure there are better uses for that beautiful mouth."

Her elbow jabbed me in the stomach, knocking the breath from my body. I let out a breathless laugh. She had fight in her, I'd give her that. When I removed my hand from her mouth, her teeth snapped at my fingers.

"Did you actually just try to bite me? Oh, I'll remember *that* for later." I winked at her as I stuffed her mouth with a piece of torn fabric from my shirt and quickly bound her hands together. I was tempted to tie them behind her back, but she would need balance to walk through the trees. I noticed healing cuts all along her arms and hands. The bruises looked like fingerprints. If she hadn't been cursing at me and lashing out like a viper, I would've stopped to question them. High Fae magic, even at the base level, was healing, so why was she covered in injuries?

I lifted her around the waist and looped her bound hands over a tree branch low enough that she could still stand but high enough that she couldn't escape unassisted. I didn't want to leave her alone, bound and helpless, but I needed to put space between us. I needed to formulate a plan with the distraction of her seductive presence.

I left her hidden in a small clearing, tucked behind some brush. I darted back to the inn to gather her belongings from her room and supplies for our journey, not forgetting her shoes and books near the oak tree. I was gone less than five minutes.

When I returned, the fury in her eyes pierced me like a knife as I ducked under a branch and back into the clearing.

"If you promise not to bite, I'll remove your gag," I said with a dark chuckle.

She snarled—actually snarled—through the fabric.

I removed the gag as she glared at me, but she kept her teeth to herself. "Good girl."

"My brother will find me, and when he does, he'll split you from navel to nose." She was seething, her eyes molten with rage, which only made this burning inside me grow stronger. That wasn't the only thing growing.

"I'm sure he'd be a worthy opponent." I pulled her hands free from the branch overhead and tossed her boots at her feet. "You'll be needing these. We have a lot of walking to do."

"I'm not going anywhere with you."

A wicked smile came to me. "Fine. I'll just have to carry you then."

She held her bound hand in front of her defensively. "Don't touch me."

Her last word came out as a high-pitched squeal. In a flash, I'd hauled her over my shoulder. Her squeal ended in a grunt as her stomach made contact with my shoulder. She kicked against me, but I pressed my arm firmly across the back of her knees. She slammed her bound hands, rather pathetically, against my back.

"Put me down!"

I stopped, turning my head to speak over my shoulder. "Are you going to walk?"

She huffed and ground out, "Fine."

I planted her feet on the ground but had to seize her shoulder to prevent her from toppling over. "See. That wasn't so hard now, was it?"

⚲

I hadn't wanted to remain in town. We needed to stay out of sight. The risk of someone stealing Evren away in the night was too great. Her safety was my primary concern now. Over the many years of bounty hunting, I learned to trust no one. That innkeeper gave her up for a minuscule bronze.

Prick.

Also, and something I didn't want to admit to myself, that odd allure, that pull toward her that I couldn't explain kept me on edge. So, deeper into the Sacred Forest we went.

I led her behind me with a rope attached to her bindings as we moved through the trees. That sharp tongue of hers ceased once we'd been walking for a few hours. Already, the slope of the ground had begun a steady incline. I watched her from the corner of my eye as I scanned our surroundings. She was silent as she picked her way over fallen branches and rocks, paying close attention to her footing, lifting each boot, and placing it back down in a sturdy spot. It slowed our pace considerably, but I kind of enjoyed how meticulous she was being.

A bitter northern wind whirled through the trees. The frigid air stung my lungs with each breath. The higher elevation of the Qanas never saw summer. Only a few warm weeks each year, the short reprieve of spring, allowing for new growth. I knew the terrain like the back of my hand, which gave me an advantage if we were followed. Many of my training years with the Arcelia Legion had been spent patrolling this area. My knowledge of every cave, boulder, and stream would protect us as we moved further north.

The rope tightened in my hand with a taut snap, and I turned. Evren stumbled and fell to her knees but still didn't make a sound. Only a soft exhale of air escaped her lips as her knees collided with the ground. She didn't try to rise, just knelt there with her head hung low in defeat. I could see red marks where the rope was beginning to chafe her delicate skin raw.

Was this some kind of distraction?

She sure hadn't acted vulnerable or dejected before I captured her.

I stared at her for a few breaths. With two noiseless strides, I was standing before her, the rope still grasped in my hand. I couldn't read her face since she had it turned down. Silver strands of hair had come loose from her braid during our scuffle and hung in her face. I knelt and lowered my hand, slowly, tucking a curling strand behind her ear. She held her breath at my touch, turning her head away from me and squeezing her eye shut tight.

Suddenly, her head jerked up, eyes wide in alarm. She whipped her head to the left, her braid swinging into her face.

I'd heard it too. The snapping of a twig. Male voices, muffled by the trees, broke the silence. I didn't see the males but knew that they were close, and they were making no effort to disguise their approach.

Spinning on my knees, I lifted her from the ground and hauled her into a dense patch of ferns.

"Stay still," I whispered, slapping a hand across her nose and mouth, holding her tight against my chest. "One movement could give us away."

She didn't fight against me as she had before. Her petite body went rigid against me, terror paralyzing her. Her breaths came in shaky, shallow bursts. The tip of her curved ear brushed against the underside of my chin. She was quivering.

As the group of males came into view, she stopped breathing completely. Five members of the River Kingdom's Black Guard were stomping through the underbrush. I silently thanked the

Powers Above the lush ferns concealed us and the group of males appeared too drunk to follow our obvious trail and scents. Thankfully, we were downwind. I needed to be more careful.

Chills covered Evren's body, and her trembling shook me to my core. The warmth drained from her body. That profound urge to protect her filled me again, coming from somewhere deep within. Her visceral response suggested she knew exactly the kind of danger she was in. I gently stroked my thumb over her arm, attempting to reassure her. Her skin was as soft as a feather under my callouses.

Why would a random group of guardsmen be wandering this deep into the Sacred Forest unless they were looking for something, or someone, specific. I watched as they moved away from us, not bothering to hide their noise. Their unrestrained voices echoed off the trees as they faded away.

I held her close for some time. I worried she'd collapse to the ground if I released her too soon. She wasn't moving. Her body was white and cold with dread. I relaxed my arm around her shoulders, adding space between our bodies. I spun her around to face me. Her eyes were wide, and her breaths were shallow and fast. She stared unfocused on my chest as I took deep, long breaths. Inhale. Exhale. A few breaths in, then out before her body mimicked mine. Color began to return to her skin again, and, after a minute, she had gathered herself. Her bound hands pressed against my chest for balance, and she took a step back away from me.

"We need to keep moving. We aren't safe here," I murmured.

"All right." The words came out as a choked rasp, and she gave a single nod of her head.

She didn't look up at me but showed no hesitation following me this time. She trailed close to me, peering over her shoulder often.

"They were heading east to Lakeshore. And with how loud they were, we should be able to hear them if they decide to circle back to us." I tried to comfort her, offering her a somewhat friendly smile.

She nodded again, keeping her eyes on the ground to make sure she didn't trip again.

"Those males were part of the High Ruler's Black Guard. Why would the High Ruler be looking for you?"

When she didn't answer, I stopped walking, and she collided with my back. I turned to face her.

"Why is the High Ruler looking for you?" I repeated.

She looked up at me with a fierceness in her eyes for the first time since I'd captured her. That fierceness ignited a spark in me.

Powers Above those eyes.

"Wouldn't you like to know," she spat. Her lips curled into an almost snarl.

"Actually yes. I don't usually make it a habit to run errands for the High Ruler. So, if I'm risking my life to help that bastard, I'd like to know why."

I remembered how he treated prisoners during the war. After one battle, his troops plundered the nearby village. They nabbed anything they could get their greedy hands on, including the females. Those deemed worthy enough were raped before being…disposed of. Those that were too far below an acceptable station were forced to work as slaves or murdered to feed their dogs. To get information from the prisoners, he would torture them with his mind powers. And when he'd gotten all he could or when he grew bored, he burned their villages to the ground.

A shudder moved up my spine. I didn't want to think how the High Ruler would treat Evren if he somehow got his hands on her.

"I didn't ask you to risk your life." Her voice was sharp.

"So should I call out to those guards and go ahead and hand you over to collect my bounty?"

She sneered viciously at me. "Do you really think they will let you walk away with any reward? They'll just kill you, steal your money, and take me back anyways."

Ah, so she does have some brains in that pretty, little head of hers.

"At least that would rid me of you." If her look could kill…

"Why is the High Ruler looking for you?"

She just stared at me. Her mouth turned down in a firm frown.

My temper flared. Swift as lightning, I yanked the rope to pull her to me. I grasped her shoulders before she collided with my chest, pinning her back against a tree, teeth bared angrily. My fingers dug into her shoulders. A menacing hiss slipped from my lips.

"Why do you even care?" she asked, her voice full of resentment, a touch of terror in her eyes.

Her heart pounded against my own chest. She was frightened. Her violet eyes were blazing. I leaned my head down, inches from her face, our noses practically touching.

Disgust covered her face as she said, "Because I am his daughter."

PART TWO

THIRTEEN
DELRIK

The High Ruler didn't have a daughter. At least not that I had ever heard of. In fact, if I remembered correctly, the Byrnes bloodline hadn't had a female heir in centuries. Only males had been born, and they were known for ruling the River Kingdom with a strict hand. It had been over 5,000 years of their control. If she were actually the daughter of Cadoc Byrnes, why would the High Ruler want his only daughter dead? All I knew was that I didn't want to return this female to the High Ruler without knowing the whole story. I didn't want to return her at all, no matter the bounty.

We picked our way higher up the mountain, the air changing to thin and earthy the further we got from Lakeshore. We'd been walking for only a few hours, but the setting sun made the light begin to dwindle. The slight slope in the earth led down to a wall of hanging vines, I knew beyond them was the mouth of a concealed cave I'd used many times. It was easy to bypass if you didn't know where to look.

I didn't say anything. I swept aside the thick vines and nudged Evren through the opening of the cave with my hand on the small of her back. The smell of damp moss greeted us, but the cave was clean and safe.

"I'm going to gather some wood for a fire," I said, before turning and leaving her standing alone. My mind was still humming with the knowledge of her lineage.

We'd need the fire for warmth tonight. The already cooling air left the exposed skin of my arms prickle with shivers. I also needed distance from her. I needed to gather my thoughts and regroup. I wasn't one to believe in fate. I didn't want to believe in fate. It was a cruel concept. The deaths of good people, like my parents, while the likes of Cadoc Byrnes and his scum guard still walked the realm. But she had only been in my presence for a day, and yet, I couldn't help thinking the Powers Above put her in my path for a reason.

I bent to pick up a broken limb and then another. The repetitive motion eased my mind so I could think clearly. I would take her to Aramis in Arcelia—he would know what to do. Arcelia, a city hidden deep in the Qana Mountains and home to the Mountain Fae. While the Mountain Fae didn't outright defy the High Ruler as the Snowhaven Fae had in the years following the war, they refused to bow to his every law. The city was made impenetrable with heavy spells and wards, making it impossible to breach and practically invisible unless you knew where to search. Only those with pure intentions were able to pass back and forth without resistance. Cadoc had bigger issues than a group of Fae that kept to themselves without stirring up trouble. Aramis would know how to proceed. I could keep her safe in Arcelia while I figured out what the High Ruler's plan was with Evren and why she was so vital.

Darkness crept over the forest as I made my way back to the cave. Tension released from my neck and shoulders upon seeing Evren propped against a boulder at the mouth of the cave, her chin resting on her bound hands, when I returned. I half expected her to be gone.

Evren Byrnes.

That was the first time I thought of her name knowing who she really was. First rule of bounty hunting: don't get too involved. Get in, get out, and collect your bounty. I was breaking that rule as I rolled her name around in my head like a fine whiskey. The name Evren fit her perfectly.

Dumping the gathered wood on the ground and wiping my hands down the front of my thighs, I got to work on building a fire. Flames soon roared to life, chasing away the shadows and escalating cold. I rummaged through my pack, pulling out the small amount of food I'd swiped from the inn before we departed. I usually traveled alone and didn't mind living off squirrels and fish, but having Evren in tow made me self-conscious about how I chose to live my life outside my role in the Arcelia Legion. It would have to be enough to tide us over. If we were going to walk all the way to Arcelia at a normal pace, we had a few days left to travel. With my speed, I could make the trip in less than two days, but that wasn't an option.

Evren sat with her back to me, surveying the dark night. Her shoulders were hunched over, arms wrapped around her knees which she'd drawn to her chest. A small twig was caught in her haphazard braid, and her tunic hung loosely on her small frame. I knew she couldn't see anything. With no moons tonight, the woods were a hollow blackness. The orange glow of the flames, as they rippled and curled over the wood gave light to the darkness that encircled our camp. She had to be hungry. I hadn't seen her eat anything today except that apple. The vision of the juice dripping down her chin came to mind again. My blood warmed, and I had to shift my sitting position.

My fingers brushed the soft fabric of her shoulder. She flinched, *hard*, at my hand, her gaze darting to the ground and away from me, as if I was about to strike her.

Fuck.

"I'm sorry," I said, stumbling over my words. "I didn't mean to startle you. Here."

I extended a piece of bread and dried meat to her. She peered at me through her long eyelashes, and I heard her swallow. She was still leaning away from me. Her eyes moved back and forth across my face, trying to decide if she trusted me enough not to poison her. The air between us grew thick, and my eyes were drawn lower when she parted her lips. She briefly looked at the food but didn't take it.

"It's not poisoned. I promise." I tore off a piece of the bread and popped it into my mouth—nudging the food in her direction again. "You'll need your strength. We have several days before we reach our destination."

She glanced over her shoulder toward the fire, keeping her eyes away from my face again as she brought her bound hands up to take the food. She nodded a quick thanks before turning back to the shadows.

The soft singing of crickets filled the air, and the screech of an owl pierced the night. A snap of wood from the fire echoed in the small clearing in front of the cave with a crack. I'd tucked the hanging vines back to reveal the yawning mouth of the cave. The glowing flames danced their light across her turned back and shadows against the surrounding trees.

Eventually, Evren braved eating the offered food. After an arduous day of walking, she didn't leave a crumb behind. Then she laid down, curled up against the rock, her back still to me, bound hands tucked under her head. I couldn't tell if she slept or if she just lay there.

She shifted her body, changing positions and causing her shirt to slide up, exposing soft, ivory skin splotched with green and bluish marks. Bruises. Old bruises that were healing, but still bruises. It's odd that a High Fae had bruises and scrapes the way she did. The one spanning her lower back had been deep based off its coloring. Acidic anger threatened to choke me. A brutal beating or an accident of some kind. I prayed it was the latter. Whatever caused them must have been extremely painful. I couldn't ever remember a time I'd been struck hard enough to cause that kind of injury. My fists tightened in my attempt to control the growing rage that filled me. How had she received those? Did someone do that to her? Had her father done that to her? I'd seen his brutality before, witnessed it firsthand during the war. I never understood it. But to someone as innocent and pure as Evren, I couldn't comprehend the hatred that would fill someone like that.

I wanted to reach out and comfort her but wouldn't dream of it after the way she reacted earlier. So, I continued to study her. Minutes ticked by. An hour. Her shoulders began to shake—I could only assume from crying.

FOURTEEN
EVREN

The sky outside the cave was shifting from black to a deep navy as I rolled over onto my back to see the forest. Morning's first light crept over the darkness, and the sounds of the night gave way to quiet and the rising sun. My captor was still sleeping. I was relieved he was still asleep. It gave me a chance to study his face. Even in sleep, his face was etched with concern. His brow was furrowed, a frown on his lips. It reminded me of the look Adaris had on his face the night I left. I longed to reach out and touch those deep lines, to soothe them away. But I withheld the touch, tucking my hands further under my head. This male didn't deserve any tenderness from me. After all, he had kidnapped me and planned on returning me to my father. I wasn't sure when, but I knew he would. We weren't moving south based on the increasing elevation and colder climate though. I felt hot anger, rise followed by dread shivering up my spine. Why would he be taking me deeper into the mountains?

Tears trickled down my cheeks, but I didn't wipe them away. He couldn't see them with his eyes closed anyways. Plus, my hands were filthy and would leave dirt smeared across my face. I was tired of being covered in filth. I let the salty wetness fall freely, soaking into the rocky dirt my arms rested on. How had I ended up in this situation? I'd simply replaced one hell with another. I sniffed, choking back the sob that was building inside me. The last thing I wanted was to wake him.

I took a steadying breath and let my eyes roam his face again. It was almost creepy, me watching this stranger while he slept, but I couldn't help my curiosity. A raised ridge of a scar trailed over right his eye and across his cheek. His skin was tanned like he spent all his time in the sun. Several days' worth of stubble peppered his chin. The darkness matched his smooth hair. His hair had fallen away from his neck, revealing another tattoo, similar to the brand that the Black Guard had. I didn't recognize the symbol though. It looked like the ancient language I'd seen written in the Essence Scrolls. My gaze drifted over his shoulder and down his arm, to his strong hand where more symbols were inked into his wrist. I wondered what his arms looked like under his shirt and how much of his left arm was covered in ink. The linen material clung to him in a pleasing way and showed an obscene number of muscles. He was a warrior of some kind with those muscles—a body used to hard training. His hand clenched onto the bow he wore the day before so tight even in sleep his knuckles were white. Even unconscious, he was on guard. A quiver of arrows tipped in white and gray feathers was leaning against the wall behind him. The cords of his muscles pulled and shifted under his shirt as he moved in his sleep. Could he sense me watching him? My previous irritation had morphed into…curiosity? Empathy? Attraction? His lashes twitched as his eyes moved back and forth under their lids. He must have been dreaming.

I don't know how long I watched him sleep. I explored every inch of him, from his head all the way to his muddy boots. The soft warmth of the sun pooled into the depth of the cave, and a yellow ray of light splashed over his face, causing him to stir. His eyes fluttered open and a yawn escaped his lips. He almost looked charming in his sleepy state.

Almost.

I smiled to myself. Just a small smile. I wouldn't give him a full smile, even inside my head.

Too bad he's an ass.

He rolled away quickly when he realized I was watching him and grumbled something to himself. Little did he know that I had stayed awake most of the night, trying to decide if I could sneak away from him and back into the forest. With his back to me I considered running, but he was too fast. And even if

I managed to get away from him, how would I find my way back? Where even was "back?" But since these bindings wouldn't budge no matter how much I strained against the rope. I was stuck. The coarse twine had rubbed red circles into my skin as I had twisted and pulled, which now burned.

Despite the lack of sleep, I felt recharged, refreshed. My back had stopped aching, and my usual headache that fogged my mind was gone. Maybe there was healing magic within the forest itself. Some say that the Sacred Forest had residual magic from when the gods came down and created the Darkwood trees. I believed it because I shouldn't have survived to Lakeshore and I shouldn't be feeling this good after what I'd gone through the last week.

He slowly sat up and stretched his arms above his head. The muscles in his back pulled taut against his shirt. I despised the idea of following behind him like a lost pet, but what choice did I have? I could play along, make him believe I trusted him so that he would let his guard down and begin to trust me. He hadn't seemed to want to give me up to the Black Guard yesterday. Maybe he could at least be trusted to get me to a safe place. I wasn't sure how I would get away from him once I'd reached safety, but right now, I was better off following him than fending for myself. I didn't want to offer myself up to the Sacred Foret for a second time. I would use his protection until I could figure out a plan to get to Adaris.

"Can I trust that you won't run if I untie your hands?"

I managed to ignore him all morning, though it was hard when he offered me breakfast. But I looked and met his eyes with the question. His irises were almost black, melding with his pupils. He arched a cocky brow at me in question, that same brow with the dangerous looking scar.

Had he read my thoughts, or did he really just fall into my plan? It couldn't be that easy. I quirked a brow right back at him.

"Feeling a touch feisty this morning?" His voice was relaxed, and the corners of his mouth twitched.

I refused to give him the satisfaction of a response.

"No?" He clutched his chest. "Ev, you're breaking my heart. How could you not trust me? After all we've been through," he said with a shrug of his shoulders.

Over-confident prick.

All we've been through! I wanted to choke him.

We finished our meager breakfast in silence, and I sipped on some warm liquid he said was coffee, which was not satisfying at all. Watered down dirt probably had more flavor. I missed my hot morning tea. And while I was tempted to keep my back turned to him, a chill in the morning air had me moving closer to the fire. I was sitting across from him on the ground, my legs tucked under me. My tin plate sat on the ground and my cup grasped in my hands trying to warm my stiff fingers. The air was clear, and every color around me was vibrant in the sun. I never thought the forest could be this stunning. The morning dew reflected rainbows of light like crystals, and a peaceful hush covered us like a blanket. A cream flower was peeking out from a nearby rock.

I mulled my plan over in my head one more time.

Make him believe I trust him. Follow his lead to wherever he is taking me. Then, when it's safe and I'm able to pack my own supplies, slip away.

He stuffed another hunk of bread into his mouth. "Clearly, I'm safer than those Black Guardsman."

Now he must be reading my mind.

I looked at him out of the corner of my eye, keeping my face turned down. "That depends on what you plan to do with me."

His mouth stretched into a captivating smile.

"So, you do speak. Well, I could lie to you and tell you everything will be peachy, and once we make it to Arcelia, you are free to go." He dumped the remaining coffee from his cup and packed it away with his plate into the pack. "How's that sound?"

I clamped my jaw shut, narrowing my eyes at him. He was taunting me. I was tempted to lunge at him and smack that smirk off his face. But I held back. Sticking to my plan would be brutal if he was going to act like this the whole time.

Arcelia sounded familiar, but I couldn't pinpoint it in my mind. It was one of those obscure names on one of the many maps I was forced to memorize.

I studied the expression on his face. I couldn't tell if he was lying. He looked amused. I needed him to believe he could trust me. I didn't return the trust, but I really didn't have a choice if I wanted to be free of this rope. I rolled my eyes at him but presented my bound hands. Something dangerous flashed in his eyes...hunger, lust.

He uncurled himself from the ground with the grace of a mountain cat and took a step closer to me. The space between us had only closed by a few inches, but I felt those inches with my whole body. It was like a fire spread through me with each step closer. The air became charged with energy. His proximity made me flustered. This wasn't fear coursing through me. What was it? Desire, maybe? I did not desire him, but my body and my mind were having a hard time agreeing. The only thing I desired at this moment was for this rope to stop biting into my skin, so I focused on that.

He stood over me, and my neck craned up to look at him. He cleared his throat, breaking into my thoughts and tingling heat swept across my cheeks. I swallowed thickly. I thanked the Powers Above he couldn't read my mind. Or at least I didn't think he could. A grin spread on his lips as he stared down at me kneeling at his feet. My face flushed even more as he studied me with dark, smoldering eyes. A hint of power radiated from him.

It took all my effort to keep my breathing even and not squirm.

His eyes didn't leave mine as he bent low, his warm breath brushing over my skin.

"Don't I at least get a please?" His voice was barely a whisper, more of a low, sultry growl.

My lips parted, but no sound came out. My whole body stiffened as he brought his hand slowly to my face. My first reaction was to pull away, but I was frozen to the spot. My heart threatened to beat out of my chest. He didn't actually touch me, but his thumb ghosted over my mouth for just a brief, eternity-lasting second. I couldn't breathe. My gaze locked on his face just inches from mine.

Then something sharp slid effortlessly through the rope in a clean sweep. He cocked his head to the side playfully, a devious look in his eye, before tossing a dagger gently toward me. *My* dagger. It landed with a thump on the ground in front of my knees. My hand reached down to the holster at my leg, coming up empty. He must have taken it when he took me. I thought I'd lost it in the struggle. I clamped my mouth shut; the delicious haze of whatever he held over me broke. How could I have been so careless? I didn't bother to say thank you before placing it back in the sheath.

"Shame. I'm going to miss you tied up and on your knees for me." The smirk on his face grew a little as he shamelessly scanned my body and backed away.

At that, my mouth dropped open in shock. What in the circle of dark hells? I'd dealt with many males perusing stares, but never one that was so blatant with his suggestive words.

"My name is Delrik, by the way." He was trying not to laugh. He had the audacity to grin at me. He must be delusional if he thought for a moment I would succumb to that smile. I swallowed the lump that had formed in my throat. What the hell was he doing to me?

"Let's go then," he said as he picked up his pack and slung it over his shoulder.

He smothered the fire before turning north and setting off further up the mountains. I extended my middle finger to his back as I stood, rubbing my freed wrists, and began to follow.

FIFTEEN
EVREN

It had been five days of walking in silence, eating in silence, sleeping in dreary caves, and each day grew colder and colder as we climbed. At least Delrik had thought of bringing my cloak when he ransacked my room at the inn.

We had an unspoken agreement of silence. Thank the Powers. I didn't know if I could handle any more of his flirtatious comments. Every time he looked at me, I blushed thinking about his words.

"Shame. I'm going to miss you tied up and on your knees for me."

One more day of travel before we reached our destination. Or at least that's what Delrik had said the night prior as we made camp. Arcelia. I didn't even try to guess how many miles we'd walked so far.

Over the last five days, I'd had plenty of time to contemplate my entire existence plus some.

Just one more day.

The more I repeated this to myself, the more I believed it. Just one more day. I was exhausted from the constant walking. My legs ached, and my feet were blistered. The red burns encircling my wrists, the reminder that I was being held against my will, had disappeared at least. The only evidence of the binding was the faded pink lines.

I brushed my hair away from my forehead as I stepped up on a boulder. The dappled sunlight colored my arms. The layer of sweat and dirt coating my body made everything stick to me. My hair to my neck, dead leaves to my arms as I brushed against trees. Dirt stuck to my palms each time I tripped and fell, which was often. I was practically jogging to keep up with Delrik's long strides. I pulled my cloak tighter around me and half-fell, half-jumped off the slippery boulder to follow him.

Delrik, on the other hand, moved with confidence and grace through the woods. I hadn't seen him stumble once. His beard had grown thick making him look wilder than ever. The further we went into the mountains, the more relaxed he became. He belonged in the Sacred Forest and the mountains. He thrived here. I couldn't imagine the solitude. At least in the fortress I had maids and tutors and Adaris. I was never truly alone.

I didn't mind our silence. I was used to countless hours of quiet. I didn't have anything to say to him anyway. So, when we stopped a few feet in front of me, I didn't bother looking up.

"We're being watched." Delrik's voice pierced the chilled mountain air between us. He nodded his head to a thicket ahead where a pair of yellow-green eyes prowled in the depth of the shadows, stalking us. I hadn't noticed the forest grow quiet. Even the insects were silent. Waiting…or hiding.

A low rumble came from the thicket as a monstrous creature as large as a horse stepped into view. Its sleek body moved with predatory ease as it took a menacing step forward; branches snapped beneath its massive, clawed paws. Its mighty head tilted to the side, and eyes cut in half with vertical slits zeroed in on us. Curled horns twisted upward behind its short, rounded ears that twitched in our direction. Lips curled up its snout into a snarl exposing multiple rows of knife-sharp teeth. It was like nothing I'd ever seen before. A cold shiver ran down my spine. Respect and fear coursed through me.

"Delrik." My voice cracked. I tried to swallow the lump of terror lodged in my throat.

And as if the forest knew the danger we were in, it trembled underfoot. I knew of the beasts that roamed the Sacred Forest but never in my wildest dreams could I have imagined this.

"Run." He sounded sure as he grabbed my arm and thrust me in front of him as we ran.

Its claws dug deep into the soft earth before it sprang. We bolted, Delrik was right on my heels. Our pounding footsteps rang out in the silence. Limbs of trees whipped against me, slicing my arms and face. I tried to duck out of the way, but it was useless. I heard the beast as it advanced behind us, Delrik pushing me to go faster. There was a break in the trees ahead, the sun shining. The light glittered on the frost that hung on every surface giving the clearing an ethereal glow. I didn't realize it was such a beautiful day.

I tripped, the ground coming up quickly, but before my face smashed into the ground, Delrik had lifted me from behind, urging me forward, faster. We'd never outrun the thing.

As we broke through the trees, my feet slid into the dirt, and I skidded to a stop. There was a ravine in front of us. I scanned my surroundings, but there was nowhere to go, no way to escape. Trapped. We were going to die. Right here in these damned woods with the bright sun mocking us overhead.

Delrik's head whipped around in my direction, eyes wide. Protection in his eyes. He spun to face off the beast as it burst from the trees.

"Delrik, no!" I screamed in terror.

But he didn't listen to me, didn't hear me. The male before me transformed from the bounty hunter to a well-honed weapon of a warrior. Delrik was quick on his feet for being so large. His body was pure precision and stealth. He drew his bow from his back and nocked an arrow in the time it took me to exhale. The muscles in his chest rippled as he pulled the string back, a silent reminder of how lethal he could be. The arrow whistled as it soared through the air. The beast swerved but not fast enough. The arrowhead grazed its shoulder. A roar reverberated through the trees. My arms flailed out for balance as the ground shook beneath my feet. The great beast trembled with anger and pain before it set its sights on us again with malice and bloodlust.

Delrik didn't wait a second to see where the arrow hit. The moment he released the arrow, he turned quick as lightning, scooped me from where I stood, and ran along the edge of the ravine. I clung tightly to his neck, and he carried me effortlessly. The beast gained on us, barely slowed by its injury. Again, Delrik halted and turned to face the beast. He reached down my leg and took my dagger from its sheath. The animal lunged for Delrik. Fear gripped me as I crouched behind him. I raised my hands above me, bracing for the deadly impact when something came from inside me, without me controlling it. A force, like a wall of hot air, surged from my hands and drove the beast back, sending it crashing into a tree.

I looked down at my hands in confusion and shock. Had that force come from me? My mother's powers. Had I just summoned my mother's powers? Delrik looked at me with the same shock and confusion.

The beast lay limp on the ground for a moment before it stood and shook off the shock. Blood caked the mahogany fur across its shoulder from the arrow. It moved in a wide arc, circling us like the prey we were. Delrik mirrored the motion. Focused, a snarl came from his lips. I slunk back into the shadows away from the beast. The beast lunged. Before the beast's feet could leave the earth, Delrik lunged to swipe the blade across the beast's throat. A clean swipe. Its throat split open and dark inky blood poured onto the ground in spurts. The body made a hollow thump onto the ground. Silence.

Delrik stood frozen in front of the still-twitching body. Blood poured from its injuries, soaking the ground. The dagger slipped from his bloody fingers into the dirt, and he dropped to his knees. The creature's thick blood dripped from him where he'd been sprayed. His body was heaving with exertion. He had a deep gash on his arm from running through the forest. His blood mixed with the beast's in a pool of shining onyx.

☥

I peeled myself from the ground and stepped from the shadows where I cowered.

"Delrik?"

He didn't respond to me as I made my way to him. His back was to me, so I pressed my fingers to his shoulder. He swiveled onto his feet, snatching up the dagger and holding it high, eyes wild. I stumbled away several steps, panicked he would attack me. His face softened when he saw me. He dropped the weapon to the ground again. A flash danced across the sky above us followed by a roll of thunder. Rain began to fall.

I knew he was a hunter, but seeing him kill, did something to me. And I could tell it did something to him. He didn't enjoy it. There was turmoil etched all over his face. I could see the pain it brought his spirit, even though the beast would've killed us. I took a step toward him, not too close, but close enough to slip my hand into his. My breath caught in my throat, and my heartbeat accelerated as I stood in front of him. A ripple of power tingled up my arm where his skin met mine. He exhaled slowly, trying to calm himself.

"Are you all right?" His voice was raw and husky.

"I'm fine." At least physically.

He'd saved me. He'd risked his life to protect me.

Delrik stepped in close, dropped his head low to meet mine, and brought his bloody hands to either side of my face before pressing his forehead against mine. His body was warm with only inches between us. I could feel the weight of his emotion on me. I was tempted to pull away from him, but I couldn't. I let him lean there with me, offering the only comfort I could and secretly relieved he was alive and safe. The metallic smell of blood that invaded my senses was already being carried off by the rain and wind.

SIXTEEN
EVREN

We remained motionless, Delrik's bloodied hands grasping my face, for several long minutes, like I was somehow anchoring him to this world. A stillness settled over us. His breathing steadied after what felt like an eternity. The sounds of the forest slowly returned to my ears as we stood there. Rivulets of icy rain dripped down the two of us.

When he took a step back and dropped his hands, my cheeks grew cold, and my chest ached from the withdrawal.

"Delrik, are you alright?" I said into the air between us.

Something haunted his eyes as they wandered over my face. He stroked his hand through his thick beard as he watched me intently, eyes crinkling a touch from the glare of sun trying to break through the clouds. Then, he turned, picked up my dagger, and knelt beside the slayed monster.

Delrik's voice was a soft whisper as he asked the Powers Above for forgiveness for spilling lifeblood within the Sacred Forest and to let the body bless the creatures as it was returned to the earth. He brought his hand to the beast's body, splaying it into the fur, speaking an ancient language I didn't recognize.

"Delrik?"

He removed one of the teeth before wordlessly standing and striding into the deep trees again. He never turned to see if I was following or not—but I did.

We hadn't made it more than five minutes before we stumbled upon a den. The stench wafted through the air of the rotting, partially eaten bodies littering the den floor. Flies buzzed around our heads. Neither of us got too close, pausing only for a moment.

"Osomals never hunt this far west, much less make a den." He seemed to be speaking more to himself than me. "A den means breeding."

I'd never heard of an osomal before. My stomach churned at the thought of more of those monsters lurking within the forest.

♀

Delrik hadn't spoken a single word to me. Not even one. At first, I willingly gave him the space he silently requested. But as the hours went on, we continued to climb. The muted light from the sun had moved from one side of the sky to the other as the day passed and we hiked away from the osomal den. We found our way into a narrow passage with sheer cliffs on either side. The rain turned to icy pellets and then to thick, fluffy snow.

When we didn't stop for lunch and Delrik's pace increased, my irritation grew. He didn't even bother to check when I tripped and fell a dozen more times. My jaw ached from clenching my teeth with frustration. I hadn't done anything to deserve this silent treatment. Hell, I didn't even want to be here.

Snow flurries flew in circles around us in the gusting winds of the mountains, and ice on the path crunched under my feet. My legs were stiff from the cold and protested with each grueling step. My cloak was soaked from the rain and was useless with the piercing cold. We had been walking all day without a break. I didn't know why he was pushing at such a fast pace. How much longer would we climb? Dusk was settling in fast, and I still couldn't see anything in front of me other than a barren passage nestled between the steep walls of the towering mountains.

Delrik didn't slow at all, even as the ground grew steeper with each step. His legs had to be at least a foot longer than mine. For every step he took, I had to take three. His feet were sure and true while I stumbled on every rock, twig, and tree root that existed on the side of this awful mountain. The trees had grown sparse, unlike the dense forest below.

Evergreens had replaced the oaks, elms, and Darkwood trees of the Sacred Forest, and uneven rocks replaced the tree roots. My hands were covered in cuts, bruises, and blood from repeatedly falling, and I could still smell the stench of the osomal smeared across the skin of my face and neck from Delrik's hands.

I suddenly slammed into Delrik's back, not noticing that he had stopped walking. My feet slid on the rocky path as I stumbled backward a few steps.

"A warning that you were stopping would've been nice," I said through gritted teeth.

A flash of dark eyes as Delrik shot a gaze over his shoulder at me.

Oh, now he can see me.

I rolled my eyes. He had stopped at a large fallen tree that blocked our path. It came up to his navel, which meant there wasn't any way I'd be able to climb over it without his help.

An unintentional whimper of defeat escaped me. He didn't turn around again or say anything, but I heard him try to hold in a derisive laugh. Apparently, he had regained his smug arrogance during his brooding and stalking up the mountain. I stiffened and clenched my fists tight, my nails digging into my palms.

Prick.

He effortlessly climbed on top of the rotting trunk, then turned to offer me his hand. He pulled me up onto the fallen tree. He still grasped my hand as I jumped down onto solid ground on the opposite side. I felt his thumb brush against my knuckles before dropping my hand, sending tingles across my skin. I paused as he moved ahead, taken aback by the familiar motion. My hand buzzed from the contact. What was that for? And why did my skin react so much to his slightest touch?

I dragged my gaze from my tingling hand and back to the passage stretching out before me and deflated. There was only a barren, rocky passage and nothing else. My body let out an involuntary sigh. I wanted to curl up in a ball and sleep for a year. Delrik could just leave me here, and I'd succumb to the forest. I looked around but didn't see any place to take shelter for the night. Just steep walls on either side of us, casting shadows across the daunting path. A lone Darkwood Tree stood tall, oddly out of place at this elevation. Above us, its branches were bare, like a skeleton stark against the evening sky. Delrik reached his hand out, brushing the fresh snow off the trunk to reveal a carving etched into its bark. He pressed his hand against the carving and bowed his head, muttering that ancient language again under his breath. I knew he wasn't High Fae, but now he was chanting incantations. Who was this guy? Was he some kind of conjurer?

My mind whirled as before my eyes, glistening in the air like moonstone, two ivory towers appeared, buried deep within the summit of a mountain, and the setting sun glinted off the tall towers. I blinked at the brightness. I hadn't noticed the river as we hiked through the mountains, but I recognized the smell of it now. It was like the river waters of home, but up here in the mountains, it smelled fresher, cleaner. The waters were pristine and azure. Milky-tipped rapids spotted the river as water crashed against rocks lining the shoreline. Other stretches were smooth and fast flowing. I heard a low rumbling of falling water. Looking for the source, I saw a cascading waterfall off in the distance. The waterfall seemed to pour into the city itself, its rushing sounds a melody of peace and serenity.

This must be Arcelia. I thought back to the Fae histories that my rather frumpy-looking tutor had drilled into my brain. After the War Across the Sea, the Mountain Fae had secluded themselves up here in the Qana Mountains. While the Arcelia Legion had helped my father during the war, they preferred the quiet of the slopes. My Father was glad to be rid of them, as he mentioned on multiple occasions. He never spoke highly of them. Though many Highborn families came from Arcelia, they were too soft, too forgiving, according to Father. They kept their city hidden with spells and enchantments. It was almost impossible to find unless your guide knew these cliffs. Apparently, Delrik was one of those somebodies.

Two regal-looking figures appeared in the passage before us. One on a black stallion, and another on a shimmering, gray-dappled mare. Both wore heavy cloaks made from beautiful, emerald fabric. Exquisite gold thread reflected the sun in fine detail. Thick fur lined the edges and the hood. The one on the black stallion removed the hood of his cloak.

Mountain Fae.

The male's thick auburn eyebrows, matching his hair, knitted together with such sternness. He had a commanding presence about him. His mouth was in a hard line. The black ink of a tattoo on the side of his neck matched the one Delrik had on his neck. It took all my effort not to turn and run. Instead, I sidestepped to stand partially behind Delrik. He protected me from the osomal; maybe he'd protect me from these Fae.

When the male laid those jade-green eyes on Delrik, his scowl melted away, making way for a smile.

"Delrik!" His arms lifted into the air, and his voice boomed as if rejoicing for the arrogant male that stood guarding me. He didn't dismount but rather trotted closer and grasped Delrik's arm in greeting. I timidly peered around Delrik. As the newcomer moved closer, I noticed a vicious-looking longsword at his waist.

"I should've known it was you. No one uses the Kiscarine Pass anymore. It hasn't been used for over a hundred years." His features relaxed as he spoke. He clearly knew Delrik well. And Delrik obviously knew how to bypass the Mountain Fae's borders.

The male studied Delrik, scanning him up and down, seeing the smeared blood, dirt, and Powers knew what else caked to us. I'm sure we were a sight to see. "What happened to you?" His nose crinkled as we pulled back a touch. "You smell quite unpleasant."

"We came across an osomal. He gave us a little trouble."

The male raised a skeptical eyebrow that shifted to concern when he realized Delrik wasn't joking. He looked imposing up on that stallion.

"We haven't crossed an osomal in...well, I don't remember." He paused and turned toward the east, like he could see through the mountain itself. "Something is drawing them from the east. There's a dark presence in the forest. More dark creatures have been spotted closer to the city." The male's lips forced a tight line. "Come, you can tell me all about it. Stay for a few days. It's good to have you home."

Home? How was this his home? Delrik wasn't High Fae. Did the Mountain Fae not care? The only common Fae and lower beings allowed in Rivamir were those that worked the lowest of jobs. Crossbreeds were treated as lower beings or shunned completely.

It was then that the male peered over Delrik's shoulder and down his straight nose at me. His proud jaw was perfectly curved, and his high cheekbones gave him a handsome, yet fierce, look. My spine straightened like a steel rod as I had been taught, hands clasped primly behind my back. I hated that this politeness was so ingrained in me that I didn't even think before my body reacted. I didn't owe any of them respect, and yet it was an unconscious reaction.

I fought the urge to redirect my eyes away from him, to nod in respect. Instead, I held his gaze, trying to stand at my tallest. The massive black stallion took a step closer, and I fought every muscle in my body not to retreat a step. The side of his mouth turned up slightly at my clear defiance of decorum, but only for a moment. The male leaned into Delrik and spoke softly. I couldn't make out the foreign words clearly before he raised his voice again.

"I don't know who you brought with you, but I like her," the male said.

I didn't bother hiding my shock at such a blunt comment.

"Come," he said as he turned and galloped off.

Delrik peered over his shoulder at me, a lazy smile flitted across his smug face, before following him. It was annoying how Delrik kept smiling at me. He'd been as cold as stone to me the last several hours, and now he was...smiling at me?

"Don't mind Aramis. You'll get used to him."

Aramis? As in Aramis Zathrian, High Ruler of the Mountain Fae?

Delrik started walking, following after Aramis. He paused when he reached the second person. I'd almost forgotten the lean figure there, frozen like a statue. Their eyes met. The person bent down, reaching a slender, gloved hand to Delrik's face, and brushed a thumb gently over his cheek—a female. I couldn't see her face, but Delrik recognized who it was. He grasped the slight hand and held it to his face before placing a chaste kiss on the knuckles. Jealousy surged through me at the familiar gesture. He'd never shown those manners to me.

The female straightened taller than before and, though her face was shadowed in darkness, her piercing gaze in my direction sliced through me like ice. She lifted her chin a touch before she turned her horse and galloped off after Aramis.

SEVENTEEN
EVREN

As we walked through the mountainous city of Arcelia, we drew quiet whispers from those that saw us. A few greeted Delrik, but most slipped into the shadows without a sound. I thought this was his home. Maybe they were shying away from me. The streets were smoothed stones, winding through towering pillars protruding from the mountainside. The surrounding buildings and homes were smooth and glossy stones with wisteria climbing up the sides. Aramis Zathrian and the female were waiting for us near a carved arch leading into one of the towers.

We followed them up a winding staircase and down a side open air corridor, Aramis leading the way, Delrik and the female walking side by side. I kept a healthy distance from the pair. She didn't remove her cloak until we entered what appeared to be an apartment. Aramis opened a wide door, carved with the same intricate carvings from the tree in the woods. I sucked in a breath of shock when I entered the apartment. It was astonishing. The entryway opened into a grand room. The doors of a balcony lining one whole side of the room were flung wide open despite the cold, though no cold came from the outside. It overlooked an impressive view of the sapphire river running through the city. The small rapids glittered in the sunlight.

I took a step into the room that looked like it had been carved directly from the mountain itself. The wall opposite the windows was sheer stone, soft and gray, that had been polished smooth, just like the floor. A fire crackled and popped inside the fireplace.

I took a shaky breath, wringing my hand under my cloak. The sheer size of the room and the vastness of the city was overwhelming. Before, the mountains had been a mystery. Now that I was here, I saw that they were more full of secrets than I could have ever imagined. An entire sleeping civilization lived nestled on the side of the cliffs.

Delrik and Aramis chatted to themselves by the entrance as I moved further into the apartment. Though the female kept her face shadowed, I could feel her eyes bore into my back when I turned away. I did my best to ignore her. I couldn't hear what they were saying. Not because they were far from me but because I was too enthralled with my surroundings. I turned in a small circle, looking up at the ceiling and the floating lights above that kept the room bright.

The ceiling was jagged like the stalactites in a cave, but there was so much beauty in the sharpened points. Oversized couches sat close to a fireplace, reminding me of the library at home. My heart ached for the familiarity of my old life, but I vowed I'd never return to that prison. I took a step closer to the fire roaring before me and raised my hands to the heat. The cold retreated from my fingers and face as I leaned in close to the flames.

"Evren." Aramis's voice made me jump. "You can come this way. I'll show you to your room."

He must have raised his voice to be sure I heard him. He swept his arm toward the front door leading back into the corridor for me to follow. I walked to him, but as I passed by Delrik, a hand, quick as a flash, stopped me. His fingers were firm on my upper arm but still gentle. What was he doing? I looked down to his hand then back to his face. His eyebrows rose, a smirk appearing on his lips. I was thankful for the long sleeves of my cloak so his skin wouldn't touch mine again.

"She stays with me," Delrik said, his voice low and husky.

I balked. He was insane if he thought I'd be staying with him. "Um, no thank you. I don't even know you."

"We can rectify that easily."

I was about to snap back...

"Delrik." The female spoke for the first time, practically interrupting me, a sound of pure reprimand. Even with her face half shadowed, her dark jade eyes were firm on his face. "You can't be serious."

Yeah, what *she* said.

He couldn't be serious. I was thankful someone else saw how ridiculous he was being.

Words echoed in my head from Adaris. "Males can be predatory, Evren. Even the ones that seem safe."

Delrik was far from safe.

"But we've had such a lovely time the last few days." He drifted a step closer, the movement as graceful and predatory as a jungle cat. I retreated a step away attempting to slow my breathing, but he didn't let go of my arm. A flirtatious smile curled his stupid lips. He winked at me before turning to Aramis. I wanted to smack him square across the face, but I could barely breathe. "Plus, I don't trust that she won't sneak away in the night," Delrik said coolly.

He didn't trust me. He thought I'd run.

Aramis pulled in a slow, deep breath and held it, contemplating. "Fine. She can stay in your guest suite then. And I'll have guards posted to watch her." He waved his hand into the air between them.

Um...Excuse me. What?

"Guards! Where would I even go?" I yanked my arm away from Delrik's grasp, pushing past him, and storming away from them back toward the fireplace. "I wouldn't survive an hour in that stupid forest."

"Thank you, Aramis." Delrik didn't even bat an eye at me, simply ignored my small outburst.

"It's not every day that you bring a female home, Delrik. Play nice," Aramis said as he and the female left us alone, closing the door behind him.

I whipped around the moment I heard the door click, spinning fast on the balls of my feet. "You can't just lock me in here with you." I sneered.

"Oh, don't worry, I won't be staying. Just going to bathe and then go find some food."

My stomach moaned, giving away my own hunger. I looked down and realized how filthy I was, covered in five days of dirt and grime from the hike. Dark blood was still caked on my hand that Delrik had held. I'm sure my face looked even worse. The rain we'd trudged through had only rinsed the top layer of filth away.

Is that smell coming from me?

I could use a bath too. And some nourishment. But I seethed from Delrik and his condescending tone. I clenched my fists tightly, trying to control myself. There was something about him that made me lose control over my emotions, and he knew it. My frustration reignited, and I felt my skin growing hot, like someone was pouring molten rock through my veins.

Movement in front of me made me glance up. Delrik was walking away and toward an open door off to the side of the sitting room. His back was to me as he lifted his bow and quiver off his shoulders, resting them against the door frame. Then, reaching behind his head he lifted the collar of his shirt up and over his head and off his arms before he tossed it into the room on the floor. My jaw dropped open. The muscles in his back and shoulders contracted and moved with the motion. Battle scars ran across his back and down his right shoulder, matching the one on his face. The swirled tattoo of ancient symbols I'd seen on his forearms flowed all the way up his left arm and shoulder. Color crept across my cheeks and down my neck.

So that's what his arms look like under his shirt.

Why was I watching this male who kidnapped me and was holding me captive? And better yet, why was I enthralled by the shape and hardness of his back? He kicked the door shut behind him. The dull thud of its closing echoed off the stone walls.

I huffed and turned away abruptly, frustrated that my body was betraying me. Why was it so hot in here all the sudden? While I'd read romance novels thanks to the servants leaving them lying around, I'd never been around other males besides Adaris. It wasn't allowed. At least it wasn't allowed until Father decided that I needed a bondmate. Then I was thrust into the world of courtship and marriage proposals. None of the males I was introduced to gave me the same reaction as Delrik just did. Powers, none of them came close to looking like him either. They were all my father's age, and honestly, were repulsive. Especially Renwick.

But Delrik...I puffed out an exaggerated breath. My face heated again as the vision of Delrik's bare back flashed into my mind, stirring something deep inside in my center.

EIGHTEEN
EVREN

I turned back to the sitting area and spotted another door. It mirrored the one Delrik had disappeared into. I moved toward it, my boots clicking on the stone floors, and poked my head inside. There was a large bedroom with a towering four-post bed.

Thank the Powers Above. I was so tired of sleeping on the ground. The bed and the mountain of fluffy pillows was the most inviting sight I'd ever seen. I want to toss myself onto the bed and weep. I was half tempted to run full speed and throw my body into what I'm sure paradise would feel like. But I knew if I started to cry, I wouldn't have been able to stop. Not to mention I'd have ruined the fabrics with my soiled clothes. There was a vase of flowers on the side table like a guest was expected. Or did they just keep flowers out all the time? The room was warm and cozy despite the opened French doors in the main space, a fire roaring in the fireplace.

What is up with these Mountain Fae and having the doors open to the cold like this?

I walked to the doors and closed them. Flanking the doors were floor-to-ceiling windows that covered the entire wall. Thick velvet curtains framed the wall of glass. I looked out the windows onto the patio covered in snow. Up here, at eye level with the peaks, I could see the powdery snow that blanketed the mountainside spotted with towering evergreens. The mountains disappeared into the glowing clouds of the sunset. It was exquisite. Wariness crept over me with the doors closed. My hands lingering on the brass handles. Remembering the invisible rope burns on my wrists indicated my status. Although they were gone, the ache lingered under my skin. I felt like a trapped animal. Granted, I'd been trapped in a gorgeous tower by an infuriatingly beautiful male. But still I, was trapped.

I stood, admiring the scenery for a long time, trying to press my anxiety down. I breathed in the quiet and let it sink into me—until my stomach interrupted my train of thought with a grumble. It was the distraction I needed to bring me back to my sad reality. I really needed to find some food.

But first, a bath.

I tore my gaze from the scenery and turned to find the bathroom. A marbled bathroom was attached to the bedroom behind a large sliding door. In the center of the room was a massive clawfoot tub. It could easily fit at least three people. It took all my self-control not to strip off the mud-sodden clothes right there in the doorway. I stepped inside the bathroom and pulled the door closed behind me.

Hot tendrils of steam rose from the water as it filled the tub. I was thankful the Mountain Fae adopted plumbing like at home. Only the wealthier cities in Illoterra had plumbing and hot water at the ready. I dipped my toes into the water to test its temperature. It was perfect, hot enough to make my skin prickle. I sighed as I lowered my battered, aching body into the deep water. The raw cuts and blisters burned in the hot water for a few seconds before the water melted away the pain. This tub really was enormous. My legs stretched out straight in front of me, and the water was deep enough to cover my shoulders, coming right up to my chin. I leaned my head back against the cool edge of the tub and closed my eyes. The soothing water seemed to wash away everything—all my worries, all my questions, and I could just be. My sore muscles relaxed and I sank even deeper into the water. Steam eventually filled the bathroom, fogging up the large mirror over the sink. It was like I was floating in the clouds on top of these hidden mountains.

♀

I don't know how long I sat in that tub. After a long while, the water began to cool. I sat up and leaned forward, bringing my knees to my chest. Then I remembered where I was. I was sitting naked in this elaborate bathroom, in a hidden tower in the mountains, held captive by a pompous male I hardly knew. So why was I so content? Why did I feel safe? This was the first time in years that I wasn't afraid of what came next.

I loosened my hair from its braid and dipped my head back into the water. Bits of dead leaves and dirt were stuck in the tangles. My long silver strands had become so dirty that they almost appeared brown at the ends. I let the heaviness of my hair pull me completely underwater before rising again, wiping my still bloodied face clean. I reached for a bar of soap that was on a nearby shelf and began to scrub the grime off my now relaxed—still bruised and cut—body. I rinsed the lather from my hair and let the suds run down my body. I glanced around for a towel. I located some freshly folded towels next to the sink. Pulling the plug in the tub, I stepped out. Dripping water as I tiptoed over to the shelf. I wrapped the plush fabric around myself.

I dared to peek into the mirror that hung above the stone sink. I cringed at the dark circles under my eyes from the long journey and restless sleep. I walked from the bathroom and back into the bedroom. I poked my head out into the main room to see if Delrik was still there. I didn't hear him, and my mood dropped. I shook the thought of him from me and closed the door to my room, turning the lock with a loud click. Why should I care or be upset with his absence?

I stopped short when I saw the heap of muddy clothes on the floor and immediately knew I was not going to put those back on. I rubbed the top of my foot against my calf, thinking. I considered throwing them in the fire.

What was I going to wear? Delrik hadn't grabbed my spare clothes. I moved to the wardrobe, hoping to find a fresh pair of pants and shirt. The apartment was clearly Delrik's, and based off him going into the other room, this was his guestroom. I doubted there would be anything in it. What I actually found inside was a line of dresses. Not extravagant dresses that I had worn back home, but simple beauties. I caressed one of the silk gowns with my fingers and let the fabric slip through them. I spotted a chest of drawers in the corner. Maybe there would be pajamas there. I walked over to it and pulled open the top drawer. I found a pair of silk pajamas that were the softest thing I ever felt. I smiled at them, dropping the wet towel to the floor, before pulling them on. The luxury of the silk caressed my curves and made me feel like a queen. The shorts were not my normal loungewear, but I didn't care. I'm not sure how everything I needed appeared, but I wasn't going to complain. I was too tired. Honestly, I could get used to this. I wondered if the Mountain Fae would let me hide out here for eternity. At least here, in the safety of the mountains, I could live that long. With Renwick as a bondmate, I didn't see myself lasting longer than a decade. I wouldn't want to last longer than that if his past cruelty was a glimpse of my future.

Night had taken over while I lounged in the tub and my eyelids felt as heavy as lead. But my hunger overruled my exhaustion. I picked up my dagger from the desk where I'd left it while I bathed. I popped my head out the bedroom door again to see if anyone was around. It was empty so I slipped out, bare feet padding across the stone floor carved out of the mountain. It must have been enchanted somehow because it was warm despite the frigid temperature outside.

The fire was still roaring in the fireplace, so I flopped onto the end of the couch closest to the heat and curled up into a ball. I watched the flames dance an orange glow across the walls. They were mesmerizing—drawing me in. A plate of food and a glass of some kind of wine was left on the coffee table next to my…sketchpad! I was certain that it was lost. I was famished and devoured the food, barely tasting it. I didn't have the energy or the willpower to move back to the bedroom, so I settled into the lush cushions.

This room was rather cozy, despite its size. It was decorated differently than the rooms that filled my home in the river lands, but I found that I loved it. The soft creams and navy were a contrast to the harsh stone of the mountain. The small globes of light floating along the ceiling had dimmed, giving off a soft light. The large windows let in the rays from the twin moons and stars studded above. I stared at the vast blanket of stars that twinkled like they were painted over the mountains. The river was a glossy black line cutting through the city. A glittering city sprawled below, mimicking the stars above. The streets below were silent, peaceful, sleeping. Calmness came over me like a wave, dragging me into a deep slumber.

NINETEEN
DELRIK

I needed a walk through the city streets to clear my head before returning to my apartment. My fast pace made the night air whip across my face. I welcomed the cold as it stung my skin. I shouldn't have pushed Evren to stay with me. Maybe I should've given her space. Powers Above knew I could use some space. And yet, I wanted to keep her close. I was being drawn to her like a moth to a flame. Something suspicious was going on, and I didn't want to risk her life in any way. It was the very essence of me, an oath I swore to myself. All those unspeakable acts during the war…I shook away the thoughts and increased my pace. I'd repented to the Powers Above, but it wasn't enough, couldn't be enough. Nothing I did would ever be enough.

I hadn't realized I'd made it all the way to my favorite spot, a clearing along the river's edge. Sighing into the fresh air, I let the view of the serene mountains and the water overflow my senses. The night was effortlessly beautiful, just like Evren. Which made it impossible to focus on literally anything. I welcomed the cold mountain air. It was refreshing after a long summer in the south. A summer of bounty hunting. The smell of the fresh dusting of snow and the sound of the rushing water was like a lullaby soothing my frayed nerves.

When I returned to the apartment, I found an empty plate sitting on the table. I knew she had been hungry. I heard her stomach rumbling the entire hike today, but we had run out of food. I actually gave her the last of the food for breakfast, having nothing for myself. She was too proud to ask for dinner though. I didn't want her to be humiliated or embarrassed, so I made sure the servants left dinner out where she would find it and fresh clothes after her bath.

I'd been sitting in my own tub when I heard the rushing water from her faucet. I heard the hiss that escaped from her, assuming it was burning from the cuts all over her. Mine sure as hell burned. High Fae were supposed to heal quickly, and there was no doubt that her blood was as pure as it could be. Even being part human, my Fae blood meant that my injuries healed at a faster rate than most. In another hour, they'd be gone. It was odd that she was covered in bruises and cuts that hadn't healed when I found her. Another piece to the puzzle that stumped me.

I drained my tub shortly after that. Sitting just a wall away from her, knowing she was naked while I soaked was almost unbearable.

☥

I didn't see Evren asleep on the couch at first. The room had grown dark with only the moons shining a narrow, silver path along the floor. The embers glowed softly in the fireplace. A whimper came from the darkness. So quiet. And then another. She was curled up in a tight ball, arms wrapped around her bare knees. The silk shorts and cropped shirt she wore left little to the imagination. Silent tears trailing down her cheeks. The moonlight made her pale hair and skin look ghost-like. Her face scrunched into fear, her lips moving, pleading.

Right as I turned to head to my bedroom, she cried out softly, "No. Please no. Not again."

I froze. Pain lurched through my body at her words. Another quiet whimper and I turned to see her mouth open in a silent scream. No sound came from her, but her delicate features twisted in agony. I rushed to her, kneeling by the couch. Cold sweat coated her contorted face and down her arms. My hands hovered over her body for a split second. I didn't know if I should touch her, wake her. Then I placed my hands on her shoulders. She shuddered at my touch. I yanked my hands back.

Icy fear gripped me as her head snapped back. A sound came from her throat like she was struggling for air, gasping for another breath. She brought her fisted hands to the sides of her head, digging her hands into her hair. The dream clawed at her mind, choking her from the inside out.

"Shh." I tried to soothe her.

I stroked the back of my fingers across her forehead and down her arm. This time, she responded to my touch, leaning into my hand. Her body was seeking the comfort I was offering, accepting it. I took a deep breath. I'd be that comfort for her. I needed to be that for her. I cupped my hands to her face and stroked my thumbs across her cheeks, wiping away the tears. Her thrashing turned to shuddering tremors, and then slowly eased. I pushed the hair back from her face. She settled deeper into the couch, relaxing her clenched hands. Just as quickly as the nightmare began, the pain on her face disappeared and was replaced by calm sleep.

I took a deep breath as I sat back on my heels. I watched her sleep for a few minutes before pulling a thick blanket off the back of the couch and draping it over her. I knew she had nightmares. I'd listened to her the last few nights battle with whatever demons were inside her mind, but none had been this bad. I was tempted to sleep on the floor next to her but knew she wouldn't like waking up to me in the morning.

Then, I noticed that dagger beneath the pillow. She sure was a feisty little thing. Maybe I shouldn't have given her that dagger back. She might slaughter me in my sleep if I wasn't careful. I smiled as I kissed the tips of my fingers and then touched them to her forehead before standing and retreating to my own room.

I collapsed into my bed, not bothering with changing my clothes.

TWENTY
EVREN

I woke up enveloped in cozy warmth. A thick blanket was draped over me, its heaviness a soothing presence. I didn't remember falling asleep the previous night. My eyelids were heavy, and my eyes were dry and scratchy. I massaged my hands over my face, keeping my eyes firmly shut against the bright morning light streaming through the windows.

Another nightmare. They plagued me most nights but since running away they had decreased, if not in number but in intensity. I'd grown used to waking in a pool of sweat, my screams ringing in my ears. At least I didn't wake Delrik with my screaming last night.

Sometimes the nightmares were vivid hallucinations of my encounters with Renwick. Other times they were simply hazy dreams of pain and fear.

It was probably sheer exhaustion from walking miles each day that had me sleeping deeper. But this time, something was different—a soothing voice protected me. A calming presence. It pulled me from the darkness, drawing me to safety, and surrounded me in warmth.

The savory smell of breakfast encouraged me to open my eyes, blinking as my eyes adjusted. Mist curled in and out of the mountain peaks. Again, the thought of being inside a cloud came to mind. The doors off the balcony were open, but the cold didn't come in. Gray and white peaks jutting into the endless blue sky. The soft ringing of wind chimes tinkling in the breeze drifted through the open doors. Birds chirped off in the distance, and the hum of activity filtered up from the street below. Arcelia was growing on me with each passing minute.

I flung the blanket off and swung my legs to the floor. Stretching my arms over my head, I scanned the apartment. Delrik was nowhere to be seen, thankfully, and his bedroom door was shut. I didn't want to explain why I had fallen asleep out here on the couch or why my dagger was hidden beneath the cushion.

I stood and spotted breakfast spread on a small table. I hadn't heard anyone come or go, but then again, I had been sleeping. Adaris used to joke that a stampede of centaurs could tear through my bedchamber, and I still wouldn't wake. The memory of Adaris made me smile.

I made my way over to the spread and popped a piece of ripe melon into my mouth. I moaned as the sweet flavor spread across my tongue. Sausages sizzled in a serving dish, and a steaming bowl of oatmeal with cinnamon sprinkled on top sat on a serving platter. Without hesitation, I plopped down in the chair and began loading my plate. As I reached for a teapot. I paused, handheld in midair. I noticed the cuts that had covered my hands last night were gone. I lifted my hands before me, turning them back and forth before my eyes to examine. I stared down at my bare legs and they were smooth and healed—not even a red line where deep gashes had been.

That's odd.

Maybe the water from my bath had a healing potion in it. Even my aching muscles and joints had ceased their throbbing. That could be explained by the hot water. But the cuts I received while running from the osomal surely would have still been there.

I rushed into the bathroom and yanked my pajama shirt over my head, dropping it to the floor. I stood staring at my naked torso, turning slowly. My skin pebbled at the intrusion of cool air. All the bruises from Renwick were gone. Last night they were there—faded to light greens and browns marring my creamy skin but still visible. And now they had vanished. Even the dark circles under my eyes had disappeared.

I gulped, not sure if I should be fearful or thankful. I'd never healed myself before. I had relied on the healers skilled hands and tonics.

Not wanting to dwell on this new discovery, I quickly grabbed my shirt and stepped away from the mirror.

I returned to my breakfast, my stomach churning with hunger just enough to distract me. Maybe Delrik could shed some light on this when I found him later.

I picked up the glass of juice sitting in front of me now, praying to the Powers Above that it didn't taste as bad as those healing concoctions Mother used to make me drink every morning. I wrinkled my nose at the memory. They had tasted horrible, but she insisted. I had been a sickly child, prone to chills and fainting spells. The healers insisted that strengthening potions and herbal teas were required to keep me alive. They weren't very effective, in my opinion, for warding off illness. Some days I could barely move from my bed. And even on good days, climbing my tree took every scrap of strength I had.

Now that I was thinking about it, I hadn't felt faint or tired in several days. Not the way I used to, even with the miles of hiking. I lifted the glass to my lips, tipping the juice into my mouth. A little laugh slipped from my lips as I tasted the sweet liquid. It was the most divine thing I'd ever tasted. Adaris would love this place. I sighed, remembering that I'd left my brother behind. I'd left my mother behind.

I used to love having breakfast with Adaris and my mother, back before Father came home from the war. Back before she changed. We would sit in the small breakfast room and eat grapes, strawberries, ham, and potatoes and laugh and chat. Would I ever share a meal with Adaris again?

♀

Once my belly was full and I could not bear to eat anymore, I went to the bedroom. I was looking forward to trying on one of those gorgeous silk dresses. It fit as well as the pajamas, I would be set on clothes for my escape. Not that I was in a huge rush to leave Arcelia. Not yet. It had been so long since I'd worn a gown of any real beauty. Life back in the River Kingdom felt like a lifetime ago. While I loved exploring the grove at home and picking flowers in our gardens, I was only steps away from a hot bath and clean clothes. The life of traipsing through the woods like Delrik's was not my particular cup of tea.

It would be nice to feel like a lady again, even if only a short while and even while being held hostage.

This place was enchanted somehow because a smile came to my lips for the third time in one morning.

TWENTY-ONE
DELRIK

"So, who is she?" Aramis asked, popping a piece of cheese into his mouth.

Someone that has turned my world upside down.

I was surprised he waited this long before asking questions. I laughed to myself. We sat in a large open-air courtyard sharing a meal. A small dome of warm air surrounded us to prevent the light snow from falling on us.

I swallowed my bite of food, taking my time before answering. "Evren is the daughter of High Ruler Cadoc Byrnes."

"Cadoc Byrnes? I haven't heard that name in a long time," Aramis said. "I didn't realize he had a daughter. I know of his son."

"You do have yourselves buried up here in the mountains. And I didn't either."

Aramis laughed. "Yes, it's been nice not having to deal with the outside world and the politics that go with it."

Aramis Zathrian was the High Ruler of the Mountain Fae and had been for as long as I could remember. My father had told me he had ruled for over 500 years. But what drew me to him most was his compassion for all creatures in the realm—from the lowliest sprite to the most powerful Fae. He viewed and treated them all equally.

After the war, he secluded his people from the rest of Illoterra to keep them safe. Spells of the most ancient kind kept unwanted dangers from discovering the hidden city of Arcelia. He told me once, long ago, his own father had protected these mountains the same way from The Great Chaos. Aramis would do everything in his power to guard us once again.

"She's being hunted by the Black Guard like a criminal. She has a bounty for her return. Dead or alive."

Aramis studied me. I tried to keep my face neutral, but he could see right through me. He'd always been able to tell when I was hiding something from him. Heat filled my cheeks, so I turned my attention back to my plate.

"That does seem odd," Aramis said quietly after a while, his fingers steepled against his chin. "I have felt a shift in the magical balance over the last few years. So have some of the priestesses. I wonder if she is part of the activity?"

I huffed. The priestesses living in the Temples of Anruin that sat outside the city all seemed a bit batty to me. Their main purpose was to translate and teach from the Essence Scrolls, assist with ceremonies and offerings to the gods, and basically irritate the hell out of me. They were always going on and on about the balance of light and good. The Powers Above had banished The Great Chaos thousands of years ago. And besides the War Across the Sea, all seemed "balanced" in the realm to me.

I hadn't felt a shift, but then again, I wasn't in tune with the magical stability of the realm. I'd skipped those lessons during the brief schooling I'd had. Technically, I didn't even attend school, only eavesdropped. I never understood how all the creatures in the realm were tethered together, creating a precarious balance between light and dark. How one small event could cause a massive shift, the tipping of a scale.

I replied, "I don't see how she's related. I mean she is just a young High Fae female."

"Why don't you stay here for some time? Rest. And I'll see if the priestesses have any ideas."

Aramis was being cryptic, and I didn't like it.

I leaned forward onto my elbows and placed my head into my hands. "What aren't you telling me?"

"I don't know anything. I just have a feeling you were meant to find Evren," he said with a chuckle.

"You and your feelings." I waved my hand through the air. Aramis rolled his eyes at my theatrics.

I had missed him. Aramis was like a father to me. And by that, I meant he didn't let me get away with any shit and was always straightforward with me. I appreciated that about him. There weren't many in my life I could truly count on. I felt that I owed him. And I would spend my life repaying him for his kindness.

I felt Aramis straighten suddenly and I looked up. Evren was standing on the path leading to our patio. She'd changed into a long gown and wore a cloak with fur lining the edges. Her hands were tucked into deep pockets. The smooth skin of her cheeks was pink from the cold. Her hair was braided into a knot at the base of her neck. She looked rejuvenated after a night of rest. She halted the moment she saw us. Her full lips came together in a pout. She swallowed hard. I could see she was nervous. She took three small steps backward in an attempt to retreat, but Aramis stood before she could turn away. He waved a hand to a seat next to me, inviting her to sit.

"Evren. Good morning. Please, come join us." Aramis bowed gracefully to her. Always a picture of perfect manners. It took everything in me to not roll my eyes at him again.

"I...I couldn't. I mean...I already ate, but thank you High Ruler," she stuttered and offered her own little bow.

"Please." He pulled the chair out from the table. "And no need to be so formal. Please call me Aramis."

The wind whipped around her as if it were pushing her closer to us. The gust pulled a wisp of hair from its knot. It danced across her face before it caught on her lips. I followed it with my eyes, unable to draw my attention from her mouth. She bit into her plump bottom lip nervously. I imagined biting into that lip myself.

Aramis cleared his throat, and I shifted awkwardly in my chair.

Damn, he'd caught me staring.

I swore I could sense him holding back his laugh. I looked back down at my plate. She hesitated for a moment longer before coming to sit across from me. Not the chair next to me that Aramis had indicated. She sat as far on the edge of her chair as possible to keep space between us. But even that distance couldn't prevent me from feeling the heat radiating from her body. The snowflakes on her hair started to melt from the dome of our protective bubble.

"Did you find the breakfast I left for you?" I asked after she'd sat. I kept my eyes down, still, a touch embarrassed Aramis had caught me gawking.

"Um, yes. Thank you," she mumbled. She pushed her hands deeper into her pockets, narrowing her eyes at me. She seemed surprised that I was the one who left the food.

"I heard your stomach growling in your sleep. It kept me up all night. So, I had someone lay food out for you." I was in a playful mood. Being home had that effect on me.

She didn't find me charming. She was clearly immune to my wooing skills. In fact, she seemed agitated.

"If I had known that, I wouldn't have eaten." Rage shot through her eyes.

Slaves. She thought I meant a slave prepared it for her.

"We don't have slaves here," Aramis reassured her, patting her arm.

Of course, he knew what she had meant.

"All the servants here earn fair wages and are free to come and go as they please," Aramis said.

Slavery was common across Illoterra since the Fae came into this world. Lower creatures, such as nymphs, sprites, dwarves, and even some humans were forced to serve under the powerful High Fae. Even non-magical Fae were forced to work. But it wasn't until The War Across the Sea and Cadoc Byrnes that slave conditions worsened. Aramis detested the practice and had forbidden slavery within his kingdom.

She seemed to visibly relax. "Oh…good." Her cheeks flushed with heated embarrassment. A beat passed. "I apologize for snapping."

I had a hard time not smiling at the bright color of her skin. The softness of those lips. I wanted to reach out and touch her like I had last night. The bright blush would be beautiful under me, too.

Powers Above, what is she doing to me?

A beat of awkward silence passed.

"Byrnes, huh?" Aramis broke the silence.

Evren shot me a look like *why did you tell him.*

"So, you've met my father? How unlucky of you." She scoffed, that anger returning.

Aramis had indeed met Cadoc Byrnes. Aramis had led the Arcelia Legion during the War Across the Sea, me alongside him. Many of the kingdoms in our realm had fought against the uprising of the Raven Fae clans. The clans had grown tired of dominated trade routes and vital resources being shipped from their continent to Illoterra. So, they had taken to slaughtering village after village, sparing no one and leaving only ruin in their wake. It was the first time in history every creature of the Illoterra had come together. Fae, centaurs, and more stood strong. But since returning, Cadoc Byrnes had been stirring up trouble and taking advantage of the instability. No individual stepped up to rule over Illoterra. Each territory separated and went their separate ways. Cadoc had been slowly spreading his control outside the River Kingdom ever since. He would go to the ends of the earth to create a throne and seat himself on it.

Aramis simply nodded. "I'll leave you two to catch up." Then he rose from his seat, winking at me as he turned and walked away.

TWENTY-TWO
EVREN

Why would Aramis bother inviting me to sit if he was just going to leave with Delrik? And I saw that wink. Did he think he was being funny? I shifted in my seat, trying to create even a miniscule amount of space between Delrik and me.

"I see you found some fresh clothes too, eh Ev," Delrik said from behind me.

Although there was an underlying tease, his thoughtfulness caught me off guard. First the food and then the clothes. His whole demeanor had changed. More at ease, relaxed since we'd arrived in Arcelia yesterday. His cockiness was on a whole new level.

I lifted my chin and said, "Yes. Thankfully, they are about my size…Ev?"

I looked over at him and saw a playful smirk on his face. He was charming but arrogant. The dirt and days of travels that had smeared his face were gone, along with the thick beard that had overtaken his face. Only smooth bronze skin remained. His hair was freshly combed back as it had been that first day, showing his pointed ears. Half was tied back with a piece of leather, and the rest rested on his shoulders. My eyes wandered over this new male in front of me. He had completely transformed. He could easily pass as High Fae rather than the vicious bounty hunter or warrior, even with his slightly shorter ears. His tunic was emerald green and his knee-high boots were no longer smudged with mud. Wildness was replaced with civility.

Don't let him fool you, Evren.

In a flash, his hand shot out. The chair between us was gone, and he was grabbing the seat of my chair. It lurched forward, the wood scraping on the stone catching me off guard. A startled cry came from me as my body jerked from the chair. My hands darted out to catch myself, grabbing for anything to steady myself. Delrik happened to be the anything my hands made contact with. He was leaning in and was now mere inches from my face, his knees pressed against either side of my thighs and my hands spread on his thick legs.

"Well hello." His dark eyes held me captive for several breaths before his lips twitched.

I yanked my hands back like he'd burned me.

"Let's walk," he said. He reached out and offered his hand for me to stand. He squeezed my hand before releasing me. He took a step away and clasped his fingers lightly behind his back. "I saw you admiring the river when we arrived yesterday."

My hand grew cold after he dropped it, and I found myself wishing he'd grasp it again. I quickly stuffed my hands deep into my cloak pockets, shaking the thought from my mind.

"Yes. It reminds me of the river at home."

"The River of Naraina feeds all the rivers and streams south of the Qana Mountains."

I nodded, not knowing what to say.

"Naraina. It means touched by the gods. Legend says that the water is poured directly from the god's hands to nourish our city and the surrounding kingdom." He paused. "We will stay in Arcelia for a bit longer if that's alright."

His dictating my next move irritated me a bit, but I didn't mind staying in Arcelia if it meant I was safe. I didn't plan on following him when I left anyways.

We stepped outside the invisible dome and soft, weightless snow flurries landed on my face. They glittered in the sunlight. I reached out a hand to catch one. I watched as a fluffy flake landed on my palm, melting the instant it touched my skin. The River Kingdom rarely saw snow. Most of the snow I'd seen was sloppy and wet and dirty. But the snow here was as pure and white as lace.

"Evren."

Every muscle in my body jumped in response to his voice so close to me.

"Sorry," I muttered. "You want to stay here? How long?"

I followed Delrik down the path away from the tower housing the apartment and further out into the trees. I looked over my shoulder back to the courtyard. I wasn't sure if I wanted to be alone with him again in the woods. Every time we were together, something bad seemed to happen.

"I don't know. It's what Aramis recommended." He shrugged as he spoke, kicking a stone, smooth from the river, at his feet.

Really? We're just going to stay put just because the high and mighty Aramis said so. I stopped walking and put my hands on my hips. "And you trust him?"

"With my life." Delrik's face turned serious. And whether he knew it or not, his chest lifted a fraction higher.

I nodded in understanding. I didn't know Delrik or Aramis. I trusted that they wouldn't betray each other. I, on the other hand, wasn't so sure that they wouldn't somehow betray me. But I had to at least pretend to believe him. Or maybe I was beginning to trust him. The smallest amount. He seemed—almost good. Genuine.

I felt a draw to stay close at least, something deep inside telling me he would keep me safe from the Black Guard and my father, and I couldn't explain why. This didn't need to be a setback. A mere detour. I could use the safety and rest before setting off for my new life. A life that had no plan or direction. I groaned internally. I needed to at least work on making a mental plan.

"What are you thinking about?" he asked, a line forming between his brows.

"Nothing."

"You're lying...tell me."

I shook my head, the smallest of movements.

We stood and held each other's gaze for several moments. Intense and serious and heavy. The snow flurries fell around him, melting on his hair, his cheeks, clinging to his cloak.

"Okay. My future." That was all I would give him for now, but he seemed to accept it as an agreement to carry on.

We moved down the path in silence until we came upon a circle of children playing in a snowy field, wooden sticks clutched in their hands. Their joyous voices filled the air. A memory flashed before my eyes. Adaris and I lay in the grass laughing so hard our stomachs ached, gripping our make-believe swords. I fought the melancholy filling my gut, the twinge threatening to overwhelm me. He would love it here, and yet he wasn't with me. I didn't even know if he was still alive.

Delrik stepped into my view, his thumb touching me, brushing my cheek. I wasn't sure if he was brushing away a snowflake or a tear that had escaped. My heart pounded as my skin burned from the contact. I ached for more of his touch.

"Go explore. I'll show you the river another time. And no sulking. You're safe here, Evren. I promise." His face smoothed with gentleness.

I sucked in a sharp breath, trying to remain composed. I couldn't show weakness. He gave me a quick nod and then ran into the circle of younglings with a wild-sounding cry, making me jump. The children all clapped and cheered when they saw him, then scattered while laughing as he chased them around. My head tilted to the side as I watched them laugh. He caught one of them and tossed the boy into the air. And I couldn't help but smile.

TWENTY-THREE
ARAMIS

She resembled Cadoc. Not in an obvious way, but rather in the way she carried herself. The way she held her shoulders back, her chin high. But there was kindness in her.

Cadoc Byrnes dominated any room he was in and demanded respect and honor that wasn't due. He was a male that wanted to be seen, wanted to feel powerful. He liked to be worshiped. Cadoc commanded the most powerful legion in the realm. He was a tyrant. He believed in the unpolluted bloodlines of the High Fae and did anything he could to prevent the dilution of High Fae power. Even Cadoc thought he was higher than the Powers Above.

Cadoc filled his Black Guard and his kingdom with those families with long lines of powerful magic.

While he didn't force lower Fae out of his kingdom (he did need them, after all), he offered little support and protection for them. The majority lived in squalor.

Cadoc was smart too, conniving. It's one of the main reasons he's so dangerous. He didn't become High Ruler overnight or with a violent uprising, but rather a slow take over. His rule over Illoterra spread like a slow disease, territory after territory. Treaties were made, bondmating pulled together warring territories, and bribes became commonplace. Many didn't realize they'd given up their freedom until it was too late. Most of the south was under his watchful eye now, except the Arden Valley and the Wildlands. Thankfully he'd stayed away from the Sacred Forest and the mountains, but I knew once he'd secured all of the south, he'd move north.

Evren was the opposite of her father. I had only interacted with her briefly, but her essence was pure and golden. She radiated joy.

I watched as she walked from the west tower toward the city's center. Even though it was ice-cold outside and a wintry wind swept from the mountain peaks, Evren had perched herself on a stone wall near the bustling market. She held a sketchbook in her hands, tapping a pencil against a blank page. Her legs were tucked under her skirts, and her cloak hood hung down her back. She lifted her hand and twirled a piece of silver hair between her fingers as she gazed at all the creatures great and small milling about the square, going about their everyday routines.

The sun was high in the sky, warming the last few days of fall before winter came in full force.

Her hand froze and a broad smile spread across her face, reaching her eyes. She released a quiet laugh at a pair of younglings dancing around their mother as she handed them a cinnamon bun. There was so much light in her. Her aura practically glowed. How she came from Cadoc Byrnes, I had no idea. How she had survived so many years in his presence and not be completely ruined, only the Powers Above knew.

I moved closer to her, and her eyes met mine.

"Oh, Aramis, hello," she said with a sweet smile.

I'm not sure what I had been expecting, but it wasn't a warm, kind greeting. Her demeanor was so different without Delrik around. I knew he hadn't been cruel to her. Cruelty wasn't in his nature despite the rumors that floated around, but she had raised her guard around him for sure.

"Evren," I said as I bowed my head in her direction. "May I join you?"

The curl sprung free from her fingers and patted the wall next to her, scooting over in an almost childlike way to make room for me.

"Are you enjoying your time in Arcelia?" I asked.

"Yes, I am. It's such a beautiful city. Thank you for letting me stay."

"Of course. All are welcome in Arcelia."

We sat in mutual silence for several moments.

"So how did you find yourself in Delrik's company?" I asked, testing the waters. I wasn't sure how much she'd open up to me.

She looked sidelong at me and plastered a knowing glower on her face. "I'm sure he told you all about our…um… introduction."

"That he has." A pause. "He told me that you're in trouble. That's why he brought you here. He thought I could help you."

She turned back to the crowd. Her posture drooped an inch, and she released a long, slow breath. She was closing up. This was more what I had expected from her.

"I'm glad Delrik brought you here to Arcelia."

She raised her eyebrows and let out a joyless laugh. "Are you? The daughter of an enemy?"

I smiled at her. "Yes. Delrik wouldn't have brought you here if he didn't believe you needed protection."

She scoffed at me. "Sure. That's what his plan was." Her lips were in a thin line, her eyebrows pinned together. Rage wafted off her and the air around her seemed to pulsate. "He snatched me out of a tree!" Her voice rose with each word.

"He told me you were on the ground when he grabbed you." I bit my lip, holding back a smile.

Fire danced in her eyes, like molten violet, as she whipped her head toward me. She snapped her sketchbook closed and slammed her feet onto the stone path, before storming off.

"Evren." I jumped off the wall and rushed after her, reaching out for her arm but not actually touching her. Delrik mentioned she didn't like to be touched. "I'm sorry. For my comment and the fact that Delrik gets his sense of humor from me."

She didn't look at me but slowed her pace a touch. I kept my steps even with hers.

"My bondmate doesn't find my humor funny either," I said, trying to coax a smile from her. "She reminds me of it often."

She continued to walk, weaving in and out of the people. I wasn't sure where she was headed; I don't think she knew. After several minutes, her pace slowed back to normal as her anger evaporated. She huffed and stopped dead in her tracks, hands clutching her sketchpad against her chest.

"He thinks I need protection?" she asked wearily.

I simply nodded in response. There was no more anger in her voice. More along the line of confusion. Her knuckles turned white as the grip on her sketchbook tightened.

I took a deep breath and laid a reassuring hand on her arm, risking the contact. She didn't pull away.

"Did you know that your father put out a bounty for you? Delrik didn't know why your father wanted you dead or alive, but he couldn't simply return you to your father."

Her eyes narrowed. She had no reason to trust either Delrik or me.

"He put a bounty out on me?" She drummed her fingers on her sketchpad once. "I ran away from home," she said.

"Why?"

She didn't answer at first, just resumed walking, stopping every now and then to investigate shop windows or carts along the street. The chatter of the market filled the air, but her silence was heavy. I loved being around my people and being reminded of what I had the privilege to protect. I waited patiently for her to share her thoughts. Sometimes you just had to be silent.

"My life was…difficult at home."

"Ah. Well, Delrik may understand more than you think."

"He knows nothing of a difficult life," Evren said dismissively. She didn't have any anger in her voice. Only sorrow.

"He was orphaned at nine. His parents disappeared into the Sacred Forest and never returned. By the time he came to me, they had been gone for years."

"Came to you?" Evren asked.

"My daughter had been sneaking food from our kitchens for weeks, and I couldn't figure out why. We finally spotted a scrawny boy, maybe fourteen years old. He had been an orphan for several years. We don't actually know how long it was. He only spoke to my daughter, but he told her that his mother was High Fae and his father was half-human half-Fae. They were on the run from the High Ruler."

"My father."

I nodded before continuing. We began to move outside the city and down a quieter street. "They left him in a cave to gather food one morning and never returned. It took us months before we knew what had happened to his parents. He was so angry those first years. But once he came of age, he joined the Arcelia Legion, learned to control that anger, channel it, and found an outlet for it. He made a vow to spend the rest of his existence protecting our home and any being that needed help. That's why he insisted on fighting in the war. He was so young but insisted. He became a powerful asset too. And now he is one of the most respected commanders in the Legion."

"He fought in the war?"

"He did." I tapped my eyebrow. "That's how he earned that scar. One battle was particularly ... bloody. Delrik took a poisoned iron sword to the face and shoulder to save a friend. After the fighting had ended, he used his speed to get all the injured Fae off the battlefield and to the healers. It wasn't until after every single soldier was seen to that I got him to sit still long enough to be tended to himself. By then, the wound had begun to heal, but the poison was trapped inside and left a scar that even the healers couldn't remove."

As I spoke, she sank down on a nearby bench, staring at her feet. I took a seat next to her.

"His every step in life had been shaped and shadowed by the sorrow of losing his parents and the horrors of the war. He's all too familiar with the pain of loss and not being able to do anything to save those important to him."

"I didn't know."

I patted her arm gently. "He may seem tough on the outside, but he's a big softy. He hides it all with the mask of his charm."

TWENTY-FOUR
DELRIK

"**I** can show you how to use that." I tipped my chin to indicate the Darkstone in her hand.

I could see my offer caught her off guard. Evren was spinning the dagger clumsily in her hand. When she heard my voice, she missed the handle, and it fell to the ground. She sat on a rock outside the courtyard near the west tower. The carpet of green moss at her feet was dotted with melted snow here and there.

I had kept my distance from Evren over the last weeks, just observing her. I wasn't sure if it was for my sake or hers. Although she was still untalkative with me and avoided me when possible, I would often catch her staring at me with a softness on her face. I rolled my eyes. Aramis must have gotten to her. I'd seen them walking together every now and then. He never told me what they discussed, and I didn't ask. I was glad she had someone to confide in, though. I hated to think she would be lonely. She was relaxed around him and was usually smiling. Her smile was radiant and warm like the sun.

"It won't do you much good if you don't know how to use it," I said, probing again, taking a step closer. "Come on," I said, extending my hand to her. A peace offering. She looked at my hand and then into my eyes.

Damn. Those eyes could pierce my spirit.

"I won't bite," I said, waggling my eyebrows, then my fingers at her.

She hesitated a moment. "Promise?"

Was she making a joke?

"Fine," I said with a dramatic eye roll. "Let's get started."

She bent to pick up the dagger and handed it to me.

⚰

Thump.

The dagger sank deep into the poor tree we'd been using as a practice target. She strolled over with an air of confidence and yanked it from the trunk that was covered in gouges. I'd yet to see this side of Evren, the confidence, the joy. And it made my foolish heart trip over itself. A feeling coiled tight inside me, the sensation spiraling tight and latching itself to me.

We'd spent the last few hours bickering with each other playfully which was a change of pace compared to our usual cold encounters. By the time the bell tower rang, she could throw the dagger with impressive accuracy. She was a quick learner.

"Excellent," I said.

She stared down at the blade in her hand, almost caressing the deadly weapon with fondness. Tears filled her eyes, and her lips trembled before she pinched them tight and wiped the moisture away quickly.

I nudged my shoulder against hers. "Oh, come on. The tree will survive, I promise. You're not that good yet."

A laughing cry escaped from her. She tipped her head back, blinking rapidly. The smooth column of her throat caught my attention.

"I'm sorry," she said.

I studied her for a moment standing next to me. We hadn't been this close since that first morning I'd brushed the tear from her cheek.

"It clearly means a lot to you," I said, nodding to the blade.

"It belonged to my brother, Adaris. He gave it to me for protection."

I realized then that I didn't know how she ended up in Lakeshore, all alone and without protection. I stayed quiet, hoping she would keep talking. Her voice was so beautiful, I didn't care what she said, as long as she kept talking. She eyed me from the side.

"He gave me his dagger for protection two years ago. Adaris helped me escape from home after we learned my father decided I needed a bondmate to help extend his control in the surrounding territories. My brother always looked after me. I wouldn't be alive today without him." She took a shaky breath, averting her eyes. "He told me to wait for him in Lakeshore and we'd find some way to get away from our Father."

I'd never had someone like that in my life. I had Aramis and his bondmate and his daughter, whom I considered my sister, of course. I trusted them with my life, but I didn't reciprocate the feelings the way Evren did with her brother. I'm not sure if I knew how. I kept myself distant from others. It was easier. I couldn't be hurt if I didn't get too attached. I didn't deserve the happiness that Evren felt anyway. But maybe having someone in my life like Evren could be good. To let someone in.

"I'm sorry," I finally said.

"For what?"

"I didn't know who you were. I didn't mean to separate you from your brother."

She let out a sigh. "I know."

We were both quiet for a time. "Who taught you to use your bow?"

Clearly, she was changing the subject. I no longer had the curved Darkwood bow strapped to my back. I didn't need it here. Arcelia was the most secure city in the Illoterra.

"Aramis. I fought with the Arcelia Legion during the War." The Arcelia Legion served with loyalty and unrivaled bravery while Cadoc's force ruled with power and fear. "It is one of my highest accomplishments to be a commander in the Legion."

She nodded at me, looking sad. "So, you've met my father too." Her voice was barely audible. "I'm sorry." She took a shaky breath. "It seems that a lot of people's lives have been affected by him for the worse."

I knew she wasn't apologizing to me for simply knowing her father. I knew she was talking about my parents. For some reason, I wasn't angry that Aramis told her about them. The thought that she felt responsible for her father's actions broke something deep inside me.

TWENTY-FIVE
DELRIK

It had been several months since I had been home. I had come to realize why I missed being here so much. Here, I didn't have to pretend to be someone I wasn't. Here, I could relax. I didn't need to constantly be on guard. Here, I didn't have to face criminals and kill. Here, I could just be.

I was surrounded by the family that had taken me in when I thought I was alone in this world. With the revelation of opening myself up to these relationships even more, I was floating on air. Seeing how Evren's love for her brother, even in their separation, gave her strength, made me wonder if I could have that too. Just maybe.

I heard young ones playing off in the distance, and I smiled. They were always so fun to play with. By the time I had come to Arcelia, I had been hardened by fighting to survive in the mountains. Over the last hundred years, those layers had slowly broken down though. At first, the younglings were wary of me, but I proved my worth. I became a worthy opponent for their swordplay and games of kingdom-building. Sticks transformed into longswords. Pinecones became giant boulders they'd catapult over the fortress walls. Whether I was the scary giant coming to slay their sheep or a harrowing dragon that flew them to fight their enemies, they begged me to join in. And it was like reliving the childhood I was never given.

I found myself in my favorite spot along the river just a mile north of the city. I often found myself here when I needed to think or when I first returned from hunting. No one ventured up this way. The small clearing was tucked into the trees that had tapered away from the river's edge. I'd been here since before breakfast, slipping out before Evren woke. After spending the afternoon with her yesterday, I felt more confused than ever. Hours of being surrounded by silence is what I needed to get her out of my mind. She'd softened to me just the smallest amount. I couldn't deny the otherworldly attraction to her any longer. We kept gravitating to one another. Her presence was exhilarating but also terrifying.

The afternoon sun shone on my face as I sat near the river, tossing small pebbles into the racing water. My mind wandered between past memories and my current dilemma. Why did Aramis insist on speaking to the priestesses? He clearly knew something he wasn't telling me. And how did Evren fit into the picture?

A movement in the shadows next to me drew my attention. A lean, hooded figure appeared from the trees, like a thief in the night. Nazneen.

"I was wondering when you'd come to see me again," I said smoothly to the hooded shadow.

The wraith-like figure glided over the stony path toward me with grace and elegance, hidden in plain sight. A heavy black cloak was draped over strong shoulders and hung to the ground. Tight riding pants hugged lean, muscular legs, and the hilt of a sword could be seen poking out from under the heavy fabric. A piece of fabric covered her nose and mouth to keep out the bitter cold, revealing only sharp jade eyes from under the hood, lending a dangerous appearance.

A gloved hand released the fabric from her face, revealing a long neck and a bright smile. And her neck had the same tattoo as Aramis and me—the symbol for the Arcelia Legion. Her hood dropped to her shoulders. Dark auburn hair was swept back into a tight twist. Her elongated Fae ears were pierced with hoops that scattered up their length. My heart filled with warmth at her presence.

"I thought you were avoiding me," I said.

"I've been out riding patrol in the mountains…and I was avoiding you."

"It's been weeks." I turned back to the river.

"There has been a surge of activity close to the city. We've had to double patrols lately. Several people have gone missing, and a maimed body was found last week. It was unrecognizable."

"There was an osomal den right outside the Kiscarine Pass," I said, tossing a small rock into the water.

"I knew you killed that osomal on your way here. We believe there are more." Her hand casually rested the hilt of her sword that was strapped to her narrow waist. "I guess that accounts for the missing people."

She ran a hand across her forehead, brushing back tendrils of hair then strode soundlessly toward me. She didn't hesitate as she took a seat next to me and looped her arm into mine. I bumped my shoulder against hers. She leaned her head on my shoulder in return, her hair tickling my face. With our closeness, I could see the soft creasing of her eyes as she smiled at me. She always smiled with her whole face.

"I've missed you, brother," said Nazneen in a quiet voice.

I swept the hair away from her forehead and placed a kiss on the top of her head.

"Well, you pretty much bolted right after I returned." I topped my mocking tone with an eye roll. "So that's on you."

She pinched my arm, but I heard a giggle.

"I was a bit…irritated," she confessed.

The sun arched across the sky, just like the day I first saw Nazneen Zathrian. How had 100 years gone by so quickly? Sitting there with her made me remember the vivid memory like it was yesterday.

That day, the sun had been shining brightly too after several days of heavy rain. I was just a boy, fourteen, maybe fifteen years old. I had found a small cave that wasn't prone to flooding and had waited out the storms. Almost four days without anything to eat had me stealing food from the first house I came upon. Nazneen caught me stealing pears off a tree in her family's courtyard. She didn't rat me out. Each day after that, she would sit food out for me. It became a secret routine of ours.

Her parents eventually took me in after finding me sitting in their kitchen while Nazneen read to me one afternoon. I was worried they'd kick me out, but instead, they made me a part of their family. Nazneen had been like a sister to me growing up. She picked on me ruthlessly, just as any sister should, and I loved her for it. Well, as close to love as I'd allow myself. She was the first person I ever considered family.

Nazneen was also fiercely protective of me. Which accounts for how cold she was to Evren upon our arrival.

"Evren, huh? How'd you find her?" She raised her eyebrows.

"I didn't find her. I kind of just stumbled upon her." She glared at me. She knew I was lying. She could read me like a book. "I don't know, Naz, there is just something about her, something powerful and something alluring."

"Why is it that you always seem to find chaos in the realm? You practically gravitate to it." She poked me in the side, and I feigned pain, grimacing.

"I can't help that the Powers Above have deemed me worthy of chaos."

She tossed her head back and laughed. What a glorious, familiar sound. She looked at me with skepticism.

"Really. I thought she was just another fugitive on the run. But the longer I am in her presence the more I *need* to protect her." I raked my hands through my hair, rubbing the back of my neck.

She patted my arm with her hand. "Delrik, sometimes fate takes over when we don't follow our destiny."

"Have you been talking to your father?"

"I haven't even seen him yet. I wanted to find you first."

Mountain Fae were always going on and on about destiny and fate and balance. They were so connected to the universe. None of it made sense to me. If any of the nonsense were true, then why had my parents been murdered? Was that their destiny? If so, then fuck destiny. This is why I avoided digging too deep. It only brought pain.

I was unworthy of finding that kind of happiness, and she knew that. We had discussed it many times. Especially after all I'd done during the war. There was no way the fates or the Powers

Above would see me worthy of anything but a life of service to the realm.

We chatted and caught up with each other's lives, falling back into our comfortable sibling roles. She nagged me about being gone too long, and I goaded her by saying she needed a break from being in my shadow. Evren appeared across the river, walking along a path. She didn't notice us; I didn't even think Nazneen saw her.

She had donned a long cloak that fluttered with her feet as she moved along the snowy ground. Her pale cheeks were flushed. The deep, layered greens of the evergreens surrounding her made the violet of her eyes stand out even more than usual. Silver unbound waves of hair rustled in the light wind. She was a thing of beauty against the winter-white landscape around her. She stopped on the path and tipped her face up to the sun, closing her eyes. I couldn't tear my eyes from her face, and my stupid heart skipped a beat. The corners of Evren's mouth turned upward in a slight smile. Those beautiful full lips. A wisp of hair floated across her face, and my eyes followed it. She took a deep, relaxed breath.

When she realized I was no longer paying attention to her, Nazneen followed my eye line. She motioned between the two of us.

"Even I can sense the connection between you two." Her voice snapped me back to reality. "The fates are dragging the two of you together, no matter how much you resist."

"What are you talking about? There is no connection." I shook my head a little, pretending to act nonchalant.

"Sure, Delrik. You can't predict who the fates select for you. Just give in already."

"I'm not going to give in to anything."

"There is a strong force drawing you two together. It's practically tangible. I saw the way you moved around each other, the way you watched her that first day." She wiggled her eyebrows at me. "Cough cough, bondmate."

"You know I won't ever have a bondmate. I mean, look at me. Who wants an orphaned brute with an unending kill list as a bondmate? I'm the last thing she needs in her life."

Naz pinched me again. "Don't talk about my brother that way."

"Also, she hates me," I said, trying to keep the sadness from my voice.

My gaze swept back to Evren. I'd seen how bondmates were with each other. The otherworldly connection. The kind of bond that could bring you to your knees with breathless love and adoration. I saw it in my parents, and I saw it with Aramis and his bondmate, Calia. But that wasn't in my future and never would be.

"I can't give her that Naz. I don't have a single thing to offer."

"Have a little faith, brother."

"I envy you and your confidence in following your destiny," I said to Nazneen.

At the sounds of our voices, Evren looked toward us. We'd been caught spying. I hadn't been spying, of course. She was the one that stumbled upon us, after all. She pressed her lips into a thin line, erasing any trace of that smile. She looked so serious anytime I was around, so withdrawn. Except for yesterday. She'd let her guard down for just a few hours. I wished there was a way I could get her to smile like she did then. Her smile was like a ray of light.

Then Evren did something completely unexpected. She began to make her way across the little footbridge to Nazneen and me. Normally she would turn and go the other way but not today. Maybe yesterday was a turning point, after all. The intensity of her stare pierced me, and I felt it everywhere.

Nazneen held in a laugh as she watched me watch Evren, her eyes bouncing to Evren then back to me. I was tempted to shove her off the rock into the river. But I knew she'd retaliate. Females never fought fair, especially my sister.

Nazneen turned her gaze to Evren, her back going a touch rigid, eyeing Evren up and down. Was that jealousy I saw on her face? Nah. She wouldn't be jealous. She was too confident in herself to be jealous. But Naz was not happy with how Evren was glaring at me. Once a protective sister, always a protective sister.

"As I said, you can't resist," she whispered to me. I rolled my eyes. This thing between Evren and me was not a good idea and was not going to happen, no matter what Nazneen or the Powers Above thought.

Well, it could be good. It could be *very* good.

Maybe I should jump in that river to regain my senses.

The cold water could do me some good too.

Nazneen pushed off the rock and stood to speak to Evren.

"We were never properly introduced." She threw a withering gaze at me. "I'm Nazneen." She bowed her head slightly before reaching for Evren's hand.

Evren hesitated a moment. I knew she didn't like to be touched. Or at least, she didn't like it when I touched her. But after a beat, she slipped her hand from her cloak, removed her glove, and grasped Nazneen's hand.

"Evren."

Nazneen was taller than Evren by several inches, but Evren stood straight and held eye contact with her. She sure wasn't timid toward other females, not even one who was clearly a Legion soldier.

"I see you have my brother under some kind of spell," Naz said, her face serious.

Evren didn't even skip a beat. "Us sorceresses love our spells."

Naz burst out a belly laugh. Evren actually made Naz laugh.

"Oh, I like her, Delrik." She spoke over her shoulder to me, still gripping Evren's hand.

"Brother?" Evren questioned.

She leaned to the side past Naz to stare at me, her violet eyes meeting mine. Now they were both glaring. I looked back and forth between the pair.

Shit, I'm in trouble.

"Don't listen to anything Naz says. Everything is a lie." I stood abruptly and slung my arm over Nazneen's shoulder. "In fact, she was just leaving."

"But I...OUCH!" Naz yelped.

I pinched the back of her arm right before she could finish her thought.

"Fine," she grumbled. "I need to go see Father and Mother anyways."

Nazneen reached up on her toes and planted a kiss on my cheek before landing a sisterly punch right in my gut. I doubled over with a faux groan. Evren snorted as she attempted to hold back a laugh that bubbled up. I swung back at Nazneen, but she ducked out of the way, scooping up a handful of snow and tossing it right at my face. I ducked in time and it grazed the top of my head before slamming into a tree behind me.

She smiled before saying, "I'll see you at dinner, brother."

Then she disappeared into the trees, as quietly as she'd appeared.

Evren watched us with a sad, pensive smile on her face. The smile slipped away to a pout, the corners of her mouth turning down. I knew she missed her brother. I couldn't imagine the pain she was enduring, not knowing if he was alive or not. I wouldn't put it past Cadoc to…no, I wouldn't even think it. I realized then that I would do anything to carry that burden for her.

TWENTY-SIX
EVREN

We stood in mutual silence along the snowy bank of the river watching the water rushing, cutting, and slicing its way through the rock. Snow covered any surface it could, leaving the landscape a crisp white that sparkled in the sunlight. The moment Nazneen left, the awkwardness set in. I shifted from foot to foot, unsure if I should stay or leave. I started walking past the river's edge and toward the west tower, but kept my pace relaxed. A few seconds passed before Delrik followed, easily catching up and striding beside me. His fingers brushed lightly against the back of my hand as we turned a corner. I realized I hadn't put my glove back on when I felt his fingertips on my skin. It sent ripples of heat up my arm, then down my spine, and fluttered deep in my belly. He must have sensed my reaction because a devilish grin came to his face.

"Isn't your hand cold?" he asked.

I quickly plunged my hands deep into my cloak. I felt pathetic, falling for that stupid smile he had planted on his stupid face. Why did my body react this way to him? I couldn't ignore his presence. Since the first time he touched me in Lakeshore, my body had been able to sense him. Whenever he entered a room, my body immediately and involuntarily gravitated towards him, like a force was pulling me to him. Even today, I was mindlessly wandering, and still, my feet led me directly to him.

Our eyes met for the briefest of moments before I turned back to the path, my heart quickening. I increased my walking pace to put a small amount of space between us. He must have noticed because he stopped walking. I'd made it a few steps in front of him before he said my name.

"Evren." His voice was barely above a whisper.

I paused, hesitating for a breath, a split second.

My hesitation hung in the air like a thick fog. Then he was there. Delrik appeared before me, rotating me with him so we were off the path, hidden from view behind a stone archway. The whole movement happened in less than a breath, or it would have if I'd had any breath left in my lungs. He moved so fast at times he almost disappeared and reappeared wherever he wanted. It took me a moment to orient myself, arms reaching out to steady myself. I backed away a step, my back colliding against a stone wall. He placed each hand on the stone on either side of my head, caging me in with his arms. I did my best to avoid his eyes. Those eyes. This close, they were midnight blue rather than black with chips of sparkling onyx around the middle. I felt so small with his towering form above me. His hard chest brushed against me, and warmth spread down my tummy toward my thighs.

"What are you doing to me? I can't seem to stay away from you." His voice was husky, and his dark eyes, like twin sapphires, had grown hungry. Shadows swirled in their depths. They were on me, searching, pleading almost.

This was too much. I couldn't think straight with him this close to me. When he was inches from me, I only wanted the distance to disappear. And then it did. He moved a fraction closer until his chest was pressed against me completely. This lack of control was overwhelming, threatening to suffocate me. Fear pulsed through me, along with something else. A vision of Renwick's face flashed in my mind. He was the last male that was this close to me, and I fought the panic rising in me.

But then an unknown feeling quickly trumped that panic. I lifted my chin more so I could look at him better, practically nose to nose. For two breathless seconds, I studied his face. The arch of his brows, the sharpness of his jawline, a dimple in his cheek. The scar across his face did nothing to take away from his beauty. Powers, he was fucking beautiful. He was looking down at me through lowered, thick eyelashes. His tongue darted out to wet his lips. A simple movement made electricity flicker through every nerve in my body.

The bodice of my dress was too tight as my heart pounded against my rib cage, my breaths rapid and shallow. I forced myself to take a deep breath, placed a shaking hand on his chest. The hard planes of his chest were smooth and warm under my palm, even through the layers of clothes. With gentle but firm pressure, I pushed him away.

"I can't." I mouthed the words. I was too stunned to speak.

He was much stronger than me. Overpowering me would have been easy, but he gave in to my request and took a reluctant step back, putting space between our bodies. My body was cold where he had been against mine. I unpeeled myself from the wall, stepping sideways away from the stone, giving myself an escape, afraid of the amount of emotion behind his eyes. Not afraid of him, but afraid of how the emotion, the nearness of his body, made me want to alter my entire plan of safety to be in his arms again. My body felt empty without his weight against me and disappointment spread through me. I didn't know if I could handle the physical touch he wanted to give me but I craved it all the same. Momentary madness. That's the only thing that could explain my increased heart rate.

We stood there, staring at each other, both breathing heavily. My hands clutched the edges my cloak tight, holding on for dear life. His eyes searched my face, questioning me. The longer the quiet lasted, the more tension grew. Not a bad sort of tension, but rather a good tension. I've never had a male accept my denial of their advances. But he stopped when I asked him to. I didn't even have to ask him. I didn't know what was more startling to me, the way he respected my wordless request or how the desire to have him was filling me. The more I told Renwick no, the rougher he became. There was something different about Delrik. I might just give in, but I didn't want another person to have so much control over me. Not again. I would never surrender that freedom. I just found my freedom, well, sort of. I didn't know exactly what Delrik wanted from me, but I didn't want to surrender myself to him just like that. Or did I?

My head tilted in curiosity. Without a word, I turned and walked away.

TWENTY-SEVEN
EVREN

After a long day of exploring the city in the snow I wanted nothing more than to snuggle up by the fire with a glass of wine and drown out the never-ending thoughts in my head. Over the last four weeks of being in Arcelia, my desire to escape had transformed into contentment. Arcelia felt like home.

I'd found a pair of thick leggings and wool socks in the wardrobe and I couldn't resist the softness of them; so I slipped my feet into a pair before tucking my legs underneath me on the couch, settling into the cushions to watch the sunset outside the wall of glass. The light seemed to linger even after the sun slipped away, smearing the sky in multihued color.

"This place seems to be growing on you." Delrik's voice came from the entryway.

I rolled my eyes. Another thing I'd grown used to. I'd learn to accept the fact that Delrik now showed up out of thin air without any warning. He still popped up at least once a day to pester me about something or other. Even though he'd kept his distance since I denied his advances, that didn't mean much. He didn't have to be close to me to make my heart rate increase. He didn't even need to be in the same room. I found my mind drifting to him at the worst times. Like when I was drinking my morning tea or soaking in that monstrosity of a tub.

I pulled my oversized cardigan down over my hands, tucking my fingers as deep into the wool as possible without setting down my wine glass, trying my best to keep my eyes on the flames to hide my excitement at his presence. I hadn't seen him at all today.

"I'm not sure what you mean," I replied.

He smiled as he strolled over and sat on the couch opposite me. He let out a long breath as he propped his booted feet onto the coffee table between us. Even with the furniture being oversized, he seemed too big for the couch. I bit my lip to cover my smirk at the thought. I didn't respond, rather, I turned toward him, recrossing my legs, bringing the wine glass to my lips and taking a sip of wine, my eyes not leaving his. I ran my tongue across my bottom lip as I rested my wine glass in my lap. We sat in the quiet for several long minutes, just looking at each other. A piece of wood cracked in the fireplace sent embers dancing into the chimney.

"Do you believe in fate?" My sudden change of conversation made him pause.

"I'm not sure." His face turned thoughtful. "I guess if I did, I wouldn't be very happy with the Powers Above."

I turned my gaze back to the fire, watching each flame leap and dance, free from constraint, free from discipline. I longed to reach out and caress the flames. Maybe this was my fate. To forever be under the hand of another while longing for freedom. I hated to think that I was fated to have a life of being controlled. Aramis and Delrik were so kind to me but I'm sure if I tried to leave, they would stop me. At least with Delrik, I wasn't in pain anymore. Physical pain, that is. Though the pain of this emotional longing would be difficult to fight for the rest of my life. I had no doubt if I gave into that longing, only unhappiness awaited me on the other side.

"Are you going to dinner? Aramis has always been a fan of grand dinners. He'll use any excuse to have a celebration."

"And what are we celebrating tonight?"

"The Harvest, obviously."

"And what did you harvest that we need to celebrate?"

"Nothing specifically within the city, but the Mountain Fae always celebrate the Harvest since it's the turning point of the seasons."

I sighed. The last thing I wanted was to be gawked at. It hit too close to home, reminding me of the fortress. The company of the flames of my fire was more appealing, but I couldn't repay Aramis's kindness by ignoring the invitation. I'd never met someone who was so generous to a complete stranger, especially when that stranger's father was a murderous ass.

"Why don't you want to go?"

"It just reminds me of my past. Not happy memories."

Delrik was quiet for a while. "You don't have to go, Evren."

I shook my head. "I'll be ready soon. I'll meet you there." I sighed.

"Perfect."

"What? You aren't going to escort me to make sure I won't run away into the night," I said with a look of fake shock on my face. I nudged his leg with my socked toes.

Delrik dropped his feet to the floor, leaning his elbows on his knees. I swallowed as I felt him shift closer to me. I had no reason to sense that shift in his body, but I did. The slightest movement and the atmosphere changed.

"Did you just touch me with your foot?" He raised his eyebrows.

I pulled my foot back to the safety of my cushions and bit down on my bottom lip.

"Did you just poke me with your fuzzy little foot?"

"Um…Maybe…?" I replied, bringing up my wine glass again.

"Game on, Ev."

I choked on my sip of wine. "Excuse me?"

I hadn't realized that my playful jab would be an open invitation to his games, bringing down the invisible barrier I'd created. My moment of weakness opened the door for him. That last barrier I had so thoroughly created around me plummeted to the ground in a split second. And I didn't mind at all. I bit into my lip again, trying not to show my delight.

He reached over across the table and plucked my bottom lip out of my teeth, holding onto it with his thumb and finger.

"I'd like nothing more than to lick this lip."

My mouth dropped open in shock. He winked, released my lip, stood, and walked out of the room without looking back.

TWENTY-EIGHT
EVREN

The grand entrance hall of the eastern tower glittered from floor to ceiling. It was dazzling. There was no other way to describe it. A grand piano sat in the corner. Soft music floated through the air. An enormous crystal chandelier hung from the ceiling with fluttering orbs of light. I nearly moaned at the rich smells from the dinner that wafted through the air. Too bad I was so nervous I probably wouldn't be able to eat anything. The rotunda above my head was a beautiful dome with intricate paintings on every visible surface. A polished banister swept up the grand staircase to the floor above where art hung on the walls. Beneath the mezzanine were grand doors leading to a reception hall.

    I tugged at my dress, trying to cover my bare skin. I wasn't used to the deep necklines and plunging backs of the gowns I'd found in my wardrobe. My dresses at home covered as much of my body as possible, covering the bruises from Renwick. This gown was nothing like my old ones. I couldn't even wear a corset underneath. Its soft velvet caressed each curve and arch of my body. The black neckline dipped low, but not as low as the back where a deep V scooped low down, revealing the small dimples at the base of my spine. The shoulders were fastened with jewels and lace flowed down my arms. The fabric was so light it almost felt like I was wearing nothing at all.

My whole body flushed scarlet as pairs of wide eyes from the small group of gathered Fae turned to me. I felt vulnerable under their intent stares. I clearly didn't belong here. An unpleasant sinking feeling entered my gut. The attention gave me flashbacks of being scrutinized at the dinners in Rivamir. There, my presence was simply ornamental, and those memories were bubbling to the surface again. Stern looks from Mother. Uncomfortable conversation. Clammy wandering hands. I was paraded around like a prize horse and gawked at by males. I was simply something to claim, something to possess. My pulse quickened. I thought I was comfortable in Arcelia, but being in a crowd took all my confidence away. Why had this been the only formal gown in the wardrobe?

I was about to turn to leave when Delrik appeared at my side, towering over me. His hand splayed across the small of my back. The tips of his fingers dipped just under the edge of the fabric. His woody citrus scent swept over me, surrounding my senses like a safety blanket. If you had asked me last week, I would've said I wanted nothing but to have space between us. But right now, I welcomed the warmth of his strong, calloused hand on my bare skin. It didn't give me my confidence back but at least I wouldn't faint. Or if I did, he'd probably catch me. Well...maybe. I leaned into his hand.

"Breathe." His nose brushed the curved shell of my ear as he leaned into me to whisper.

He was so close, the warmth of his breath against the back of my neck, which made breathing almost impossible. Before my brain could process his words, my body obeyed.

Delrik had changed his outfit as well, looking more dignified than ever before. His tunic and evening coat the colors of the Arcelia Legion showed off his muscled chest and arms, a longsword strapped in ceremony at his waist. Even his boots shone to perfection, reflecting in the light of the candles. He looked the part of a true High Fae and a valued Commander in the Arcelia Legion.

"You ready?"

I struggled to swallow and nodded. "Um...sure...I think," I stammered, a bit dizzy but I didn't budge from the spot.

Delrik applied gentle pressure to my lower back, urging me forward. Shivers from the skin-to-skin contact rushed up my spine, and I struggled to breathe for a completely different reason.

"I won't let you trip. I promise," he said.

"How did you read my mind?"

Delrik's chuckle was sultry as he led me into the reception hall to a spot at an elegant long table dominating the room. I saw Nazneen sitting next to Aramis at the opposite end, and she gave me a broad smile. I tried to smile in return, but the amount of anxiety I was feeling made for a poor attempt. I swallowed, trying to focus on not tripping. One heeled foot in front of the other. My blood pounded in my ears, making everything a muffled commotion. I was reliving my worst nightmare as all eyes turned to me.

Aramis's commanding voice drew attention to the head of the table. Everyone returned to their conversations, leaving me to release my held breath.

Delrik pulled a chair away from the table, and I sat, my shaking legs thanking me as they collapsed under me. Delrik took the seat next to me and draped his arm over the back of my chair in a possessive way. He thumb rubbed a smooth circle over my shoulder once before he drummed his fingers on the wood. His closeness was pure intensity. He reached over my plate to grab a piece of fruit off a nearby tray, his body brushing against mine, and I followed the movement back to his mouth. I quickly looked down at my plate and tried to control my nervous breathing, but his nearness made my body hum.

Throughout dinner, his eyes followed my every movement. His eyes lingered on me often. My cheeks burned at his close inspection. I didn't speak during dinner. I was too nervous. Too nervous to eat much too, preferring to stick with my glass of wine. I pushed my food around in circles until a server dressed in Arcelia colors removed my plate from the table.

I could do this. The meal was almost over. Delrik and Aramis took turns distracting everyone so I didn't have to be a part of the conversation, drawing attention away from me. I needed to remember to thank them for their kindness after this horrible ordeal was over.

Suddenly, the piercing sound of glass shattering on stone echoed throughout the cavernous reception hall. A flash of flame and pain crossed my mind. My body jerked away from Delrik, shrinking into myself.

Silence.
One second.
Two.
Three.
Laughter.
Laughter?

"I'm sorry Finley. An accident of course." It was Aramis's voice. Calm and collected.

I peeked through my squeezed-shut eyes to see Aramis drying the table with a cloth from a spilled goblet. It appeared to have rolled off the table and crashed to the floor.

Then Delrik's touch was there, gentle and reassuring. He carefully pried my quivering hands from the dark wood table and replaced them in my lap. He didn't release my hands, his one enormous hand covering mine. He moved his thumb in a small circle on the inside of my wrist until my breathing returned to normal.

Shame filled me, replacing the unadulterated terror. A blush crept down my neck and across my chest.

"I'm sorry," I whispered, barely audible to anyone but myself.

TWENTY-NINE
DELRIK

I could've sworn there were fingerprints left in the wood of the table—*burned* into the smooth surface. The charred spots were smoking a bit. I could taste the fear in the air around her. I knew her life before winding up in Arcelia wasn't the most comfortable, but I'd never seen anyone react to broken glass in such a way before.

    I shook the thought from my head as I pulled my tunic over my head in preparation for bed. Evren had been absolutely stunning tonight. It was wonderful being able to be so close to her, being able to touch her. And the best part was she didn't shy away from me this time. Her skin was so soft and creamy, begging to be touched. I couldn't help my eyes drifting down the long curve of her spine. Powers Above, her gown hugged all those luscious curves. I shouldn't have been having such thoughts. She seemed comforted by my presence, even if it was only because of the party.

I climbed into my bed, and my head sunk into the soft pillow.

☥

I couldn't stay asleep. I tried to, but my mind was racing. Thoughts of Evren kept coming into my dreams, and I woke, restless, trying to escape from her presence inside my head. I'd fall asleep just long enough to dream. Then I'd be shaken awake. I let out a frustrated sigh and raked my hands through my hair. I didn't want to be attracted to her. It was a distraction. But I couldn't deny it any longer. First thing tomorrow, I'd find her and give myself fully to this consuming desire.

I'd followed her from the party back here to my apartment to make sure she was okay, but she'd closed herself in her bedroom. I had pressed my ear against the cool door but heard nothing.

The air around me was thick and suffocating even though there was no fire lit in my room. It was stifling. I kicked off the blankets. A thin layer of sweat had formed on my bare skin. I strode from my room into the main seating area in hopes the cold mountain air would calm my burning skin. I noticed a pair of heeled shoes discarded on the floor beside the couch. Evren kicked them off as soon as we returned to the apartment.

I wanted to check on her but when I went to her door, it was already open. I turned and saw Evren standing on the balcony. I almost turned to go back to my room, but I was captivated by the view.

Evren stared off into the darkness, her back to me. The sky was painted like a dream around her. The midnight black sky was dark as pitch except for the stars that danced in the sky. Like dancing balls of fire, they shimmered above the peaks. She just stood there, being beautiful. Nothing could ever compare to the night sky now that I'd seen her against it. And she didn't even know the effect she had on me.

The last several weeks I had done everything in my power to maintain distance between us as she'd requested, but I couldn't help reaching out my hand to her. Since she was the one that broke down those barriers with that adorable foot of hers. I just wanted to be beside her.

Her hands were flat on the stone railing, head bent, shoulders slumped forward. If I didn't know any better, I'd think she was sleeping. She was so still. Almost in a trance. Her breaths were slow and shallow. I moved a step closer to get a better view. She still wore that ebony gown. I was glad she had decided to wear it tonight for dinner. I wasn't sure what Naz had put in her wardrobe, but I needed to thank her. I much preferred females in dresses. I preferred how *this* specific gown showed off Evren's grace and softness. Though come to think of it, those pants were nice on her shapely hips while she was sitting in that tree.

A maid had pinned up Evren's hair on top of her head for the party tonight, showing off her long, delicate neck and the pale skin of her beautifully bare back. So many twists and braids knotted to perfection. I dragged my eyes from the knotted silver of her hair and down her back. A trail of diamonds winking in the moonlight on a delicate chain flowed down her spine from the necklace she wore. The dress dipped low, and I couldn't help but stare at the slight arch of her back. She was stunning. She had been so quiet at dinner, hadn't spoken a word to anyone, and had slipped away as soon as the meal was over. But I didn't blame her. Dinner parties weren't really my thing either. I only attended when Aramis insisted. He said it was good for the citizens of the city to see my face, to remember who I was, one of the top commanders in the legion. I much preferred the shadows. That's one of the reasons why I stayed away from Arcelia for chunks of time.

I watched her in fascination as she picked each pin from her hair, loosening the mountain of silver curls and slowly shaking out her long hair. The thick waves tumbled falling to her waist. She twirled the strands around her fingers, her head tipping to the side, twisting it into a tight rope before pulling it over her shoulder, and exposing her skin again.

Powers Above, her back was delicious.

I wondered if her soft skin would blush that wonderful color under my fingers. She'd let me touch her this evening. Would she let me explore her body the way I craved? Would she shiver under my fingers? I imagined trailing my fingertips in light circles down her spine, lower and lower. I'd give anything to worship her body with my mouth. My heart pounded wildly inside my chest as I imagined my lips moving down her throat to her chest, sweeping my tongue down her stomach to her navel and then lower. A fire lit inside me.

Get it together!

Evren's body heaved as she took a deep breath, drawing me away from my lustful thoughts. She drummed her fingers against the stone, then lifted her chin to the sky, eyes closed. The moonlight made her pale face glow. Her dark red painted lips were full and begging to be kissed as they parted slightly with an exhale. The stars were bright tonight. So bright. They seemed to send sparks along her fingers, down her spine, along the hem of her dress, making every inch of her skin glow.

I blinked. The sparks had turned to shining, flames tipped with violet. They grew, slowly at first, sweeping down her spine. Where her fingertips lingered, and flames moved across the balcony. Fingerlike tendrils of flame spun around her, threatening to engulf her completely. The hem of her dress smoldered, and flames licked at her bare feet. She turned to me, spinning in a half circle—unseeing. Her arms extended down and her palms facing out. Her palms held balls of orange and lavender fire. Her veins illuminated with fire through her translucent skin, and her eyes glowed like violet embers. I stood frozen, not knowing if what I saw was real or if one of my nightmares was coming to life.

THIRTY
EVREN

Standing there in the quiet, I took in all that was around me. Tonight's dinner had been so overwhelming. I was still coming down from the anxiety. I hated that Delrik had seen my weakness, my pathetic loss of self-control. I was usually better at hiding my anxiety, but I'd let my guard down. I'd grown too comfortable here.

There was so much beauty here in Arcelia, and I longed for its beauty to fill me. I wanted this peace to be my future, to be my entire life. Maybe Aramis would allow me to stay permanently. The stars' light reflected off the river below me, twinkling. I tipped my face up to the moons, closing my eyes, taking in the tranquility, letting it fill me completely. I'd never felt a calmness like this before. A calmness that was so true, so pure. I could relax completely and release all the pent-up fear from the last eighteen years of my life. The fear of disappointing my father and dealing with the aftermath. The fear of my mother's rejection. The fear of the abuse. The fear of Renwick controlling my future. This peace was what I'd been searching for, and it was finally within grasp. I would never again give in to the darkness. I'd never surrender to its suffocating pain and control.

Warmth started to grow from within, and I reveled in it. The feeling of safety and control, of resilience and power. I heard something whispering, a voice calling to me. It was powerful. It was fierce. I wanted that power to consume me, to smother the fragile creature I had been. I was so tired of being weak. My palms turned upward, begging that warmth to spread through my body.

※

Something firm slammed into me. It jolted me roughly, shook me. It pulled me away from that warmth, that security, that calming.

No.

A distant voice called my name. This other voice, interrupting my peace, was full of fear and dread. I recognized it though. I knew that voice. Delrik. I tried my hardest to ignore him, to find that warmth again. How could he feel such dread when I felt so much power?

My eyes flickered open, and Delrik was there—yelling my name. He yanked me away from the balcony, breaking into my meditation. I looked down, and I was engulfed in flames. Flames came from my hands, my feet; my whole body seemed to be glowing.

Then, in an instant, they were gone. Smothered out. The night grew dark and cold without the flames to heat it.

No.

I clenched my hands to the necklace resting on my chest. I needed that warmth. Why had it gone? I turned, frantically searching for flames, wanting them to consume me again.

The only evidence of the flames that moments ago engulfed me were the singe marks on my gown and the two scorched handprints left on the balcony where I had been leaning.

Delrik's eyes locked on mine. I could still see the sleepiness that clung to his face, but he was frightened. His face was etched with panic. His bare tattooed chest heaved. He had a tight grip on my shoulders. His fingertips were painful almost. He shifted me to his chest. My hands and cheek were smashed into him. A fine dusting of dark hair traveled across his chest and down his stomach past his navel. I suddenly stiffened at the embrace if that was what you could even call this. Tiny flecks of burning embers danced around us on the night breeze.

Delrik held me tightly, pinning me against his body, like if he let go of me I would burst into flames again and drift away like the embers on the wind.

THIRTY-ONE
EVREN

"I've always had dreams of fire, ever since I was a little girl. Why does it matter?" I couldn't understand why Delrik was making such a big deal out of this.

"Except this time, you weren't dreaming. And I'm assuming you've never lit yourself on fire before, have you?" Delrik said in a sarcastic voice.

I watched as he paced back and forth, hands raking through his sleep tousled hair. He did that when he was frustrated. The hair thing. I smiled, recognizing his unconscious movement to be something familiar now.

"How can you be smiling right now!" He bellowed at me before letting out a groan and returning to his pacing.

"Delrik." Aramis's voice was calm.

"And how can *you* be so calm!" Delrik boomed back, his eyes wide and wild.

Those startled eyes jumped back and forth between Aramis and me.

Delrik, as soon as he'd gained his composure, had dragged me from our apartment. His apartment...not ours.

"We need to wake Aramis now," he had muttered to himself.

I'd barely had time to grab a cloak draped across a chair as we swept out into the night. I didn't realize it was Delrik's cloak until we'd arrived outside Aramis's residence. We were a site to see—he was shirtless, and I was clad in a smoldering evening gown, both of us heaving trying to catch our breaths.

I wasn't afraid of the fire. In fact, the flames had burned all my fears from me, leaving behind in their wake an air of confidence. I felt empowered and secure. I didn't have the answers. And I didn't really care.

Aramis and Delrik looked back and forth at each other before looking at me again. I hated being the center of attention like this. We all knew the answer to Delrik's question.

No, I had never lit anything on fire before. Especially myself.

A minute passed. Then another.

"Did you have training in your Fae powers when you were growing up?" Aramis asked.

"Of course, she did." Delrik answered for me.

I pursed my lips at him, turning in his direction.

"Really? And how would you know?" I asked.

He snapped his mouth shut.

Of course, I had. My father insisted that it was part of my regular education. I had never quite grasped my powers though beyond the basics. I could make objects float, and I could light tiny balls of Fae light in the lanterns in our dim library. Sometimes I could make tiny spheres of water dance in the bathtub. But other than that, my powers were nonexistent. I knew I would eventually come into my full powers. I just didn't know when.

Maybe this was that. My tutors had told me Fae powers matured at the age of twenty-five, and now I was only a few months away from my twenty-fifth birthday. I never had any reason to question them.

I cleared my throat. "Of course, I had training." I paused, embarrassed. "But nothing came of it."

"Until now," said Delrik.

"Your father or mother never spoke of such strong powers to you?" Aramis asked.

Why did he have so many questions? I didn't have the answers. Letting someone in was foreign to me. Being the one that needed help filled me with weakness again. The confidence left behind from the flames began to flicker out, replaced by the fragile female I had been.

"They would've known if you possessed powers of this level," he said, more to himself than me. "Powers this strong couldn't be hidden. They would've manifested at an early age."

"My brother's powers became apparent at a very young age. But my father didn't know I had powers." My words trailed off. I knew they weren't true the moment I had spoken them into the universe.

Had they known? Had my father known I had stronger powers than most? And if he did, even if he had suspected it, why had he not told me? Had he been hiding it from me on purpose? My father was a cunning man so I wouldn't put it past him to pull the wool over my eyes. But why? And did my mother know? I needed to know why. I felt a strong urge to understand. I refused to be this delicate, demure, weak creature any longer. I'd had a taste of what strength could come from within me. I would not let anyone overpower me ever again.

Aramis's eyes darted between Delrik and me, as if he were debating if he should share his thoughts.

"Arden Valley," Aramis muttered to himself.

"I'm sorry?" I tilted my head in confusion.

He spoke up and again said, "The Arden Valley."

"Aramis, we aren't going to the Arden Valley," Delrik said.

I looked between the two males. "Why not?"

"Because it is one of my most unstable and dangerous areas in Illoterra," Delrik stated. "The Arden Valley is the only thing separating the Wildlands from the rest of Illoterra."

"And...?" I asked, waving my hand in the air for him to elaborate.

"Do you know what's in the Wildlands." He yelled as he flung both arms into the air before scraping them through his hair. "The osomal that nearly killed us? They thrive there. Not to mention countless other dark creatures. And tribal wars are in constant motion. It is one of the places Cadoc's laws and orders hadn't been able to penetrate."

"Evren, have you heard about the Supreme Elementals?" Aramis asked, drawing my attention away from the furious Delrik.

"Yes, of course. I read about them in the Essence Scrolls as a child. I don't remember the exact details. But my father said that the Supreme Elementals have all but become extinct due to cross breeding and the fading pure bloodlines."

"Ha!" Delrik let out a sound that was half amusement, half crazed.

Aramis shot his adopted son a glance before continuing. "Supreme Elemental powers are not passed from generation to generation. They are gifted to the individual based on their worthiness and projected fate."

"Powers Above!" Delrik's brows shot up. "Wait. You think Evren is a Supreme Elemental?"

Aramis and Delrik had been watching me, studying me while I swirled my thoughts around and around in my head. I finally lifted my head to them, and they could see the change in me. Something that was dormant inside me began to awaken. I lifted my hands out in front of me, palms facing the ceiling, and attempted to summon flames to my palms. A weak, sputtering spark, just a slip of a flame, tickled my fingers.

It wasn't much but it was something.

"You possess great power, Evren," Aramis said. "Great power, indeed. And I know someone in Arden Valley that should be able to answer all the questions we have."

THIRTY-TWO
EVREN

Delrik followed me back to our shared apartment in silence, keeping his distance but following my every move. Anger flooded me, fear seeping back in.

His voice was jagged and rough from all his yelling. "Are you sure you're alright?"

No, I am not alright!

I wanted to laugh. Me? Powerful? Important? I could barely summon a globe of light to read my books at night.

I turned on him quickly, lashing out. "What's it matter to you? I thought I was just a bounty."

What would happen now that Delrik knew I possessed such power? Surely, he would use that to his benefit. Surely, he'd return me to my father now and collect his reward. With my elemental powers so strong, he could easily seek to bargain for a higher price. Every other person had used me. Why would he be any different?

"I want to help you," Delrik said. His hands were raised in front of him like he was trying to calm a scared animal.

"But why?" I scowled at him, crossing my arms over my chest. My head was beginning to throb. I pressed my warm fingers to my temples. I briefly wondered if they were warm from the flames that were pulsing through my veins. They had been warm even when wandering in the snow, I realized, even last week. Come to think of it, the frigid temperatures of the mountains didn't seem to bother me anymore. How long had my powers been growing without me even being aware?

"Please." He sounded sincere.

That sincerity made me pause.

I studied his face. I was too exhausted to argue with him. I suddenly felt drained. I needed to lie down. I needed to be quiet for a bit and process all this. This internal battle of strength and weakness. Dark and light. Fear and courage. I released a heavy sigh.

Delrik ran his hands through his hair, frustrated. What was he so frustrated about? He wasn't the one that just found out he could light themselves on fire.

"Ah! You infuriating female." His voice was husky and strained. He looked up at me, and the fierceness in his eyes penetrated my spirit. "I don't want anything to happen to you. I can't let anything happen to you."

I watched him take a slow, deep breath through his nose as if to steady himself. Thunder rolled across the mountains in the distance.

At that exact moment, I wished there was no space between us. My pulse began to race, and my chest grew heavy. Suddenly my dress was heavy and smothering. The anxiety of the future tried to seep in, but something was different. Some had shifted like it had when Delrik had me pinned to the stone archway.

Something felt right. He felt right. A mix of emotions danced behind his dark eyes. I wanted to know his thoughts. I wanted to remove all the worry and pain for him. And as if he had read my mind, he began to move toward me. Raw energy filled me from somewhere deep inside. Those walls that fell earlier today were still absent, letting him close in. And he wasn't even near me; he was still all the way across the room.

He took a step toward me, with purpose. My anger softened as he took another step.

He paused a few feet from me, waiting for me to say something. Waiting for my permission. Or waiting for me to deny him again. I was standing on the edge of a cliff, and the ground was about to give way. I only had a moment to decide. Would I back away or jump?

My anger dissipated with that pause. I knew I could trust him then. That he wouldn't do anything to hurt me, and he wouldn't take advantage of me. My belly fluttered with something warm and fuzzy and foreign. The way he looked at me, taking in every inch of my body, left me feeling exposed, but also comfortable, like he could truly see me now.

I inhaled his woody scent. His chest was still bare, and the sculpted muscles shifted up and down with each breath. A chest carved from years of graceful and powerful swinging of a sword. An image of a fierce Qana mountain cat was inked into his skin. Its sleek body was built for stealth and speed. Just like the male standing before me. My whole body shivered, and that uncertainty I had been feeling slipped away on the breeze through the open doors. He unclasped the cloak and slipped it off my shoulders. It pooled on the floor at my feet.

The moment came to walk away.

And then the moment passed.

Powers Above, I wanted his closeness with such urgency. It should've scared me. I wanted to feel his powerful hands take my entire body. I wanted to see if the rest of his body was as sculpted as his chest. I could sense his growing arousal every second we were together.

Delrik said in a husky voice, "I am going to kiss you, Evren."

"Okay," I whispered back, anticipation building between the thread of space between us.

I took a timid half-step toward him, hardly a movement. But it was enough of an answer to that unspoken question for him. Our bodies collided with such force I had to take a step back again.

One of Delrik's hands cupped my face, his thumb stroking my lips. I felt the entire length of his body against mine. He was standing over me, his height advantage quite apparent with how close he was.

But his lips didn't meet mine. Not how I expected. He kissed the corner of my mouth, turning my head to reach my jaw. I tilted my head back further, giving him access to my neck. I felt him smile against my throat before he trailed light kisses down my neck to my collarbone.

My blood was roaring in my ears. He pulled back to look at my face, and I gazed back at him. His eyes dropped to my mouth, and he lowered his head. Warm and soft, his tongue swept across my bottom lip, coaxing my lips apart, tentative, seeking my approval. My lips parted, giving him access. His tongue floated across mine, and my knees buckled in the most wonderful way possible.

He buried one of his hands into my hair, tugging gently, guiding my head back further to deepen the kiss while the other snaked across my hips to grasp my behind. My arms wound around his torso, tracing their way across the soft skin of his back. My fingers curved around his waist. The ridges of his firm, toned stomach pressed against the softness of my dress. Ugh, that thin barrier was infuriating. I didn't want it between us. I just wanted him.

His mouth, soft and demanding, had me questioning everything. I thought I knew what I wanted. Freedom from my father and control over my own life; no longer a pawn to whatever game my father was playing. But his body flush against mine made me want something more, something I'd never dreamed I could want. Something I never dreamed I could have. It coiled deep in my gut, and an ache that was crying to be filled. I had contented myself with safety and didn't think the fates would grant me happiness too. Especially now that, even though he knew of my powers, that *I* knew of my powers, he still wanted nothing more than just me. And I wanted to drown myself in him completely.

He pulled away abruptly with a sharp gasp of breath, the weight of him disappearing, leaving me off balance. My lips formed a pout. Instantly, I felt empty.

"Delrik." I spoke breathlessly, his name like a plea, a prayer to the Powers Above.

A hiss came from his lips as I pressed my body against him again, a wish for him to continue. I wanted more of him.

"Greedy female," he said with a mischievous smile.

He leaned his forehead against mine, both of us breathing the same air heavily. Our hands were clasped together on his chest between us. I'm not sure how long we stayed that way, but he eventually gave me a gentle kiss on my forehead. He reached up and twirled a piece of my hair around his fingers and gave it a playful tug.

"Goodnight, Evren."

He turned away and walked to his bedroom and quietly closed the door.

PART THREE

THIRTY-THREE
ARAMIS

The sun had just begun to light the sky. The cream stone of the towers encircling the gardens swirled with lilac hues as the light bounced from the whitened landscape. A fresh layer of snow from last night left the air crisp and clean. A pair of birds caught my eye as they fluttered across the sky. Delrik was preparing the horses and supplies to make the trip to the Arden Valley. Evren stood in the center of the bare branches and bushes, spinning in a slow, slow circle to take in the full morning. Her long travel cloak swirled around her as she spun. She had the free spirit of a child seeing the world for the first time. It made sense since she'd been locked in Cadoc's fortress her whole life. I marveled at the joy that radiated from her this morning. She was a light that this realm needed, especially as the unknown darkness continued to spread.

I turned to Delrik and said with a fatherly tone, "Please be on guard. And stick close to the known roads."

Delrik rolled his eyes, and he checked the horse's saddle one last time, straightening the saddle pad and tightening the girth. Supply sacks were strapped behind each saddle carrying food, bed rolls, extra horse blankets, and temporary shelter from potential harsh winter winds that like to come without warning. These mountains were not kind to travelers. The horses stamped their feet in anticipation of the journey, and their warm breath created puffs of clouds in the air. Evren smiled at them and rubbed their noses with affection.

The Arden Valley was a several days' ride from Arcelia. It would not be an easy trip, especially with the new snowfall and the bounty still out on Evren. I'd sent soldiers out past the wards of the city to check if Cadoc was still searching for his daughter. They'd reported back that not only had the reward doubled if Evren were to be returned alive, but Black Guardsmen were scattered over every inch of the realm within 300 miles of Arcelia.

"Of course, Aramis. We will be cautious," Delrik said.

"It's important to remain unseen."

Delrik dropped his head with a sigh. I knew I was being overbearing, but I couldn't help it. "I know, Aramis. I know the risks. I know what's at stake, and I will keep her safe."

I raised my hands in surrender. Of course, he knew all these things. I'd trained him myself. Sometimes when he looked at me, I still saw that young, scared boy Nazneen brought home. This morning, however, he stood tall and confident. I could see the strong warrior he had become. Brave and smart. Compassionate and honest. A true Arcelia Legion Commander. And I couldn't imagine anyone else leading our legion and protecting Arcelia. He had never failed at anything he set his mind to, and he would not fail in his mission to help Evren.

Nazneen stood back, leaning against the stone wall, arms crossed, and a scowl plastered on her face. Her twisted auburn hair was slung over her shoulder, and she toyed with the ends. She looked thoughtful, focused. She only looked this determined during training or battle. Delrik was her best friend and her brother. She was loyally protective over him, so her change in demeanor was not a shock. Especially after learning about Evren's powers over breakfast this morning. She liked Evren but was wary of her developing elemental powers and curious about why Cadoc wanted Evren back home so badly.

She watched the pair like a hawk, her eyes sharp and focused. It was that focus that made her a great warrior and spy—she was a shadow and a thief, the finest in the legion. She helped pave the way for many other female warriors too. She shifted her weight off the wall and came to stand beside me, her boots crunching on the icy ground. She gave me a nudge, handing me a sheathed sword.

I cleared my throat. "I have something for you." Then I lifted the weapon, presenting it to Delrik. "This was my father's and his father's before. It goes back to the first forged weapons in the realm. It served me well during the war. I'd be honored if you carried it with you," I said.

Delrik looked at the sword, then to me, his eyes wide with shock. His fingers reached out to touch the sheathed blade but withdrew. A small puff of white cloud from his exhale hung in the air. Evren was watching him, curious, but didn't say anything. I saw her hand beneath her cloak reach out to him, but she didn't touch him.

"The Warblade of Silverlight," he said under his breath.

It is told in the old stories of the Mountain Fae that the blade was impregnated with wisdom from the Powers Above and brings guidance to those that wield it.

"It has protected our family for centuries. And I know it will continue to protect you, my son."

"But it's supposed to go to your heir." He looked to Nazneen.

Her smile was gentle as she said, "Then I guess you better bring it back home...preferably with you in one piece."

I handed it to him, and Delrik took it from me. The scabbard of the longsword was made from wood older than the Sacred Forest and was engraved with the ancient language of the gods. The pommel and grip were simple, unlike so many swords most High Fae carried. Only a single sapphire was set in the handle surrounded by small diamonds. They reflected the morning sun brightly. I watched as Delrik withdrew the blade to examine it. The blade itself was pure Lilura Steel from the depths of Mount Lendorr. It was lighter than any steel ever made and its blade deadlier than any poison.

Delrik's voice broke as he sheathed the sword again and tried to speak. "I promise I will return it to you." He lifted the sword to strap it to his back, the hilt peeking from behind his right shoulder.

I reached out, and we grasped each other's forearms firmly. He gave my shoulder a squeeze before pulling me into a hug. I knew he wasn't of my blood, but he was honorable, and I considered him my son. I trusted the Powers Above when they brought Delrik to our home. I trusted that he was made for a great purpose. I just hoped he could recognize that truth before it was too late. And his connection with Evren may push him onto that path. Only the Powers Above knew.

"I have been and always will be proud of you. And we will see each other again soon," I said to him.

Delrik gave Evren a leg up to her horse, his fingers lingering on her hands when he handed her the reins. Then he tightened the leather sheath at her calf where a dagger rested. She shifted in her saddle, finding her balance. A blush creeped across her cheeks as Delrik leaned in and whispered something low to her.

Evren giggled before clearing her throat and turning to me. "Aramis, I don't know how to repay your kindness," she said to me, a gentleness on her face.

"Oh, dear child, you will be welcomed here in Arcelia for all your days," I replied.

The smile that she gave me illuminated through the entire garden, or her elemental powers surged just the smallest amount with her joy, I couldn't quite tell. She'd learn the full range of her powers soon, and I knew that she would find answers she needed in the Arden Valley.

Yes. She was truly a light, pure spirit. I gave her a deep bow.

Nazneen waited until Evren was settled on her horse before she spoke.

"Brother, be safe. And please don't be gone for so long this time."

Delrik wrapped her in a tight hug, resting his chin on her head. Her body relaxed into his hold. They embraced each other for several moments before reluctantly parting. He kissed her forehead. She squeezed both his hands and then came to stand beside me, looping her arm through mine. She was holding back her emotion with each wobbly breath.

"Don't let anything happen to him…please." Nazneen spoke to Evren, the hardness on her face softening a touch.

Evren simply nodded at Naz before saying, "I promise."

"Come on, sister, you know I love to attract chaos." He winked, raked a hand through his hair, and effortlessly swung his leg over his horse.

Naz pressed her lips together as she held back a laugh.

He gave me a quick nod before kicking his horse into a gallop, Evren following behind him. Their horses' feet crunched in the snow as they disappeared over the horizon.

THIRTY-FOUR
EVREN

We had agreed with the new knowledge of my growing powers, it was best to expedite our journey in search of answers. So, two days after the night of the dinner, we packed up our supplies and prepared to set off on horseback to the Arden Valley. It was a crisp, clear morning. Snow covered every surface. Even the air seemed quiet. Morning mist hung over the water's surface of the river. Mornings like this had become my favorite.

I had crawled out of bed and moved to the common area. The apartment was dark since the sun hadn't risen yet. The embers in the fireplace glowed, and I sat there lost in them until the sun made its appearance. I'd grown to cherish the exact moment the sun peeked over the horizon—lavenders, pinks, and gold smearing the sky like it was a canvas. I sat with a hot mug of tea curled up on the balcony—wool socked feet and all—lingering and watching the city come to life below me. I truly hoped that one day I would be able to return to Arcelia and call it my home. Maybe even a future with Delrik.

Delrik and I were wearing thick wool cloaks lined with fur against the cold. I'd traded in the gowns I'd been wearing for thick riding pants and boots. Even then, the bite of the mountain air crept over my skin.

Delrik checked all the straps on the saddlebags before he checked the sheath strapped to my calf. His fingers lingered on my leg, and their heat spread through me, even through the thick pants. I smiled down at him, and he winked in return.

"I'm looking forward to another kiss like the other night, by the way." His voice was low and husky.

We'd had hardly any time alone the last two days with having to prepare for our sudden departure. And the time we did get together was full of delicious tension and whisper-soft touches disguised as accidental grazes. He hadn't kissed me again...not yet.

I watched silently at the family exchanges as they said their goodbyes. I felt like an intruder, glimpsing what very few ever would. So, I remained still and quiet. Nazneen's mood toward me was off this morning. Aramis must have told her about my developing elemental powers. I couldn't blame her for her wariness. After hearing about my father's role in the war, I even questioned why he would keep such a thing from me.

We rode in silence as we crossed the quiet streets. Most were still in bed at such an early hour. Delrik slowed the horses' pace the closer we got to the border of Arcelia and where the protective wards ended. A bridge stretched out before us, barely wide enough for one horse to pass at a time. It arched over a deep crevice in the mountains, so far below that I couldn't see the bottom. I slowed my horse to a stop. Delrik assured me that these were the finest horses in the legion and would be able to easily make the trip to the valley. However, now facing the icy stone death trap they called a bridge, I couldn't help but imagine myself plummeting to the unforeseen depths.

I was trying to think of anything to keep my mind off the drop…and the thought of the other night flashed through my mind. I hadn't slept much the last two days, not after what happened. Between the horrible dinner, my powers deciding to make an appearance, and Delrik's mouth on me, I couldn't get my brain to shut off. Even in my exhaustion, I kept replaying Delrik's lips trailing up my neck. I could still taste him, still feel the weight of him leaning against my body and his hands traveling across my skin.

A cough broke into my thoughts.

"Hey Ev, are you planning on following?" Delrik asked with a smirk on his face showing off his dimple. He was almost halfway across the bridge but had stopped and turned around in his saddle. "You're thinking about me, aren't you?"

I shot him a dirty look, gulped down the bile that was creeping up my throat from the sheer drop before me, and refused to look down as my horse's hooves clopped onto the bridge.

We cleared the bridge and the powerful enchantments protecting Arcelia, my skin zinging as we passed through the magic. The plan was to follow the winding lower ridge of the Qana Mountains across to the east and into the rising sun. The ridge was the safest and fastest way to get to the valley. Safe as in it was too treacherous for most and there would be less chance of coming across the Black Guard. The ridge cut straight across the realm and wasn't frequented by travelers. But Delrik's knowledge of the mountain made it our best option.

We rode in silence, me following closely behind Delrik. This was much better than walking, though I wasn't sure my hind end wouldn't agree by the evening.

My eyes wandered the landscape. Dense trees as far as my eyes could see. I was seeing the forest in a whole new light. The trees were silent sentinels guarding over us. The towering pines stretched their branches high into the air—a sea of overlapping hues of greens. The snow wasn't thick on the ground, unable to penetrate the canopy overhead and as the path became more overgrown, we slowed our pace.

After a few hours, we stopped for lunch along a fast-flowing stream, allowing the horses to rest. I braced my hands on Delrik's shoulders as he lifted me from my horse. His large hands almost covered my entire waist. Those hands that had held me possessively to him. When his hands left my waist, liquid warmth pooled where his hands had been, and I wanted him to touch me again.

Delrik walked to the water's edge where the water lapped against the smoothed pebbles at his boots. He bent down and dipped his hands in the water and splashed his face and neck. I watched as rivulets of water slipped below the neckline of his shirt. The memory of his muscular chest came to me. I kept my face down in case he turned and saw me watching him. I crouched down to pull food out of the pack and to start a small fire for warmth. Although there wasn't as much snow here as in Arcelia, there was still a light dusting on the ground.

I heard movement behind me, a snap of a branch and a rustle of leaves. The horses nervously stamped their feet and whinnied at the unfamiliar sounds. I turned around in time to see a massive, leather-covered hand come at me from above, grabbing my face, covering my mouth and nose, the other hand fisted at the back of my head buried in my hair. My hands went to their wrist, trying to free myself as panic coursed through me.

I could only let out a muffled scream from the hair being torn from my scalp as I was pulled to my feet so that I was face to face with the attacker. A shadowed face turned from me to face Delrik as he whipped around. A cruel smile appeared on the half-hooded horrifying face.

I struggled against him, my eyes wide in fear as I recognized the male under the dark hood. Fear and magic flared in my chest; uncontrollable fire spreading, but I didn't know how to use it.

"It seems you let your guard down, my pet," the male purred viciously, twisting his face. "Tsk tsk, that wasn't very smart now, was it?"

I didn't need to see his whole face to know who he was.

Renwick.

THIRTY-FIVE
EVREN

Renwick wrenched me hard against him, twisting me so my back was to his chest as he clamped a hand tightly around my throat, eliciting a strangled gasp from me. My toes barely touched the ground making it impossible to balance myself.

No. Not again. No. No. No.

His other hand wandered down to my breast and then slid across my stomach. My insides churned at his touch, and flashbacks of those hands doing unspeakable things to me crossed my mind. It was nothing like Delrik's touch. Renwick's touch promised agony.

"Still just as beautiful as ever, even dressed like low life filth."

"Let her go," Delrik said harshly. My eyes shot to him. He was standing now, but frozen, not wanting to elicit a more aggressive response. I could see him weighing his options. His jaw was set, and his eyes were murderous.

I tried to shake my head and warn him to run but I couldn't get a sound past Renwick's hand.

Renwick laughed cruelly. I could smell the sour sweat on him, and his breath was hot against my ear as he ran his tongue up the backside of my neck. I hated when he did that. It was his way of staking his claim, marking me with his scent. No matter how much I scrubbed myself, his smell lingered long after my bath. I tried to pull my head away, but he tightened his grip on my throat. Black spots covered the edges of my vision briefly.

"Let. Her. Go," Delrik said, more calmly this time, though I could see the tension on his face. His hands were fisted at his sides. Even with his speed, he wouldn't risk attacking with my life being threatened.

A low evil chuckle came from Renwick. "Oh, I don't think so. She's coming with me."

He took a step back, my toes dragging in the dirt as he pulled me with him. I gripped his forearm tightly.

I refused to go back with him. I refused to let him win. I would have rather died than let him touch me again.

"Though," Renwick paused, "it would be more enjoyable to let her watch me kill you before taking her back home." His hands tightened on my throat again, lifting my feet completely off the ground. "You have made my life very difficult over the last several weeks."

Renwick spun me around and I didn't see the blow coming. His arm swung, hitting me hard, the back of his hand striking me so forcefully my legs buckled beneath me. My head snapped to the side, and a sharp pain cut across my face. My body crumpled in a heap. I saw black spots again as the agonizing pain spread to my temple. Warmth dribbled down my lip, and I tasted blood and dirt that had caked to my face. I brought my hand to the side of my face. The blow shocked me. He'd never hit my face before. He'd said he didn't want to ruin my beauty with bruises.

Before my knees even hit the dirt, Delrik leapt at Renwick. But Renwick was faster—he reached out an unrushed, calm hand. With his powers, Renwick slammed Delrik into the rocky bank of the stream. His body made an awful sound as it crunched to the ground. The breath whooshed from Delrik on impact, and I felt the air leave my body as if my body was connected to his.

I didn't think it was possible, but I had almost forgotten this pain. Almost forgot this helplessness. Almost forgot the shame. I tried to crawl away from him, but he shoved me into the ground with the heel of his boot on my back. The rocks sliced into my hands as I attempted to scramble away.

"No, no, no," Renwick said in a mocking tone as he grabbed the back of my head, lifting me by my hair.

He pulled me back, up into the air and into him again, and placed a thin blade at my throat. I froze. I stopped fighting the restraint. I felt the cold tip as he lightly pressed it down my neck to my collarbone, drawing a line of blood. I gritted my teeth but didn't cry out. I wouldn't let him see my fear. Before, my cries had just made him more excited. I wouldn't give him that satisfaction.

"I need you to watch me slaughter *him* like the animal he is," Renwick seethed.

Delrik struggled to catch his breath as he lifted himself from the ground.

Renwick tossed me to the side into a nearby boulder. My limp body collided with the solid rock, and I heard a sickening snap in my chest. I heard the bone break before the blinding pain shocked me.

Renwick let out a low laugh before attacking again, this time choosing to use his fists instead of his power. He had told me once that he preferred to feel the life leave someone's body with his hands. Delrik rolled out of the way just in time. Renwick crashed into the stream, splashing water into the air.

He whipped around, growling in frustration, arm thrust into the air. Delrik's body flew through the air as if he weighed nothing at all. This time, though, he was expecting it. Delrik landed on his feet, touching the ground for a split second before his punch knocked Renwick back into the water. They moved so fast I couldn't keep up with their blurred forms. My head spun from the pain and dizzying movements.

Renwick reached out again with his mind and grasped Delrik around the throat, strangling him. He lifted Delrik's struggling body into the air, and he drifted, floating a foot above the ground, right into Renwick's outstretched hand.

"Renwick, no!" My voice came out shrill and strangled. I pushed myself up to my hands and knees, trying to fight the urge to pass out from the pain that made it nearly impossible to take a breath.

Delrik couldn't escape Renwick's grasp. Renwick slammed Delrik into the shallow water, kneeling over him, his knee pressing into his chest. He towered over Delrik, holding his head submerged, his lips curling in a self-satisfaction. Delrik's speed was useless once Renwick got his hands on him. Renwick's strength overpowered him completely. Renwick laughed as Delrik fought against the grip on his neck, holding him underwater. Hands clawed wildly at Renwick's hands, arms, and face. Hate twisted on his disgusting face.

I couldn't take a deep breath without a sharp pain splitting my chest in half. My eyes burned with tears and dirt and blood, but the panic building in me burned more.

Then I heard his voice.

"Your father didn't tell you, did he? How was he planning to use you?" Renwick peered over his shoulder at me, still on my hands and knees next to the boulder.

I didn't want to hear anymore. I hated his voice. I hated his face. I hated his very existence. I saw Delrik's hand grab a fistful of river rocks and then he threw them into Renwick's cocky face. He yelled angrily, rearing back just enough that Delrik's face broke through the surface of the water, and he took a gasping breath.

Renwick was quick to push him back into the stream.

I didn't leave time to second guess myself as I forced myself to my feet. Each breath sent a tearing pain through my entire body. I preyed on the distraction, reaching for my dagger strapped to my calf. I took two breaths to steady myself as Delrik had shown me. I tossed the dagger end over end in the air so that the blade landed in my palm.

Breathe. Focus. Never surrender.

Another painful breath. As I exhaled, I released the fear. It was replaced by fury—fiery, powerful anger. I would not let his monster steal any more joy from my life.

I took a sure step forward, grinding my teeth at the pain as I drew my arm back. Then, with all my might, I released the blade from my fingers. A stream of yellow and orange fire trailed after the dagger through the air, straight and true, right into Renwick's back.. It embedded deep into his flesh, hitting the mark. Renwick reared up and screamed, thrashing in pain, reaching backward for the blade that he couldn't reach. I ran at him and grabbed the hilt. I twisted it deeper into him.

I felt a sly smile come across my lips. Finally, payback for all the fists, all the hidden bruises, all the mental torture, all the pain he inflicted on me over the last two years. I felt power and control sweep through me, propelling my courage further. I let that darkness seep into me. Renwick turned and peered into my face. Fire flickered to life in my palms, shooting sparks to the ground and his eyes went wide with surprise.

Renwick dropped to his knees in front of me. Blood bubbled from his mouth.

"You will never touch me ever again," I snarled.

I grabbed his shoulders and slammed my knee into his face. A satisfying crunch of bone reverberated through my body. I straightened and placed my hands firmly on my hips. I felt zero remorse as his corpse slumped face down into the dirt in a crumpled heap.

Delrik sputtered as he scrambled to his feet. Water splashed as he tripped and fell before finally making it to the shore.

"Evren, run."

I didn't think twice about obeying before I ran for our horses. Delrik was on my heels in an instant. His strong hands gripped my waist, practically throwing me into the saddle. He smacked my horse's rump, and it took off into the trees. I tried to call back to Delrik, but I was struggling to hold on as my cracked rib barked in pain. My horse followed along the stream at a breakneck speed.

Suddenly, out of the corner of my eye, I spotted Delrik galloping several feet away. His horse swerved closer, and he reached out for my reins.

"Woah." His voice wasn't rushed or fearful as he gently pulled back on the reins. My panicked mare slowed, her chest heaving from the exertion beneath my legs. I patted her sweaty neck in reassurance.

"What the fuck," Delrik said under his breath.

Our horses slowed to a canter and then to a walk. Delrik was looking around us, scanning the trees for another ambush.

"We need to keep moving, find somewhere to take cover. He may not have been alone."

I had rid the world of one small evil and I was glad of it. A shift in the balance back to the light. The male that had terrorized my every waking moment and even my dreams for the last six months was gone. No longer did he hold power over me. And he never would again.

"He was definitely alone." I sat up straighter in the saddle and stretched out my neck, wincing at my injuries. "He always works alone."

⚲

"I'm going back to see if Renwick is actually dead, and if he isn't, to make sure he does die. You wait here." Delrik spoke matter-of-factly.

We'd found a rocky overhang not far from the clearing. It gave us enough coverage while still allowed Delrik to keep an eye on the surrounding area. I stayed on my horse in case we needed to get away again, but I was not going to just sit and wait to be attacked again.

"I'm going with you." I moved my horse in front of his.

"No." His hand landed softly on my shoulders and I cringed at the sharp ache in my chest. "I'm not going to put you at risk again."

"I'm at risk staying here alone."

He glared at me with his lips pressed into a thin line and a grim look on his face.

I crossed my arms over my chest. I wasn't budging on this, and Delrik knew better than to fight with me about it.

Our horses picked their way back along the stream to where we had been ambushed. I prayed to the Powers Above that there was still a body on the bank. At the same time, I didn't want to see the damage I'd inflicted. We stopped just on the edge of the clearing and dismounted our horses.

"Evren, you don't have to look. Just turn around."

"No. I need to see it for myself. I need to see that he's dead."

Delrik nodded and squeezed my hand in support. "I'm right here." Then we stepped into the clearing.

The mangled, bloody corpse had already been picked over by the beasts wandering the forest. They'd wasted no time on letting a free meal go to waste. It had maybe been an hour. Ivory bone protruded from what used to be a leg, the other half of it across the clearing like something had attempted to drag away the fresh kill. His face was unrecognizable.

Suddenly a wave of nausea took over, and I hurled my breakfast and what appeared to be ash onto the ground next to the fallen body. Delrik was there quickly, holding back my hair, and wiping the clamminess from my forehead with his shirt. Of course, he'd hold back my hair. How chivalrous.

I gasped for air between heaves. My ribs protested with anger with each heave. Although they were broken, I'd felt and heard them crack, I could feel them already knitting back together with my healing power.

Delrik handed me a canteen of water, and I thoroughly rinsed my mouth and face with the cool liquid.

This must be how everyone reacted to death the first time they saw it, the first time they took a life from another. Or, at least, that's what I told myself to soothe my unease.

I looked at the dead male next to me—still feeling no remorse. I only felt relief. He would never again lay a hand on me. A shiver ran down my spine and I shook my head before I looked up and found Delrik staring at me. My chest rose and fell with rapid breaths. The searing pain was more of a phantom pain than before. Had I really healed myself that quickly?

Delrik slipped his hand into mine and squeezed it gently. A charge sparked between our hands, but neither of us pulled away. We stood, holding hands on the bank of the stream for a minute. A purplish bruise was rising to the surface of his skin. And his knuckles were split open, dripping blood, running down my fingers. Apparently, I could now heal myself faster than him.

Blood began to flush across my cheeks, and I dipped my head down to avoid looking into his eyes. He had watched me kill someone. For the second time, I had lost control of myself, and he'd witnessed it. I tried to pull my hand away, ashamed, but he wouldn't let go. He leaned his head down into my field of view to look into my eyes again. A smile of gratitude—and something else—on his face.

"I could bow at your feet for saving me," he said.

I couldn't resist the temptation of him being so close. I leaned in and pressed my lips quickly to his. A split-second decision. As I pulled away, his lips followed as he leaned into me, refusing to break the contact. His tall, warm body tangled with mine, all arms and legs, as our mouths devoured each other. There was nothing sweet or slow about it. Knowing that only chance and luck had us both standing here now instead of dead. I laughed against his mouth when I finally came up for air.

He purposely brushed a growing arousal against my stomach, and a moan escaped from the back of his throat. Apparently, my saving his life evoked quite a…um…physical response.

I quirked a brow at him. "Now who's being greedy?"

THIRTY-SIX
RENWICK

That. Fucking. Bitch.

One moment, I'm crushing the life from that damned bounty hunter's body, and the next, everything is blinding pain. She fucking stabbed me! She buried a damned dagger in my back! And then had the gall to break my nose. When I get my hands on her I'm going to beat the living hell out of her and then rip her heart from her chest. I don't even care what Cadoc wants anymore.

"Sir, can I get you anything else?" one of the low-life guards—a new recruit still in his probation year—asked me as he hovered nearby. I was crouched next to the water, rinsing the dried blood from my hands.

The healer standing behind me let out a whimper. Blithering idiot. If he weren't so useful, I wouldn't have kept him around. He followed me as I stood and propped against a low rock so he could finish healing the wound. I'd straightened my nose with a snap on my own and wiped the dried blood from my face with my ruined tunic.

The guard was standing several feet away as if he was afraid to get too close. Little did he know I didn't need to touch him to kill him. My hand reached out, and my fist closed slowly. The young male started gasping, clawing at his throat. A malicious smile twisted my mouth and then I snapped his neck with a simple squeeze. His body made a sickeningly satisfying sound when it smashed into the rocky ground. There was nothing I loved more than the crumbling of bones being crushed in my palm and snuffing out the life of my victim.

The other guardsmen took several steps back, averting their eyes from their deceased comrade.

"I'm almost done, sir. Then we can return home," the healer stuttered.

I waved my hand in dismissal.

Captain Whitt appeared before me with a small pop. The ability to blink from one location to another wasn't a common gift. The power made Whitt invaluable to the Black Guard and helped him climb the ranks quickly. It did *not* make him one of my favorites though.

"General Ashewood. They haven't gone very far. Would you like me to go after them?" the captain asked.

"No. We will return home and update High Ruler Byrnes. I have information to pass on to him."

"Finished sir," the healer interjected, scrambling back behind the guardsmen.

"About damned time." I stood, brushing the leaves and dirt from my pants and pulling my blood-drenched tunic on over my head. I could still feel the skin around the freshly healed wound pulling as I moved.

"Let's go," I said to the group. I stomped over to Whitt, stepping over my pool of my own blood soaking into the ground. I let the fact that I almost bled out fuel my fury.

Whitt asked, lifting his chin toward the dead male, "What about Avery's body?"

I picked up the damned dagger that bitch impaled me with. I recognized it as the dagger Cadoc gave to that pretentious son of his when he completed the Trials. The kid didn't deserve it. I could've easily passed the Trial if I'd been allowed to compete, but only High Fae were allowed to enter. And even with my unique powers, I was not considered High Fae in Cadoc's eyes without knowing my lineage.

I rolled my eyes and stomped over to Avery's body. Using my foot, I rolled Avery over onto this front and into the pooled blood and drove Evren's dagger deep into this back. "Leave it for the beasts."

⚲

My ears popped, and my stomach dropped.

Fuck I hate blinking.

Suddenly I was standing in front of Higher Ruler Byrnes in his study. The healer, Captain Whitt, and the other guardsmen knelt behind me. The temperature in the study was sweltering. I looked down at my bloody and muddy boots and grinned to myself about the mess I was making on the priceless rug. Cadoc thoroughly enjoyed flaunting his finery and riches whenever he could, and I secretly reveled that I was soiling the rug.

"So, you got stabbed by my powerless daughter, eh Renwick?" His voice was slick and domineering as he lounged in his chair with his feet propped on his desk.

I lifted my head to meet his gaze, holding it for several seconds before inclining my head in greeting. Bastard was so cocky sometimes.

"I have new information pertaining to your daughter, sir," I stated, trying to hold back my distaste just speaking of her.

"You're dismissed."

I knew he wasn't speaking to me. Everyone behind me darted to the door. Cadoc waited until the door closed before dropping his feet to the floor. He leaned forward in his chair, the leather squeaking under his girth, and looked down at a map on his desk. A vein popped out on his neck and his jaw clenched.

"My apologies sir," I said in a honeyed voice.

"It's lucky that she missed your heart and Captain Whitt stumbled upon you during his scouting."

I ground my teeth so hard I thought they would crack. "Yes sir."

"You have new intel," Cadoc said without looking up from that damned map he was so obsessed with.

I was so tired of being his errand boy. For weeks all I'd done is run all over this fucking realm chasing after a female that's supposed to be powerful but is instead a weak little bitch. I'm the fucking Head of the Black Guard. General Ashewood. And I'm better than this.

"I followed her trail from Lakeshore to the outskirts of Arcelia, but I couldn't get past Aramis's wards."

"Paranoid bastard."

"I posted guards on every road leading out of Arcelia to alert me of any movement." I fought the urge to shift my feet. The stench of my own blood filled my nostrils. "I thought they'd somehow missed something, but three days ago, I caught her trail again leaving Arcelia on a remote road deep in the mountains. I followed them for a few hours…"

"Them?" Cadoc interrupted, his full attention finally on me. I hated when he interrupted me. "Yes, sir. A male was with her. That crossbred legion commander, one of Aramis's favorites. Delrik Valhar."

His face curled in disgust. "Ah, that orphaned kid Aramis took in."

"The very one. Well, he's following her around like a lovesick puppy. They're heading to the Arden Valley."

"Interesting." He was now pacing back and forth behind his ostentatious desk.

Did he really need a desk that large?

"Arden Valley…Arden Valley…What's in the Arden Valley?" he asked.

"I don't know, sir, but I overheard them discussing supreme elemental powers." Cadoc's eyes grew wide. "I also believe the girl's powers have started to develop."

Cadoc's step froze, his foot suspended in the air. His whole face grew as crimson as the Byrnes Family crest.

"Seriously!" His voice shook the windows. "Of course, her powers would develop after she runs away."

"I witnessed it myself. She's untrained, but they are strong."

He picked up an iron fox statue from the corner of his desk and hurled it across the room. It smashed into the marble mantle, breaking off a chunk, before falling to the floor. Even though iron was known to deplete Fae magic and could even cause death, Cadoc insisted on keeping this chunk nearby. I'd catch him stroking the metal when we were deep in discussion.

"We should just let her go to the valley and have the wildland tribes take care of her," I said with disdain leaching from me.

"We can't let that happen."

I finally broke my stance and raked my hands across my face. "Why is she so vital to your plan?"

"That doesn't concern you," Cadoc bellowed, his face growing redder by the second. How was that even possible? Even the tips of his fucking beloved pointed ears were red.

"I'm Head of the Black Guard!" I raised my voice. "I *need* to know your plans."

Pain. Sudden, crippling pain. I fought against Cadoc's invasion of my mind. I pushed back but the near-death blow had weakened me. I crumbled to the floor and knelt at his feet. I wouldn't give him the satisfaction of hearing me scream.

Cadoc's voice echoed inside my head—cold and full of wrath. *Remember who you're speaking to, Ashewood. Remember where you came from. Remember how I brought you from slavery to the highest you can ever be.*

And then the pain was gone. Blood leaked from the crescent moons my nails had dug into my palms. I used the back of my hand to wipe the sweat and spit from my mouth.

Fucking bastard.

One day, I will make him pay for all the shit he put me through. I knew he wanted me to go through the bondmate ceremony with her, but he refused to tell me why. Maybe he thought he could control her by controlling me. Cadoc always had a false sense of control. Manipulating him into thinking I was simply a pawn to be used was easy enough. I spotted his weakness the first time he offered his hand after a group of kitchen boys kicked the shit out of me for slipping soapy water onto the floor. I would exact my revenge on Cadoc Byrnes. One day.

"What's next, High Ruler?"

THIRTY-SEVEN
DELRIK

"We should keep moving." My body was still pressed against her, molded to her.

She moved away from me, then bent down to retrieve her dagger from Renwick's bloodied carcass. The creatures of the forest had already made the body unrecognizable. She sucked in a sharp, painful breath with the movement. I knew she was injured, but she was healing quickly, much faster than me. Her body was no longer peppered with cuts and scrapes, like it had been when I had first stumbled upon her. I'd noticed the first week in Arcelia that all her injuries had healed.

Her boots crunched on the rocks that littered the riverbank as she stood and walked to the stream to rinse the bloodied blade. My head cocked to the side as I watched her. Her reflection peered back at her from the clear water. Dark blood splattered her face and hair, a stark contrast to her pale skin and silver hair. She was almost the exact opposite from the female I'd first encountered back in Lakeshore. She was no longer the meek, vulnerable creature I'd kidnapped for ransom. She'd morphed into something more. Not full of confidence, not yet, but I could glimpse what had been hidden beneath the years of neglect and abuse.

My father had once told me it was tradition for human hunters to smear their prey's blood on their faces after their first kill. Seeing her covered in her enemy's blood made my own blood grow warm with pride. She splashed water onto her face, rinsing away the proof of the kill.

"What did you mean earlier that he was definitely alone?" I asked.

She spoke through her hands as they scrubbed at her already clean face. "He always worked alone." Then she dunked her hands into the water and scrubbed at the dried blood under her nails.

He always worked alone? What did that mean? Maybe she was closer to our attacker than I'd realized. I helped hoist her onto her horse before turning to my own.

We didn't bother hiding or moving the body. The creatures lurking in these woods had already started feasting on the evidence of his worthless life. It would be gone by nightfall.

We rode side by side as the horses picked their way along the path.

"How did you know him?" I asked as we rode away.

"He is...was the head of my father's Black Guard."

That's where I recognized him from. He wasn't the Head of the Black Guard during the war, but he'd clearly proven himself to Cadoc. I'd done my best to avoid working near the Black Guard during the war.

She paused, eyes darting quickly to me as if she were hesitating to go on. "My father selected him as my bondmate. We were supposed to go through the blood binding this coming winter."

I brought my horse to a halt with a pull on the reins.

"Bondmate? Him! That horrible bastard? Your father was going to let that happen?"

The idea of Evren being permanently bonded to that male made me see red. Then I remembered the bruises I had seen on her body when we first met: the deep purples and the fading greens and yellows, the cuts up and down her legs, the scrapes all over her hands and how her nails were broken. Had he been the one to do that to her? What sadistic male enjoyed beating young females? Of course, Renwick was the Head of the Black Guard. Cadoc *would* pick such a monster to stand by his side and would want him to be engrained into his family. The sudden urge to kill something else now burned from within.

Maybe I should go back and smash his head in with a rock so bad that even the gods in the afterlife wouldn't recognize him.

"It was Father's plan all along. According to Adaris, his goal is to have connections all over the realm. He even wanted Adaris to be bonded with a female from the wildlands in hope of swaying them. Renwick was just his selection for me." She shrugged her shoulders and looked down, almost ashamed of the lack of empathy from her father.

Then, she dropped her voice in a low, husky tone. "Your duty is to marry a wealthy male from a strong family and produce tons of tiny male offspring that will continue on long after you have passed." She furrowed her brows and scowled.

Wow. She did truly resemble her father when she made that face. She let out a joyless laugh.

"Is Renwick even from a High Fae family?"

"I don't think so. I think he was just more my father's best friend whom he could trust. Plus, he has a rare power."

I'd experienced that rare power firsthand. My horse let out a snort and tossed his mane, frustrated that we were standing still. I nudged him gently in the side to walk on. We rode side by side in silence for a few minutes.

"Did your father know how Renwick treated you?" Deep down, I already knew the answer before I even finished asking the question. Fuck, I didn't want to actually hear it come out of her mouth.

Her face reddened, and she turned her gaze away from me, pretending to look out into the trees.

"I saw all your bruises." My tone was flat. My stomach turned sour. "That first night in the cave. What did he do to you?"

"What did he *not* do to me?"

"Did he…force himself on you?" I looked down as all the blood drained from my face.

"Thank the Powers Above, no. For some reason, that was a line he didn't cross. He'd come close a few times but always stopped or was interrupted. I think the torture of holding that above my head was his plan." She took in a shaking breath. "I tried telling my father, but he didn't care. And why would he? He treated me practically the same way."

Painful silence stretched between us.

"My father didn't speak to me those first few years after he returned from the war. In the beginning, I tried to get his attention. I would bring flowers from the garden or a new book I was reading from my lessons. I would ask questions during meals and sit outside his office waiting for him to appear. I was only seven, and I couldn't figure out what I'd done wrong."

She took a deep breath to steady her brittle voice.

"One afternoon, I stumbled into his study, not realizing he was in a meeting. He struck me so hard I fell to the floor."

Tears began to spill down her cheeks.

"That was the last time I sought him out. But as I grew older, something switched in him. He seemed more...invested in me. He was more interested, although I wasn't sure why. He insisted I begin my higher education and learn to control my powers. I realized he was shaping me, molding me into a suitable bondmate." I saw the shiver that went down her spine.

I clenched my jaw in muted rage.

"I learned to stay out of his way to avoid his wrath. I was invisible to him most of the time anyway. But with Renwick...it was harder."

If I were being honest with myself, that didn't truly surprise me. Cadoc was known for his sick sense of humor and his love for power and gore. I'd seen it with my own eyes during the war. He'd torture for the entertainment of it. He would use iron shackles and knives and cages to torment and torture all the Fae and lower beings he captured—burning them and slowly draining their powers away. It was the reason I'd refused to join forces with him when he offered me a position in the Black Guard.

"I thought the powerful High Fae families believed bondmates were destined by the Powers Above. Didn't your mother have any say in this?" I asked.

There was a veil of melancholy on her face.

"My father was more concerned with breeding power and strength into our bloodline than nursery stories of fated love. Bondmates aren't real. And my mother had no power when it came to him.

Especially when it came to his violent outbursts. He was very clear about what was to happen in his kingdom and didn't take kindly to opposing views, even from his own bonded mate."

Darkness began to cover me as I started to truly grasp the pain on her face, the kind of hell she had lived through, and what path she was heading toward for her future. No wonder she had run from Cadoc.

"I'm glad I snatched you out of that tree in Lakeshore," I said.

The corners of her mouth tipped up. "Me too."

Silence hung between us for long minutes as we continued through the forest. "I would never be cruel to you for entertainment, Evren. Never."

"I know."

We rode until the sun started to slip below the horizon. The orange glow cast stripes of color through the trees. Fireflies danced off in the distance, leading the way down the path to a safe resting place.

♀

"Let's camp here tonight." My voice broke the heavy silence that hung between us.

We stopped in a glade, tied up our horses, and began unpacking our rolls of gear for the evening. Night had already come, and I shivered at the chill. Evren gathered pieces of wood and kindling for a fire. Using her foot, she cleared away a bare spot, then crouched down on the ground, dropping her pile near her feet. I could see she was focusing hard on her upturned hands when a small spark ignited in her palms.

It flickered for a brief few seconds before the cold night air extinguished the faint light.

She let loose a heavy sigh.

I squatted beside her. "Have you ever tried to summon your powers before?"

She side-eyed me with a look of exasperation on her face. "Up until the other night, I believed my powers to be low magic consisting of hovering feathers and making spheres of water in the tub." She huffed a sardonic laugh and trailed a twig through the dirt.

I waggled my brows are her. "The tub, huh?"

She smacked me playfully on the arm. "I don't think I'll ever be able to control this amount of power."

"You will. It just takes time." I brushed my knee against her leg. "Right now, your fire is connected to your emotions."

Evren leaned back into my touch, and warmth spread from the contact. "How do you use your powers? Your speed seems to be second nature."

"Well, after 120 years, it should be."

She blessed me with a small smile.

"My mother was the one who taught me to control my speed." I don't know why I'd said that. I'd never talked about my parents with anyone, not even Nazneen. I arranged the wood pieces and leaves she'd found for the fire. "It was the gift she passed on to me."

I let out a small laugh. I can't count the number of times I broke some item or another sprinting through the house as a youngling.

"What about your father?" she asked.

"He only had low magic. He was half-human."

"What happened to them?"

I stayed quiet. Even after all this time, it was still hard to think about. I knew Aramis told her they'd been killed, but she was asking for more.

"I'm sorry," Evren began to stand. "I shouldn't have pried."

"No," I said quickly, reaching for her hand and tugging her back down to keep her on my level. "It's fine. Honestly, no one ever asked, except Aramis. And it was too fresh then." I sat back on my heels and rubbed my dirty hands down my thighs. "I told Nazneen I didn't know exactly what happened to them, but I lied. I saw it all. They were captured by the Black Guard and murdered. Well, at least my father was. My parents told me to hide when the guardsmen showed up at our house. My mother pushed me towards the forest and told me to run. I hid but I saw everything. I was nine."

I closed my eyes at the painful memory.

"They killed my father for trying to protect my mother. After witnessing the Black Guard during the war, I'm thankful it was quick. They took my

Mother, said she was being taken to Rivamir to pay for her crimes of crossbreeding with a human. I'd never see her again. I can only assume she is dead too. I've never felt so useless in my life."

Evren slid her hand on top of mine. Warmth flowed over my fingers. "I'm sorry, Delrik. I'm so, so sorry."

"You don't have to be sorry, Evren. You aren't responsible for their deaths."

She squeezed my hand.

"I've never told anyone about them."

"What were their names?" she asked.

"Elliot and Morgan Valhar."

She smiled at that, and for the first time since that horrible day, I felt a weight lifted from my shoulders.

"Aramis told me that he and his bondmate took you in," she continued.

"Yes. I owe Aramis and Calia so much. He allowed me to join the Arcelia Legion and taught me to channel all my anger and sorrow and vengeance into something useful." That potent, raw pain had slowly lessened over the years with the skills I'd learned under his watchful training. "There is no knowing where I'd be without them. And Nazneen."

Evren pursed her lips, and I laughed. Naz had been a little standoffish since Aramis told her about Evren's elemental powers and tried to not leave us alone together.

"Seriously, she'll be fine. She's protective is all. She was there for my lowest lows...so she hovers."

"Fine. I'll give her some time to come around," she said as she brushed her hair away from her face.

"Okay." I clapped my hands together. "Let's try again. When you do feel your fire, where does it come from? Your heart, your hands?"

"It can't be that easy."

"Just try it," I said, tugging at the end of her hair.

She thought for a moment, closing her eyes and searching within. She was the most beautiful thing I'd ever seen. I caught myself leaning closer to her. Then she pressed one hand to her chest and the other to her stomach, "Here. I feel it here, deep down. And it extends out from there."

"Alright. Take a deep breath. Focus on where you want the energy to go. Picture it flowing from you into the wood."

She rolled her eyes but took a deep breath, extending her hands before her, palms up.

A line formed between her brows, and her eyes shone brightly.

Suddenly, instead of sparks, pure flames of orange and yellow ignited on her upturned hands. A smile spread across her face. The glade was illuminated in bright light.

She held her palms to the wood, and even though it was damp, it lit quickly. She shook her hands and the fire disappeared. The wood crackled as the flames roared, consuming the wood.

"Not gonna lie, that was a bit impressive," I said as I handed her a canister of water and a sandwich wrapped in paper. She sat back onto the bedroll and kicked off her boots.

"It was easier than the other night. I can sense the flames under my skin more now. Not a burning, more like a constant humming presence. Like they are flowing through my veins."

I nodded and sat down beside her, leaning my back against a tree trunk.

"Thank you for today," I said.

I picked at my own sandwich. I should've been the one to save her, not the other way around. I'd never come against anyone or anything I couldn't overpower. My speed allowed me to eliminate any threat. This was a first for me. I knew the Fae that Cadoc kept close to him were strong, I'd seen their powers in action during the war, but Renwick took me completely by surprise.

Evren didn't say anything, just sat quietly with me, knee to knee, and stared into the fire. The flames cast dancing shadows across her face.

"What did he mean by my father planning to use me?" Evren wondered out loud. "I mean, I know he wanted me bonded with Renwick to help spread his control, but I feel like I'm missing a piece of the puzzle."

"I'm not sure. Do you think it has something to do with your powers growing stronger?"

"I didn't even know I had these powers. If he knew, he showed no indication." She paused. "I need to find out. Will we actually find answers in Arden Valley?"

I had no idea. I shrugged and leaned closer to her, hoping that my presence would offer her some comfort. "Aramis seems to think so."

She leaned her head on my shoulder. I brushed back her hair and kissed her temple.

That night, we slept curled into each other. Her head tucked under my chin and nestled against my neck. Her chest was pressed flush to mine. My thigh tucked between her legs and our ankles crossed. Her warmth wrapped around the two of us. Her body seemed to radiate heat, making the fire almost unnecessary.

Being in the forest again felt familiar and safe. The insects chirped, and the evergreens rustled in the nighttime breeze like a soothing lullaby.

I watched Evren sleep, her delicate lashes rested on rosy cheeks. Her skin was as pale as moonlight. I held her close, breathing her in—jasmine and honeysuckle. She was temptation in the purest form, and I wanted it to consume me whole.

THIRTY-EIGHT
EVREN

We rode another four days to the Arden Valley, stopping for more breaks than the previous days, taking our time. I grew more comfortable riding my horse and became better acquainted with Delrik. Like how he preferred the snow and that the scar on the back of his hand was from Nazneen from when he tried to steal a biscuit from her plate at breakfast. I learned the curve of his lips and the shape of his jaw. The weight of his hand resting on my leg while we rested became as familiar as my own.

    We had spent each night tucked close into each other. I had discovered that if I concentrated enough, I could emit enough heat for the both of us to not freeze. And with him near, and Renwick truly gone from this world, my nightly bad dreams had vanished. The connection between us grew stronger, but both of us were too afraid to speak of it. It was easier keeping it quiet and not risking anything.

On the fifth day of riding, we started our descent from the mountains, picking our way down the steep slopes of the switchbacks. Snow no longer covered the ground, but winter was following us. A light current whipped through the trees, and in response, the branches released their remaining leaves into the air. Reds, yellows, and golds, all floated on an unseen current of air. This far east, there were less Darkwood trees scattered in the Sacred Forest, replaced with towering elms and oaks. Birds flitted from branch to branch, twittering away at each other. Small animals skittered across the ground in search of food before the first winter snow fell. Even with the clouds rolling in threatening rain, I could see the beauty of such a place. I saw life in every nook and cranny. I understood why Delrik preferred being in nature rather than in the city. But I still needed a bathtub and bed.

My horse's hooves crunched on the fallen, browned leaves that littered the forest floor. Peace filled me, a sense of calm. All the things that had been plaguing my thoughts during the days and dreams at night ceased to be as the forest lulled me into relaxation.

On the last day of our journey, we shared my mare just to be close to one another for warmth, the other following behind. The weather had shifted for the worse, and rain was beating down on us. Our cloaks were useless against the downpour. We were both soaked to the bone, but we persevered. Delrik rode behind me, his body against mine, one arm around me gripping the reins, his other hand resting on my thigh. The rain cooled my flushed skin—flushed from having Delrik so close. It was a welcomed distraction.

I refused to think about the male behind me. I was absolutely *not* thinking about his firm chest pressed against me. I was absolutely *not* imagining his fingers traveling higher up my thigh. And I most certainly was *not* wishing he'd press his lips to the side of my neck.

As if he could hear my thoughts, I felt him start to draw slow circles with his thumb on my thigh. I took a quick look over my shoulder; his face was blank as if he didn't even realize he was doing it.

I tipped my head up to the sky and let the ping of water droplets bouncing off my face help my mind ignore the heat rising under his hand on my leg. I let out a rush of air to calm my wildly beating heart.

The thought of my powers growing stronger within me was the only thing that could distract me from those lustful impulses. Ever since the night on the balcony, I had felt the surge of magic getting stronger each day, and I couldn't ignore it any longer. Powers I thought I didn't have. Powers my father thought didn't exist or hid from me. As a child, I had always been weak. Maybe that's why my parents had kept me isolated all my life. My father was probably embarrassed at my lack of powers. Or maybe it was for a more ominous purpose. Renwick had mentioned my father using me, but for what purpose?

I needed to learn how to focus and control my newfound magic. I'd practiced summoning and extinguishing my flame every time we stopping riding. I prayed to the Powers Above that Aramis's friend in the Arden Valley had answers for my future.

Delrik leaned in, letting his warm breath on my neck bring me back to the present. I sucked in a breath as a shiver went down my spine. I felt his eyes on my face as I tried my best to ignore the yearning building deep within me, and I couldn't help but smile into the rain. I knew he was feeling a similar desire. I felt his breathing falter, and my smile grew wider. A surge of heat radiated from my body, and I felt his response in the form of his arousal grow against my backside. He traced his fingers across my stomach, barely touching me. The sensation was more decadent than chocolate.

♀

"Halt. And lay down your weapons." My shoulders stiffened, and I felt the color drain from my face at the rough, unseen voice.

I knew we could potentially run into trouble. Aramis had warned us over and over. I thought, though, after dealing with Renwick, the Powers Above would be on our side for the remainder of our journey. We were so close.

Delrik straightened to his full height in the saddle behind me to look past me, and I felt his chest rumble with...with laughter? What was happening?

"Really, Vidarr? Is that the best you have? It's the cheesiest line. You could smell us a mile off." Delrik's cheeky voice rang with friendship. I immediately relaxed, knowing we weren't in any danger, but my heart still pounded relentlessly in my chest.

Delrik jumped off the horse and moved toward the shadows. A pair of sparkling golden eyes shone into the fading dusk. A centaur stepped into the clearing—a large, dark bare chest blending into a thick bay coat. A leather strap ran across his chest with a quiver and bow strapped to his back, a long spear in his hand. His broad smile greeted us as he scooped Delrik off the ground into an embrace. The centaur towered above Delrik.

I had learned about the centaur tribes in the Arden Valley when I was younger, but I'd never met one before.

The centaurs are too proud for their own good; they're just animals. My father's voice bounced around in my head.

Although the centaurs had roamed the forest over the last thousand years, this valley held sacred powers to them. And they were willing to do anything to defend it. The Black Guard had tried several times to take the valley but failed each time, at least according to Adaris.

I was coming to realize many things that I had only read about in books. So much of the world had been hidden from me. I felt so far removed from what was real. My home had truly been a fortress to keep everything out and to keep me in. I was so small and insignificant to the expanse of the realm.

"Were you expecting us?" Delrik asked.

"The stars told me to expect a visitor. It's just a wonderful surprise that the visitor is you." Vidarr clapped a hand forcefully onto Delrik's shoulder, making him stumble a small step. His eyes were amiable and full of humor.

Delrik turned toward me, still frozen on horseback, the reins limp on the horse's neck. I'm sure I looked like a drowned rat. Delrik, on the other hand, was just as drenched but still managed to look like a warrior, all handsome and fierce.

"This is Evren Byrnes." Delrik smiled at me and gave me a wink. "Evren, this is Vidarr Fanenos."

I didn't dismount the horse. The height gave me the confidence I was lacking. Plus, I didn't trust that my quivering legs would support me. I couldn't seem to control them. I forced a smile. I didn't want to be rude, but I was intimidated by this Vidarr, no matter how well Delrik knew him.

Vidarr nodded his head in greeting, offering a kind smile, before leading Delrik down a slight slope into, what I assumed, was Arden Valley. The trees still hid most of the landscape, and with the setting sun, it was growing darker by the minute. The horses followed Delrik without hesitation, so I had no choice but to tag along too.

The trees parted, revealing the sprawling valley that opened before my eyes. The wide meadow had a stream running through the middle. Thin trails of water branched off like fingers stretching into the browned grasses blowing in a breeze. They twisted this way and that, moving as if they were breathing in the wind. My gaze swept across the golden-brown landscape as I took it all in. I followed the stream up toward the mountains to a small waterfall pouring water over the cliff feeding the stream. Round yurts of all sizes were scattered throughout the valley, some in small groups and others standing alone. The sun-bleached canvas of the yurts was stretched taut and wrapped over their wooden frames. Smoke pipes poked through the roofs, and strings of smoke puffed out in thin clouds. I spotted a young centaur child picking flowers in the field. She had a crown of the orange blossoms woven into her hair.

Vidarr led us deeper into the valley, to their tribe. When we reached the outer edge of the meadow, I swung my leg and dismounted my horse, rubbing my hand gently down its soft neck. I didn't see Delrik appear at my side but felt him tug slightly on the end of my braid.

"Ev? You coming?"

Vidarr and Delrik continued walking toward the center of the village. Sweeping peaks encircled the entire valley. I brushed my fingers through the waist-high beige fescue that lined the path, soft and damp on my fingertips from the rain. The storm clouds had passed just in time for the last of the sun's rays to turn the entire valley a rosy golden hue.

"Let's rest and have dinner." Vidarr's deep voice carried back to me.

The sun had dipped down behind the mountains, and the first stars were beginning to appear in the deepening indigo sky. Fires dotted the landscape like flickering lights. Their flames dancing in the dusk reminded me of the fireflies from the woods, and I relaxed into the peacefulness. Every place Delrik brought me proved that maybe the world wasn't all the pain and destruction that I had known it to be.

⚲

We ate smoked rabbit and roasted vegetables around a fire with spiced wine with Vidarr's family. I listened to stories of the centaur tribes and how they came to settle in the Arden Valley, living by the stars in the endless night sky. Delrik and Vidarr swapped stories from the war, some heavy, some lighthearted. They spoke about how Aramis had bridged all the territories in the realm with Cadoc during the war to create a united front and the pranks the troops would play on each other during the long years away from home to keep morale up. The centaur whose head was tipped back laughing across the fire seemed like a completely different male than the fierce warrior from the tales. Delrik was no longer the closed-off, brooding male I'd met months ago and more like the mischievous male I had come to know. There was a devious spark of playfulness in his eye as I looked over at him, and he gave me a lopsided smile.

"I wasn't sure why Aramis decided to fight alongside Cadoc, but I trusted him. But it worked out in the end. Well, until now." Vidarr paused. "Our scouts have seen more of the Black Guard recently, camping in the smaller villages. The bastards have even tried to encroach on my territory. They usually don't venture this far east."

"They've been combing the lands looking for Evren. She's Cadoc's daughter," Delrik explained.

"Ah." Vidarr mulled over the information.

"Have you heard any rumors or whispers about his plans? Aramis suggested you may be able to help."

"I haven't." Vidarr grew serious, the mood of the group shifting. "But I know someone, something, that may provide the answers you're searching for. There is an ancient creature that lives nearby that knows of dark legends. I can take you there."

Based on the look on his face, I wasn't so sure I wanted to meet this ancient creature.

"What kind of ancient creature?" Delrik asked.

Vidarr replied, "Alux is older than any creature in the realm. It's believed that she has been here since the beginning of time, but no one actually knows how she came to be."

"Alux?" I asked. "I've read about her. An ancient one that seduces her victims by conjuring visions and luring them to her with her voice. Then once she had them in her grasp, she'd peel the flesh off their bones and bathe in their blood."

"That's the very one," Vidarr confirmed.

"That sounds *exactly* like the kind of creature I want to hang out with," Delrik said, trying to ease the tension that had grown.

My grip tightened on the ceramic mug of spiced wine I was holding. I shivered at the thought of Alux, or maybe it was the chilling autumn night. I wanted answers, but seeking them from such a horrid creature didn't sound appealing. I'd been around enough darkness to last me a lifetime.

"And although she can't actually see the future, she has spiritual connections in the past, present, and future that give her unexplained knowledge."

"How do you know exactly where she is?" I asked.

"She's been trapped in the Wasted Shallows for as far back as our histories go. No one knows who banished her there or why."

Well, it looked like we were going to the Wasted Shallows.

THIRTY-NINE
DELRIK

The sun had set long ago, and plans were in place to visit Alux in a day or two. We had to prepare an offering first, in hopes that she would give us the answers we wanted.

I leaned over to Vidarr and whispered, "It's getting late. We should probably rest. We've had a long journey."

"Yes. Come, I have a place for you," Vidarr said.

I stood from the ground and offered my hand to Evren. She looked up at me through her lashes and placed her hand in mine. As we walked away from the circle of light from the glow of the fire, Evren laced her fingers through mine. My heart tightened at the familiar gesture. She drew herself closer to my side and shuddered. Our clothes were still damp from the earlier rain even after sitting beside the fire for a few hours. The night was dark, barely lit by the two crescent moons in the sky.

Vidarr showed us to a yurt tucked into the hillside, further away from the tribe's tents. I was grateful that it was further from the village for privacy. From the outside, the tanned canvas was weathered with a small circular structure with a flap for a door. It would make do for our short stay.

I pulled back the flap, holding it open for Evren to enter. The interior was larger than it appeared from the outside. A large bed sat on one side with a small table beside it. The bed was covered in thick furs and woven blankets. A mountain of pillows, more than anyone could ever need, were piled high against the headboard, which was intricately carved with mountains, trees, moons, and stars. A wood-burning stove filled the space with a comfortable warmth. After sleeping on the ground for the last few days, that bed was a welcome sight. The ceiling was a curved lattice of poles crisscrossing the cone shape.

"If you need anything, let me know. There's a washroom through there," Vidarr said, pointing to the sectioned off area. He clasped my shoulder again. "I'm happy to see you again, Delrik. It's been too long. Be sure to rest, my friend." Then he gave me a not-so-secret wink.

Vidarr bid a blushing Evren goodnight with a nod before silently slipping out. I dropped our packs to the dirt floors which were covered with panels of wood and a thick navy and cream rug. Opposite the bed sat a small table and two chairs with a lantern sitting in the middle that gave off a warm, soft glow. Evren was standing near the table and ran her hand over the smoothed surface.

I was frozen to the spot upon seeing Evren. We'd been riding for days, and yet she looked magnificent. Her legs had filled out, making her pants fit snugly over the muscular curves. The luscious flow of her hips up to waist was begging to be caressed. Her dagger clung tightly to her calf in its leather holster. The buttons of her shirt were partially undone, dipping low. Each rise of her chest was tantalizing.

She'd unlatched her thick, wool travel cloak and draped it over the nearby chair. The long sleeves of her top were rolled to her elbows, leaving her wrists exposed.

How could wrists be so beautiful? The long locks of her silver hair were pulled back in a twisted braid, tied at the end with a strip of leather. I wanted to pull the end of the tie and release the strands one by one and run my hands through the length.

She stood, wringing her hands in front of her, and I could see them shaking. She was nervous. Then she looked up at me through her dark lashes, violet eyes dancing with apprehension and lust.

"You can bathe first if you'd like." I motioned toward the washroom.

She pursed her lips and placed both hands on her hips, causing one of those seductive hips to jut out to the side. I couldn't help it as my eyes zoned in on the curves.

"Do I smell bad or something? Have *you* looked in a mirror recently?"

Damn those hips look divine.

I took a stalking step toward her, a wolfish grin on my face.

The stern expression on her face wavered. "What are you doing?" She dropped her hands and they hung loosely by her sides.

Another step.

"Stop!" Her voice was breathy, and she raised her hands in front of her.

Her mouth told me to stop, but her eyes gave her away. They dropped to my chest, then slowly took in every part of my body as I stepped closer, telling me to come closer.

Another step.

She squealed as she turned to run. I don't know why she bothered. There was nowhere she could hide. But the idea of catching her was exhilarating and heightened my desire even more.

A playful growl came from deep in my chest as I sprang like a jungle cat and sent her tumbling to the ground. I rolled her to her back and planted my knees on either side of her waist. I entwined my fingers in hers, pushing them into the rug above her head. My weight pinned her to the ground. I leaned close, barely an inch from her lips. Her eyes darted back and forth between my eyes and my mouth. I hadn't tasted that mouth since the day at the stream.

"Oh, come on, Ev. I don't smell *that* bad." I kissed the tip of her nose. "There's no need to run from me."

She shrieked again and tried to wriggle out from under me.

"Babe, do that again," I said, grinding my hips into her, mimicking her movement.

Her eyebrows shot up. "Delrik!" My name a mere gasp over her laughter.

"Fine." I rolled off her onto my back, propping my hands under my head. "Go bathe. I'll be waiting."

FORTY
EVREN

I had never felt like this before, emotions so deep, the draw to be near someone. I didn't know if I wanted to allow myself to experience feelings this intense. I knew once I opened myself to Delrik completely, I would not be able to close that door again, and that scared the hell out of me. I couldn't keep him off my mind. I couldn't stop looking at him, wanting to reach out and touch him. There was something about him, and I wanted it to fill me, body, and spirit.

  I stood in the washroom, wringing my hands again, trying to steady my breathing and trembling hands. The space was small. A copper basin sat on a wooden table, and a matching copper tub was in the middle of the room. The spring water in the tub was cool and clean. I was able to warm the water with my magic. I was almost as dirty as the day I'd arrived in Arcelia.

This time, I didn't soak in the hot water. A shelf with two fluffy towels and a fresh bar of sweet-smelling soap was tucked in the corner.

Nervous energy filled me, and I couldn't keep still. A strange new sensation settled deep in my belly, all tingly and warm. I'd never been with a male before. Thankfully, Renwick had never stolen that from me. I'd overheard the maids talking about their exploits though. I'd heard the grunting and muffled cries of pleasure through closed doors. I'd seen the books deemed inappropriate, yet, still, they somehow managed to find their way into the library. I wasn't completely in the dark. And if Delrik could make me feel so weightless and free with just the kisses and soft touches he'd gifted me with so far, I was curious how else he could make me feel. I washed quickly and scrubbed my teeth before dressing in clean clothes and slipping back into the main room.

Delrik sat at the table unlacing his boots. He stopped mid-movement when I pulled the tent flap back leading from the washroom. I stopped at my bag to grab a brush and began untangling my hair. Then I pulled it over my shoulder and loosely braided it again. Fresh linen pants flowed down the length of my legs, pooling at my feet, and a soft, sleeveless shirt clung to my still damp skin. How amazing it felt to be clean again. Delrik's gaze roamed over my body, and I clenched my legs together tightly. He must have noticed because a small primal sound came from him. He took his time looking at every inch of me. Chills trailed after his gaze, serious and quite intense. The instinct to cover myself with my arms surfaced, but I pushed it back. I didn't want to hide from him. I knew I was safe with him.

When his eyes made their way back up to mine, I could see a shadow of something in them. They were dark with want. His shirt was open at the top, exposing a glimpse of his chest. I had the urge to reach out and trace my finger along the curve of his collarbone as it dipped down his sternum.

He stood and moved a few strides closer to me with a lustful look on his face. He didn't touch me, not at first. I was so used to his quick movements that the slow, deliberate motions made my entire body twitch with eagerness. I didn't know where to look. I didn't know what to do with my hands. Silence stretched between us for a beat, time both speeding up and slowing down. He was standing before me. Then he spread his broad hands across my hips, squeezing gently, his fingers pressing into the linen.

A whimper slipped from the back of my throat. Powers Above, he wasn't even touching my skin, and I was already having trouble thinking and breathing. He leaned his forehead against mine. His eyelids fluttered closed, and his lips moved closer to mine.

He dipped his head to catch my mouth. His breath quickened as did mine, and his lips grew greedy against my mouth. He pulled my hips flush to him, and I felt a hard length pressing against my stomach. straining against the buttons holding all of him back, leaving little to be imagined. He rolled his hips against me before pressing his thigh between my legs.

My body reacted on its own, moving closer to him, my back arching. As his lips explored my face, his hands reached down to untie my freshly washed and braided hair. The soft, damp waves loosened. He sunk his hands deep into the locks, giving it a gentle tug to tip my head back so he could kiss my throat. I moaned softly as his tongue slid across my chin.

He lifted my shirt over my head, exposing my skin to the night air. He pulled his head back to take me all in, and I felt my skin prickle and my nipples harden under his stare. The side of his mouth twitched slightly. He brought his mouth lower and then his teeth tenderly grazed over my nipple, flicking the sensitive flesh with his tongue. I sucked in a breath as he moved to the other breast, his hand replacing his mouth cupping the fullness of my breast. My head dropped back, and my eyes closed in pleasure. I tangled my fingers into the thick, silky waves of his hair, holding him to me.

Powers Above, his mouth was glorious. Everything and nothing filled my head as I drank in his touch like I had been deprived water.

I longed to feel his skin on my hands. I untucked and lifted his shirt, sliding my hands along his waist and then up his back. The battle scars stretching across his skin were ridged under my fingertips. They were only a part of his story, a part of what made him who he was. And I wanted every part of him. I wanted every sadness. I wanted every scar and the ugliest memories. But I also wanted all the good and bravery and kindness. The cotton of his shirt slid smoothly over his skin as he lifted his head from my chest, standing to his full height, to pull his shirt over his head. The defined sun-kissed muscles of his stomach pressed against me. His skin was warm against mine. My fingernails scraped across his skin, leaving light red streaks in their wake. His muscles rippled under my hands, a reminder of how much strength and power lay beneath. Wetness began to spread between my legs.

He shifted his weight into me, and we walked back together, not wanting to part as he continued to lavish my breasts and neck with attention. The back of my legs hit the soft blankets of the bed, and I fell back onto the plush mattress. Delrik pulled his bottom lip into his mouth as his eyes roamed my half-naked body sprawled before him. The desire to cover myself was nonexistent now. I let him see all of me. His arousal at seeing my body was obvious now, straining. It twitched when my eyes landed on it.

He leaned over me, pressing my body further into the furs, and whispered against my mouth, "I'll be back."

With a swift kiss, he pushed off me and strode to the washroom. His eyes danced with mischief as he peered over his shoulder. He paused his stride.

And then his pants hit the floor.

He was naked!

Completely naked—in all his masculine glory. Bronzed skin. Sculpted muscles.

My breath caught in my chest, and his grin turned wicked.

Powers Above.

He winked and then disappeared into the washroom.

"Tease!" I yelled, and his laugh rang out into the air.

☥

Delrik made quick work of bathing, taking no longer than ten minutes or so. Then he was back standing before me. Lounge pants hung casually on his hips leaving his upper half exposed. I'd moved up to the head of the bed and snuggled into the down stuffed pillows but not under the blankets. His eyes were deep and dark as they stared me down from across the space, like a predator stalking its prey. And I was defenseless against him in the best way possible.

Then, that speed. In the blink of an eye, he was standing at the foot of the bed.

"Comfy?" he purred.

I wiggled deeper into the plushness. "I am."

Excitement pulsed through my veins at his nearness. He grabbed hold of my ankles and yanked me towards him. I slid from my reclined position to my back again, and he hummed with approval. My stomach flipped with excitement.

His fingers pulled at the drawstring of my pants and hooked his fingers in the waistband that held my pants on. His eyes met mine up through his lashes, waiting for permission before continuing. I nodded. As his lips curved into a thankful yet seductive smile, he slid my pants off my hips agonizingly slowly, ensuring that his fingers lingered on my skin, leaving a blazing trail. I squirmed in hopes of making him move faster, lifting my hips and then one leg at a time as he peeled the linen off my burning skin. The sight of him kneeling between my feet had my heart beating wildly.

His eyes grew darker as his hands brushed my thighs. He scooped his hands around the back of my legs and up to my behind, pressing his fingers deep into my flesh. He was still wearing his pants, but I didn't care. I just wanted his mouth on me.

As if he knew what I was wishing for, he lowered his head and pressed a kiss to my stomach, dipping his tongue into my navel. His mouth made its way up my body, licking and kissing, until his lips were on mine again. His length, still bound inside his pants, rubbed against me, sending shudders to my core. When my breath stuttered, he quirked a brow and rolled his hips into mine. I couldn't help the moan that escaped from me.

"Has anyone ever touched you, Evren?" His body hovered over mine. He dropped a kiss to my collarbone. "Touched you with passion I mean?"

Another kiss, followed by a sweep of his tongue between my breasts up my sternum.

"Never." The word came out on a shaky breath.

"Hmm," he hummed with delight. "Good. I want to be the first."

Kiss.

"And only."

Kiss.

"Forever."

Powers I wanted that too. I only wanted him. At his words, my power thrummed in my chest like it was responding to him too.

Then his fingers were touching me, their calloused roughness on my sensitive smoothness, gently trailing down my exposed skin to the junction of my thighs.

"Delrik!" I gasped as his fingers swept through my wetness.

"My Evren," he said brokenly, "you are so beautiful."

A whimper came from me as his finger stroked me again and again, circling and teasing. With each stroke against my most sensitive flesh, my insides curled tighter and tighter. My head dropped languidly to the side. He kissed the side of my neck at the same time he dipped a finger into me. I sucked in a breath at the unfamiliar invasion.

"So perfect," he purred as he watched his finger pump into me in slow rhythmic movements.

He pressed he heel of his hand against me, and I shuddered at the glorious friction. I wanted more, but I wasn't sure what I wanted more of.

"Delrik." My hips ground into his hand, craving the friction his palm gave.

"Yes, my dear?" he said. He lifted off me and dropped his head to nip at the inside of my thigh.

"Please."

The building pleasure in my belly was growing higher with each roll of hand against me.

"Please?" Another nip of his teeth, then a kiss to soothe the pain. "What do you want?"

"More."

"More?"

"Yes," my head nodding.

Then his hand was gone. My body clinched around the emptiness.

I began to protest until I saw what he was doing. He stood abruptly. He removed his pants. My eyes shot wide. I'd never seen a naked male before. Well, besides Delrik's bare ass a few minutes ago. I knew the mechanics of sex, but *that* was not going to fit inside me. His cock was thick and hard. He wrapped a hand around himself and stroked slowly while I watched in awe at the splendor that was Delrik Valhar.

Then he was back on top of me. Would I ever get used to his speed? Skin to skin, his whole body pressing down on mine. He didn't pause or wait for me to give him permission; he already knew I wanted him. My wetness beckoned him. He nudged my thighs wider and settled his hips between them. I could feel the thickness of him pressed against my opening and I grew nervous.

What if he didn't like it? What if I did something wrong? How will know...

"Whatever your thinking—"

Kiss.

"—Stop. I've got you Evren."

Kiss.

I swallowed and nodded. My eyes fluttered closed as I tried to relax.

He pushed into me just a little. I sucked in a sharp breath, and my nails dug deep into his shoulders. How the hell was this going to work?

"Relax Ev," he purred and kissed me below my ear and nuzzling into my neck, sinking further into me until he met resistance.

He groaned. The fullness and the sound of his pleasure made my inner muscles ripple with pleasure. I wanted more of him. I *needed* more of him. I couldn't get close enough to him. He held still, waiting. His arms quivered with the effort. My hips moved forward on their own accord the barest amount. My body knew exactly what it wanted and how to get it.

"This might hurt at first," he said, his voice ragged with restraint as he hovered over me.

I nodded, holding my breath. "I know."

Without further warning, he plunged into me, deep and hard. My face contorted, and I sunk my teeth into the flesh of his shoulder with the sudden sharpness. My whole body was rigid with tension.

"I'm sorry," he whispered as he showered my face with tender, unrushed kisses. Delrik remained motionless as my body acclimated to every bit of him. He swore softly under his breath as he waited for me patiently, savoring each moment.

Half pleasure, half pain. The burning slowly started to subside.

I felt him throb inside me, fighting his instinct to take me, and pleasure skittered through me. My hips rose as I pulled him tentatively closer, deeper into me. My body was trembling as he pulled out and then pushed all of himself back inside of me. The pain dulled, replaced by tightening and intensity. He wrapped one of my legs around his waist so that there was even less space between our bodies.

We moved together, slowly at first, finding our rhythm, and matching our pace. We moved faster as pressure began to build in my core. Delrik kissed across my chin and down my throat. I was riding higher and higher. I didn't know how I could take it anymore. I was going to burst at the seams.

"Delrik," I begged. I pulled him closer.

He cupped my cheek and dragged his thumb across my bottom lip. "Let go, baby. Just let go."

So, I did.

I exploded around him, my inner walls clenching around him greedily. My body shook with pleasure. I felt like I was falling, floating, and he was the only one that I wanted to catch me. My head tipped back in ecstasy, and Delrik raked his teeth against the pulse point in my neck. Then his groans of release matched mine as we unraveled together.

Our heaving breaths were ragged as he collapsed on top of me. I welcomed the weight of him, using it to bring me back down to earth.

After a moment, he rolled off me. I whined in protest, missing the feeling of him, the weight of him, but then he pulled me close to his side and wrapped his arms around me. With my back to his chest. He traced the tips of his fingers over the curves of my body as we both drifted into blissful and sated sleep.

FORTY-ONE
DELRIK

P_owers Above, this bed is the most comfortable thing I've ever slept in._

I drew Evren close to my chest and buried myself into the furs and blankets. Her silver hair spilled across her shoulders and the pillow. She smelled so wonderful, that jasmine and honeysuckle that I'd come to know so well. I nuzzled my nose into her hair, breathing her scent, now entwined with mine, filling my lungs. I wanted it imprinted on my very spirit. Her skin was so soft and smooth under my touch.

She settled deeper into me, melting into me, her warm breath and soft snores hitting my chest. She must've rolled over sometime in the night. I lay in the silence, listening to the world outside. Even in the early hours of the morning before the sun rose, the valley was a flurry of life. Crickets chirped. Bats swooping to and fro. Frogs from the stream called to each other.

Is this how Aramis felt about Calia? How my parents felt about each other? This undeniable urge to protect and comfort and cherish. I knew she didn't believe in bondmates, and if it weren't for witnessing it myself, I didn't think I would either. But the longer Evren was near me, the more I couldn't deny that there was something *more* about her. She had dragged me into her gravitational pull against my will. I gave myself up completely last night. She was now the center of my heart and spirit, and I couldn't imagine ever leaving her side. I couldn't endure it. I would rather experience death a thousand times than be separated from her ever again.

She grinned, eyes still closed. "Are you watching me sleep?"

She blinked open er eyes. We were still chest to chest. Her hand delicately grazed over the raised scars across my face and shoulder. Typically, anyone even looking at them bothered me but not Evren. She understood my scars because she had scars too. Hers were just hidden deep within. I wanted to heal those wounds, those deep scars and make sure she never felt pain like that inflicted by her father and Renwick again.

"Yes. I am watching you sleep."

She blinked drowsily.

I hadn't realized the sun had risen. I was too focused on the magnificent being in my arms. I couldn't remember the last time I'd slept so well.

"Well, that's a little creepy."

I felt her smile into my chest as she traced the line of hair down my stomach to my navel. My blood thrummed. I didn't think she knew how seductive that touch was, what it was doing to me. A low growl escaped me, and her hand froze. Then she giggled. Maybe she *did* know what she was doing.

"Naughty girl," I said as I pulled her on top of me, settling her so that she straddled my waist.

"I don't know what you're talking about." She placed an open-mouthed kiss on my shoulder followed by a playful bite before pushing herself upright. The blankets fell from her shoulder, and she was exquisitely exposed. Light filtered in from the makeshift windows of the tent and bathed her naked body in a soft yellow glow. She lifted my left arm to her mouth and kissed the inside of my wrist where my tattoos started and then trailed kisses all up my arm, back to my shoulder and across my chest, saving the last kiss for my Legion mark on my neck. Her rose-pink lips were swollen from last night.

"I find these *very* attractive, just so you know." Her voice was angelic and light.

I released another low growl. "Hmm."

It seemed that I'd opened a very interesting door completely unexplored. This was going to be fun. I sat up, pressing our chests together, and nipped at her bottom lip teasingly.

"Come on. Let's find something to eat. I'm famished. If I don't eat soon, I'll end up devouring you."

We sat in front of a morning fire, eating breakfast, and watching a group of rambunctious younglings play in the chilly water. They hid in the tall cattails, jumping out at one another in some sort of game. Their laughter flitted through the air. The stream meandered through the valley before curling and disappearing into the woods to the east. An early morning breeze rustled the grass and a piece of Evren's hair drifted across her face. The sun was warm for an autumn day, and clouds floated high across the sky. This would probably be one of the last warm days before the weather shifted.

I watched as Evren made small talk with Wren, Vidarr's bondmate, but I wasn't listening. I was trying to find a way to steal Evren away all for myself, like the selfish male I was. I wanted to spend the day just being together without being chased by deadly beasts, insane Fae, or our pasts. I wanted to spend the day kissing her and showing her, in every way, how important she was to me. I wanted to pick wild berries with her and feed them to her one by one. I wanted to dip our toes in the stream and watch her draw in her sketchpad as I rested my head in her lap.

Powers, I sounded like a lovesick youngling.

After breakfast was finally over, I led her down to the stream at a slow, leisurely pace.

"How long have you known Vidarr?" she asked me.

She was twirling a violet-blue flower in her fingers. She'd spotted the tiny trumpets outside our tent and couldn't resist plucking a few from the vines. Wren told her the morning glory flowers were a symbol of innocence and love. They were the exact color of her heavenly eyes I'd been drowning in since day one.

"We met during the war. He wasn't the tribal leader at the time. It was passed on to him when the old leader was killed during a battle. He was younger than most leaders but stepped up when he was most needed. After the war, he'd brought the tribe here to the Arden Valley, and they've been here ever since."

She stopped walking and looked at the sky, spinning in a circle. "It's beautiful here. I can see why they stay."

"It's the best place in all Illoterra to see the stars."

She side eyed me and cocked a brow.

I said, bumping my shoulder into her playfully, "Well, not right now. I meant at night."

"It's almost as beautiful as Arcelia," she mused. "You prefer the mountains, though, don't you?"

"I don't care where I am as long as you are there too," I said.

Her violet eyes suddenly met mine, and she blessed me with the most gorgeous smile this world has even seen.

Shit. She has captured me. And I don't even want to escape from her grasp.

She swished her hips as she walked away, teasing me. My heart nearly stumbled as she bent over and picked up a smooth pebble and tossed it lazily into the stream. Her hair blew in the breeze—wild, free, and unbound. She brushed an errant wisp from her eyes as she stood. She had a grace about her that reminded me of a bird soaring through the air, an elegant creature full of strength and beauty.

Then, in a breath, she disappeared from sight.

"Evren?" My heart stopped dead, and fear nearly knocked the wind out of my chest. "Evren!"

I moved to where she had just been, my feet moving fast. Too fast. I tripped on something and came crashing down toward the ground and landed right on top of Evren. Her laughter rang through the air. Her hair fanned out in a silver arch around her head.

Laying in the tall grasses, hidden from view, everything was gleaming in the sun. She rolled on top of me, settling between my legs. Her mouth claimed mine—soft and sweet. Her hands delved into my hair, and her tongue swept in to explore my mouth. She tasted like honey from our breakfast, and I moaned into her mouth.

I held her close, squeezing her waist. When we parted, she looked down at me with such joy.

Then I slapped my hand on her butt. "You, my dear, have a great ass."

Her eyes popped wide, then crinkled in the corners as she laughed. What an exquisite, bewitching sound.

FORTY-TWO
EVREN

The night air bit my skin. I was settled between Delrik's knees and against his chest. With a blanket wrapped around us, my power kept us both cozy as the autumn day gave way to an almost wintry night. Vidarr had invited us to dine with his family again. The fire was now just glowing embers. The sky above was painted with stars. I knew the stars above were the same as the ones in Arcelia, but I couldn't help think there was something different about tonight's sky.

Delrik ran his fingers through my hair. When he reached the ends, he picked up a curling wave and wrapped it around his fingers. When he saw me watching, he gave the curl a playful tug, before leaning down and kissing my shoulder. After an evening of passion and a day's worth of teasing, I was wound up, aroused and flustered and wanting to give in to the building tension.

"I see the harmony of the cosmos has poured some of its tranquility out for you," Vidarr said with a sidelong glance at Delrik.

His bondmate, Wren, smacked his shoulder. "Vidarr Fanenos! Don't pick on them."

"I'm just saying. The Powers Above have a plan for these two. I know you can sense it, Wren."

"Pardon my bondmate, he doesn't know when to keep his thoughts to himself," Wren apologized.

The pair were nestled against each other, their long legs tucked beneath them. Vidarr was running a finger across Wren's shoulders and looking longingly at her. Their sleek coats glowed in the starlight.

"Oh, that's ok," I said, waving my hand through the air. "I know all that stuff about fates and bondmates isn't real. Just some nursery stories for little ones."

Hush descended around the circle, and I suddenly felt nervous. The cup I'd been sipping paused halfway to my mouth.

Shit. I didn't know all the customs of the centaurs. Had I said something insulting?

One of the young centaurs snickered behind his hands.

It was Wren that finally broke the awkwardness. "Oh, hon. That's not true. Bondmates are most definitely a real thing." She looked up at

Vidarr and cupped his face lovingly. "Otherwise, I would've gotten rid of this brute ages ago."

My mouth went dry. "But...um...my father said it was just a myth. A story." I sat up, turning around, and looked over my shoulder to Delrik, searching for confirmation.

His small smile made me aware of how foolish I'd been for believing anything my father said to be true. Heavy embarrassment filled me. I wanted to hide under a rock until daybreak. The way everyone was looking at me made me feel even more pathetic than ever. He kissed my forehead as if to reassure me.

"I've seen it. Bondmates. It's real Ev," he said gently. "First with my parents, and then with Aramis and Calia."

I thought about it. I'd seen Aramis and Calia and how they revolved around each other. "How do you know if someone is your bondmate?"

Wren was the one that answered me. "The tie between bondmates...it's a deep connection, a gift from the gods. It goes beyond love, beyond lust. It's about unwavering trust and respect; about shared lives and magic. A gift to bind two forever in life and death."

I was confused. "Then how would Renwick have been my bondmate?"

"He wasn't. No matter what your father told you." Delrik's eyes darted up to Vidarr's. "However, there is a ritual, a blood ritual, that is done between bondmates to bind them together in body, spirit, and magic to make them stronger." He tucked a piece of hair behind my ear. "Maybe your father thought that the blood ritual would bind you and Renwick together. And if he knew about your powers, he may have believed Renwick would have access to your powers."

"I didn't know the blood ritual would mean I would share my powers. Would that have even worked if it weren't the fated by the gods?"

"I don't know, but that's one thing I want to ask Alux. And your powers are only shared if you want. It's not like they are divided equally or anything. It's the ultimate act of trust to share your powers with your bondmate," Delrik said.

I turned to Wren. "Did you two do the blood ritual?"

She shook her head. "No. Centaurs don't have magic like the Fae do. Our gifts come from the stars."

I simply nodded and toyed with a piece of my hair. This was a lot of new information, and I wasn't sure how to handle it. I hated feeling so helpless and ignorant about my own life.

Delrik turned to Vidarr. "Speaking of Alux, can I help you set the trap tonight?"

"What trap?" I asked.

"We need to bring Alux an offering. So, we are going to trap an osomal," Vidarr explained.

I nearly jumped out of Delrik's grasp, but he grabbed ahold of my waist before I could get anywhere.

"Are you crazy! The last one almost killed us."

"Only crazy for you," was his response. So cocky. "And that one took me by surprise. We are the ones setting the trap this time, not the other way around. Plus, the more dangerous and deadly the creature, the more willing Alux is to part with information."

He was insane. And he was going to get himself killed.

"She does have very refined tastes." Vidarr winked, then nudged Delrik.

I just rolled my eyes. They were so childish.

"One of my scouts located a den not too far from here," Vidarr said.

"I want to go with you." I turned around in Delrik's arms to see him face to face.

His mood shifted so quickly. "No, it isn't safe. I won't put you in the path of another osomal," Delrik said.

"But I can protect myself. Protect *you* with my powers," I said as I waggled my fingers in front of my face.

"I'll be fine, I promise," he said, smoothing back my hair and kissing me. I blushed and darted my eyes to the other pair sitting across from us. "I also don't want you to accidentally burn my eyebrows off."

I pinned him with a stern look before settling back into his chest. I wrapped the blanket tight around me with a huff even though I wasn't cold at all. He had a point. I had no idea how to target my powers. I was still learning to summon them when I wanted. "Fine."

"Then we will leave around midday tomorrow after we have the osomal," Vidarr said.

☥

I paced back and forth in front of our bed the entire time Delrik was gone with Vidarr. Knowing he was potentially coming face to face with another osomal made it impossible to sit still.

I tried to distract myself from what tomorrow would bring. While I was ready to get answers, I was also not mentally prepared for the impending bad news that I felt looming over me like a bad storm. I didn't want to have any regrets. I didn't want to waste time on things that didn't matter. I wanted to spend time with those I loved. I was tired of living my life according to the will of others.

When I tired of pacing, I practiced my magic by summoning floating balls of fire while sitting cross legged on the floor and then smothering them out between my hands. I studied the majestic glowing orange and golden flames, rotating the flames to see them from all angles. I wanted to learn every aspect of this divine, yet dangerous power.

When Delrik finally returned, he swept me into his arms. And like he could read my mind, Delrik said, "Whatever comes tomorrow, we can face it together."

He wrapped me tight in the safety of his arms and poured everything into a kiss that shook me to the core. And for the first time in my life, I felt hopeful for the future. It was at that moment that he became the center of my world.

FORTY-THREE
DELRIK

Anticipation gnawed at my insides as we moved deeper and deeper into the woods and further into the mountains. The dense branches tangled above our heads. It was midday, but there was hardly any light filtering through the crowded birch trees. The bark of the trees was cracked and peeling, like skin sluffing off a corpse with russet pulp seeping through the cracks.

Back in the valley, the sun had been shining when we set out, but snow blanketed the earth here. As if they knew of some impending danger, the birds and insects had become silent, and the whole forest stood still. A layer of ice encrusted pale branches above, making the trees sag with heaviness.

I sensed Evren's nervousness. She'd tossed and turned most of the night, murmuring in her short bursts of sleep. I disliked that I couldn't have control over the dreams that haunted her. I'd take them from her if I could. That's why I had wanted to ask Vidarr for specifics about the osomal without her nearby.

I shivered from the memory of slaying the beast. Vidarr had set a trap early this morning to capture the offering. When the osomal was lured in, we knew it needed to be killed. Not just for Alux, but for the safety of the village. I'd helped him cut it to pieces, not feeling guilty about killing it this time. The beast's body would be used to feed the tribe. No part of the animal would be wasted. Alux would be given its head. Vidarr had thanked the Powers Above for the provision and safety.

♀

"Do you trust this Alux creature to tell the truth?" I asked Vidarr as we moved through the forest south of the tribe.

"Though she is known to deceive her victims, we will bring a gift. The offering will encourage her to be truthful," Vidarr replied.

"I feel like this has all been my fault." I hung my head between my shoulders. If it hadn't been for me, she'd probably be nestled in a quiet village. Her father would have looked, of course, but I doubt he would've found her. I'd come to realize how cunning she truly was. And if her brother was planning to meet up with her, he probably would have done a much better job at keeping her safe.

"Cadoc would have found her. You know that. He has his ways. It's better that you found her when you did." He laughed to himself. *"Though if she had her powers, she probably would've set you on fire."* His sense of humor was an acquired taste.

He's right—she would have set me on fire and danced around my burning body.

"You're awfully comedic this evening," I pointed out.

"I can't wait to capture this bastard. He's been stalking our livestock for weeks. And this is the perfect reason to end him." He paused briefly.

"You must forgive yourself and move on. Clearly, she has," Vidarr said to me patting my shoulder.

I sighed. I knew he was right. I had started to believe that there could be something more for me. But the longer I was separated from Evren, the more my doubt grew. Not doubt in her, but in myself. How could I be with her if I couldn't even protect her? Renwick overpowered me so quickly. If it hadn't been for her, I could be dead. Now we had to deal with Alux and whatever outcomes she foresees. I knew I was unworthy of such a marvelous creature.

☥

Evren must have realized my thoughts had drifted because she squeezed my hand tightly until I made eye contact. Her brows were drawn together with uncertainty, questioning my thoughts. I brought her hand to my mouth and pressed her open palm to my lips. With that simple movement, I could see her shoulders relax a little. My body followed suit, as if we were one. If she stayed by my side even knowing my weaknesses and my past, then I would have a true chance at happiness in this life. *We* had a chance at happiness. My whole being was enchanted by her, no matter how much I was undeserving.

My body was still reeling from the past few days. Flashes of Evren's back arched in pleasure streaked through my mind, her lips parted in a sigh and her hair tousled from our many joinings.

Vidarr silently led us through the trees. The snow muffled the sounds of our feet. Our tracks were the only evidence of our presence. The air grew heavy, and the light dimmed with each step we took.

"The Wasted Shallows is only a mile ahead," he said over his shoulder to me.

Vidarr had the head of the osomal strapped to his shoulders. Evren had kept her eyes diverted from the decapitated beast for the entire hike so far. Its hollow eyes, though dead, seemed to track her every movement, sensing her, drawn to the power swelling within her. And in response, her elemental flame was on alert. I could feel its power.

The stillness was eerie, and I couldn't stop the fear that was creeping in. Dark shadows shifting through the trees caught my eye, but when I turned to look, they were gone. Or had they even been there? I love the forest, but this place…this place was a dead space where no living being could survive.

The closer we got to the lake, the colder the air became, like the warmth was being sucked from the world. Noxious sulfur filled the air. We broke through the trees to see a lake. Pale shards were scattered across the frozen ground. Shards of bone. The Wasted Shallows wasn't frozen over, but ice skirted around its edges. It stretched out in tendrils toward the center of the lake. The water was opaque and as dark as obsidian. A mist hovered above the surface of the water and at the bases of the surrounding trees, making it difficult to see if anything were to attack us. We were completely exposed and vulnerable. I didn't like it one bit.

A short, hooded figure emerged from the air itself, floating above the center of the lake. It moved slowly, almost painfully, walking on an invisible surface above the water like it were solid, its back hunched and with a staggering gait. It couldn't have been taller than four feet. Its faded, tattered cloak hung loosely on the lithe body and billowed behind it as it moved, almost like smoke and shadow. Ice followed in its wake, making crackling sounds as it spread.

I looked over at Vidarr with furrowed brows. He even had a touch of uncertainty on his face, and his hand was poised on the hilt of his sword. I mimicked him and kept Silverlight within easy reach. I flexed the muscles in my legs in preparation to lunge if necessary.

The figure stopped walking several feet away, just out of reach of my sword.

"Alux," Vidarr said in greeting. He slung the heavy osomal head off his back and dropped it at the edge of the water. "An offering."

The dark creature gave a slight nod but didn't speak a word. Her body, instead, turned toward Evren as if she was the only person standing on the edge of the lake worthy of her time.

The sound that came from beneath the hood set my hair on edge. It wasn't really a voice. The ancient hollow intonation overlapped with a child's high-pitched ring. Too ancient. Too all-seeing. And yet, musically sweet and hypnotizing. This was how she lured in her prey. Terror rippled up my spine, and the fine hairs on the back of my neck stood up.

"I know who you are. I've seen you, girl. I have been waiting for you. I knew you would come eventually."

The figure took another hobbling step closer to Evren.

"I felt you come into this world, growing stronger with each day. At least until your seventh year. Seven years after your birth your power halted and...disappeared. Not completely. I could still taste it, but it was muted, almost nonexistent. But now, here you are, more powerful than *I* even predicted."

The hooded head gave Evren a slight bow in respect. Though, to me, it didn't seem that the creature showed anyone respect. I couldn't contain the protective snarl that curled from deep within me. I stepped a fraction closer to Evren.

"Ah! I see you found your bondmate as well. He smells divine." She dragged in a slow, elongated breath, as if she could taste the air. I could hear the hunger in her rattled breath; practically feel her teeth wanting to bite.

"How do you know who I am? What do you mean 'grow stronger'?" Evren questioned, taking a step away from the hooded being. It took everything in me not to wrap my arms around her, pull her into me, and protect her from Alux.

A small giggle came from under the hood. Like a child. The sounds made my spine straighten, like when you hear a sword scrape a stone. "You're telling me you haven't felt the power growing inside you?"

Evren, confused, took another step back, closer to me. This time, I reached for her, not quite grabbing the back of her shirt.

"How about I show you," Alux replied.

I didn't know what Alux meant, but I knew I didn't want to find out. I wanted to turn and leave as fast as possible. We'd find another way to find out about Evren's elemental magic. The creature took another fragile, hunched step closer.

Gnarled hands appeared from under the shadows of the tattered robes. Long, spindle-like fingers lifted the hood back, revealing a child.

A child?

The young girl before me looked no more than fourteen. That was no child though. Her face was smooth and plump, so unlike her withered hands and decaying body. Golden, blonde hair swept down her back in long curling waves. A twisted crown of bone sat snuggly on her head, and an amulet of pure darkness rested in the center of her forehead. Her beauty was captivating. I could see how she could persuade her prey to walk right into her grasp.

The only thing distinguishing her from a beautiful, young girl was her eyes—empty, endless voids of black.

She smiled with her delicate, child-like mouth and tipped her head to the side like a curious feline. Then she opened her hands, and summoned darkness.

PART FOUR

FORTY-FOUR
EVREN

Darkness engulfed us, like a shadow that unfurled around our bodies, concealing Alux from view, and deadening every sound. It quickly spread as it surrounded our feet holding us in place. It worked its way up our legs until we could no longer see the lake or woods around us. A disembodied laughter swarmed my senses as it grew darker. The scent of mud and decay wafted from the stagnant water, filling my nose. I coughed at the thick, suffocating musk. I reached out a hand to touch it, but there was only air. My pulse pounded in my ears. I could see the silhouettes of Vidarr and Delrik standing beside me but that was all. Delrik slid a reassuring, protective hand around my waist.

Then the shadows whispered my name.
Evren.

A noiseless hiss. My mouth went dry. Could Delrik hear them too?

The creeping umbra drew me deeper, and a voice of darkness murmured deep into my spirit, beckoning me to step closer to see. Without realizing it, I stepped forward into the yawning gloom. Delrik's hand tightened on my hip, not letting me get too far from him. Then a vision played out in front of my eyes. The shapes were so lifelike I was tempted to reach out and touch them. The apparitions poured over me and penetrated my very being. I felt it in every fiber of my body.

The ancient one spoke:

"A long, long time ago before time even existed, the Powers Above reigned overall. They created creatures of all manner, including the gifted High Fae, and let them wander the realm."

As she spoke, images appeared from within the smoke, playing out the history of our lands.

"Centuries passed without war and strife. But there were those that were displeased that only the High Fae were offered the strength of the gods powers. They called themselves The Guild. They revolted, gathering all their lesser powers together to create The Great Chaos in the world. They released evil creatures into the realm to throw off the balance between dark and light. The Chaos didn't care who was powerful or not, who was rich or poor. Its only desire was to claim as many lives as possible to feed itself. The gods fought against the evil and used ancient spells and enchantments to contain the dark magic to the circle of dark hells. The evil creatures that the Great Chaos created were gathered and confined to Rochris Islands. The Powers Above hunted down all the members of the Guild and their supporters. They killed them and trapped their souls within the Darkwood trees of the Sacred Forest.

All but one. The sole surviving Fae secluded himself for centuries, causing him to become even more deranged and mad.

"One day, a High Fae couple crossed paths with the one surviving Guild member while traveling across their kingdom. Instead of devouring the couple alive, they begged the Guild Fae to let them pass and made a bargain. The High Fae couple promised their firstborn child in exchange for their safety.

"When they finally had a daughter years later, they had forgotten the bargain. The Guild member bided his time, waiting for their daughter to mature into her High Fae powers, wanting to take her at her strongest.

"On the twenty-fifth year after her birth, he retaliated with a curse and cashed in on his bargain. Their daughter was condemned with the supreme elemental power of fire. The fire magic overwhelmed her, and she burst into an eternal flame. No healer in the realm could save her. She fought against the curse, but in the end, the eternal flame consumed her, body and spirit, and she was no more.

"The Guild member warned that due to their betrayal, all females born into the family would forever be cursed with the eternal flame. Generation after generation, only male offspring were born into the bloodline. Only one female was born during those years. As a precaution, the patriarch had her killed to hide the shame of the curse.

"Time passed, and it was believed that the fire-cursed bloodline was lost. However, soon after the War Across the Sea began, I felt a shift in the realm, an imbalance of dark and light. A child was born of the ancient bloodline. A female child. Almost twenty-five years ago."

The darkness faded away, and the lake reappeared in front of us, and Alux stood before me. Her empty blackened eyes bore into my soul. I shook my head in disbelief. She couldn't mean me. I had studied the bloodline of my family. Nowhere in the library or genealogy texts held in the temples did it tell of a curse on my family. There were no females born into the Byrnes Bloodline, only males.

Until me.

A wicked smile stretched across her youthful face like she could hear my thoughts. Unease gripped me. Of course, there wouldn't be proof of children being murdered. There wouldn't be proof of a shameful curse. Father had been enraged when he found out I existed. His daughter. The first female of the Byrnes Bloodlines in generations. He hated me. He hid me away. But if the curse would eventually kill me, why had he kept me alive?

"Am I that child?" Terror shook my voice. I knew the answer before I even finished the question.

Alux simply curled her full, pink lips into a wry grin. Her face held all the confirmation I needed. The truth weighed heavy as stone on my shoulders.

The darkness swirled around us once again, faster this time, and a new vision came before us.

A vision of the future. A vision of *my* future.

Alux's voice spoke into the shadows, and my father materialized before me. "Cadoc will use a blood binding ritual when he selects the ideal male for you. The blood ritual will give your bonded access to your power, thus giving your father access to it. You, my dear, will be used as a weapon that will burn this realm to ash." Bloodlust flashed on her face. "That is, if he can figure out how to prevent the eternal flame from consuming you first."

Fire and smoke and death surged around me in the shadows, images that would forever haunt me. My whole life had been a lie. I would either die in an eternal flame or I would have my power wielded as a weapon, leaving me where? Imprisoned and bonded to who? I had killed Renwick. Would Father just replace him with another one of his lackeys? My mind grew fuzzy and it had nothing to do with the shadows.

I didn't want to hear anymore. I just wanted to forget, but I couldn't forget. I couldn't unsee what Alux showed me. I couldn't stand it any longer. So, I turned and started to walk away. Away from the dark shadows and into the mist of the birch forest. Delrik tried to grab my wrist to stop me, but I ripped my arm away from his grasp.

My feet struggled in the snow, but I pushed faster and faster. The cracked bark on the trees became a blur. Pieces of ice snapped off breaking branches as I pushed them aside. The bitter cold stung my face and eyes. I did the only thing my body could do. I ran—away from that creature, away from the vision, away from the future that I knew, without a doubt, would come true.

FORTY-FIVE
EVREN

I ran until my legs couldn't stand it anymore. I caught myself on a birch tree, hands slamming into the cracked, white trunk. Warm blood dripped from the slices, but I didn't feel the pain.

I gulped giant breaths of air but still couldn't breathe. My fingers moved to my throat, trying to remove the invisible hands squeezing. My throat constricted, choking off the oxygen I desperately needed. My lungs were burning despite the heavy rise and fall of my chest. My heart was pounding in my chest, ears, and stomach. If I had anything in my stomach, I would have heaved it onto the forest floor.

My legs shook, unable to keep me standing for one second longer. I collapsed to the ground as my knees gave out, and leaves and twigs snapped as I hit the earth. The snow melted against my hot skin and soaked into my pants, but I didn't feel the cold. My attempts to refill my lungs with air were useless. Defeat hung like a cloud over me, that sense of hopelessness. The air was thick and quiet against the hectic flurry of visions dancing in my head.

Finally, the tears came, and shaking began to wrack my body. Silent sobs released the pressure that had built up in my throat. My chest still burned from the effort of taking a single breath. I had tried so hard to escape from the control, escape from the pain, but I could never get away. This power would control me; it would consume me and, ultimately, destroy me. And if it didn't destroy me, if somehow my father was able to harness these powers, I would forever be his prisoner.

I knew that he would do anything to drain every ounce of my magic from me, and when he was done, he'd dispose of me. I'd seen him do it with other Fae, powerful Fae. He befriended them and used them until it no longer benefited him. Then they'd disappear forever. And I was no different.

A twig snapped and my head jerked up to see Delrik moving slowly toward me, hands raised in front of him like I was a wounded animal that would flee at any moment.

"No," I mouthed, but no sound came out. "I...I...I...I can't." I dug my hands into my hair, pulling at the roots. Anything to take away the unceasing reality of my future.

He stepped over fallen branches, and his boots crunched on icy leaves with each step closer. I couldn't pull him into this darkness. I couldn't destroy him with me. I shook my head at his advances, trying to step away, forgetting that I was already on the ground.

I felt empty, hollow, inside. He didn't deserve this despair. It was like we were on opposite sides of the world. A gaping hole swallowing up everything stretched between us, and I couldn't get to him without drowning him too. I was damaged beyond repair.

I didn't fit into this world. I was simply raised to be used as a weapon. That was my fate. Not Delrik.

He stepped closer to me. I wished the earth would swallow me right then, right there. I turned my face away, ashamed of the uncontrollable torrent of tears. They were proof of my weakness. I had been weak all my life, but now my weakness was going to ruin another. It would ruin someone I'd grown to cherish. My bondmate. I couldn't let my powers harm Delrik or my death be another one added to his long list of sorrows.

The tears dripped from my cheek, the fresh cuts stinging as they flowed along the curves of my face and off my nose before hitting the ground. They left streaks on my face as they washed away the grime that coated me. I hung my head, my hands in my lap. A single tear landed on my hand, and it sizzled before turning to steam in the wintry air. Delrik's gentle fingers hooked under my chin and tipped it up to look into my eyes. He framed my face with his broad hands. Tears continued to stream freely. Tears of knowing that my father was going to sell me to the highest bidder and steal my powers and imprison me. Tears of hopelessness. Tears of despair.

FORTY-SIX
DELRIK

As soon as Evren turned to run, Alux disappeared back into the endless depths of the lake, the osomal head also gone. She had given us the answers we needed, even if they weren't the ones we wanted to hear. I followed Evren but kept my distance. I knew she needed time. Time to process everything she'd seen, everything I'd seen, but I needed to comfort her. I needed her to know she wouldn't face this alone. I pushed away what Alux had said about her magic consuming her. I couldn't think about that now.

I found her kneeling in the snow and dirt, shoulders slumped in misery. The memory of her the first day I found her flashed in my mind. Defeat. Agonizing defeat.

There was this heaviness around her, more than before, hanging in the air. I made my way to her, slowly. I bent down on my knees in the soft snow in front of her, pulling her hands from her face, tucking my chin to look into her eyes. Her eyes used to have such life in them. Now they were muted and dull. That sparkle had been extinguished, and it was like a knife to my heart.

I clung to her in a desperate attempt to provide any relief I could. I knew it was nothing. Nothing I did would ever comfort her or take away her pain, but I would try. I pulled at the tether binding our souls together, praying to the Powers I could keep her from falling into the recesses of her mind.

I drew her face closer to mine and lightly pressed my lips to hers. She didn't respond at first. Her blank stare passed through me like I wasn't even there. Another kiss, and still just a vacant look on her face.

"Please Evren, come back to me," I pleaded, my voice cracking. "Please."

I kissed her a third time.

Her shoulders sagged, and her chin relaxed into my hands. I wasn't sure if I had made the right decision in kissing her until she slowly parted her mouth, offering herself to me. My tongue swept in, claiming her as my own, reassuring her that I was there with her, that she wasn't alone anymore. She would never be alone again.

"There you are." I kissed the tears off her cheeks before pulling back to see her.

We knelt in the forest together, knees touching; and our foreheads pressed together. Snow began to fall in fluffy flakes around us, but a bare circle of earth surrounded us from Evren's magic melting the snow. Her magic was protecting us from the cold. It was a living entity thriving inside her, and we'd figure out together how to let Evren and the flames live together in harmony.

I offered a hand to her, silently urging. She gave me a small nod, and we rose, hand in hand. Without any words, I slowly led her back to the valley away from Alux and the knowledge we'd just learned. I couldn't see Vidarr behind us, but I knew he followed, watching for unseen dangers that lurked near the shallows.

With the small contact of her fingers, longing hummed throughout my entire body. It wasn't a physical longing. It wasn't a wild lust. It was something new, an urgency that went much deeper than lust. I would never leave her side again. I would stand by her and fight with her to change her future. I didn't realize I wanted something like this for myself until she showed me what I was missing. And her touch just reaffirmed that she was what I'd been waiting for my entire life. And I would do anything to save her. Anything.

FORTY-SEVEN
EVREN

"What will make you happy?" Delrik asked. We were tucked in bed, our bodies fatigued from the day, but we found comfort in the presence of each other. His arm was draped over my bare hip. His calloused fingers traced small circles across my smooth skin. My head rested on the plush, feather pillow, Delrik facing me. His dark eyes were hooded with seriousness.

I was taken aback by the question. I had never truly considered it. The only time I'd ever done anything with the intent of making myself happy was running away from home. And running from my father and Renwick was for survival than to make myself happy. Further than that, I had no plan for the future. If Renwick didn't eventually kill me, the ever-closing walls around me would have. I didn't know how my mother withstood the isolation of our home. She was as much a prisoner as I had been. No wonder she was a shell of a female now.

A piece of wood cracked in the stove heating our yurt. I leaned in and kissed his shoulder, more for my own comfort than anything. The warmth of his skin under my lips and his woody smell grounded me. I focused on the hope that bubbled in my chest. I've never felt safe with anyone, except Adaris. That has all changed now. I didn't know yet how I would remove these elemental powers from me, but I knew Delrik would be by my side.

I scooted closer and nestled myself into his chest, needing his closeness. His closeness prevented me from overthinking. He was a lifeline securing me to this world and kept me from spiraling. I trailed my finger down the planes of his chest. I traced the snarling mountain cat inked into his pectoral, lost in thought.

"Ev?"

I forgot he'd asked me a question.

"I'm not sure," I finally replied.

Exhaustion washed over me, bearing down. I knew what I had to do. I had to go back. I sat up abruptly.

"I have to go back," I said.

"What?"

"I have to go back."

"Go back? Go back where? To Rivamir?"

"Alux knows more than she told us. She must."

I threw the covers off and jumped out of the bed.

"Evren, you can't just go back." He sat up, the blankets pooling at his hip.

"Yes, I can. And I will. Right now." I pulled on my pants and shirt and stood with my hands on my hips facing Delrik. "I refuse to accept that I am fated for a death by flames. I refuse to be a pawn to anyone anymore. Not even the grand plan of the gods and fate."

I sighed, walked over to him, and sat on the edge of the bed. I pulled a pillow to my lap and picked at a tassel on its corner.

"I have never once in my life had control. I've always been told what to do, where to go, who to be with. I am reclaiming my life, starting with you. I'm choosing you." I pressed a kiss to his stunned lips. "And if that means I have to go back to Alux and demand answers so I can survive, I will." I brushed the back of my fingers lightly over his cheek.

His face softened into my hand, and his eyes scanned my face. "Okay. Then I'll go with you."

♀

I didn't falter as we returned to the Wasted Shallows. My steps were sure and confident. I didn't slow my pace as we got closer to the gloom and darkness. When the murky water came into view, I pushed through the last line of birch trees and into the waiting mist. Delrik stood at my side and held my hand tight.

"Alux!" I called out through the coldness.

Silence.

"Alux, I have more questions."

Still silence.

"I know you can hear me." Anger lurked under the surface of my words.

A sudden sharp gust of wind whipped through the air. Delrik suddenly released my hand and groped at his throat. He gasped and dropped to his knees.

"Delrik!"

I collapsed next to him, searching for whatever was attacking him. Horror shot through me, and my heart pounded in my ears when I noticed thick vine-like shadows wrapped around his neck and clawing their way into his mouth. Black lines veined out from his mouth, eyes, and nose like cracks in his skin.

The same cold, dead chortle from before curled around me like a house cat. "I see you came back. Foolish girl."

"Let him go!" I spun around on my knees, but Alux was nowhere to be seen, just her harsh voice wrapping all around me, coming from every direction. The ice-covered trees caused my scream to echo over and over.

"Now why would I do that?"

I couldn't stop the shudder that crept down my spine as if those long spindly fingers were biting into my skin.

"Please!" I wailed. I clutched at Delrik's face. "Please!"

Delrik's eyes suddenly went wide with terror as he looked over my shoulder. I followed his line of sight. Alux hoovered a foot from me. Her precious, angelic face peered down at me from above. Her head was cocked to the side in such an innocent and peculiar way. Her beauty was almost unnatural. Her hair draped over her shoulder in a golden sheet that reminded me of the sun-kissed grasses in the valley. The temperature dropped and ice formed, a thick layer along the ground around us. Her shadows hovered innocently over her shoulders like their extensions weren't currently strangling the life from my bondmate.

"You didn't bring me a present this time." Her voice was hypnotic. Her mouth tipped into a disappointed pout, her bottom lip poking out. "So, I figured your bondmate would do as a nice replacement."

She bent, reaching past me to Delrik, and curled a boney finger under his chin. Her cloak slipped up her arm exposing withered, decaying skin that was so transparent I could see the bone underneath. I pulled away from the stench.

Delrik's lips were now a dull ice blue. I lunged for the hem of her cloak. The tattered fabric disintegrated in my fists. It smelled of mildew, sweat, and death.

"I'll do anything! Please, just don't hurt him."

"But he smells so delectable." She stretched out the word. Her tongue darted out of her mouth like a snake as if she could taste him already. "Even with the human blood polluting his veins. Humans aren't as delicious as Fae. That odd tang of metal salt. But humans tend to scream more which I do love." Her eyes flared with delight with each word.

My stomach roiled, aware of the shards of bone scattered around us.

"Alux please! Anything." I couldn't hold back the plea.

"Fine." She waved her hand through the air in exasperation, and Delrik dropped down to his hands and knees, breathing heavily. "Though you're ruining all my fun."

"Evren, don't." His voice was raw, rasping. "We can't trust her."

"You should listen to your bondmate, girl." Her face had returned to that serene child, her deep pools of solid ebony eyes drawing me in. What was this creature, and how did she ever come into being?

"I won't let you harm him," I bellowed at her, sparks flying from my hands and smoldering out in the ice and snow.

The power rising higher and higher in my blood was intoxicating. It skittered across my skin like lightning across the sky. I wanted to lose control and let it consume me just so I could make Alux pay for laying her hands, or shadows, on Delrik, but I was afraid of that eternal flame. Instead, I put my body between her and Delrik and pushed the power back down.

Alux unhurriedly batted at the glowing embers that landed on her cloak. "Calm down, deary. You're going to burn down my forest. I have no intention of eating him." A sly look spread on her face. "Not today at least. As long as you help me."

I eyed her suspiciously. What could I possibly do for her?

"Help you with what," I asked wearily.

Alux drifted in a circle, a beast hunting her prey, her rotting hands folded within her cloak. "Something was stolen from me a longtime ago, and I need you to find it."

"We don't have time to..."

Alux cut me off. "*If* you succeed in finding what was stolen from me, then I will tell you how to save yourself."

I paused. So, she did know a way for me to survive the fire curse. My heart fluttered with the possibility of a future, but I needed to focus.

"But...if you fail," she said as she reached out a withered hand to Delrik again.

"Wait! I haven't agreed to anything." I screamed, but it was too late.

Delrik's head snapped back, and his arms splayed wide. His mouth was pried open by an unknown force, and a scream worse than death itself came from him. Black, swirling shadows dripped from Alux's extended hand. Shadows crawled through the air like serpents. These were different than before, thick and oily. They slithered across the frozen ground. When the encroaching darkness reached Delrik, it climbed up his body and poured down his throat, stifling the unearthly sound. Then, just as fast as it started, it was over. Delrik lay on the ground again. His body was weak from the invasion, and his breathing was shallow. But he was still alive.

"What did you do to him?" I asked as I cradled his head in my lap. He'd turned pale, and his skin was clammy.

"If you fail or betray me in any way, I will give you to Cadoc myself and let the elemental fire consume you. And your bondmate here,"—She pointed a finger down at Delrik,—"will be consumed by the shadows I've gifted him. You have nine days to return."

I turned back to Delrik and saw the skin of his upturned right palm was charred black, dark as onyx, as if he had laid his hand on a branding iron. I picked up his hand and brushed my thumb over the darkness that stained his flesh. It was cold, so unlike the rest of his body, but smooth to the touch. The shadows slithered in constant motion like they were trying to break through the barrier containing them.

Alux left me with no choice. I couldn't let Delrik meet the same fate as me. I couldn't let those shadows suffocate the life out of him. Even if Alux was lying to me and didn't know how to save me, I had to find whatever was stolen from her to save

Delrik. I scooped my hands under his shoulders and helped him sit up.

"What was stolen?" I asked, my voice low and controlled. I had to stay in control, even with my magic fighting to rip me apart from the inside. I wrestled it back, hiding it away for now.

"Ah. See? You aren't as foolish as I thought." Alux brought her fingertips together under her chin and smiled, her hollow black eyes burrowing into me. "As I said, something was stolen from me a long time ago. A ring. And I want it back."

"A ring?"

"Yes, girl. A ring. An invaluable one. The Ring of Teris."

"Do you know who took it?"

"Yes. Yes, I do. Cadoc Byrnes."

FORTY-EIGHT
DELRIK

The sun was already high in the sky when we returned to Arden Valley. The light was harsh compared to the dark forest we stepped out of. We wandered down the path that led to the village. I shivered despite the warmth of the sun's rays. Whatever Alux put inside me had taken root. I wanted to collapse into bed and sleep for a week, straight, but I couldn't do that. I looked down at my hand and felt the sickening darkness penetrating every part of me.

Nine days. I only had nine days to save Evren.

We bypassed our yurt and went straight to Vidarr. He was near the stream helping a kid to string a bow. Targets were placed at various distances away. The boy watched Vidarr's hands closely, memorizing each step. He'd always had a knack for teaching. His patience was endless. When Vidarr was finished, the boy nodded his head, took the bow from Vidarr's hands, and removed the string. Then he methodically repeated the process he'd just learned. Vidarr clapped the boy on the shoulder and turned towards us when he heard our approach.

"Where have you been?" Vidarr began mischievously, waggling his eyebrows at the two of us. Then he looked at us closer, scanning us from head to toe. "What happened to you?"

Vidarr motioned for us to walk back to the center of the valley so we could speak freely.

"We went back to Alux," I replied.

He stopped mid step and shot me a stern look. "Tell me everything."

Over a lunch of bread and smoked fish we told Vidarr everything that had happened with Alux: how she could save Evren, the stolen Ring of Teris, the curse she'd placed on me. I had expected to remain weak, but I felt myself returning to normal as I ate and rested. My body became mine again, though the shadows stayed active on my palm. One of the centaur healers hovered over me. She kept poking me here and there, mumbling to herself before shaking her head. Eventually she settled on handing me a tea that smelled awful.

"Vidarr, this is dark, ancient magic. I've never even read about it. There is nothing I can do," the healer said. "This tea will only help soothe his sore muscles."

Vidarr simply nodded to her. She bowed and departed.

"It seems like we have no choice but to find this ring," I said, taking another large bite of my food to get the earthy herbal taste off my tongue.

"Why is the ring so special to her?" Vidarr mused.

"I'm not sure. She didn't tell us anything more than what it looked like," I replied.

"And you believe Cadoc still has this ring?" Vidarr asked.

"Yes." Evren's voice broke in. "He still has it. He has never taken it off." She turned to stare into the distance, her hands fisted together in her lap. "I remember the ring. I remember when he came home from one of his trips with it. His trip had been secretive, not even Renwick went with him. That was the day he told me I could start training my magic."

Silence spread between the three of us. We watched a flock of birds drift across the blue sky on the light breeze rippling across the valley. Their wings were stretched wide, catching the air under their feathers and gliding to and fro. Evren shifted her food around her plate. She was observing me closely, tensing every time I shifted to get more comfortable, scanning my body for injury.

"Ev, I'm fine," I reassured her. I rubbed lazy circles on her back with my uncursed hand.

"You aren't fine." She glared at me, snatching my hand up and forcing my hand open, prying my fingers back one by one. "You aren't fine. We have nine days to figure this out."

Her gentle fingers ran across my hand before she brought my palm to her lips and pressed her mouth to the darkness.

"I don't care what I have to do. I will go to the ends of the realm and further if I have to." She climbed into my lap, straddling my legs, and wrapping her arms around my neck. She leaned her forehead against mine. "There is nothing in the world I wouldn't do to save you."

Out of the corner of my eye, I saw Vidarr had turned away to give us some privacy with a smirk on his face. So, I kissed her, deep and hard. My tongue swept across hers, and she tasted of pure light and goodness and honey. All my life I thought the Powers Above were unfair, unjust. But having Evren in my arms, even if it was just for a short time, made it all worth it.

Sliding my hands under her thighs and cupping her ass, I lifted her, and without breaking my lips from hers, I carried her all the way back to our yurt.

I yanked back the flap and stormed inside. I pulled back from the kiss and looked into the depths of her amethyst eyes.

Mine.

"Evren, are you sure you want to do this? You have no idea how dangerous your father is. I've seen what he's capable of."

"What choice do we have?"

"You always have a choice."

She dropped her legs from my waist, her mood shifting to frustration in an instant. "I'm not afraid of him anymore."

"You should be! We can find another way to stop your power."

Evren pushed away from me, turning her back and scrubbing her hands down her face. When she whipped around, flames danced in her eyes. "We are going!"

I swiped my hands through my hair and growled through my teeth. "You are so infuriating! Just stop and let's talk about this."

She spun on her heels again and tried to walk away.

"Evren," I called after her, and she stopped dead in her tracks.

"I won't let you die! I can't watch you die, Delrik." Her hands were fisted at her side, but I could see flames licking out between her fingers. I couldn't see her face, but I could hear the plea in her voice.

I deflated a little. "Evren." It was just a gentle whisper.

"Didn't you hear her?" She choked on a sob. "I am your bondmate." She turned slowly and looked at me. "I will never let anything hurt you."

I knew she hadn't believed in bondmates before, thought they were just a myth. But hearing her say those words, speaking the truth I'd known deep down since the moment I laid eyes on her, shot pure heat down my spine and had me hardening.

"I will never stop searching for a way to save you. I will never surrender. And if that means I must risk my life, I will," she said.

In a blink of an eye, I had her wrapped in my arms, pushing my hands into her hair and devouring her mouth. We were both covered in dirt and tears, but I didn't care. I needed her now. It was all clashing teeth, fabric tearing, pleasure and pain as we took out our fears on each other while fully giving into the bond we'd been fighting against for so long.

I walked her backwards across the space until her ass bumped the table. I spun her and pushed her down so her stomach was flush to the table, not bothering to remove her shirt. I yanked her pants down to her ankles and kneeled behind her. Black lace underwear greeted me. I traced the edges of the fabric where it met her creamy skin.

"Were you wearing these for a special occasion?" My voice was low and husky.

She sucked in a sharp breath and wiggled her hips through the air. "Maybe."

"Where did you even get them?"

"I may have packed them before we left Arcelia."

I feathered kisses and fingers up the back of her thighs and across the softness of her ass. A moan came from her that made my cock harden more almost to the point of pain. I stood and gave her ass a firm squeeze, relishing in how her flesh gave way to the pressure of my fingertips. I wanted to leave my marks all over her thighs and ass. I swiftly unbuttoned my own pants, pushed the flimsy lace aside, and I drove into her. Hard.

Her scream of pleasure filled the air. With a fistful of her shirt, I pinned her down to the mahogany surface. She whimpered with delight at each thrust, spurring me on. Powers Above, every little sound she made was music sent from the gods.

She tightened around me, and her knees began to shake. She raised up on her toes to let me in deeper as she reached above her head. Smoke curled from under her fingers where she clung to the edge of the wood. She turned her head to look back at me over her shoulder, but her hair covered her face. I brushed the silver strands from her eyes, and those flames were ablaze.

"There are no beings in this world that will keep me from you, Evren." I thrust into her. "Tell me you are mine." Another thrust.

"I'm yours," she said breathlessly. "Forever."

Her inner muscles gripped me as she let go, spiraling around me. Pleasure pooled at the base of my spine. Building, building, building and then blessed release.

I growled with contentment as I leaned down and placed a kiss on her spine. "Always."

PART FIVE

FORTY-NINE
DELRIK

It took us nearly three damned days to reach Rivamir. Although the Sacred Forest and our horses hadn't changed from our last journey, something ominous hung over us. The Darkwood trees grew thicker as we got closer to the River Kingdom. We only stopped long enough to rest the horses and eat, not wanting to risk being caught on the road.

Now that we were standing on the bank of the Great River, the fortress loomed like a sleeping beast in hibernation. When it woke, it would be ravenous.

How were we supposed to sneak inside without getting caught? It was impenetrable. The torrent of the rapids crashed against jagged rocks, but the roaring did nothing to drown out my thoughts. In the darkness of the moonless night, I could barely see the black water. I turned to look up at the expansive fortress again. The only sign of life were the golden windows dotted along the walls. This monstrosity of a house had been Cadoc's pride and joy. He had bragged about its impenetrability all throughout the war. How no creature could pass into the River Kingdom without first crossing the river.

And yet, Evren had escaped its confinement. The gods were on her side that night. If she found a way out, then we could find a way back in.

Evren shuddered next to me. "I never thought I'd be back here. At least not by choice." She let out a joyless laugh. "I figured if I did come back, I'd be kicking and screaming."

I reached for her hand and laced my fingers through hers. She squeezed my fingers tight. Warmth spread into our joined hands as if her power were reacting to my touch. I balled my other hand into a fist, the one marred with shadow. The unworldly coldness churned against my skin. I let the cursed shadows fuel me and drive me to push forward.

Over the last three days, the shadow's ever-moving tendrils had slowly crept up my wrist and were now writhing across my forearm. The inky black crawled closer and closer to my heart each day. I didn't want to know what happened when they reached my heart. I found myself staring into its hypnotic depths while I laid awake at night, unable to sleep.

"This way," Evren said as she tugged me away from the shore of the river and toward a cluster of trees. Our feet were soundless on the carpet of grass.

"Where are we going? The bridge is that way."

"There is a tunnel that leads directly into the fortress. The Black Guard used to use it, but it floods every spring when the mountains thaw or when large storms roll through. Father gave up maintaining it. Said that anyone stupid enough to use it deserved the watery death. Only two guards will be stationed at its entrance. We should be able to get past easily."

"Is that how you escaped before?"

"No," she said, shaking her head. "There was rain coming and we didn't want to risk getting trapped down there if the tunnel collapsed."

"How did you get out?"

"I swam across," she said with a flippant wave of her hand.

"Whoa. Wait a moment." I dragged her to a stop. "You swam? As in, you actually willingly jumped into that water,"—I pointed into the death rapids,—"and swam across?"

"It was that or face the blood ritual with Renwick." She gave a half shrug. "At least the water would've been a quick death." She tugged my hand again. "We need to get out of the open."

Circle of dark hells. I couldn't wipe the shock from my face as I followed her, my hand still gripped in hers. My bondmate faced certain death to escape this place.

We reached the small cluster of trees and pushed through the growth. Two rounded boulders sat precariously on the edge of a sheer drop off into the water. They weren't higher than my waist and were covered in damp moss that was blackened by the night.

Evren stooped and picked up a fist-sized rock. She tossed it lightly in her hand, testing its weight, before saying, "You ready?"

She unsheathed her dagger. It had taken time for her to learn its balance and how it moved, but now she handled the blade like an extension of her body. I followed suit by unsheathing Silverlight. The hilt vibrated with what seemed to be excitement in my palms.

Then Evren mouthed *one, two, three* and tossed the rock over the boulders. I watched it arc up and then down into the night. Its clang echoed as it bounced down the invisible opening.

"Hey. Who's there?" a gruff intoxicated voice called into the night.

"It's no one you fool. It's never anyone," another voice said, sounding equally intoxicated.

"How did we get stuck guarding the tunnel again?"

Grunts of exertion and shuffled footsteps came our way as two overweight, sluggish guardsman popped into view over the boulders. I almost laughed at how easy this was going to be. Evren's dagger flew, accurate and true, with a whistle and landed with a solid thump in the first guardsman's chest. I didn't leave time for the other male to cry out before I plunged my sword into his throat. It came out the other side of his neck dripping with blood.

In three seconds flat, they were both gone, and I was more turned on by my bondmate than I ever had been before. She was graceful and beautiful, a weapon of violet and silver. I reached for her, gripping her by the nape roughly, and dragged her to me. I crushed my lips to hers quickly, and when I pulled back, she snapped her teeth at me playfully.

"This way," she said. She bent, placed a foot on the guard's chest, and pulled her dagger from his flesh. She wiped the blade clean on his uniform. Then with a shove, the deadened body rolled off the embankment and splashed into the water below. I followed suit and rolled the second body into the torrent. The sound of the river drowned out their bodies hitting the water.

Evren picked her way over the rocks like an agile cat. My boots slipped on a moss-covered rock and my knee cracked on the stone. I scrambled to regain my footing. Evren stifled a giggle and then disappeared down into the hollow black of the tunnel. I looked around one last time as I drew in a long breath. The river's current roared and the pitch of night surrounded us. I was about to go into my enemy's home and steal a prized possession. My life and my bondmate's life were at risk. So, for the first time I'd ever remembered, I prayed to the Powers Above to let us come out on the other side of this ordeal alive.

Evren's head popped out of an almost invisible split in the boulder. "Are you coming, or am I doing this alone?" And she vanished again.

I didn't hesitate as I squeezed my body through the narrow gap between the boulders. I had to duck down to prevent my head from scraping the ceiling of the tunnel entrance. Moisture filled my nostrils and made my skin slick. The mildew-covered ground below me slanted steeply down as the tunnel moved parallel to the river. Our footsteps echoed around us. We didn't need to stay silent since guards weren't expected to patrol this area, but I remained alert. The corridor stretched out in front of us before taking a sharp turn. If we were moving parallel to the river, the turn would lead us beneath it. Even with my Fae sight, I strained to see in the heavy darkness, and I trailed my hand along the damp wall as a guide. I pushed the image of Evren being trapped down here out of my mind.

Once we turned and began moving under the river, droplets of water dripped from the ceiling above me.

I don't know how long we walked. A minute. An hour. Time slowed with each step.

Eventually, the ground angled upwards again. I could see a soft flickering light above us. Our feet moved up a sharp slope when a set of stairs appeared. Evren nodded and began to climb the crumbling stone steps. These stairs looked like they'd seen better days. After several minutes of steep climbing, we stepped through a doorway, coming out on the other side to a hallway and the faint light of sconces. Dark, reddish wax ran down the walls and pooled on the carpet, reminding me of a puddle of blood.

Evren followed my gaze to the wax and ruined carpet. "I don't know why he insists on using candles when there is electricity here." She rolled her eyes.

We were tucked into a small hallway. I poked my head out to look down the hall, but Evren pulled me back.

Evren surveyed our surroundings carefully. "We're near my father's office on the first floor. We need to move to the entrance hall at the other end of the house," she whispered.

She grabbed my hand and led me down the hall, our boots muffled on the runner that spanned the corridor. We didn't pass any servants on our way, but Evren still moved with caution. In fact, the whole fortress seemed eerily quiet and empty. Something was off.

We dipped into another alcove. She knew every nook in this fortress. Evren pressed her back flush to my chest in the cramped space, and I purred into her hair. She reached back and smacked my chest. How did she still smell so good after marching through the forest for three days?

"Focus!" she whispered as I buried my nose into her neck, breathing deeply. "I need to find Adaris. You stay here."

"No." My voice turned stern. I wrapped my arms around her waist, holding her against me. "I'm not leaving your side. Not here."

"I'll be fine. It will be easier to sneak to his room if it's just me."

I stared at her, not wanting to give in, but she had a point. She knew this fortress. She knew where to hide and how many servants there were. It would be easier for her to hide alone than for the two of us together.

"Fine," I finally said, reluctantly releasing my grip on her. "But if you are gone longer than ten minutes, I'm coming to find you."

"Fine." She pushed me back into wall and planted a soft kiss on my lips. "I'll be right back."

She stepped into the candlelight. At the exact moment, on the opposite end of the hall, a female appeared.

FIFTY
EVREN

My heart stopped in my chest. It literally stopped for one, two, three beats before starting with a sputter.

My mother. Arabelle Byrnes. Standing directly in front of me. It was like seeing a ghost. I'd seen her in this space so many times—the wood panels, the crimson carpets, the globes of lights, but she was the last person I'd expected to run into.

So much for remaining unseen. I started to retreat back into the alcove and into Delrik's protective presence.

"What are you doing here?" Her voice was clear and strong and firm, sounding just like how I remembered from my childhood. I stopped short, confused.

"Mother?" My voice sounded weak as it carried down the hall, almost childlike.

Suddenly Adaris appeared out of nowhere, turning the corner to stand beside her.

"Adaris," I said breathlessly and took a step forward. "I…"

"Stay back." Adaris's voice was like a shard of ice. His hands were fisted by his side, and his eyes were focused on something above my shoulder.

I froze.

Was he talking to me? He wasn't talking to me.

I felt movement behind me, but before I could say anything, Adaris was running at me. My body slammed into the wall, and he caged me in protectively from an unseen threat, using his body as a shield. What was he doing? Had someone snuck up behind me?

I peered under his raised arm and into the dark alcove where Delrik was waiting for me. Adaris couldn't see Delrik tucked into the recess, just knew that someone was there. A conjured knife appeared in his hand out of thin air.

"Who are you?" Adaris demanded. His tone was as harsh as the look on his face.

"Evren," Delrik said, stepping into the light tentatively, reaching one reassuring hand toward me, the other floating upward to Silverlight strapped to his back.

"Adaris stop!" I huffed angrily, trying to push my way past him, back to Delrik, but he wouldn't budge. "Adaris!"

Adaris shoved me back into the wall, away from Delrik.

That was the *wrong* move, but I didn't have a chance to warn either of them.

Adaris reached for Delrik's shoulder, but in an instant, Delrik had him pinned to the wall, his forearm pressed against his throat, teeth bared. The tip of Silverlight was pressed into the underside of Adaris's chin, and the knife was abandoned on the floor. An angry hiss came from the two Fae males.

"We have to get out of here." Delrik's voice was commanding, ignoring Adaris's struggles completely.

I stumbled over my words, still trying to grasp the fact that Adaris was right in front of me. And my mother. My knees felt weak.

"Delrik." He didn't hear me through his protective fury. All he saw was someone he didn't know put his hands on me—his bondmate.

Adaris caught on before Delrik and stopped his struggle against Delrik's hold.

"Delrik," I said, more soothing. I gripped his arm and gave it a firm squeeze. His glazed over eyes met mine. I could feel his magic vibrating in response to the threat. Even though Delrik looked like he was ready to remove Adaris's head, I could see absolute terror underneath. "He is my brother. That's Adaris."

Delrik blinked as he processed my words. He released the pressure of Adaris's neck a touch, just enough for Adaris to catch his breath and speak.

"Little sister, you didn't tell me you found yourself a bondmate." Adaris's voice was choked but he still managed a smile.

I shot him a look. "Really, Adaris? Now is not the time for jokes."

Delrik snapped his teeth inches from Adaris's face, and my idiot brother just grinned. He was really going to start something if he wasn't careful. With our bond so fresh, he'd become feral when it came to shielding me from danger.

I looked around. We'd already made too much noise. A servant was bound to stumble upon us soon if we didn't move this reunion to a more discreet location. Delrik released Adaris and possessively drew me into his chest with his arm across my chest.

"Who thought you'd go for the controlling, overprotective type," Adaris said, straightening his clothes. He ran a thumb under his chin where Silverlight had nicked his skin. The wound healed with the touch. He gave me a wink. I punched him in the arm as hard as I could.

He rubbed his arm with a grimace. "Dang little sister, you've gotten strong."

I couldn't believe Adaris was standing in front of me. I took a shuddering breath. The weight of Delrik's arm across my chest was a steadying force against the emotions threatening to crash into me.

My mother cleared her throat behind us. "I'm sorry to break up this reunion, but we need to move. We aren't safe here." She had moved closer but was still several feet away.

"She's right. We can't trust anyone. Even the walls have ears," Adaris said. He looked up and down the hall.

"Let's go upstairs. Hurry. And stay quiet." Mother turned and walked away without checking to see if we were following.

Delrik was still looking back and forth between Adaris and me, not trusting I was safe. We didn't have time for proper introductions right now. I stepped out of his grasp and took his hand. I pulled him along, following Adaris and my mother.

"Your mother?" he mouthed when I looked back at him.

All I could do was shrug in response.

I was worried about following Mother. Could I trust her to keep her mouth shut? I knew Adaris wouldn't put me in harm's way though, so I followed without question.

We climbed the familiar staircase to the third floor, down the carpeted hall, and took the first left. I could walk the route with my eyes closed. My fingers glided along the smooth wood panels, tracing the decorative crown molding, just like I had when I was a child. We bypassed my old bedroom and slipped through the door Arabelle was holding open. One by one, we noiselessly stepped into Adaris's room.

Adaris turned the lock with a loud click that echoed off the elevated ceiling and stone walls of his room before turning to me. "Why did you come back?"

With the better lighting I was able to take a good, long look at him now. Adaris looked haggard. His eyes were set in deep, dark shadows, giving away the worry from the last few months. A thin sheen of sweat covered his face. His hair was dull and his clothes rumpled, like he'd been wearing them for days. What had Adaris endured from our father? His eyes were down on his hands—cuticles torn and scabbed. His back lifted in a deep breath before he spoke. That air of confidence dissipated and was replaced by melancholy.

"You shouldn't have come back," he said.

With three quick strides, I had him wrapped in a tight hug. I held him as he buried his head into the crook between my neck and shoulder. I saw Delrik flinch at Adaris being so close, but he stayed quiet. I could tell he was unsettled, but Adaris was my brother and best friend. And the ache of missing him crashed into me like a tidal wave.

"I can't believe you're alive. Father sent the Black Guard after you. Even Renwick went. Someone almost killed him. We don't know who. Whitt found him hanging on by a thread. I knew if he almost died then you wouldn't stand a chance."

I pulled back from him so I could look in his eyes. "I'm okay. I'm safe."

He shook his head with confusion. "How did you survive?" he asked.

Everything suddenly weighed too heavy. I couldn't begin to process all that had happened and attempt to explain it to him. I would, one day, but not right now. I released him and returned to Delrik's side. He tucked me into him and smoothed a hand across my hip.

"I'm not really sure. Maybe a bit of luck," I answered hoarsely, looking up at Delrik. "And fate."

"Wait." Delrik's chin jerked up. "Did you say Renwick was alive?"

FIFTY-ONE
ADARIS

Praise the Powers Above, Evren was alive. And she looked so healthy—full of life and strong. The last time I'd seen her she was so pale and thin and covered in bruises from Renwick. I wished he had died in that damned forest. Unfortunately, Whitt and the healer were able to save him.

Now Evren was here.

I needed to keep Cadoc and Renwick away from her. I needed to figure out why she was here and then get her as far from the River Kingdom as possible. Mother paced back and forth in front of the windows with her hands clasped tightly together and pressed to her mouth. Nervousness radiated from her.

"Renwick is alive. Captain Whitt found him with a dagger plunged deep into his back and his nose smashed in. They were able to get a healer to him and they brought him back here."

"Fuck," Delrik exclaimed.

He turned his focus to Evren and raked his hands through his hair. She was three shades paler with worry plastered on her face; her whole body was unnaturally motionless. He tipped his head down and whispered something against her ear, soothingly rubbing her arms up and down while he took deep breaths. Evren mimicked the breaths like she was trying to center and calm herself. With each breath she took, I could see her shoulders relax.

"He's even worse now. He doesn't even bother to hide his sadistic nature anymore," Adaris said. "Not from the staff or the other guardsman."

Guilt raked over my nerves. Seeing Evren standing in my room reminded me of all the ways I had failed her. I should've tried harder, searched longer. I should've scoured the entire realm, not resting until I found her. But when I returned to Rivamir to gather more supplies after failing to find her in Lakeshore, Cadoc had sunken his talons deep into me.

"Don't get me wrong; I'm beyond happy to see you..." Evren twisted her fingers. "But..." She blinked back tears and whispered, "Why didn't you come? I waited for you."

Delrik gently brushed against Evren and laced his fingers through the ends of her hair. He was still looking down at her, completely entranced by her.

I rubbed my hand across the scruff on my chin. "Evren,"—my face dropped—"I'm so, so sorry. I wanted to be with you. I tried to get to you. I searched for you for weeks. I combed the forest looking for any sign of you. I refused to believe you were dead. I would have kept looking if it weren't for Father." I paused, taking a breath.

Evren reached out and squeezed my hand.

I audibly swallowed back the emotion building. I pulled my hand from Evren's and turned away so she couldn't see my shame as I told her why I failed her.

"Father...he kept me here. He broke me, Ev. He stripped me of my rank, my title. He used his power to trap me here. I fought for as long as I could, but eventually, I broke. Just like he broke our mother."

Cadoc's control over my mind and how much he could torture with a simple look was unfathomable. He didn't even need to be in the same room to enforce his will on me. He swore if I didn't obey him, he'd kill Evren when he found her and make me watch while he did it.

I'll break her slowly, piece by piece. And there will be nothing you can do to stop her endless pain.

After watching him torture Arabelle for so many years...I couldn't let him hurt Evren. Back then, I could've left, could've saved myself, but I would never leave Evren and Mother behind. They were powerless against Cadoc. At least with me here, I could attempt to draw Cadoc's rage away from them. So that's what I'd done. I stayed and done my best to shelter them from his line of fire. But Cadoc's rage was immeasurable since Evren left that night. No one could protect us now.

"Mother?" Evren turned to Arabelle, who was shifting from foot to foot. Her mouth was drawn in a straight, grim line. She'd stayed quiet and distant while we'd talked. She swallowed thickly and stepped away.

"I'll go find some food. You both look starved," Arabelle said before she slid from the room on ghostlike feet.

Evren asked as soon as the door clicked shut. "Can we trust her?"

"Yes. Of course, Evren. She's your mother," I said.

"She may be your mother, but she hasn't been a mother to me for over a decade."

I saw that shudder go through her. I knew Mother had been powerless to protect Evren from Cadoc and Renwick. I'd heard her crying in her room the first few years, but over time, it became easier for her to stop fighting and just submit to Father's will. Mother, once joyous and caring, had decayed before my very eyes to a shell of person, all while Cadoc tortured and controlled her mind.

"That's the most she's spoken to me in years." Evren released an aggravated breath.

"Evren...," I sighed. "I'm sorry."

"There is nothing for *you* to be sorry for, Adaris. You weren't the one that ignored me most of my life."

I let out a breath. I didn't want her to blame Arabelle. I'd rather her place that blame on me.

"She's been under Cadoc's mind control since he came home from the war." I couldn't look at her. I should've been able to protect them both somehow.

Her mouth fell open. "What?" Her legs went limp, and she would've hit the floor if Delrik wasn't holding on to her so tightly.

I looked Delrik up and down, a pang of protective jealousy coursing through me, but he still had his eyes focused on Evren. He guided my sister across the room to the bed and sat down next to her.

"How long have you known?" Evren asked in disbelief as she stared at her feet.

"Since the very beginning."

"You knew all these years that he was using his powers to control our mother and you didn't tell me?" Evren rubbed her hands down her thighs. Power rippled off her.

"I figured you were safer the less you knew."

"Safer!" Her eyes shot to my face and pierced me with a glare that could turn me to stone. I could've sworn I saw flames flash brightly in her eyes. "There was nothing safe about this house. Nothing."

I dropped to my knees before her. "Evren. Please forgive me."

She sighed and cupped her hands against my cheek. Her hands were so warm, almost hot, like she'd been holding them to a fire. I searched her face for the forgiveness I sought. And, of course, it was there. This female I knelt before was still my little sister, but she'd grown to be kind and loving despite all the horrors she'd endured that I couldn't protect her from. I'd missed her so much.

"What happened to you? Did he hurt you?" Her voice was like salve soothing a wound.

Being under Cadoc's control was even worse than the Trials. For the Trials, I'd chosen to give up my powers, but with Cadoc, my powers were confined inside me. They were there, begging to fight back, straining to be released. I didn't want to tell her all that though. I didn't want to tell her how he made me endure days without food. I didn't want her to know how he made me watch him torture the lower Fae and beings his Black Guard brought home for information on her whereabouts. I didn't want her to find out about how he'd regularly forced me to slice cuts into my own arms with his iron knife he so fondly played with just to find joy in my screaming.

I shook my head.

"Mother has had it worse. The night you escaped, I could hear Cadoc and Mother fighting. There was so much destruction from them unleashing their full powers against each other. I thought they were going to bring down the whole fortress the way it shook on its foundation."

"I can't remember the last time I saw her use her powers," Evren said, shaking her head in disbelief.

"The rage she felt from you disappearing gave her enough strength to break out of Cadoc's mind control. But Mother was no match for his wrath. He wore her down, blow by blow. She had been weakened by the years of his invasion into her mind, and she could only fight for so long before he had control of her again." I scrubbed my hands across my face. "Mother's screams echoed through the dungeons for days. She was almost unrecognizable by the time he'd grown bored with torturing her. Why he kept her alive, I don't know."

I'd seen many prisoners displayed as a warning after Cadoc was done torturing them. I shuddered at the memory. "Now he doesn't have to keep her controlled. She assumed you were dead too. So, she stays quiet and out of the way. I don't even think he remembers she is here."

FIFTY-TWO
EVREN

Adaris hung his head low.

"I don't know what to say." I couldn't believe all this pain was because of a cursed power that ran through my blood.

Delrik stroked the back of my hand, trying to calm me. I was sure he could hear my heart trying to escape from my chest. A crackle of energy danced in my palms, but Delrik didn't release my hand. I hoped that my fire wasn't hurting him, but I couldn't ask him, not right now.

All this time Mother was being controlled by Cadoc. There was nothing she could have done about Renwick's behavior or Father's outbursts. She couldn't protect me even if she wanted to. I'd hated her for so many years—for the absence, for the callous comments. Guilt started gnawing at my stomach, making me want to vomit.

Mother reappeared with a tray full of food and set it on the table in the sitting area. I stared at the woman that was my mother in awe. Though she was thinner and looked pale, she moved with the smooth elegance of her Highborn blood. She looked alive. In my memories of her, she was always stiff and unnaturally rigid with a forlorn look on her face.

How had I not seen that she was so different from the mother in my early years? How had I been oblivious to her sudden shift in demeanor? My heart ached deep in my chest that I'd had so much anger and resentment toward her for all these years.

I covered my mouth with the back of my hand to stifle a sob that threatened to escape. I stood, not bothering to hide the tears that flooded down my face like the dam had finally broken. I walked to where she was sitting primly on the couch. She stiffened as I grew closer but didn't pull away. I hesitated for a beat, standing in front of her, before bending down and wrapping my arms around her in a hug. Her rigid posture melted away.

"Mother?" I asked.

"Evren." Her voice was shaky as she returned the affection, clinging tightly to me for the first time in seventeen years. "Shh. It's alright. Everything is alright now, baby. Don't cry."

She pressed her hand to the back of my head like she used to when I was little, and I snuggled deeper into her warm embrace. We stayed locked together for a long time.

"Come, you need to eat," she said as she wiped the wetness from my face. Her face glistened with moisture too.

She ushered me to the couch across from her. Patting my arm gently, she put a plate in front of me. I was choking back tears, trying to not let them cascade down my face any longer. I hadn't realized how hungry I was until I smelled the food. My mother began to pile food on my plate.

"Shh." Delrik appeared by my side and knelt. Both Mother and Adaris startled at his swiftness. "Deep breaths. You have to stay in control. Especially now." He spoke quietly so only I could hear. He took my hand from my lap and kissed my palm. His eyes said *don't reveal your powers; we don't know if they can be trusted.*

So, I took several deep breaths before looking up to meet Adaris's eyes. He was watching me, watching us, a look of suspension on his face.

"Are you finally going to introduce us to your ... friend?" Adaris said changing the subject.

Delrik snarled and leaned a half inch closer to me. He still had a grip on me, the trembling of his hand controlled as his own power moved up my arm. I almost laughed at his territorialism.

"This is Delrik, my bondmate. Delrik, this is my brother, Adaris, and Arabelle, my mother."

"It's lovely to meet you. I assume you are the reason my daughter is alive and safe," my mother said.

"She doesn't need me to protect her. I simply have the honor to do so," Delrik said through gritted teeth, still facing off with Adaris.

Adaris wasn't backing down, but I had a feeling it was to get a rise out of Delrik more than anything. Neither of them made a move to greet each other. The air became thick with aggressive tension.

"Oh, stop it, both of you. We have more important things to worry about." Mother said, her hands on her hips in a motherly way. "Like, why did you put yourself at risk coming back?"

She turned her attention between Delrik and me. Then she pushed a plate toward Delrik with a sweet smile. He took the plate and nodded with gratitude.

I looked at Delrik before I spoke. I ran my fingers up his forearm, following the darkening mark of Alux's curse. The shadows moved away from my fingertips as if they were retreating from my flames. Adaris didn't miss the movement, whether it was my tender touch or the shadows that grabbed his attention.

"We are searching for something. Something that is required to save my life and his," I said.

"So, your powers have finally developed then?" Mother asked, a little stunned. She dropped back onto the couch.

I snapped my head in her direction. "So, you *did* know about my magic?"

"Of course, I did," she replied and crossed her arms over her chest. "I did everything I could to keep them hidden and prayed to the Powers Above that Cadoc never figured it out. But then you ran away, and I knew there was nothing I could do to protect you anymore. Your fate was set."

"What do you mean kept them hidden?"

"I gave you herbs, Bloodthorn, to be specific, that suppressed your powers, to keep them from growing." She didn't show any sign of remorse in drugging her own daughter. "That tonic you drank every morning."

"You were poisoning her?" Delrik asked, shocked, glancing down at the food she'd placed in front of us as if he could taste the herb hidden in his food.

"I knew if Cadoc found out about the strength of your magic, he would kill you. He believed in that wretched curse, and with how he reacted when he met you, I didn't want to risk anything." She took a deep, steadying breath. "His father had killed his sister when she was born for the very same reason."

"He had a sister? I never knew that."

"And why would you? The shame of a cursed offspring would reduce his control of the kingdom to nothing. And it was common knowledge that you existed. You couldn't simply disappear. So, I convinced him that you were powerless. Well, at least for the elemental curse. You were seven when he met you and you had no signs of any kind of power." She took a breath and continued. "At the first sign of your powers growing, I began the Bloodthorn. The small amount I gave you every day was enough to keep you weak. That weakness kept you safe."

My mother sat straight and proud. My mouth dropped open in shock. All this time I thought I was broken, a flaw in the High Fae bloodline, but I was really being poisoned by my own mother.

I stifled a laugh with my hand pressed to my mouth. I couldn't help it. What mother poisoned her own child? And for more than fifteen years!

"That was why I'd started growing stronger after I ran away. That's why my body began to heal itself. The poison must have filtered out of my system the longer I went without my morning tea." I just shook my head. "I don't remember my powers developing when I was young."

Arabelle smiled. "You were playing in the garden on a cold winter day. You'd abandoned your cloak in the ground beside you and were sitting in a simple short sleeve smock. Snow fell all around you, but before any flakes could touch your skin, they melted in the air and evaporated. Even the stone pavers under you were free of snow."

Delrik squeezed my knee. Warmth from my power warmed his hand in response.

"Bloodthorn," I said thoughtfully. One little plant had such a drastic effect.

"Cadoc knew it was only a matter of time before you developed some form of magic, and he still believed it was the fire curse. He searched all over the realm and even across the sea on the western continent, searching for a way to hide the shame of the family curse. If you developed powers before he found a way to hide them, he was planning on…disposing of you by some accident or another. Cadoc did eventually come across someone. A powerful male, who told him there were two possible ways to keep you alive and potentially harness your powers: the Ring of Teris or the blood binding ritual between bondmates."

"How would the blood ritual keep her alive?" Delrik asked.

"When bondmates complete the blood binding ritual, they are bound by body and spirit … and magic. Whatever powers are in one person can be shared with the bonded mate. The male told him that if the elemental flame was shared it could potentially be manageable and wouldn't destroy you or your bonded."

That was why he was rushing to find me a bondmate. If he didn't perform the blood binding ritual before the elemental flames grew to full power, I would be destroyed by the flame. But it still didn't make sense.

"But why Renwick? He wasn't my bondmate." I asked.

"Renwick is his most trusted, his Head Guard," Adaris explained. "Renwick would have access to your powers. Cadoc controls Renwick, thus he could control your power and use it to expand the River Kingdom and take over the realm the way he wanted. The bondmate was simply a decoy, a front for the other kingdoms in the realm. Combining Fae families with powerful magic created a united front," Adaris said.

"It wouldn't have worked since they weren't really bondmates," Delrik stated. We'd already gone over this with Vidarr.

"I think Cadoc was willing to try anything," Adaris answered. "And I guess we aren't going to find out now." He raised his eyebrows and nodded at our joined hands.

Delrik stiffened and positioned his body between me and the rest of the room. His chest rumbled with a barely contained growl.

I couldn't let my father get hold of such dangerous powers. There was no telling how he would use them. My head began to pound as exhaustion washed over me. The air in the room was growing heavy and I wished I could be outside to let the night cool my blood.

Without a word, Delrik rose, pushed open the doors to the patio, and returned to my side.

"What about the Ring of Teris," I asked.

"The Ring of Teris is a powerful, ancient object able to harness the powers of anyone that goes against the person in possession of the ring if they so desired. It is supposed to contain the power within it until the one that wears it needs to use the power," Mother explained.

"Cadoc was going to wait until your powers grew to full strength and then trigger you to attack him so he could steal them from you," Adaris said. "With the ring he would be able to contain the power and then use it for whatever his twisted mind came up with."

Mother rolled her eyes. "Cadoc hasn't removed that ring from his hand in fifteen years."

I looked at Delrik, and he read my thoughts. This was the exact ring that Alux had sent us to retrieve. We couldn't let her get her hands on it, no matter the costs. There was no telling what she'd do if it was returned to her and she escaped from the Wasted Shallows, what evil she'd bring upon the world.

"Did your father ever mention what his plans were once he had the elemental power?" Delrik asked Adaris.

"Not to me. He and Renwick would seclude themselves in his study for days at a time discussing secret shipments and trades, but when I asked about them, he brushed me off. When I did happen to overhear their conversations, they spoke of cities and names I'd never heard of. I can only assume they are on the western continent, based off the ships coming and going."

Delrik spoke up. "I wonder if it has anything to do with them slowly taking over the realm one village at a time."

My head was swimming, and I desperately needed to sleep.

"You both need to rest," Mother said as she stood. She patted Delrik's shoulder and leaned to kiss me on the cheek. "We will talk in the morning at breakfast."

We decided it was safer for us to stay in Adaris's rooms for the night. Even with Cadoc away on a trip, the servants and guardsmen still roamed the fortress. At least tonight, we could rest since he wouldn't return until tomorrow. We had until then to figure out how to get the ring from Cadoc without killing ourselves.

Adaris excused himself to walk Mother back to her rooms down the hall, giving Delrik and me some privacy. The two of us undid our weapons and hid them under the bed. The only weapon we left visible and easily accessible was my dagger set on the side table.

Delrik and I stepped into the washroom together. Soft globes of light hung on each side of a framed mirror. The frame was made of twisted steel that formed replicas of the grove trees and rushing water and sly foxes hidden within them, their eyes glowing crimson with rubies. Delrik was worried about leaving me alone, not trusting I was truly safe. The moment the door closed behind me, his hands were in my hair, leading me backward until I hit something solid. The cold marble of the counter bit into me as he pressed me against it.

He reluctantly pulled away with a ragged breath. "I can't keep you safe here, Ev. We need to get away from Rivamir."

I ran my hands up his chest and over his shoulders, looping my arms around his neck. "I know. And we will. We came all this way. We can't leave empty handed. As soon as we get that ring, we'll disappear." I turned my head to kiss the shadows on his forearm. They darted away from the contact of my lips on his skin.

He blew out a shaky breath. "It's not worth the risk."

"I will not let you die to save me. I won't."

Delrik pressed his mouth to mine, almost desperately, like he could somehow change my mind. "You are a stubborn female."

"But I'm *your* stubborn female."

A possessive snarl rumbled in his chest. "Yes, you are."

Delrik released me, and we took turns cleaning off the three days of travel. Fresh scents of soaps and oils filled the washroom, and steam fogged the mirror. The hot water did so much more than cleanse my body. It shifted my mood and allowed me to relax. I stood in front of the mirror with a towel wrapped around me and wiped the fog with my hand to clear a space to see my reflection. Delrik was behind me, his long, powerful body pressed into me. His lips ghosted over the smoothness of my shoulder and up my neck. He took a deep breath. "Jasmine and honeysuckle," Then he kissed me on the side of the head before pushing away from me to dress.

When we'd finished dressing, we rejoined Adaris back in his room.

"Evren, you can sleep in the bed. Delrik and I will take turns standing guard," Adaris said.

Delrik pinned Adaris with a look that suggested he wasn't going to take orders from him. I chuckled to myself as I towel dried my hair. It had gotten so long over the last two months. I guess being poisoned with Bloodthorn had stunted me in more ways than just my magic. Delrik took the towel from my hands and continued squeezing the water from the strands. Then he ran his fingers through the length before braiding it and draping it over my shoulder. He'd watched me braid it over and over and, after many attempts, mastered the weave himself.

A fire was lit in the hearth, and Adaris was standing near the mantle with a glass in his hand. I climbed into his bed and tucked my feet beneath me. The sights and smells of his old room flooded my mind with memories.

We used to play hiding games when I was little. As I grew older, our games shifted into puzzles and chess, or simply reading by the fire well into the night.

I settled into the blankets and cushions, all varying shades of reds and silvers, as Delrik brought a wingback chair to sit next to me. He placed a hand on my knee, offering his warmth and comfort. The weight of his hands was exactly what I needed right now.

Adaris took a sip from the glass and placed it on the mantle before tucking his hands into his pockets. "So, do you have a plan? Besides stealing the ring, that is."

"I'm open to suggestions," I said.

"He isn't even here right now."

"That gives us some time to really make a plan instead of just running into the fire headfirst," Delrik said.

"And what about after you get the ring? You need to get as far from here as possible." The seriousness in Adaris's voice reflected the difficulty of the task ahead.

"We need to get it back to Alux and figure out how to break this curse," I said to Delrik.

The room became quiet, and the sound of the water filtered in through the opened doors.

Delrik's face turned pensive. "We could do the blood binding. We are bondmates. Maybe it would be enough. Your father believed it would work with Renwick, so why not for me?" he said.

My eyes shot to his face. It was a crazy idea. Not the blood binding part. I'd do anything for him. I wanted to be bound to him for all time. But the thought that we could somehow control the supreme elemental fire. It literally consumed the last Fae it inhabited. I didn't know if he truly understood the risk of binding himself to me.

"He is your true bondmate. I say it's worth a try," Adaris said.

"But what happens if the power is still too strong? What if it consumes us both?" I cringed at the thought of Delrik burning alive in my flame.

"It won't. Between the two of us, we can contain it."

Both males sounded so confident. I climbed off the bed and into Delrik's lap, my knees on either side of his thighs. If it worked, if the two of us could control the elemental flame together, I would be free from my father forever and be able to stay with Delrik. His fingers brushed stray pieces of hair that had fallen from my braid away from my face and leaned in to kiss me.

"Ugh you two are so gross." Adaris flopped down onto his back on the couch in front of the fire and flung an arm across his eyes. "Thank the Powers for not bringing him home *after* the blood binding. You'd be even worse."

I grabbed a pillow off the bed and threw it at him. It landed with a flop against his face before bouncing onto the floor. Adaris let out a laugh, and how wonderful the sound was. I shifted in Delrik's arms so my legs hung over the arm of the chair and rested my head against his chest. I began to relax as the sound of the crackling fire and the steady thump of Delrik's heartbeat soothed me to sleep.

FIFTY-THREE
DELRIK

I stood with Evren sleeping peacefully in my arms and placed her gently in the bed. I didn't bother covering her with the blankets. She didn't get chilled anymore with the fire flowing through her veins. I stood, staring down at her for a moment.

Adaris was sprawled on the couch with his newly refilled glass pressed to his forehead, eyes closed. He was definitely not sleeping though. I could see his eyes moving beneath his eyelids and he was humming some sort of tune to himself. Thin scars covered his raised arm, and the paler skin glowed almost white in the firelight. Evren had mentioned he wasn't old enough to fight in the war. I wondered how he'd received so many cuts. It looked like each cut was made from a similar blade, in exact, measured movements, and somehow prevented from healing. I'd seen Cadoc use iron and salt to torture his victims and slow the healing process during the war. I averted my eyes before he caught me staring.

I walked to the glass doors that were still open to go onto the balcony. The air was warm compared to the mountains and smelled of brine from the sea. I couldn't see the Kamson Sea with the dark sky, but saltiness hung in the air. I'd never liked the water. The crossings back and forth from the war were treacherous, mentally and physically. The salt reminded me of war and death. I released a long breath, pushing the sea and war out of my mind, and leaned against the balcony wall.

Evren agreed to do the blood ritual with me. I didn't think I could be happier than the first time I heard her call me bondmate. I prayed to the Powers Above that it was enough. I'd risk everything if I could give her a chance to live. However, no matter how many times I ran the situation through my head, I couldn't figure out how we would get the ring off Cadoc's finger. Arabelle had said he never took it off. And with his mind control powers, getting close enough would be nearly impossible. Breaking free from Alux's shadows would be pointless if I couldn't save Evren too.

I looked down at my hand and arm. The black, rippling shadows were now above my elbow.

"So, what's the story with that?" Adaris was leaning against the door jamb.

I looked over my shoulder at him, and he lifted his chin to indicate my arm.

"It's none of your concern."

"If it affects my little sister, then it is my concern." He pushed off the jamb and walked to stand next to me.

I held my arm up and turned it slowly in front of me. The serpentine shadows twisted and taunted me. I nearly felt the scales of snakes under my skin even though the shadows were smooth to the touch. I swear if they had actually been snakes, they'd be striking my face with their venomous fangs. "Just a small gift, a token of gratitude for retrieving the ring for Alux."

"Isn't the Ring of Teris the ring that trapped her in the Wasted Shallows to begin with? Giving it back would release her."

"Isn't that just a myth. Anyways, giving it back will save Evren's life."

"You'd be releasing that monster upon the realm."

I whipped around to face him, facing off with the only other male that Evren has ever loved. My face twisted into a snarl. "But my bondmate will be freed. And that is the *only* thing that matters to me." I took a step closer so that our bodies almost brushed each other. "I would die if I had to. Anything to save her."

Adaris's mouth flipped up into a smile. "Well, at least I know you're serious about her and not after her powers."

I wanted to rip his throat out. Nothing about this was funny. The only reason I had not broken every bone in his face was because of Evren.

Suddenly, I heard a pop. A form shifted in the room behind Adaris. Adaris fell forward like he was shoved through the doorway and stumbled into me. A muffled scream and a crash had me running back inside but I slammed into something hard and unforgiving. A shield blocked the entry. I slammed my fists against the invisible force and screamed Evren's name. Evren's eyes were wide in panic for a second before she lost consciousness. A Black Guardsman pulled Evren's limp body off the bed while a second held the shield in place. The bastard had one hand wrapped around her shoulders, and the other pressed a cloth to her face. Everything happened so fast. My stomach dropped like I'd jumped off a cliff.

Then, with another pop, they were gone. The shield disappeared, and Adaris and I crumbled onto the floor in a tangled heap.

What. The. Fuck.

I knew Cadoc had members of his guard that could blink, arriving undetected and disappearing just as quickly. I should've been more alert, expecting Cadoc would use everything at his disposal to take Evren back. I'd seen those Fae gifted with the power turn the war in our favors during many battles. This was the second time I'd underestimated Cadoc and Evren had paid the price.

My heart pounded in my ears in panic as I surveyed the scene. The room was a disaster. The table was flipped onto its side, and a chair lay shattered into pieces on the floor. The bedding was shredded to pieces. Feathers were still floating through the air. My mind swam with panic. Bile burned my throat. Evren had put up a fight, but she was gone.

"Adaris." My voice boomed through the room. "She's gone."

Adaris darted into the hallway and sprinted down the carpeted corridor. I ran for the bed and pulled Silverlight from under it and followed him. He crashed into another door, and it burst open, the wood splintering as he smashed through the lock.

I heard him say *Cadoc found Evren,* and then Arabelle was by his side.

The three of us stood for a moment, looking around us, not knowing what to do next.

"Fuck!" I couldn't help the curse.

"What happened?" Arabelle asked.

"He just took her. I was standing there, and he appeared. He just took her, blinked right before my eyes," I said.

"Damn it!" Adaris cursed.

Then, a switch went off, and Adaris froze. His body was suspended, trapped—one arm outstretched, his head turned in a strange direction, his face completely blank. But his eyes…his eyes were terrified and wide in warning. Then he jerked unnaturally as he turned on his heels and walked away.

Just walked away.

"Adaris?" I called after him. I started to follow him.

What in the circle of dark hells is going on?

A gentle hand on my arm stopped me. "Don't." Arabelle had gone pale. "He's under Cadoc's control. He's been summoned. We need to follow him, but we can't be seen."

"Will he lead us to Evren?"

"Most likely."

She patted my arm before she straightened her dress and followed Adaris down the hall.

FIFTY-FOUR
EVREN

My body was stiff with pain. How long had I been out? I was sleeping and felt Delrik shift me to the bed. I squeezed my eyes tight, not wanting to wake. Or were we with Alux? I couldn't remember. Or was I in the Sacred Forest? Everything was scrambled in my head.

I heard movement, so I rolled over sleepily. I cracked my eyes open expecting to see Delrik sitting beside me, but the body looming over me was one of my worst nightmares come to life.

Dread coursed through me like I'd been struck by lightning. Before I could react, a cloth-covered hand clamped firmly over my mouth and nose. I tried to take a deep breath, but the air through the cloth covering my lips was sickeningly sweet tasting. I instantly recognized the scent:

Doloryum—a powerful drug made of the Dolor herb that grew wild across the River Kingdom. If slipped into food, the herb was deadly. But when crushed and added to olive oil, the aroma would temporarily paralyze and sedate the victim. The healers had used the drug for the many injuries I'd gotten as a child. The cloying smell was firmly embedded in the memories of being sedated to be stitched up or to break a fever. A figure shadowed from a mask covering his face loomed over me.

I tried to fight the male pinning me down to the bed, before the Doloryum overwhelmed me. I thrashed and kicked. My foot made contact with something hard, but the drug was too strong. My movements slowed and everything blurred. A veil slipped over my mind, and everything went blank. The last thing I remembered seeing was the fuzzy outline of Delrik before all the air surrounding me closed in.

⚲

An aroma so familiar and comfortable filled my senses, and I didn't want to open my eyes. Leather and books and stone and salt. The feather pillow under my head was soft and luscious. If I could roll my eyes with them closed, I would. I snuggled deeper into the cushion, trying to ignore how strange my body felt.

The fuzziness of a dream was clearing—half Fae and osomals and ancient creatures and fog. I frowned, not wanting to wake but also not wanting to relive the nightmares. I searched for anything that would bring the safe warm feeling back.

As I came to, a haze hung on all my senses. It couldn't have all been a dream. It was too vivid, too lasting in my mind. My mouth was dry and stale. I furrowed my brow in confusion. My head pounded heavily and I winced at the pain. Why was my head killing me? Even the low buzzing sound pulsing in my ears made me wince. The world swayed under me like I was falling. Even while laying still, I felt unbalanced. I cracked one eye open. My vision blurred in and out of clarity. I blinked, trying to bring the room into view.

I was in my father's cavernous study, curled up on one of his couches. A massive mahogany desk covered in rolls of maps was the central focus of the room. Dark wood panels lined the walls. Two wingback chairs stood before the fireplace. In the fireplace, there was a strong fire, making the room stuffy and unnaturally warm. The dark marbled stone of the mantle was missing a chunk along the edge like someone had taken a sledgehammer to it. Thick curtains covered the windows blocking any potential light from seeping in. This was the only room in the house that I had avoided at all costs. I'd only been here once, and I didn't know why I was here now. My father's hulking form was masked in shadows, his elbows propped on his desk, and his fingers folded together under his chin.

The Byrnes Family crest hung above the fireplace—crimson and steel. Power and fear. Cadoc swirled a crystal tumbler of amber liquid in his massive hand when he caught me watching him.

Chunks of memory filtered back to me from the previous night—harsh hands grabbing me, the too sweet smell of the herb, a fading handprint bruised into my arm, the shock on Delrik's face.

I needed to get out of here. Terror pulsed through me as his cold eyes landed on me. Cadoc looked more sallow than usual, like the last two months had stolen away his "youth". An involuntary shiver skittered across my skin that had nothing to do with being cold.

"Welcome home, my dear." His voice was deceptively level, so painfully charming. "I've been looking everywhere for you. Why did you leave?"

I didn't trust my father in the slightest, especially with the savage gleam he had in his eyes.

I stifled down the fear overwhelming me. My mind said to move quickly, move away, but my body was slow to react. My limbs felt heavy, sluggish. I was suddenly aware of how exposed I was in my simple night dress and tugged at the hem.

"What happened? How did I get here?" My words sounded slurred.

Shit. Did I say that out loud?

"You've been causing a lot of trouble for me." He stood, moving in that calculated way he did around his desk, and took a step toward me. "I had Ashewood track you. He followed your trail to

Arcelia, but he couldn't get past their damned wards." He took a sip of his drink. "I will burn that city to the ground one of these days just to spite Aramis. How dare he keep me out. He's always been a cocky, self-important prick. When Ashewood didn't return, I sent out a search party. They found him deep in the mountains." Rage flashed across his face.

A figure moved through the darkness behind Father's desk. It stepped closer, coming into the light.

Renwick.

I tried to scramble to my feet and back away from him, but my muscles refused to respond. Everything was moving in slow motion. I had never seen so much fury, so much hatred in his eyes. My limbs finally moved, so sluggish. I strained as my father stepped toward me. I was barely able to push myself up, leaning heavily on the arm of the couch. Somehow, I got my feet under me and stood on my wobbly legs.

"You aren't looking well, my daughter. You should sit back down." He shoved me roughly onto the couch.

The sudden movement made my stomach flip, and my vision blurred as the room spun around me. Renwick tucked his hands behind his back and came to stand at my father's left shoulder.

"I know everything." My voice was raspy; my throat burned from the lingering effects of the Doloryum.

A mirthless laugh came from Cadoc. "You do, do you? What, did Alux give you a glimpse into the power slowly eating away at you?" He tipped his head back and laughed. A cold sound. "Stupid creature. Did she tell you what would happen when you couldn't contain that power? How it would consume you?"

"How do you know about the fire power?"

"You wouldn't have come back unless you needed something."

Unease curled my insides, and acidic bile rose in my throat. "You will not steal my power from me. I will never give it up." My voice was finally coming back. I couldn't let him win.

I tried to rise again.

The crystal tumbler in his fist suddenly shattered, spraying shards of glass in every direction.

"Your weakness was always such a disappointment. It disgusts me, really. If I could take the power only, I would. But I'm stuck with you. Just like I'm stuck with your mother and stuck with Adaris." Cadoc raised his fist in the air, the ring glinting in the firelight. Renwick smiled from behind him. "At least until I can be sure this ring actually works."

Suddenly, something hit my mind; Cadoc was trying to push past my mental barriers using his powers, trying to control me, slowly torturing me from the inside out. He had controlled my mind many times before to assert his will. He preferred it over his fists. He didn't like to get his hands dirty. I had to resist him. My mind resisted his advances.

"You *have* gotten strong," he hissed. "But not strong enough."

I couldn't hold him off any longer. The Doloryum cast a haze over me. A glorious haze that welcomed me, beckoned me into the oblivion of relaxation. Father suddenly broke past my defenses; my body collapsed and convulsed on the ground at his feet. My body contorted in ways that weren't natural as sharp pain coursed through me. My head snapped back at a painful angle. My fingers stretched, then bent. My back contorted itself until I was splayed prone on the floor. My heels banged on the floor as I convulsed. I clenched my teeth, refusing to scream. I didn't want to give him or Renwick the satisfaction of hearing me scream. Renwick had always loved when I screamed.

He released me after an agonizing minute that seemed to last longer than an hour. I cowered on the ground like the scared child I was. I couldn't bring myself to look at him. Instead, I stared at the floor. A long crack snaked out from under the carpet, across the floor toward one of the high windows up on the wall. I could see that the place I once considered home had truly been my prison. That high window didn't even look out over the landscape surrounding the house, but rather toward the sky. And the thick curtains were always drawn, keeping any view blocked. The old stones were chipped, cracked, and worn away with age. Heavy steel doors with deadbolts were on every exterior wall, and guards were posted day and night. Not even animals dared live in the twisted, tangled trees in the grove. The grove of trees I had loved to explore were surrounded by high walls. Not to keep others out, but to keep *me* in, to keep me hidden, to keep me imprisoned. If everyone forgot I existed, no one would know I needed to be saved.

The weight of the realization crashed down on me—harder than any blow the monster I'd once called father had ever given me. Harder than the punishing swings of Renwick when he believed no one was looking.

I was crushed by the reality that had come into my view at last. I would not survive this. Nothingness surrounded me. Emptiness gnawed at my very spirit, swallowing it until I was hollow inside, threatening to suffocate me. I'd been condemned to a life of torment. A fate worse than death. All I wanted was for this to be over with as quickly as possible. I just wanted him to end me. If he killed me, then I could escape, and he couldn't use me as a weapon. And if I were gone then he wouldn't be able to get to Delrik. There was no need to pretend this would end any other way than my death. He was just putting off the inevitable, just another way to torture me.

Again, he attacked.

FIFTY-FIVE
EVREN

Cadoc stood over me, staring down with a sickening smile on his face as my body recovered from another mental assault. I'd lost count of the number of times I'd passed out and awoken to his grinning face. I would never escape. This would be my life forever. I wondered how long I could possibly live that way, a prisoner being constantly drained.

Devastation, emptiness, and defeat ripped through me. I covered my mouth with both my hands in an attempt to hold myself together, but it wasn't working. I felt everything. Literally, everything tore through me.

Then I heard a throat being cleared from the corner near the window. From the shadows, I could see a tall male, sitting with his legs crossed, hands resting on his knee. Then he stood. His face was bloody and mangled, but his violet eyes were still the same. The same eyes as mine.

Adaris.

I reached a shaking hand toward him, but he didn't move to me. He didn't speak a word, just watched me with clouded, glazed eyes. Foreign, distant, and pained. His face was full of remorse, but all he did was stand immobile. Cadoc looked between the two of us, still smiling.

Adaris stood submissively before Cadoc. I shook my head, but the throbbing started again with a vengeance. His eyes were the only evidence my brother was still within the shell he'd become as they ran over my face in a silent communication that I couldn't understand.

"Thank you, son, for helping me find her. If you hadn't searched so hard, she would've been lost." Cadoc turned to Renwick. "And you, Ashewood."

Renwick bowed his head. "Of course, High Ruler. I couldn't let such a valuable asset get away."

I clamped my jaw down tightly, fisting my hands at my sides. "You!"

Though Adaris had told us Renwick was alive, I was surprised to see he appeared to have no lasting effects from my dagger. A spasm streaked behind my eyes. "I stabbed you." I didn't want to believe he had survived, even though I knew he had.

"Enough." Cadoc's voice broke in. Despite the harsh tone, his face was serene.

Adaris flinched at the sharpness, taking a step back toward the window, away from Cadoc.

My heart ached as I watched my brother. I could only guess the hardships he withstood for my sake. And he was as trapped as I was right now.

"All I wanted from you was your obedience."

Pain.

"A show of unity to prove to the realm that I am truly in control."

Pain.

"Your brother finally came to see my ways." Cadoc sneered.

Adaris winced—his face was pale, drawn. What had Father done to him? Disgust covered my face. Disgust for Cadoc's hatred and disgust that Adaris was forced to submit to such evil. But Adaris wouldn't submit, not on his own. Cadoc was forcing him, using his powers to control him.

Pain—blinding, razor sharp pain—shot through me again, and this time, I couldn't hold back the howl that tore from me. My back arched, my toes curled tight into my feet, and my hands clenched into fists so tight that my nails drew blood from my palms. My body lifted from the ground and hovered before him in a twisted knot.

Are you ready to obey, Evren? His deep voice thundered through my head, echoing like he was surrounding me. *Obey like your brother, and I'll let you live.*

I pushed against Cadoc's intrusion, but my attempt was useless. He'd gripped my mind in a vice and warped it until I couldn't see straight.

Release.

Quiet.

My lungs sucked in much-needed air, and my body fell limply to the ground. A layer of sweat covered my entire body. I stretched my fingers trying to regain my equilibrium. I felt Cadoc's heavy boots vibrate through the floor as he drew closer, but I was too breathless to stir. I felt pressure on my hand and looked up.

Renwick, not Cadoc, was standing above me, his boot resting on the back of my wrist.

"Renwick, don't." Adaris's voice was forced through gritted teeth. I could hear the pain he was in fighting the control our father had on him.

Cadoc reached a casual hand toward Adaris, closing into a quick fist. Adaris went rigid, eyes wide.

My eyes flicked to Renwick towering above me. Pure evil. He was pure evil. I heard the bones in my hand snap before I felt the pain. Penetrating pain. A scream ripped through me. I tried to hold back my tears as my stomach plummeted with nausea, all the blood draining from my face as pain radiated up my arm.

And then something threw Renwick away.

It was Arabelle. My mother.

Cadoc roared and flew at me, but Arabelle blocked his blow, her hands raised in front of her, holding an invisible shield before us. Her powers.

That was the first time I ever remembered my mother doing anything to protect me. She turned to look over her shoulder at me. Her hands shook with the effort to maintain the wall of air she'd created. It was like the last seventeen years hadn't happened. Her eyes were bright, clear, vibrant. The mother I had cherished and loved in my younger years was there with me, and she poured every ounce of her magic into protecting me from the monster she bonded.

Cadoc attacked, but the barrier my mother had around us stood strong. I felt it quiver under his blows. Sweat dripped from her forehead, and blood trickled from her nose and ears. Her arms were slowly giving way with the effort of holding against him.

When Cadoc finally broke through, the moment he pierced her barrier, he lunged and went straight for her throat. His hand gripped her, and my mother's mouth opened in a silent scream, the sound cut off from the pressure. Cadoc's eyes found mine. They were angry slits, and a depraved smile curled his lips. Mother kicked as Cadoc lifted her body effortlessly from the floor, her hands reaching to claw at his face. Her nails left bloody streaks on his cheeks.

Crack.

The sound reverberated in my ears, and my skin turned to ice.

Cadoc crushed her neck in his powerful hand like a mere twig snapping under a horse's hoof. My mother's body went limp.

Arabelle's body dropped to the carpet next to me with a nauseating thud. Her head was twisted at an impossible angle. Her eyes were wide with shock and lifeless. The light behind those violet eyes was gone. And I'd never see it again.

A pulse of energy surged through the room like a ripple in the water as a sob welled in my throat. I held my broken hand to my chest and scrambled back against the wall, away from her lifeless form.

I gave into the ripple of power and pain as darkness overcame me.

FIFTY-SIX
DELRIK

I lost track of Adaris quickly. He was moving faster than I anticipated, and this damned fortress was a maze of turns and dead ends that slowed my pace. All the halls looked the same to me. I knew she had to be somewhere within the fortress. We were already bonded to each other. No blood ritual was needed to tell me that. I didn't know where Evren was exactly, but I could sense her essence like a string stretched taut between the two of us. All I had to do was focus and follow the path the gods had given me. I climbed up several flights of stone stairs and down another winding darkened hallway. Arabelle was right on my heels, and as we turned a corner, I saw a faint glow, a sliver of light, from a door down the corridor that stood ajar.

I was going to murder Cadoc once I got my hands on him. No, that would be too easy. I wanted to hear him beg for his life. I wanted the satisfaction of seeing his face when I ran my knife deep into his gut over and over. I wanted nothing more than to wrap my hands around Cadoc's throat and squeeze the life out of him. With my speed, Cadoc would never see me coming. He wouldn't stand a chance.

An agonizing scream pierced the air and my blood ran cold. Before I could react, Arabelle heaved past me, bursting into the room. I watched in shock as she dove between Cadoc, seething like a viper, and Evren, a crumpled mess on the floor. I could now see where Evren got her boldness and determination. I took a step into the room just as Cadoc broke through a wall of protective magic and Arabelle's neck snapped.

Just like that, Cadoc snuffed out Arabelle's life. His eyes slid to mine. Cruelty distorted his features. This is the male I remembered from the war. From behind him, Renwick stalked forward.

"Ah. The faithful mutt has followed his bondmate."

I snapped my teeth with a snarl. I didn't risk taking my eyes off the two males. Evren was still breathing, unconscious but breathing.

"Hello, Delrik. It's lovely to see you again." Cadoc's voice was silky smooth as he gave me a mock bow. "I see you've formed somewhat of an attachment to my daughter." He clutched at his chest. "Too bad she's already spoken for."

I was seething, but I held my ground.

Renwick walked to Evren's side. I tracked his movement, fighting the urge to reach for Silverlight on my back. He eyed her bare legs greedily as he nudged his boot against her slack hand. It was swollen and turning a shade of purple. Her hand was splayed and bent all wrong from the wrist down.

"What did you do to her?"

It was Renwick that spoke this time. "She was giving us a little...trouble. I was just encouraging her to cooperate like the good pet is she."

"That's enough, Ashewood." Cadoc looked down at his daughter sprawled on the floor and back to me. "You know there is a simple way to end all this."

"How?"

"I could really use your skills in the Black Guard. You'd be an excellent commander."

"Fuck you," I spat at him.

"Aramis has been holding you back all these years. I've seen what you're capable of. You could be so much more."

"Fuck. You."

"Such a wide vocabulary," Renwick mumbled under his breath as he picked a piece of lint off his pristine uniform.

Adaris still stood in the background, frozen in place like a statue. His eyes darted between Evren and me.

Pop.

The male I'd seen take Evren appeared beside Adaris. He looked Adaris up and down, assessing him with pure disdain. Then he kicked Adaris in the back of the knee, forcing him to collapse onto the floor, panting, as if the act of falling released him from Cadoc's hold. Renwick's vicious cackle filled the air.

"We should give him some time to think about how badly he wants his bondmate back," Cadoc said. He bent down and so gently, like a loving father, brushed the hair away from Evren's sweaty face.

And then they were gone, whisking Evren away to Powers knew where, leaving Adaris and me alone in the study with Arabelle's lifeless corpse.

FIFTY-SEVEN
EVREN

My eyes popped open, or at least I thought they had. I blinked a few times and realized I was surrounded by darkness. Or semidarkness. The more I blinked the more my eyes adjusted. The ground below my cheek was rough and cold. My head and body ached. I tried to push my hands against the stone floor to sit up, but pain shot through my broken hand. A yelp escaped my throat.

Where was I? I shivered as a biting wind gusted through the window high above my head. My thin nightgown did nothing against the cold. There were no stars in the dark sky. A gloomy moonless night. The smell of rotting flesh and moisture hung in the air. My ankles were bound in shackles. Iron shackles. Their coldness leeched the magic and energy from me.

A door in the distance opened, and a soft yellow glow appeared. I squinted my eyes as the sudden light from a torch came into the room. Not a room, but a cell. I was in a cell of some kind. Vibrations of power hummed through the space as heavy booted steps moved towards my cell.

"I hope you slept well." Cadoc spoke into the dimness.

I didn't move, didn't speak, just stared at the cloaked shape of him. With the torch stretched before him he was still cast in darkness.

"Come now, Evren. You know you can't run away whenever you please. At least down here, I know you'll be safe."

A guardsman unlocked the cell door, and Cadoc stepped inside, taking up every bit of space with his menacing presence. I scrambled to get away from him, on my knees with my mangled hand against my chest, the shackles clanging together as I pushed my feet against the moist floor. My bare knees scraped the stone. He squatted in front of me. Dancing light reflected off the curved black metal of a dagger. It was my dagger; the one I'd been carrying for the last few months. The one I plunged into Renwick's back. Cadoc tossed the dagger into the air and caught it by the hilt.

"Your brother didn't appreciate the gift I gave him for his Trial if he just threw it away on you." He raised a brow. "At least you had the good sense to take care of it."

He withdrew a second, smaller knife from a hidden place in his cloak. The coldness of the iron tainted the air before I saw the thin blade. He held it up in the torch light. "I prefer this blade though." He slipped my dagger into its sheath at his waist. "Besides, I wouldn't want to contaminate such a precious blade with your filthy, cursed blood."

He ran his thumb over the edge of the iron blade, admiring its deadly sleekness. Cadoc leaned forward, and I flinched away from him, but he grabbed the back of my head, knotted my hair painfully in his fist to keep me still.

"Tsk tsk tsk," he said.

He stroked the flat side of the knife down my cheek, almost lovingly. Its iciness seared into my skin just with its touch. So cold it burned. He dragged it lower until the tip was pressing into my collarbone. His wicked eyes met mine and held them. He pressed the blade's tip into my skin, dragging the corrosive blade in an arc across my chest. Pain flashed through me, but I held my face still, biting the inside of my cheek until I tasted blood. Cadoc chuckled to himself as he stood. Disorienting waves of sickness made me sway as traces of the iron seeped deep into my skin.

"Are you expecting me to beg for my life? Because I won't."

"Ha! Oh, I'm not going to kill you. I'm going to do the exact opposite. I will keep you alive no matter what it takes." He crossed his arms over his barreled chest, the iron dagger still gripped in his meaty hands and my blood dripping from the edge.

"There's also no need to find you a new bondmate. That was only a distraction after all. A ploy to get you to play along." He bent to wipe the blade clean on my torn night dress before slipping it back into its hiding spot. "I can be very persuasive. You'll do anything to save your precious Delrik."

I sucked in a gasp. No. He couldn't have Delrik too.

"And with this,"—He held his ringed finger in front of my face,—"I'll possess your power in no time."

He stood and turned to leave.

"And if I don't?" My voice was small, but there was a sharpness in it. I forced an air of confidence, though I didn't feel it. "If I fight you?"

Never give in. The words echoed in my head, I felt more confident just thinking.

Cadoc barked a laugh.

One second, he was at the cell door, the next, he'd lifted me from the floor, my feet dangling in the air, hand grasped around my neck. The iron chains pulled taunt and bit into my flesh. Cadoc's face was inches from mine. "Like you could fight me."

I spat into his face. Speckles of drool and blood covered his mouth and nose and he recoiled.

He slowly lowered me back to the floor before he swung his fist across my face. My cheek split open, and blood trickled warmly down my chin.

"You belong to me."

The cell door slammed, and he stormed away, taking the flickering light from the torch with him.

⚲

I wasn't sure how much time had passed. I kept slipping in and out of sleep, though I tried to stay awake. Over and over, I jerked awake, throughout the night and day, preventing me from falling into deep sleep despite my exhaustion. My tattered clothes were useless against the damp, cold air. Shivers took over, and I couldn't control them as they wracked my aching body. Dried blood caked my skin where Cadoc had used my dagger to pierce my flesh. The open wounds on my face and chest began to smell, and my crushed hand was so swollen I couldn't open my fist. The iron was draining my magic and preventing me from healing.

No one came into my cell. No food or water was brought to me.

I know at least a day went by. The tiny window near the ceiling allowed a thin ray of light into the cell. I preferred the dark though. At least in the dark I couldn't see how dire my situation was.

Footsteps, quick and quiet, padding softly on the stairs grabbed my attention.

"Evren?"

I knew that voice.

"Adaris." My voice was a rasp. "Adaris," I said, trying again.

I tried to stand but couldn't. My weakened legs struggled to support my body.

"I'm here, Evren."

Keys jingled and then a click as Adaris unlocked the barred door. He held a lantern up and, using his powers, summoned a globe of light. He hung the lantern on a nail protruding from the wall.

"Circle of dark hells. What did he do to you?"

"He has Delrik. He has Delrik."

He ignored my soft whimpers as he unlocked the iron shackles from my ankles and hissed when his skin touched the metal. Then his strong arms were around me as he lifted me effortlessly and carried me out of the dungeon.

"Delrik. He has Delrik."

It took a moment for my eyes to adjust as the familiar hall of our family home came into view. I'd never been in the dungeons below our home. I hadn't even known there were dungeons deep below the fortress, but it made sense, knowing my father and the Black Guard.

I leaned my head against Adaris's shoulder, my broken wrist cradled against my chest. My eyes closed at the heaviness of my aching head and waves of nausea that rolled through me with the jostling of each step.

"Delrik," I whispered.

I didn't even care where Adaris was taking me. I was finally safe. Adaris would keep me safe. I felt Adaris bend down and set me on the soft surface of a chair. I pried open my eyes despite the dizziness. We'd made it to a servant's corridor just outside the entrance hall, the same corridor we had used to escape just six months before.

"We can't stay here. Do you think you'll be able to walk?" Adaris asked.

"Yeah, just give me a few minutes." I knew my strength wouldn't return that quickly. "We need to get Delrik."

Adaris turned when he heard movement from the shadows behind him, and I began to panic. Had someone followed us? I couldn't go back down into that cell. And then Delrik's face came into view. His reassuring hands were clinging to my face.

"There you are," he said as he bumped his nose against mine. He kissed my brow and pulled back with the most breathtaking smile I'd ever seen. Tears streaked his cheeks. He bent and kissed the cut on my cheek and then, with tenderness, my bloodied and swollen lip. "I knew you'd come back to me."

FIFTY-EIGHT
EVREN

I managed to stand and Delrik wrapped his steady arms around my waist. My legs wobbled beneath me.

"Evren." His voice held so much urgency as he buried his face into my matted hair. "Evren."

I clutched Delrik's shirt in my one good fist. It was really him.

"He told me he had you." I sobbed into his shirt. "He told me he'd use you to force me to give up my powers."

His muscular body, his woody smell, enveloped me. I buried my blood coated face deeper into his chest. He smelled of sweat and forest and home. Strong hands gripped my shoulders, holding me tight to him. Delrik tried to pry me away, but I clung to him like he was life itself. I felt like if I opened my eyes, I would realize this is all a dream;

I'd be back in that cell. Then his arm scooped behind my knees, lifting me. We paused momentarily on the threshold leading from the entry hall to the courtyard.

"The grove," I said. "There is a path that leads south to the city."

"Yes. We can cross the river from there or jump on a ship out of the kingdom," Adaris chimed in.

The three of us slipped out the front door and into the dim night. We made it halfway across the courtyard when the ground beneath us began to shake. A booming voice echoed across the house. Even the great walls of the fortress trembled at the amplified sound.

"You can't hide from me, Evren," Cadoc said. "I'll always be able to find you."

My stomach plummeted, and I couldn't stop the trembling that shook my body.

"You must go. Now!" Adaris insisted, pushing Delrik and me down the pathway toward the grove. "Run. I'll meet you there."

"Adaris. No!" I tried scramble out of Delrik's arms, but he clung to me tightly.

No. I wouldn't leave him behind. Not again. Cadoc would kill him. But Delrik didn't give me a choice. Adaris ran back toward the entrance hall while Delrik half carried half dragged me away into the coming dawn. The pitch of night was shifting to a dim gray and plum. Over his shoulder I could see Adaris standing and taunting Cadoc to divert his attention from the wide-open doors. Delrik dragged me kicking and screaming away from the house. My feet slipped on the dew-soaked grass as we moved closer to the grove. The stars above were blinking out one by one.

A scream erupted from the house, and Adaris's limp body was thrown from the front doors. He landed with a crunch on the gravel walkway. Adaris struggled to push himself up but collapsed back to the ground.

Cadoc stepped from the enormous steel double doors. "Such a disappointment."

Adaris suddenly twisted, and a howl of pain like I'd never heard before came from his lips.

"Adaris!"

Delrik tripped over a root that stuck up from the ground causing him to trip and lose his grip on me. I took advantage of his imbalance and pushed against his chest, freeing myself to stumble back to Adaris. I came to a screeching halt by his side, bending to lay hands on him. The convulsing stopped, and Adaris took heaving breaths. Cadoc's wicked laugh rang through the morning air.

"Evren, you have to go," Adaris said through panting gulps of air, his voice raw from screaming.

"I'm not leaving you. Not again."

Adaris had spent my whole life protecting me. He had sacrificed so much for me. I was no longer a child. And now, *I* would protect him. Even if it meant giving my life. Delrik would understand. He knew how much Adaris meant to me and how he'd protected me. I would be strong for him this time. I would not let Cadoc prey on him any longer.

"Evren, no. I am not going to lose you again." Delrik was pleading. He gripped my upper arm and tried to haul me up but released me quickly with a yelp. The fire under my skin refused to let him move me. It pulsed with fury on the surface, ready to be released and consume anything or anyone that crossed me.

"If I die, then I die. But I will not let *him* win," I said to Delrik. I couldn't look at him. If I looked at Delrik, I would lose my courage. If I saw the pain on his face, I'd leave everything behind, and I didn't want to. Not again.

I stood, stepping into the space between Adaris and Cadoc. Barefoot, my short night dress whipped my thighs in the warm breeze. Bruises and cuts wrapped around my ankles from the iron shackles I'd worn. My swollen cheek pulsed as I scowled at Cadoc. I wiggled the fingers on my broken hand, allowing the piercing agony to fuel my anger even more. Cadoc stood in the doorway, illuminated by the torches inside. He held the curved dagger in his hand. That dagger belonged to me. I could taste the fury that wafted from him. The fury was pure, unadulterated power, but my rage was stronger than anything he could ever feel. Renwick stood in his usual spot to the left of my father. I hated him. I hated them both.

Delrik was a blur, like an arrow shot from a bow, as he snatched the dagger from Cadoc's unsuspecting hands. Two seconds and he was standing at my back again. He pressed the dagger into my opened palm. "If you stay, so do I." And he withdrew Silverlight from his back.

Cadoc threw his head back and roared with manic laughter. "Well, aren't you two a pair."

Pain.

Not the crippling pain I felt earlier but enough to go rigid. I felt Delrik stiffen too.

You think your little dagger and bondmate can take me down? Ignorant child. Cadoc's voice came calmly through the haze of my mind.

He released me, and I fell to my knees but managed to look up at him. He was never a father to me. He was a vicious monster, and I would never let him use me. Ever. I would fight with every last piece of me.

Renwick outstretched his hand, gripped it into a fist, and with a wide, sweeping arch, tossed Delrik away from me across the courtyard.

"No!" I bellowed.

Shadows dragged across the earth as the darkness coiled around me. Thick clouds circled above, blocking out the colors of a new morning sky. Heat rose from my core, up my throat, demanding to be released. The madness surrounding me grew quiet, and all my attention turned inward. A crackle flowed across every surface of my skin. I'd felt this heat before—the flame, the fire.

I looked up at my father one last time and smiled as I greeted the eternal flame like an old friend.

With a roar of thunder, I rose into the air, head thrown back and arms spread wide. I wanted to give into the fire. The flames burned away everything—the pain, the regret—and replaced it with euphoric ecstasy and bliss. Power. Pure power coursed through me.

I ripped in half, fracturing in two, and from within, I exploded into fire.

FIFTY-NINE
DELRIK

Anger coursed through me at the sight I beheld. Evren looked so small—kneeling in front of Cadoc—covered in marks that *he* gouged into her. So small and helpless. I used the last piece of my strength to steal the dagger for her. The shadows had sucked the last drop of power from my body, and I struggled to stay conscious. Renwick smirked at me from his obedient position behind Cadoc. I was too far from Evren; I couldn't do anything to save her.

The air was thick with tension. Silent.

Evren didn't attempt to crawl away. I reached for Silverlight that was just a foot from me and pushed myself up from the ground. Chunks of gravel had embedded in my skin from where I landed.

Then, like something was blocking out the rising sun, darkness took over. Shadows crept down the outer stone walls and from within the trees, crawling across the ground. They crawled to Evren, like she was sucking all the light and energy from the world, as if she had summoned them. I looked down at my arm, thinking that the shadows in me were doing this, but they were still imprinted in my skin, swirling angrily. The gathering darkness encircled her and Cadoc, moving faster and faster. Cold sweat formed on my skin. Cadoc spoke, but I couldn't hear him from this distance and over the surging in my ears. All my effort was focused on Evren.

No. She can't give in to it. Never give in.

I repeated the words to myself, the words she'd spoken so many times. I recognized that spark in the air. The taste, the tang of pure, raw energy. The same as the night on the balcony. If she fully succumbed to the power, she would never return. It would destroy her.

Her face peered up at her father, not with fear this time, but with a burning inferno. Her lips twisted into a smile, but there was no joy—just power. Undiluted, explosive power.

Her body rose into the air, a red glow emanating from her skin. Luminous streaks covered her. She rose high above Cadoc, arms extended out, her head tilting back, welcoming the flames that I knew were coming.

With a crack, her body split in two, engulfed in fire, and a bird of fire erupted from her. The majestic bird with its broad wings beating up and down, loomed above Cadoc. He stood in awe of what his daughter had become. Sleek silver and black feathers covered her massive, powerful body and wings ablaze with molten shades of purple, orange, and yellow ending in white-hot flames. Resplendent.

"Evren." I couldn't help but whisper her name.

Crushing despair swept over me. She was gone forever. The eternal flame had awoken and swallowed her whole. And she had just let it.

I dropped to my knees and gripped my head, trying to hold back the agony. I couldn't take my eyes off the fiery predator that used to be my bondmate.

I felt that bond tug in my chest. Violet eyes suddenly flashed to me. I was struck by their beauty, their intensity. I knew those eyes. Eyes the exact color of the morning glory flowers we picked in the valley. They were *her* eyes, telling me Evren was still in there. She was still inside. Evren was alive inside the fire bird. Somehow, some way, she was alive. She turned her attention back to her father. He attempted to attack, thrusting his arms forward, sending a visible rippling wave of pain directed at her, but she didn't falter. She snapped her ebony beak impatiently at him, and he stumbled back a step.

The giant bird, her body standing taller than me, lowered to the ground. Right before her deadly talons made contact the earth, she transformed into a winged High Fae. Evren had wings of brilliant, sleek black and silver coming from her back. Her swollen face had healed, and the jagged, red edges of the slice across her chest was gone. Every inch of her skin had returned to the flawless porcelain the Powers Above had given her. All the evidence of the evil Cadoc inflicted on her had disappeared. Her silver hair billowed out behind her in curling waves of liquid moonlight on a phantom breeze.

She took a step forward, the ground smoldering where her bare toes touched. She spread her wings to their full width, easily spanning wider than the steel doors where Cadoc still stood shellshocked. Her wings arched into the dawn painted sky. Embers flickered off their tips before she tucked them in tight. Her skin glowed bright, and she wore a dress made of fluid white flames that licked the ground around her feet.

Evren took another menacing step toward Cadoc. "You live only to consume power and tear this realm apart. I will *not* allow it."

Cadoc stumbled back, tripping over his feet but catching himself on the stone steps. Renwick didn't try to catch him. Instead, the coward slipped back into the shadows of the entry hall, but not before flashing me a look. I wanted to follow him, but I'd never catch him with my powers drained, and I refused to let Evren out of my sight. Let him run like the scared bastard he was. I'd enjoy hunting him down later.

"You stole my childhood; you caused me daily pain." She clasped her hands in front of her, and thunder boomed when they made contact. "You tortured my brother. You murdered my mother."

Evren stalked closer and closer to Cadoc.

"I will never bow to you," she said. Her hands parted, and a ball of fire suspended in the air between them.

"Evren." Cadoc took a trembling step forward. "Daughter. Please. We can rule the realm together," he tried, his voice shaking.

"Liar."

"Together, side by side, we can have all the power."

"I don't seek power. I don't seek control." Her voice grew louder.

"What can I give you then?"

"Nothing. You are worth *nothing* to me."

She was only a foot from him now, and though he was taller than her, he cowered before her.

"Please."

"You have never shown anyone mercy a day in your miserable life. And if I could, I would kill you and revive you over and over, as many times as the number of lives you took." Her words were as sharp as a knife.

The ball of fire spread outward and engulfed her hand. She reached out that hand and grabbed Cadoc by the wrist. Cadoc screamed as her flame covered fingers held their vice like grip. Her focus moved to the giant ruby on his pinky as he thrashed and begged for release.

Evren smiled sweetly. "This belongs to me." She slipped the Ring of Teris off Cadoc's finger.

She released his wrist, leaving behind charred, smoking skin. His hand began to disintegrate into ash until only a stump remained.

Evren tipped her head to the side curiously. The soft curls followed the avian movement. She stared at her hand, flipping it back and forth to examine the flames dancing along her fingers. Her hand clenched into a fist, and the flame extinguished. Cadoc sagged with relief.

"You know, I never needed your approval. I wanted it. Desperately. But now, I know I never needed you."

Then she extended a finger, just one, pointing it into the air. The tip held a single orange flame.

It pulsed, bright and brilliant. She reached out and touched her finger to the center Cadoc's chest. He began to scream. His chest glowed from within as if he was burning from the inside out. His mouth opened wide, and his face began to blister and crack, and a molten blaze seeped from the seams.

"See, Father. You would never have been able to contain my power."

Then he burst into ash and soot that disappeared like wisps of smoke with the wind.

SIXTY
EVREN

I watched the ash float away into the coral and golden sky. The sun was just below the horizon, and the sky was ready to welcome the new day. I turned my attention to Adaris still on the ground. His shoulders slumped, exhaustion on his face, his body shaking. The moment Cadoc took his last breath, Adaris was released from the mental binds that had been enslaving him. His face and arms were covered in cuts and were dripping blood. Tears welled in his eyes, and his body shook with silent cries. He wrapped his arms around himself, trying to hold himself together.

    I dropped to my knees in front of him. I extended my hand to offer comfort but quickly pulled it back when I saw flames rolling just beneath the surface. I wasn't sure if my touch would burn him the way it had Cadoc. Volatile flames thrummed in my hands, all over my body.

A heaviness sat upon my shoulders, pulling the muscles of my back—a new weight I hadn't felt before. The feathered ebony and silver wings coming from my back were relaxed and glowing like embers rather than the pure flames they had been moments ago.

Then I felt him, felt his presence. Delrik. My bondmate. My body turned toward him, craving his presence. Delrik was standing, frozen in place, but a curious smile tipping his lips made the dimple in his cheek stand out. He took a confident step toward me. I smiled.

"I won't hurt you." I reached out to him. All my hesitation left me when I saw him. I knew that I wouldn't hurt him. He was mine forever.

"I know."

He limped over to me and then his mouth was on mine, our teeth and lips clashing frantically. He scattered all my thoughts that weren't of him as he lifted me from my feet, stealing my breath. A kiss so raw and fierce. I gave him everything. He pulled back and brushed his fingers across my cheek. The flames on my skin receded, leaving behind my wings as the only visible reminder of my decision to surrender to the elemental fire.

Delrik pulled me against him fiercely and kissed me again. The relief of his presence, the weight of his body against mine was perfect. He reached up and ran a gentle hand down the curve of my wing. A fiery feather caressed his hand in return.

SIXTY-ONE
DELRIK

I stood in awe of the raw beauty and power emanating from my bondmate. When I reached out to her, I expected to feel heat, but as I brushed my fingers over the feathers, the flames didn't burn me. Although the edges of her wings looked and moved like fire, they were as soft as silk and cool to the touch, like the feathers of a bird.

When the elemental power, her elemental power, reciprocated my touch, I knew that she was no longer in danger. She was made for this power.

"Well, this will take some getting used to," I said slyly.

She playfully swatted me away. "Just give me a moment. I can feel the power ebbing."

Slowly, like they were the last embers burning out, her wings disappeared, leaving behind my Evren.

I pressed my forehead against hers and breathed her in.

I felt a small weight land on my shoulder. When I opened my eyes, a small, ebony owl the exact shades of Evren's wings, no bigger than my fist, was perched there. It tipped its little head to the side, reminding me so much of Evren. The bird fluttered its tiny silver wings, stretching them and tucking them back against its side. The edges of its wings and its eyes were violet, just like Evren's eyes. I looked back and forth between Evren and the bird, marveling at the similarities.

"Um…does this belong to you?" I asked her.

The owl snapped its beak at me twice, then opened its mouth, and a small flame hiccupped from its mouth.

"I guess so," she said with a soft laugh. She stroked the top of the bird's head with the back of her finger.

"And I'm yours,"—she smiled up at me,— "forever."

I growled with contentment. "Always."

SIXTY-TWO
EVREN

We left the River Kingdom in the capable hands of Adaris. There were so many things that needed to be done to undo what Cadoc had begun, but Adaris was capable. As wicked as the Black Guard was, they recognized Adaris's secession, and Adaris had a few trusted guardsmen he put in charge immediately. They didn't falter in taking on the responsibility and accepting Adaris as the new High Ruler of the River Kingdom. He'd restructure the Black Guard over time and weed out the truly dangerous Fae from the ranks. We planned to meet in Arcelia in six months to formulate a plan going forward.

Renwick had disappeared that morning. We searched as much of the fortress and grove as we could, but to no avail. If we had more time, we could have searched longer, but Delrik only had one more day before Alux's shadows would consume him. I knew Adaris wouldn't rest until he'd found Renwick.

It was impossible to hide what had happened on the front lawn of the fortress. There were too many prying eyes to keep the elemental flame a secret. It had only been a day, and High Fae families were beginning to ask Adaris questions and express concerns about such a dangerous gift roaming free in the River Kingdom. We decided it was best to leave Rivamir for now until things settled down.

Now that I'd given in to the elemental flame, I wasn't sure how long I would survive. I didn't feel weak; quite the opposite. I felt stronger than ever before.

My primary concern was Delrik. The shadow curse had weakened him, and it was starting to take a toll. He looked weaker than he was letting on. Adaris didn't question me when I slipped the Ring of Teris onto my finger without an explanation. It was simpler to just leave it unsaid.

Adaris' new Head Guard, Garrett, offered his power of blinking to get us back to the Wasted Shallows. I'd seen Adaris and Garrett together over the years and knew they were friends. Delrik agreed but wasn't quite sure if he wanted to trust the new Head Guard. We didn't really have a choice though because he was too weak to make such a long journey with only one day left before the deadline of his curse.

Adaris and I said goodbye, holding each other tight for a long time. I knew I'd see him again, but I still worried about being separated from him. At least this time, we knew Cadoc wouldn't be a threat, and he knew I'd be in Arcelia as soon as we dealt with Alux.

I tucked my new little owl friend, Aura, as Delrik named her, into my travel cloak and held Delrik's hand in mine. I'd never blinked before, at least while conscious, and wasn't quite sure how it worked.

With one last smile for my brother, I heard a pop. My stomach bottomed out as I was pushed and pulled from every angle, plummeting through space and time. Everything spun around me in a whirling blur and then my feet hit solid ground again. I almost collapsed, but Delrik held me tight.

"That was awful." I bent to put my hands on my knees and prayed to the Powers Above I wouldn't lose my breakfast.

"You get used to it." Garrett laughed.

I looked around and saw that we'd blinked right to the edge of the birch forest outside the Wasted Shallows. I shivered at the sudden drop in temperature.

"I'll wait here. And when you're done, I will take you both to Arcelia."

Bone deep wariness had me dragging my feet through the dead brush that littered the forest floor. I knew we had to move fast. Each passing moment the shadows had eaten more and more of Delrik. The charred darkness was visible above the neckline of his shirt like it was a hand reaching up to strangle him, threatening to choke the life out of him.

Alux was waiting by the shore of the lake when we finally stepped through the tree line as if she had anticipated our arrival. We stopped several feet from the shore, not daring to get any closer. Aura swooped down and perched on my shoulder.

"So, you submitted to the elemental power," she said. It wasn't a question.

There was no physical evidence of the flame, but she could sense it. When she spoke of my power, I felt a surge of energy flow through me in warning. It fought against my hold to lash out to protect Delrik and myself. It didn't like Alux, to say the least, and ash coated my tongue.

Delrik stood next to me. He was pale, and his breathing was uneven, but he stood tall, nonetheless.

"I see you also collected what I asked you to," her otherworldly voice called to me, but I didn't sway to its seduction.

I lifted my hand, flashing a rubied finger before me, turning it this way and that. The smooth planes of the stone reflected the sparse light that was able to penetrate the canopy above. Alux smiled and began to move toward me.

"Release Delrik," I commanded, and she froze mid-step. "Free him from your curse, and it is all yours."

Alux drew her lips into a thin line, and anger rippled off her.

"He will be free of my curse once I have possession of my ring."

I stood unwavering, even with her icy glare and rage. Then Delrik collapsed, convulsing, foam pooling at the corner of his mouth. This time, I didn't flinch; I didn't move to help him.

"Enough." My voice was stronger, a force to be reckoned with.

"Do you think I'm stupid girl? Do you think I trust a Fae child and her mongrel?" She bellowed. "Give me the ring!" Her ancient voice reverberated off the trees and shook the ground I stood on.

Good. I wanted her fury. I wanted her rage. I wanted her to lose control.

"You will pay for your disobedience girl." She hissed through a seething snarl.

Alux turned to Delrik, lying in a heap on the ground, still twitching and writhing. She extended a hand and called her shadows back to her. The darkness was violently ripped from Delrik's body, returning to their master.

He was freed.

The darkness that had marred his bronzed skin for the last eight days was gone. No evidence of the curse was left behind.

Delrik stood on shaky legs, sucking in deep breaths, and grasped my hand. He rolled his shoulders with relief before looking to Alux, giving her a smug smile.

"I wouldn't be smiling if I were you, crossbreed. I am going to feast on your bodies tonight." Her tongue darted out and licked her lips.

With a twist of her scrawny wrist, Alux released an evil laugh and then struck.

I spread my arms and let the shadows wrap around me, enveloping me. Their biting strands poured into my body, trying to tear into my flesh, but they wouldn't hurt me, couldn't hurt me. I absorbed every shadow.

Every. Last. One.

Alux stood baffled that I wasn't cowering and surrendering. I lowered my gaze to meet her. Her eyes peering back at me were hollow and white. And I knew that I now possessed her voided eyes.

"What did you do, you bitch?" Alux shrieked. But her grating voice was barely audible, that of an elderly crank.

I simply raised my hand again, the ruby ring swirling with blackness.

I tipped my head to the side. "Has anyone ever told you it isn't nice to steal things from people?" My mouth curled into a smile that mimicked the one she'd given me earlier. "You were going to steal my powers from me. I can't let that happen."

"You don't know what you've done," she screamed.

The lake began to boil with her fury. Chunks of ice sunk to the murky depths and steam rose.

"Oh, I know exactly what I've done."

Alux's mouth opened wide…too wide—like a gaping hole where a mouth should've been. Her lips curled back as her teeth morphed into fangs. Her head fell back at an unnatural angle. A cry, so loud and piercing it rippled the water away from her, and all the trees surrounding the lake were flattened to the ground in a wide ring. Delrik and I struggled to stay upright with the force. I'd never heard that sound come from a living creature. It was a thing from nightmares.

Alux scraped her fingernails into the skin of her face trying to gauge out her own eyes. Her powerless white eyes. Black—oily, thick darkness—poured from the wounds.

"You'll never be able to control that amount of power." She sounded deranged and frantic.

"I know. I'm not meant to contain this much power. But my bondmate can share it with me." I squeezed Delrik's hand. "And you. You will rot here in this hellhole for all eternity."

SIXTY-THREE
EVREN

We didn't want to spend any more time in the valley than we had to. I just wanted to get Delrik home and rested as soon as possible. The shadows were gone, but they had taken a toll. So, after a hasty goodbye to Vidarr and Wren, Garret blinked us back to Arcelia. Our five-day trip took mere seconds. Aura nestled close to my chest and ruffled her feathers with contentment at the mountains of Arcelia surrounding us. After only a day, she had become my constant companion.

⚀

The sun's light bounced off the moonstone tower and snow and painted them in pastels. I gripped my cloak tighter around my shoulders. I wasn't cold. I just loved snuggling into the furs while large snowflakes fell all around me. I kicked off my boots as soon as we returned to Delrik's apartment and stepped out onto the balcony. There was a small circle surrounding my bare feet where they melted on contact.

"I've missed the smell of the mountains and the snow," I said. "I know you have too."

"I knew the mountains would become your home."

"You never said that."

"I did in my head."

I turned to walk back to him. "That doesn't count."

"Come back inside." Delrik sat on the couch and was unlacing his boots. "Aramis will be here any minute."

"But he's not here yet," I said as I made my way slowly to him and dropped down to my knees. I grazed my hands up his thighs.

He let out a frustrated breath through his teeth. "We didn't need to talk to him immediately. We could have waited a night…or two."

I reached for his boots and slipped them off his feet, tossing them toward the hearth. Delrik leaned back and stretched his legs out straight before relaxing them.

Right then Nazneen burst into the apartment, the door bounced off the wall with a loud crack. She made it five steps into the living room and stopped short.

"What the hell is going on?" she screeched as she covered her face and turned her back to us quickly.

"Really, Naz. We are completely clothed," Delrik said with a sly smirk plastered to his face.

I was still kneeling on the floor in front of him but quickly pushed myself up right as Aramis crossed the threshold.

He walked toward Delrik and me. He clapped a hand on Delrik's shoulder and then wrapped him in a hug. "Welcome home, son."

"What did that witch do to you?" Nazneen was now pacing.

"Don't call my bondmate a witch. It's rude." Delrik joked.

"This isn't funny, Delrik!" Naz had gone from disgust to panic to tears of relief in a matter of seconds.

Delrik went to Naz. He reached for her, but she flinched away from him like he was diseased.

"Naz, I don't actually have the shadows in me anymore."

"But she put them *inside* you!"

"She'll never be able to do that to anyone ever again," he said.

Naz looked between the two of us, confused.

"We took Alux's shadows." I held up my hand where the Ring of Teris glinted in the light on my finger.

"A ring?" Aramis asked as he stepped forward and reached for my hand. He touched the ring with his finger. "It's ice cold."

"Yeah, the shadows aren't a fan of my fire."

"It's the Ring of Teris," Delrik explained.

Realization dawned on Aramis's face.

"Cadoc has had it all this time. He was planning on using it to steal Evren's elemental flame."

Delrik continued to explain our entire journey in detail for them.

Nazneen eventually gave up her pacing and perched on the edge of the sofa. Once she was still, Aura swept in from outside and perched on Naz's shoulder. Naz just blinked in confusion. Aramis stood calmly taking in every piece of information.

"So that's how you escaped Alux. You took her powers using the ring," Aramis said.

"Yup. They are contained where they can't do anymore damage." I sat on the couch opposite Nazneen. "Do you have any idea what we should do with the ring now?"

Aramis shook his head. "No. I need to figure out the safest way to keep it hidden or destroy it without releasing the dark magic." He tipped his chin to me. "You can hold on to it for now. I don't want to potentially tamper with whatever spells containing the shadows."

♀

After an hour of convincing Nazneen I was indeed not secretly dying, Aramis and Naz bid us goodnight. A maid had brought us a platter of dinner—roasted chicken, garlic potatoes, steamed vegetables, and freshly baked bread. We laid out our food on the coffee table and stuffed ourselves full while sitting in front of the fire.

Delrik was lounging on a mound of blankets he'd dragged from the bedroom to make a bed on the floor in front of the fire. He was stretched out on his back with his hands laced together behind his head.

I stood to put away our dishes so we could move the coffee table for more space on the floor.

Delrik stood and added another piece of wood to the fire. The way the fire danced oranges and red across the hard planes of his body was captivating. His pants hung loose on his hips in the most delicious way. I spread my hands across his chest, resting them there between us. His hands came to mine and lifted them to his mouth. He kissed each knuckle.

He tipped my hand, and the ruby ring caught the light. "You are a beautifully cunning creature."

Then he lowered his head and pressed his lips to mine. He released my hands and sank his fingers into my hair. I unbraided it as soon as we were alone. He loved it when my hair was unbound and free. He twisted it into a thick rope around his fist and tugged gently to tip my head back. He placed a kiss on the underside of my chin and then brushed his nose along my jaw. The slower he kissed me, the faster my heart raced.

Delrik began to unbutton my shirt—so agonizingly slow without taking his lips from mine.

"Shall we move this into the bathing chamber? I could use a good, long soak in that tub," Delrik said, and he focused on his fingers as they untucked my shirt from my pants. He hooked his fingers under the hem and teased the sensitive skin of my stomach. Everywhere he touched me, my skin lit with desire. His tongue dipped into my mouth. I was turning into a puddle with just his kisses. He bunched the shirt up, taking his time, the fabric moving across my oversensitive skin. His lips finally left mine as he pulled my shirt over my head.

"We definitely should bathe before this goes too far." I laughed as I pulled away from him. "I'm covered in Powers know what."

I leaned forward into his touch again, but he'd stopped. His hands on my shoulders pushed me away, holding me at arm's length.

"What's wrong?" I asked.

But he wasn't looking at me. At least he wasn't looking at my face. His eyes were on my stomach. I tried to move, but he held on to me tightly.

"Evren." His voice was shaking.

His fingers ghosted over my stomach but not touching me. I looked down to see obsidian, charred shadows draped over my hip and snaking around my torso and then up between my breasts. I brought my fingertips to the darkness and traced the ice-cold marks. They shifted under my touch, and I yanked my hand away.

We looked at each other in shock and then looked at the ring. I held my hand forward and tried to wretch the band from my finger, but it wouldn't budge. It didn't move an inch.

Circles of dark hells. What had we done?

PRONUNCIATION GUIDE

Adaris Byrnes (a-dar-us)
Alux (al-ux)
Aramis Zathrian (air-a-mis zath-ree-an)
Arabelle Halloran Byrnes (ara-bell hal-oh-ran)
Cadoc Byrnes (kaa-dahk)
Calia Zathrian (cal-ee-ah zath-ree-an)
Delrik Valhar (del-rik val-har)
Elliot Valhar (val-har)
Evren Byrnes (Ev-ren)
Morgan Valhar (val-har)
Nazneen Zathrian (naz-neen zath-ree-an)
Renwick Ashewood (ren-wick ash-wood)
Vidarr Fanenos (vee-dar fan-ee-nose)
Wren Fanenos (fan-ee-nose)

Cities, Landmarks, and More
Arcelia (are-sell-ee-a)
Basdover Gulf (bas-dover)

Bloodthorn
Darkwood
Doloryum (Dolor) (doe-lor-ee-um)
Elementum (el-e-men-tum)
Essence Scrolls
The Fortress
The Great Chaos
The Great River
The Guild
Illoterra (i-lo-terra)
Kilnard (kil-nard)
Kiscarine Pass (kis-kaa-reen)
Lakeshore
Lilura Steel (lil-er-a)
Mount Lendorr (len-door)
Merock (mer-ock)
Menrath (men-wrath)
Mountain Fae
Osomal (os-oh-mal)
Qana Mountains (kaa-nuh)
Ramshorn
Raven Fae
Ring of Teris (ter-is)
Rivamir (riv-a-mirror)
The River of Naraina (na-rain-a)
Rochris Islands (row-kris)
Snowhaven Fae
Sacred Forest
Snowhaven
Temples of Anruin (an-ru-in)
The Uprising

Warblade of Silverlight
Wasted Shallows
The Wildlands

ACKNOWLEDGMENTS

Never in my wildest dreams did I ever think I'd write a book and actually have it published. A little over a year ago I challenged myself to write a book. From there, it has blossomed into a fantasy novel that I am proud to put my name on. I couldn't have done it alone. I owe so much love and appreciation to those in my life.

Paul, my fabulous husband—You have always supported in with all my crazy ideas throughout life. You are my partner and my better half. Thank you for the countless times you picked up after the kids, cleaned the kitchen, and folded laundry so I'd have more time to write. Thank you for listening to my obscenely long writing playlist over and over without complaint. This last year has been insane, and I wouldn't have survived it without you. I love you to the ends of the earth and back again.

My two crazy kiddos, Braxton and Berkeley June—You both inspire me more than you'll ever know. Watching your creativity grow to love reading and drawing over the last year has been the best gift ever. Thank you for encouraging me even when you didn't know you were.

"Mommy, are you writing another chapter! Yeah!" - Berkeley June

"Hey mom, can I help name your book? And the next one? There should be dragons!" – Braxton
I know you both won't be able to read this book for a long, long time, but know that you both are lights in my world.

Emily, aka Pigeon—At this point, you have been with me for literally every step. From tossing ideas around in the car while driving ten hours back home to Georgia to last minute title changes and fanart, you are a freaking rock star.

My mom, Susie—You have read and reread every single version of this manuscript. You were my first alpha reader, my beta reader, and an ARC reader. And you have kept my grammar and spelling in check like a pro. You have always told me to shoot for the stars and dream big. For that, I am thankful. I love you, Mom.

My sisters, Katie and Anna—I'm so grateful for all the calls and texts I've put you both through the last year. Katie, you spent countless hours with me on the phone while I typed and planned and rearranged plots. You also told me I'd succeed and encouraged me every chance you got. Anna, thank you for introducing me to the fantasy genre and spending so much time going back and forth on our love for all things whimsical. You are such a blessing in my life. Oh, and I can't forget my brother-in-law, Rob. Although you didn't know what Fae were when this whole adventure started, you stepped up and gave me ideas and smoothed out choppy sentences. Maybe I'll be able to turn you into a fantasy reader, after all.

My entire family, you have been beyond supportive—Dad and Karen, Roses and Grandaddy, Papa and Nana, Kerry and Ron, Emma and Hayden (loved your help with character design), Weston, Lexi, and Jillian, Holly and Charles, and Grey and Carly.

Diane, my far, far away best friend—You have been alongside me from day one, and you hyped me up and kept me going. I'm so grateful to your constant love and support. It is a blessing to have you in my life.

My fellow fantasy writer, Hayley Whiteley—(shameless plug, go check out her book Ink and Ore.) I can't count the number of times I've messaged you for help. And you have never hesitated in your generosity, kindness, and guidance. Thank you for being your awesome self.

Kaylee—Thank you for becoming my newest book friend. I have loved getting to know you this year and nerding out on all the books.

Tori—Thank you for just being you. We've gone through the last nine years together as military wives. All the ups and downs, moves and deployments. Your friendship is so valuable to me. Thank you.

The Overbooked Literary Club—What a beautiful group of women that I have had the pleasure of meeting and reading with. I've always wanted to be in a book club, and our group is the best one out there. You ladies have become friends and confidants. Thank you for all your support.

Jon & Jessica and the entire Attitude Nation Weightlifting Team - the group of women and men I have met through the sport of weightlifting brought me out of depression and carried me through the last three years of all my ups and downs. What started off as a challenge from my husband Paul to lift a barbell for 30 days turned into a massive life transformation for the better.
Jon, you have not only been an amazing coach, but your family has become our family. You encourage and challenge me, not only in the gym but also in life.

You and Jess dedicate so much to our team and for that, I am thankful.

All of my teammates past and present, your support and love and butt-kicking has helped make me who I am today. From working out on zoom calls to flying across the country to meet face to face for the first time, I have made lifelong friends in this barbell club.

Red Circle for life.

If you don't love your life, then change it. – Jon North

My editors—Kyla and Katelyn, you both were so patient with me as a newbie writer. You gave me incredible feedback that helped me not only improve this book but become a better writer. Thank you for all the time and effort you put into this project.

All of my beta readers—Liz Murray, Rio Thompson, Janelle Marie, Amie Loader, Susie Bergman, and Pat Anderson. You ladies were the first to read my book, and I am so thankful. Your honesty, suggestions, and time is above and beyond what I expected.

My fabulous ARC readers and street team—Thank you for all you have done to help make my debut book a success.

And lastly, thank you to all the readers out there. Thank you for joining me on this journey, sharing, supporting, and reviewing my book.

ABOUT THE AUTHOR

Megan L. Adams is a new fantasy writer. She was born and raised in Georgia and is the oldest of seven siblings. She's enjoyed reading and writing since elementary school. After exploring many creative jobs, she recently picked up her pen to write her first novel, *Shadows Within the Fire*. Megan currently lives in Maryland with her husband, her two children, and her golden retriever-husky mix, Toma. In her spare time, Megan enjoys drinking coffee, exploring local bookstores, and tending to her collection of orchids.

Made in the USA
Middletown, DE
09 April 2025